Throat

Clara stumbled into the hallway. ...ately wanted to hide, find a place where she could throw up or cry, or both; but not only was she at a loss for words, she was at a loss for a place to go at this late hour. Her first impulse was to run outside, follow the creek, maybe all the way to the river. She stood in the dark hall and sobbed, frustrated it was the middle of the night, and the only realistic place she could go was the room she shared with Lily.

Crying softly, she crept inside and sat on the edge of her bed. Across from her in an identical bed, Lily was already asleep. Clara unbuttoned her high-top boots and climbed under the coverlet with her clothes on. Bone-weary after the worst day she'd had since her mother died, she lay awake, trying to make sense of a senseless turn of events. Pa wasn't supposed to get married again. He hadn't promised that; however with her and Lily to take care of him, he didn't need a wife. Besides, cousins marrying cousins, one of them much older than the other, was a complete muddle of how life was supposed to be.

With a sudden start she realized she would be seeing Geneva every day. They would be living in the same house—the one Pa built for his family—and her best friend, her only friend in this place with no neighborhoods or schools was now her stepmother.

Praise for Ginger Dehlinger

Ginger has won or placed in several writing competitions. *Last Ride*, an essay describing the journey of a tumbleweed, won first prize in the 2011 Rising Star contest for Pacific Northwest writers. Her coming-of-age novel, *Brute Heart* was a finalist in the contemporary fiction category for a 2012 Big Al's Books 'n Pals People's Choice Award. A short story, *The Embroidered Sheets*, was a finalist for the Women Writing the West "Laura" award in 2013. Ginger has also published and received recognition for her poetry.

Never Done

by

Ginger Dehlinger

Never Done

Cover Art by *RJ Morris*

The Wild Rose Press, Inc.
PO Box 708
Adams Basin, NY 14410-0708
Visit us at www.thewildrosepress.com

Publishing History
First Cactus Rose Edition, 2017
Print ISBN 978-1-5092-1372-6
Digital ISBN 978-1-5092-1373-3

Published in the United States of America

Dedication

In memory of my great-grandmother,
Ella May Leaming Fell (nee Tripler),
whose life inspired this story.

Acknowledgements

Never Done was inspired by the life of my great-grandmother, Ella May Leaming Fell (nee Tripler), who handwrote her life story at the age of eighty-one. One of her descendants made photocopies of Grandma Fell's autobiography and distributed one to every family. I remember reading my copy and being impressed by the amount of detail my great-grandmother recalled and how hard she worked most of her ninety-nine years.

"I cannot say that anything extraordinary has happened to me," wrote Grandma Fell on page one, but in the rest of the 147 legal-sized pages she filled, she described a life most would describe as fascinating. Like most women of her generation, my great-grandmother didn't openly discuss personal matters. For example, all she wrote about her widowed father's marriage to a sixteen-year-old girl was, "and things didn't go well with the new young wife."

I tried to imagine what it would be like to have a stepmother not much older than I was, and "things didn't go well" didn't come close. So in *Never Done* I expanded my great-grandmother's understatement into a highly fictionalized stormy relationship that takes place between two women from their teens (roughly 1884) until the flu epidemic of 1918. I incorporated other details from Grandma Fell's autobiography in a story that moves from cattle country, to mining towns, to homes with electricity and indoor plumbing, making sure everything she and I wrote is historically accurate.

My late cousin Bob Brown had a hand in this process when he transcribed our great-grandmother's handwritten pages into a typed document. Grandma Fell's handwriting wasn't terrible, although hard to decipher in some places. I wasn't able to thank Bob in person, thus I'm acknowledging him here for the time and effort he saved me.

I also want to thank my critique group, especially Sandy Thompson and Larry Koppy, for their input during the three years it took us to work through my manuscript. My editor, Cindy Davis, was also a great help during the polishing process. And a wholehearted thank you goes to Dick Dehlinger, my most outspoken promoter and fan.

Part I

Cowboys and Clotheslines

Chapter One

A blue-gray dawn cooled the parched San Luis Valley that day as Clara grabbed a bucket for the first of many trips she'd make for water. La Jara Creek was only a stone's throw from the back of the house, but a bucket of water was a two-handed carry for a girl of fourteen.

It was the middle of July. She wore a cuffed and collared blouse, full petticoat, long linen skirt, and button-top boots. By noon she was wiping her brow with the sleeve of her blouse. Her shoulders ached and her neck had a crick in it from hanging clothes on a line she could barely reach. Taught not to complain, she dealt with the drudgery in silence, wishing she'd been allowed to go to Santa Fe.

"How much is left?" she asked her Aunt Lou halfway through the afternoon.

"Just Albert's work clothes. I put them to boiling on the stove."

Clara sighed, knowing her next task would be scrubbing the stains out of her pa's clothes. Ranch work turned even a persnickety cowboy into a dirt ball, and Albert, who worked right alongside his men, got just as dirty as they did.

"When do you think Pa and the others will be back?"

"Anytime now...hopefully before nightfall."

Twenty-two and unmarried, Lou was the youngest of Albert's sisters. Her slender frame was bent over the rinse tub as she wrung out the contents piece by piece. A few strands of her hair had come loose. She tucked the hair behind her ears, and then hefted a basket of wet sheets as if it held cottonwood fluff. "Hurry up," she said as she walked toward the clotheslines with the basket. "We need to finish before they arrive."

Clara set to work with renewed energy at the thought of her father's return. She was equally excited to see her friend Geneva. Her pa and Geneva had been gone ten days, off to New Mexico Territory to witness the marriage of his sister Alma to Geneva's brother Morris. It was a long trip by wagon to attend a wedding, however, the bride and groom were first cousins, and in 1885, first cousins were not allowed to marry in the state of Colorado.

The entire time the wedding party was away, Clara felt lost in the four-bedroom log house she'd been living in for a little over a year. She missed the sound of her pa's booming voice barking orders or sharing jokes with his cowboys, and dearly missed going outside with him after supper where he would quiz her and her younger sister on the constellations hidden in a brilliant canopy of stars.

"We are almost to heaven up here, girls," he liked to say while he and his daughters stood on the front porch staring at stars twice as big and bright as those that hung over Philadelphia. Heaven was a forgivable exaggeration for a man who'd known only the hills and forests of the East. Before moving to Colorado, Albert owned a prosperous lumber business situated on the banks of the Delaware River. He took his daughters to school every morning on his way to work, maneuvering his horse and buggy through congested streets with the skill of an accomplished horseman. Six feet tall and elegant as an ivory cane, he tipped his derby to every driver he passed. Clara always made sure she got to the buggy before her sister Lily, so she could be the daughter sitting next to him.

She missed those cool, carefree mornings, especially on Monday, laundry day. Sometimes she would accidentally drop something she just washed in the dirt and wish for a green lawn like the one behind their home in Philadelphia. She was just about to ask her pa to let her go back to her Aunt Mid's elegant house on Richmond Street when Geneva and her family moved to the San Luis Valley.

Barely sixteen, Geneva was the picture of sophistication to a girl two years younger. Her mother even let her wear perfume, and whereas Clara had been taught to speak to adults only when spoken to, Geneva waded right into adult conversations, using given names and dropping aunt or uncle when it suited her.

"Please don't call Pa that," Clara said the first time Geneva called him Albert.

"But that is his name," Geneva replied. "Should I call him Cousin instead? I have many cousins."

She did have many cousins, seventeen to be exact, including Clara, a first cousin once removed who was trying to finish the week's wash before Geneva and the rest of the wedding party returned. Using a broom handle, Clara pulled her pa's steaming clothes out of the cauldron simmering on the stove. She let the garments cool, and then used salt, lye soap, and a bristle brush to remove the stubborn stains. After a final rinse in a tub of clean water, the clothes were ready to hang.

The back of the house was in shadows by the time Clara and Lou poured out the last tub of dirty water. Clara was pinning a pair of trousers on the clothesline when the sound of horse hooves striking hard-packed dirt and the squeaks of her father's spring wagon announced his arrival. Next came his commanding voice bringing the horses to a halt. "They're back!" she cried. Lifting the folds of her skirt and petticoat, she ran from the rear of the house to the front.

She waved at the four people sitting in the wagon, her hellos reaching them before she did. Nine-year-old Lily was already on the front porch, jumping up and down like a jackrabbit. Lou stood next to her, wiping her hands on her apron. Everyone began talking at once. The babble continued as the women and girls walked inside the house and the men unloaded supplies purchased in Santa Fe: a roll of wire that had been strapped to the tailgate and sacks of flour, beans, corn meal, sugar, and potatoes stored under the seats.

"I want to hear every detail." Clara reached for Geneva's hand. "Everything—what Santa Fe was like, where you dined, what the ceremony was like." She cupped her hand to the side of her mouth. "Did they kiss in front of you?"

Geneva smiled weakly and shook her curly blonde head. "I can't talk now...maybe later." She let go of Clara's hand.

The men finished unloading the supplies, and then joined the women. Albert passed around a bag of sweets, and with the taste of honey on their tongues, the female members of the family, none yet thirty years of age, prepared a late supper. Alma peeled potatoes and

Lou seasoned the steaks while Clara and Geneva set seven plates on a hand-hewn plank table surrounded by ten store-bought chairs. The long rectangular table separated the kitchen from a living area that held a floor-to-ceiling rock fireplace and leather-upholstered furniture.

"How long can you stay this time?" Clara asked. She and Geneva arranged silverware next to the plates.

Geneva opened her mouth as if to say something, and then closed it. She placed the spoons to the right of the knives, smiling mysteriously while taking longer than necessary to make sure the silverware was straight.

"Will you be spending the night?"

Geneva stopped fiddling with the silverware. "Yes," she stated, without looking up.

The two young women didn't see one another often. It took half a day by wagon on a trail brown and rutted as a waffle to travel between their ranches. When they did spend time together, they took long walks after their chores were done, commiserating with one another over the duties their parents and this harsh new life had imposed on them. At Geneva's urging the girls usually ended up in the horse barn where they sneaked up the ladder to the hay loft, lay on their stomachs, and watched Albert's cowboys tending their horses in the stalls below.

They held whispered debates over which cowboy was handsomest, or whose facial hair they liked or didn't like. Both girls preferred moustaches that turned up at the ends like the curved horns on cattle. They called the upturned moustaches "happy" and the ones that grew downward "sad."

Sometimes Albert came into the barn while they

were there. He was never a contestant in their best-looking cowboy contests, but if he had, he would have scored well, and his clean-shaven face would have escaped the girls' facial hair comments. Whenever he entered the barn, Clara buried her face in the hay, barely breathing until he left. Geneva did the same. The girls always checked one another's hair for straw before going back to the house. It was easier to spot in Clara's dark brown braids than Geneva's blonde curls.

Alma approached the plank table with a steaming bowl of potatoes. "Supper is ready." She looked at Clara. "We are all famished. Please tell Lily it is time to eat."

Lily was on the front porch giving the rocking chair a workout. "Potatoes!" she gushed, when Clara told her what they were having for supper. They hadn't had potatoes in months, and the ones in the ground wouldn't be ready until fall. "That is all I am going to eat tonight," Lily said. She jumped off the chair and ran inside.

Clara and Lily took their customary places at the foot of the table, and Clara motioned to Geneva. "Come sit with us." Geneva gave a dismissive wave. She was at the opposite end of the table, standing behind one of the chairs. "I can wait." She fidgeted with the chair back, avoiding Clara's inquisitive stare until Albert and Morris joined her and Alma. Morris pulled out a chair for Alma, and Albert did the same for Geneva.

A pang of jealousy stabbed Clara's breast at the sight of Geneva being the recipient of Pa's good manners. She guessed her friend had gotten used to being treated like a lady during a trip lasting ten days. Throughout supper, a meal anyone living in Conejos

County would have called a feast, Clara barely spoke to Lily on her left or Lou on her right. She kept her eyes on the four people at the head of the table, envious of the way they conversed like old friends, Geneva laughing too loudly and gesturing too enthusiastically.

After everyone finished eating, Albert and Morris stood in front of the rock fireplace, smoking Pandora cigars while the women cleared the table and did dishes. Geneva got right to work in the small kitchen. Clara did the same. Alma and Lou did most of the talking while the four women washed, dried, and put away the dishes. Clara politely listened to the two sisters' prattle, assuming she and Geneva would have a chance to talk later.

"Time to call it a day," Albert said as the women walked into the great room. By then it was nearly eleven o'clock. Clara bid a cheerful goodnight to her Aunt Alma and Uncle Morris, who were staying in the guest room. Geneva lit a lantern and walked toward the master bedroom. Albert followed, a few steps behind.

Clara's heart gave a lurch. Mouth agape, she called out to them, but neither one stopped or answered. She stood for a moment, barely breathing until the bedroom door closed behind them.

Eyes wild, she rushed down the hallway to the bedroom her aunts shared before Alma left to get married. Lou was there, readying herself for bed. "Geneva is sleeping in here tonight, is she not?" Clara poked her head out the bedroom door for another look. She was hoping to see Geneva walking down the hall, her face glowing in lantern light, but all she saw was the last log flickering in the fireplace.

She closed the door and pinned her eyes onto the

back of her aunt's head. Lou let down her light brown hair, removed the hairpins one at a time, and placed them in a pink glass jar on top of a bureau. "Albert didn't tell you?" She picked up a hairbrush and brushed her hair with long, forceful strokes.

"Tell me what?" Clara held her breath.

Lou stopped brushing. "That he and Geneva decided to get married, too…as long as they were in Santa Fe." She bent over and continued her hundred strokes. "…where it's legal for cousins."

Clara clapped both hands to her mouth and slumped against the doorframe. A score of questions raced through her brain, but she couldn't assemble a single one into words. The sudden dryness in her mouth would have prevented her from asking them, anyway. She kept looking at her aunt, hoping she would say something reassuring. Instead Lou remained devoted to her nightly ritual as if nothing of consequence had happened.

Throat tight with emotion Clara stumbled into the hallway. She desperately wanted to hide, find a place where she could throw up or cry, or both; but not only was she at a loss for words, she was at a loss for a place to go at this late hour. Her first impulse was to run outside, follow the creek, maybe all the way to the river. She stood in the dark hall and sobbed, frustrated it was the middle of the night, and the only realistic place she could go was the room she shared with Lily.

Crying softly, she crept inside and sat on the edge of her bed. Across from her in an identical bed, Lily was already asleep. Clara unbuttoned her high-top boots and climbed under the coverlet with her clothes on. Bone-weary after the worst day she'd had since her mother died, she lay awake, trying to make sense of a senseless turn of events. Pa wasn't supposed to get married again. He hadn't promised that; however with her and Lily to take care of him, he didn't need a wife. Besides, cousins marrying cousins, one of them much older than the other, was a complete muddle of how life was supposed to be.

With a sudden start she realized she would be seeing Geneva every day. They would be living in the same house—the one Pa built for his family—and her best friend, her only friend in this place with no neighborhoods or schools was now her stepmother. Did that mean she would have to obey her? Would a former friend, a girl close to her own age, be telling her what to do?

Chapter Two

By the time the black ceiling Clara stared at most of the night turned gray, she had decided to return to Philadelphia. Aunt Mid, her mother's older sister, doted on her and Lily for two years while Pa was beginning a new life and building a home for his family in Colorado. Aunt Mid had house servants. Clara could see her school chums again; enjoy ice cream once in a while. She lay barely breathing, listening for sounds of the house coming awake, but the only thing filling her ears was the beating of her heart.

At the first sound of pans banging in the kitchen, she jumped off her bed and ran down the hallway, hoping to catch her pa before he left the house. The plank floor felt cool on her bare feet, and the great room smelled faintly of wood smoke. Still wearing her skirt and blouse from the day before, she hurried to the chair next to the fireplace where Albert was putting on his boots. She stood in front of him, shoulders hunched around the knot in her chest. Looking at his clean-shaven face, his forehead white above the hat line, she wanted to say something from the heart, but all she could squeeze out of her quivering lips was a pitiful, "Pa?"

Albert kept his head down. He shoved his feet into his boots, and when he stood up, he had a tough-as-jerky expression on his face. "We will not be talking about this," he said in the same manner he might close a business deal.

Clara searched his hazel eyes for a sign of compassion. Seeing nothing except stony resolve, she crossed her arms over her heart as if to protect it from further bruising. She abandoned the little speech she had rehearsed, knowing she would burst into tears if she said anything at all.

Albert noticed his daughter's puffed eyelids. Relaxing his jaw, he paused for a moment to cup her face in his hands before grabbing his hat and heading into the day.

Clara watched him walk past the front windows. When she was sure he wouldn't turn around, she wandered to the dining table and pulled out the same chair she'd sat in the night before. Although it was the same chair, the same girl wasn't sitting in it, not this woeful adolescent, wishing she were dead.

"You could probably use a cup of coffee," said Aunt Lou who had witnessed the brief exchange between her brother and niece. She knew Clara snuck a cup of coffee every morning, and a minute later she returned with a cup of the hot, dark elixir whitened with milk and sugar. "Sit for a spell," she said. "I will cook breakfast this morning."

Clara drank slowly, her torment changing to rage as she remembered how cold Geneva had been the night before, how stupid she felt for not realizing something was wrong. She was on her second cup of coffee when the door to Pa's bedroom opened and Geneva walked toward her, arms raised in a provocative yawn that strained the buttons on the front of her blouse. Her ash blonde hair, curly as fiddle fern, looked even wilder than usual.

"You're up early," Geneva said. "Did you sleep well?"

"No," Clara said, with no attempt to hide her annoyance. "Did you?"

A shameless grin spread across Geneva's face. She sat down next to Clara. "Hardly at all."

Color burned Clara's cheeks. She pushed back her chair as if to leave. "I have chores to do." The lump in her throat made even those few words difficult to say.

Geneva took hold of Clara's sleeve. "Stay. Finish your coffee. I can do everything you and your aunts have been doing, and just as well. Of course you still have to make your bed."

"My bed is already made." Clara's gray-green eyes flicked a hostile look at Geneva's blues. "Must you punish me this soon…Stepmother?"

"Punish you? You should be thrilled—free as a kitten."

"Pa depended on me and my aunts. We took good care of him. I enjoy helping him."

Geneva rolled her eyes. "You are still a kitten, you know."

Clara bridled. "And you are a cat? You do look like a lion this morning." Despite an effort to keep them still, her lips quivered. "Shouldn't you be pinning your hair up now that you are a married woman?"

Geneva leaned back in her chair. Thrusting her bosom forward, she plumped her curly blonde mane. "Albert likes it this way."

The brazenness sent Clara reeling. Again she found herself searching for words. This time a few choice insults came to mind, all of them outside the bounds of propriety. She got up from the table, cup and saucer in hand. "I will never call you Mother," she vowed on her way to the kitchen.

Chapter Three

"Nobody seems to have domestics around here," Geneva complained to Clara and Lou at the end of her first awkward day as a stepmother. "Mama taught me everything I need to know, though, when it comes to keeping house. We learned together."

Lou draped an arm around Clara's shoulders. "As did we."

"I probably need a little more practice," Geneva said, "but I will make sure Albert's household runs smooth as possible. He works outside all day. His home should be a place where he can relax.

****

The broad San Luis Valley where Albert chose to begin life anew lies between the Sangre de Christo Range on the east and the San Juan Mountains to the west—eight thousand square miles in southern Colorado and northern New Mexico. A vast ocean of scrub brush covers most of the area, although trees grow at higher elevations. Albert was drawn to the valley for its far-reaching expanses of natural grass hay. He sold his lumber business, and then, parcel-by-parcel, he purchased thirty thousand acres of rangeland to feed the cattle he accumulated lot-by-lot. With the help of Mexican workers, he built the largest house in Conejos County as well as a barn, corral, three sheds, and a bunkhouse. All of this buying and building took him two and a half years, and by the time he sent for his daughters he was running the largest herd of cattle between Alamosa, Colorado and the New Mexico Territory border.

His daughters and young wife Geneva came from fashionable neighborhoods where nearly every home had a cook and housekeeper. Clara had grown up with a Negro servant named Nettie who kept the house spotless and cooked marvelous meals, cookies every day for the children. She also did the family's laundry.

Clara was ten, Lily five, when their mother died giving birth to a baby boy who shared her coffin three days later. Nettie hung a gray silk ribbon on the front door, and everyone had to whisper for a week. Soon after his wife's funeral, Albert sent his daughters to live with their Aunt Mid, and Nettie found other employment. Clara had been exited to join her father in Colorado for what she thought would be a grand adventure in the West until she found her new life came with a passel of chores and no Nettie to do them

****

Freed by Geneva from the chores she hated, Clara changed her mind about moving back to Philadelphia. Secretly she believed her new stepmother would fail, and she wanted to be there when it happened. She didn't have to wait long. The first night Geneva cooked supper for Albert and his family she burned a skilletful of precious Santa Fe potatoes. During her first week she made rock hard biscuits, hot cakes with doughy centers, and beef liver that was dry and tough. Her cooking became a source of amusement for Clara and Lou. They kept their giggles in check until the day Geneva tried to fry corn without first soaking it in water, and kernels exploded out of the frying pan like buckshot.

Albert was in the house at the time. "What in blazes is going on?" he shouted over the barrage of kapows. He rushed into the kitchen. One of the kernels grazed his cheek, and the expression on his face was too much for Clara and Lou, who laughed until they were laughing at each other for laughing.

"Stop this nonsense!" Albert rubbed his cheek. "If the three of you cannot cook a decent meal and do so in peace, then you can eat with the ranch hands. And believe you me, a diet of rice, beans, and tortillas can be dreadfully tiresome."

Chapter Four

The civilized world still adhered to Victorian principles when Geneva moved in with Albert, his daughters, and his sister Lou. Not all rules were strictly obeyed, however adults didn't speak openly about personal issues, and children were supposed to keep their thoughts and opinions to themselves. Teetering between childhood and womanhood, Clara began using silence as a weapon. Geneva, typically chatty as a blue jay, followed suit, creating a hostile environment for the entire household.

With her husband busy with his cattle business and Lou and Clara ignoring her most of the time, Geneva focused her attention on Lily. She brushed Lily's long blonde hair every day and listened to her read, or taught her to crochet when she had a few minutes of leisure. One Sunday morning she gave the nine-year-old a set of small tortoise shell clasps to pin the hair off her face.

Clara shot her sister a look of scorn. "What did you do to deserve these? Geneva is just buttering you up."

"Why are you so mean to her?" For a month Lily had been observing the tension generated by a dying friendship.

"Why do *you* like her so much? But of course you like her. She gives you little presents and doesn't make you do a lick of work. She even makes your bed."

Lily wrinkled her brows. "Maybe you are just plain

mean."

Later that day, Clara was in the great room reading a book while Lily and Geneva sat across from her on the leather sofa. Their heads, bent over a needlework project, were nearly touching. Both had hair the color of honey, Lily's straight, Geneva's frizzy.

Clara put her book down. Their blondness reminded her of a time not long after her mother died when Lily had been chosen to play an angel in their Sunday School Christmas pageant. All of the girls wanted to play angels and wear white organza gowns and wings made with real goose feathers. Clara already had another part in the program when she asked her Sunday school teacher if she could be an angel, too.

"My mother is an angel now," Clara added to her request. "She went to heaven two months ago."

The teacher shook her head. Peering down her perfect nose she said, "Who ever heard of a dark-haired angel?" Three and a half years later, the remark still stung whenever Clara brought it to mind. With her straight brown hair parted in the middle and braided, she thought of herself as plain compared to her fair-haired sister, and their father's choice of a pretty blonde wife seemed to confirm it.

Geneva's cooking improved, and she kept the house clean, but after six weeks of washing bedding, towels, and clothing for five people, she handed that chore back to Lou and Clara. Clara was incensed. Why should this flighty, self-centered person, two years older than she was get to boss her around? Worse yet, Geneva had given her the hardest chore of the week, an exhausting all-day project scheduled for the day after a day of rest.

Several Mondays later, Clara was checking her father's trousers before laundering them when she discovered a letter in one of the pockets. The letter was signed Mildred; Aunt Mid's given name—no truly yours, yours sincerely, no cordially—simply Mildred. Clara read the letter twice, and then put it in the pocket of a different pair of trousers hanging in her pa's closet.

The next morning, Geneva was in the kitchen ironing one of Albert's shirts when Clara walked in and poured herself a cup of coffee. "Aunt Mid thinks your marriage is evil," she said, stirring in cream and sugar.

Geneva kept ironing. "What makes you say that?"

"I read it in a letter she wrote to him." Clara smiled gleefully and took her first sip of coffee.

A ripple of irritation spread across Geneva's face. She set the iron on its trivet. "I don't remember Albert receiving a letter from her."

"Pa is not obliged to show you his mail. I doubt he would have let you read that one, anyway, not when Aunt Mid called your marriage 'a perverse union.'"

Geneva gave Clara a blue-eyed glare. "That sounds like something you made up. Why would you be allowed to read Albert's mail when I'm not?"

"Pa didn't show it to me. I found it. I go through the pockets of every garment I wash before I wash them. Once in a while I find something interesting…such as Aunt Mid's letter."

Geneva eyed Clara with cold speculation. "Have you ever found anything of mine?"

"I found a lemon drop once."

"What did you do with it?"

"I ate it."

Geneva tightened her lips. "You are such a child!"

"Perverse means evil!" Clara blurted. "I looked it up in Pa's dictionary. Aren't you ashamed the people back home think your marriage is evil?"

The two young women planted their feet in the middle of the small kitchen, glowering at one another like duelists. Finally Geneva threw up her hands and said, "With everything else I have to do around here, why must I be saddled with a spoiled child? Leave me be. Go outside and play, Stepdaughter."

Chapter Five

Clara's Mondays seemed endless, yet she ran out of things to occupy her time the rest of the week. There were no schools in Conejos County, no church, friends, or books from her pa's sizeable collection she hadn't already read, some twice, *Wuthering Heights* three times. Nettie was no longer around to pester with questions all day. Clara could always go for a walk, but she didn't care to walk by herself, or with Lily who always wanted to turn back before she did.

Lou went horseback riding in her spare time, sometimes alone, sometimes with one of Albert's cowboys. She took riding lessons before moving to Colorado. She and her sister Alma, both in their twenties and neither one a beauty, had decided odds of finding a husband were better out West than in the city. They volunteered to escort Clara and Lily to La Jara when their brother's house was finished, and he invited them to stay. With them they brought trunks filled with stylish dresses and wraps, fine linens, a feathered hat or two, and their best jewelry. They wore earbobs on occasion, but the rest of their finery remained in the trunks while they went about organizing what had been a bachelor's quarters into a working household.

Women were scarce as fresh vegetables in the San Luis Valley, which made Albert's sisters enormously popular with his men. Alma was not impressed.

Referring to cowboys as "boys pretending to be men," she married her cousin Morris who owned a ranch nine miles from Albert's. Lou, on the other hand, made flirting with cowboys her favorite pastime.

Will you teach me how to ride a horse?" Clara asked Lou one boring Thursday. "We could go riding together."

"I don't have enough experience," Lou answered. "Back in Pennsylvania, I learned on a proper equestrian saddle. To ride like a lady on one of those big western saddles the cowboys use, you have to grab the pommel with one hand (I use my right) and the back of the saddle with the other. Then you have to hang on for dear life. I can do it, however I can't gallop, nor do I feel completely safe when my horse is simply ambling."

"Who taught you how to ride that way?"

"Albert's foreman showed me how. If you are truly serious about this, Clara, I will ask Vincent if he can spare the time. He's an excellent rider. Good with horses. You know who I'm talking about, don't you?"

"Oh, yes." Clara tried not to smile. Back when she and Geneva were spying on cowboys, Vincent won most of their best-looking-cowboy contests in spite of a downturned moustache that made him look sad.

A lean man of twenty-three, Vincent Reese was older than the typical cowpuncher. Lou had set her cap for him before she started falling for a different cowboy every other week, most of them several years younger. Lou asked Vincent if he would show Clara how to ride, and after making sure Albert was in agreement, he took on the task. It would be a welcome break from his routine as well as a chance to improve his standing with the boss.

He chose a gentle bay named Hero for Clara to learn on, reddish-brown with a black mane and tail. To prepare the horse for a female rider, he attached one of Clara's long skirts to the horse's pommel and then rode him around the corral until Hero got used to something flopping against his ribs.

Clara stopped counting how many times she fell, but after each incident, she dusted herself off and climbed back on Hero. One day Albert stopped by while Clara and the horse circled the corral. Seeing how hard it was for his daughter to sit sideways on a western saddle, he drove the buckboard to Conejos and bought her and Lou sidesaddles. He offered to buy a sidesaddle for Geneva who declined. "I'm afraid of horses," was the excuse she gave. "They have big teeth and clunky feet."

Clara couldn't remember her onetime friend being afraid of a horse if there was a handsome cowboy sitting on it, putting a saddle on it, or tying it to the hitching rail in front of the ranch house. Several times she'd seen Geneva, a married woman now, rush up to Vincent when he rode to the house to meet with Albert, petting his chestnut mare like she would a cat while detaining him with chatter.

Chapter Six

The sidesaddle gave Clara a huge boost in self-confidence. Designed to accommodate a woman's skirt and petticoats, her sidesaddle came with two pommels, one she hooked her right leg around, and one over the left thigh to hold her in place if the horse galloped or jumped. After using her new saddle for less than a day, she rode Hero out of the corral. She made a few trips close by the house that afternoon, and then she and Lou began riding together almost every day. When they rode at a gallop Clara lifted her face to the flood of fresh air filling her nostrils. Her half-raveled braids bounced against her back as she put more distance between her and her stepmother with every thud of Hero's hooves.

The farther she rode, the more she embraced the rugged beauty of the San Luis Valley. Exciting new vistas seemed to be waiting in ambush beyond every rise—pronghorn, elk, and bald eagles, prairie sunflowers poking their small yellow heads above the tall grass, ground squirrels and cottontail rabbits that scattered in every direction when she and Lou rode through their territory.

The summer sun was sometimes fierce enough to burn the blue out of the sky, and by September, when the valley floor was awash in yellow rabbit brush, Clara's face and hands, along with the part separating her hair into braids, were brown as a nut.

Albert's men sometimes rode with the women. Most of his cowboys were young, some as young as fifteen. They all wanted to get to know Clara, but she was only interested in what she could learn from them—how to control a feisty horse, how to determine a horse's age, breed, and disposition before putting a saddle on it, how to ride alongside a cow without spooking it; anything that would make her a better horsewoman in the eyes of her father.

That lasted until October when a young man from the Oklahoma Territory caught her eye. Curtis was two years older, a bit of information she had to drag out of a boy who kept to himself and said little. His dark hair and eyes reminded her of the Italian boys she'd gone to school with in Pennsylvania. As a way to get him to talk, she asked if he was Italian, certain he would confirm her hunch.

"No," he said quietly, "Black Dutch."

Clara heard a tinge of wariness in his reply. "Black Dutch?" She studied his suntanned face. "I have not heard of that nationality. I am Pennsylvania Dutch. Maybe they are alike." She gave the brown-eyed boy a cheerful grin, deciding in an instant he was her beau.

Like many of the men on Albert's payroll, Curtis would often be gone for days at a time, working in another part of the ranch. Even in the wilds of the San Luis Valley, the standards of polite society still applied, and whenever he and Clara were in the same place at the same time, it was usually in the company of others. They still managed to be alone long enough for a private hug a few times. On one of those occasions he'd given her a peck on the lips; a small, titillating transgression a girl might have shared with her best friend if she'd had one.

Chapter Seven

Curtis spent the winter after that first kiss in a line shack in the westernmost corner of Albert's thirty thousand acres. He and another cowboy had been sent there to ward off rustlers and keep cows from wandering onto other ranches. Their replacements arrived in March. By then Clara was on Hero again, helping her pa round up strays or move cattle from one pasture to another. She'd become good enough at working cattle she could identify which calf belonged to which cow if they got separated. There was more to learn, though, and she couldn't wait to ride with Curtis again. To her, no one—not even her pa or his foreman—sat a horse as well as Curtis, who rode as if he and the animal were conjoined.

On a cool day in May, Clara was running errands for her father's men while they branded the last of the winter-born calves. Curtis was there. So was Albert, watching from the saddle of his buckskin stallion. The air was filled with dust and pollen and the sour smell of cow manure. Calves were bawling, cows bellowing, men shouting to one another, when in the midst of the pandemonium, Clara ran after a runaway calf. When she couldn't catch it on foot, she grabbed the reins of the closest horse, put her left foot in the stirrup, pulled the back of her skirt between her legs, and straddled the horse like a man.

"God almighty," Albert muttered into his bandana, and before the day was over he was making plans to send her and Lily back to Philadelphia. He bought their train tickets, and after swearing Geneva to secrecy, asked her to prepare a special supper for the night he planned to inform his daughters of their fate. Geneva got the chuck wagon cook to shoot a couple of sage hens. She cleaned the birds herself, roasted them, and served them with hominy and gravy. Round with child, she set the meal she had sweated over on the table and then excused herself.

Albert watched his pregnant wife trudge down the hall to their bedroom. Then he sat down in his chair at the head of the table and picked up his knife and fork. "I hope everyone sitting here appreciates this meal," he said. "Geneva cooked it even though she was indisposed."

He carved one of the birds, put a portion of it on his plate, and passed the rest. Before taking his first bite he scanned the faces at the table. "I have something to say." He turned to his sister. "Not to you, Lou, to Clara and Lily." He took a bite of sage hen and took his time chewing it. His daughters served themselves, but held onto their forks, waiting for whatever he was about to say.

"I have decided you girls need to finish your schooling," he said. He directed a critical scowl at Clara. "And the only way I can give you a decent education is to send you back to Philadelphia."

A grin spread across Lily's face. Waving her fork in the air she began chanting, "Philadelphia! Philadelphia!"

Lou poked her with her elbow. "Put your fork

down, Lily."

"I have made arrangements for you girls to stay with your Aunt Mildred again," Albert continued, unblinking. "I am confident she will teach you to be ladies."

Clara slumped in her chair. Avoiding her father's not-so-subtle censure, she kept her eyes on the dent in a pewter pitcher that sat in the middle of the table. The bleakest of futures flashed through her mind—no tearing across the dunes on Hero, no chance to find out how a kiss might feel when it lasted longer than two seconds. "Please don't make me go back," she said in a small voice, still staring at the pitcher. "I like it here, Pa. I *love* it here."

Albert poured gravy on his hominy. "This is an opportunity, Clara, not a punishment."

Clara pushed the food around on her plate. No one spoke, not even Lou. When Albert's plate was empty, he stood up and patted his vest pocket. "I have your train tickets right here." He gave Clara a firm, meaningful glance. "You leave in a week."

He walked to the fireplace and lit his customary after-supper cigar. Sending his daughters back to Philadelphia would do more than give them the education he wanted them to have. It would also restore harmony to his household and avoid the turmoil he felt was sure to come when the child his wife was carrying joined the family.

Early the next morning, Clara went looking for Curtis. She found him behind the horse barn, practicing his roping, using a tree stump for a cow. She spoke in bursts, her lips quivering as she told him what her father had decreed. Curtis listened to her vent, roping and releasing, roping and releasing his motionless target. Without stopping he said, "Tonight we ride to Conejos. After dark."

Clara smiled, nodding vaguely. She had been to Conejos twice, a town about fifteen miles from the ranch. It was more a random collection of buildings than a real town, yet she'd heard there was a Justice of the Peace there. She thought it improper to ask Curtis if his plan included marriage, however, in less time than it takes to say Justice of the Peace she convinced herself he was just too shy.

"Come outside when you hear my signal," Curtis told her. "I'll have Hero with me."

For the rest of the day, Clara avoided making eye contact with everyone in her family. She went to bed early to prevent Lily from seeing she was wearing her dark green riding habit under the covers. She pretended to be asleep while her sister changed into her nightdress and climbed into her own bed. Lying still as a post, hands at her sides, ears straining the night air for some kind of signal, Clara worried a Justice of the Peace might refuse to marry her and Curtis because they were too young. That concerned her more than what her family might say if the man agreed to perform the ceremony.

At some point she dozed off. Around midnight, her eyes popped open at the sound of an explosion outside. She leaped out of bed and peered out her bedroom window. It was too dark to see anything, so she ran down the hall toward the great room where her pa, barefoot and in long underwear, was heading for the front door with a shotgun in his hands.

"Someone just fired at the house!" he shouted, and

it dawned on Clara that what she'd assumed was an explosion was probably Curtis's signal.

Geneva and Lou hurried into the great room in their nightclothes, Lou carrying a lantern. "Douse that light!" Albert ordered. "Everyone down on the floor!" Eyebrows knit, he glared at Clara, but made no mention of her being dressed in her riding habit in the middle of the night.

Lou blew out the flame, and all three women got down on their hands and knees. Albert opened the front door a crack and peeked outside. A few seconds later he opened the door wider and started to leave. Clara got up to follow, but he told her to get back down.

The five minutes he was outside felt like an hour to Clara. She debated whether to stay where she was or slink back into bed. She opted for the security of her bed where she lay awake the rest of the night, wondering what her father had found and what he was thinking.

The next morning, in either an amazing act of courage or one of youthful ignorance, the shooter stopped by the house. Clara dashed to the front door when he rode up. Albert was three steps behind.

He pushed Clara aside and opened the door to a young man standing on the porch, hat in hand. He'd never met Curtis. With Vincent doing most of the hiring, he didn't know all of the men who worked for him. "Were you the imbecile who shot off his pistol last night?" he asked. "Why in God's name would you do such a thing?"

Curtis aimed his dark eyes at his boots. "Can I talk to Clara, Sir?"

Clara tugged at her father's sleeve. "Please, Pa."

Not about to leave the two of them alone, Albert stood in the doorway, grilling the young cowboy until he haltingly admitted to his and Clara's plan.

"I threw some rocks at her window. She didn't come out, so I shot."

Albert raised his dark brows. "At the window?"

"At the sky."

With a calm that belied the storm in his head, Albert fixed a smoldering eye on Curtis. "My daughter is too young to get married. You, as well, young man. And furthermore, when I finally walk her down the aisle, I do not want to see a cowboy waiting at the other end."

Curtis put his hat back on and left. He made himself scarce after that, withdrawing from human contact like a desert tortoise in its shell. When he showed up in La Jara a week later to say goodbye to Clara, Albert made sure he didn't board the train.

Chapter Eight

Clara and Lily arrived at Pennsy station on the fifth of June. Their Aunt Mid, a widow with no children of her own, was waiting on the platform when her nieces arrived. After a kiss on the cheek for each of them, she paid a porter to load their luggage into the back of an open cab waiting in a line of horse-drawn vehicles next to the station. During the twenty-minute ride to her house, the girls sat facing the driver with Mildred between them.

Lily scooted to the edge of the seat, swapping one view for another as the cab rumbled down the variously paved avenues and streets. Clara slouched against the upholstered seat back, ignoring the gurgling fountains they passed, wishing they would drown out her sister's voice.

"Look, Clara!" Lily pointed to a store with striped awnings over its windows. "I remember that shop. Pa used to buy us ice cream there. May we go there, Aunt Mid?"

"You are probably mistaking that shop for another," said Mildred. "There are many such confectionaries all over town, which means there is one not far from my house, which means yes, we will have ice cream. Not every day, however. How about you, Clara? Do you like sweets?" Clara nodded glumly, observing without really seeing the people and buildings they passed. Aunt Mid nudged her with her shoulder. "Of course you do."

As the cab clattered up the stone block drive leading to her aunt's house, Clara raised her head. The long driveway was lined on both sides with ancient oak trees, their branches entwined in some places to form a canopy. Peering into the leafy umbrella, Clara remembered how she used to long for cool green shade after moving to Colorado where her father had sacrificed most of the trees around their house to build it. Now the leafy oaks seemed ordinary, and it wasn't cool in Philadelphia, it was hot and muggy.

Two newly decorated bedrooms awaited the girls' arrival, each with a four-poster bed and tall mahogany bureaus. Multi-paned windows welcomed daylight into every corner of the three-story house, and wall sconces lit the hallways by night. The drawing room, with its shiny maple floor and massive, round-arched fireplace, was wallpapered in blue forget-me-nots, an unassuming pattern for a room of such grandeur.

Mildred's young charges returned from Colorado looking more like street urchins than proper young Philadelphians, and the first thing she did after the girls unpacked was cut Lily's hair, badly tangled after the long train ride. Clara's hair escaped the shears, but she got a lecture about her suntan. "A lady always wears a hat in public," said Aunt Mid. "Do not let me catch you without one."

"In this heat?" Clara got a piercing look in reply.

Both girls suffered from the humidity, yet it was not even officially summer when they arrived. The temperature in their upstairs bedrooms was unbearable, and after three sweaty nights, Clara asked if she could sleep downstairs on the screened porch. Mildred allowed both her nieces to sleep there for one night and then made arrangements for them to spend the rest of the summer on the Jersey shore.

She rented three rooms in a beachfront hotel on Brigantine Beach, a small island where the days could be hot, but a cool ocean breeze brought the temperature down at night. Clara met several boys and girls on the island who were about her age. In groups of three or four they spent the summer rowing in the bay, riding the trolley, or fishing for crabs that the hotel cook prepared for their suppers. Lily found a friend, too, a boy who was good at building things out of sand and catching water beetles.

Clara kept her Colorado tan all summer because the sun hat her aunt insisted she wear rode on her shoulders whenever she was out of Mildred's sight. Lily kept her head covered, and when she and Clara started school in September, they didn't look like they were related. The city was cooler than it had been in June. As the girls walked to and from school, the lawns and gardens of the homes they passed were still green and graced with flowers. By mid-October the flowers were gone, and they were wading through red and yellow leaves up to their skirt-covered ankles.

At school, Lily became fast friends with a girl named Bella whom Clara decided was a brunette angel, if there ever was one. Convinced her own brown-haired looks were unremarkable, Clara was surprised when her suntanned face and stories about riding horses and punching cows made her the center of attention, especially with the tenth grade boys. Boys began sitting with her at lunch, waiting for her after class, sometimes asking to walk her home. With interesting things to do and young people to do them with, she hadn't thought about Curtis since her second day at Brigantine Beach.

Just before Thanksgiving, one of Clara's admirers, a boy she was particularly fond of, invited her to go to a dance with him. She asked her aunt for permission and was pleased when she said yes. Then Mildred added, "Only because I will be there playing the piano."

Clara and the boy were a trifle late arriving at the dance. They hung up their coats, and as they took their places in the quadrille, Mildred stopped in the middle of the song she was playing and said, "If you cannot be on time, young lady, you need to go home."

Clara withered. She stood for a moment in the middle of a roomful of tittering adolescents before hurrying off the dance floor, cheeks aflame, eyes lowered, grabbing her coat on the way out. Her dance partner followed.

She burst into tears the minute they reached the sidewalk. He offered her his pocket handkerchief and she hid her face in it. "We were only a few minutes late," she sobbed. Hands clenched at her sides, she headed for home. The boy matched her stride for stride, neither one speaking until they arrived at Mildred's house. They walked up the front steps, and Clara jerked open the heavy door. "Wait," the boy cried. "The bakery is open early. Let me buy you a sweet roll tomorrow morning."

Clara's mood brightened at the suggestion, and after she and the boy agreed on a time, she gave him back his handkerchief and wished him good night.

At five a.m. the next day, with her heart in her throat, she slipped into her blue linen jumper. She was soundlessly negotiating the last few steps of the staircase when her aunt called out, "Go back to bed, Clara, until we all get up," thus ending another budding relationship. After that, Clara was allowed to go to dances only in the company of her aunt, and when Mildred went home, Clara went home.

Lily watched all of this with interest, and profiting from her big sister's mistakes, she asked her aunt for piano lessons and practiced every day. Mildred knew Lily's friend Bella's parents; therefore Lily was allowed to go to parks, parties, and even sledding with her little friend as long as one of Bella's parents went with them.

Aunt Mid was strict but fair; although Clara could never understand what she had against novels. Clara spent most of the winter with her nose in a book, often unbeknownst to her aunt, a novel. Every day she wrote in the diary Lily gave her for Christmas. She spent hours at her bedroom window, watching wet snow drip off naked tree limbs, and wishing she were in the San Luis Valley where it didn't snow often, but when it did, the snowflakes formed cottony pillows on everything they touched.

She also spent a good deal of time doing homework, and completed the ninth and tenth grades in one year. Tenth grade was all the public schooling available unless she went to Normal School to become a teacher. She knew her father expected her to be serious about this last opportunity for formal education, and she finished with stellar marks in math and penmanship. She had no interest in furthering her education, and the year she'd spent walking down tree-lined streets and playing croquet on sprawling, weedless lawns made her long for the scrub brush and sandy plains of her pa's ranch.

In her diary she wrote: *If I try real hard I can smell the grass and sagebrush. I miss Hero and riding in the quiet of the morning. I miss the cows, too, but horses are ever so much smarter.*

Chapter Nine

Albert came to Philadelphia for Clara's tenth grade graduation, and as soon as she found an opportunity to speak with him alone, she begged him to take her back to Colorado. He refused. She persisted, albeit respectfully. He argued for the cultural advantages of living in a city, the potential for a husband with a college degree, an easier life than she would experience in rough and tumble Colorado. She countered with how helpful she would be, both inside with Geneva and outside with the cattle. They wrangled off and on for almost a week until the day before he was to leave.

"I have decided to let you come back, Daughter," Albert said, "however with two stipulations. One, you must promise to be nicer to Geneva. She was despondent after we lost our first child, and now she has a two-month-old son to care for. Secondly, you must promise to ride a horse like a lady."

Clara nodded enthusiastically, mustering up a yes that sounded sincere enough to get her back to Colorado. Lily, with more schooling to complete and a friend she couldn't bear to leave, stayed behind.

Albert bought a five-pound box of Whitman chocolates for Clara to give to Geneva when she saw her for the first time in more than a year. Clara made sure the gift was safe during every mile of the long train ride. One of Albert's ranch hands was waiting in the buckboard when they arrived in La Jara. With a boost from her father, Clara climbed up and sat next to the driver. Albert squeezed next to her. She cradled the box of chocolates in her lap as the ranch hand slapped the reins and the horse lurched into a reluctant trot. Halfway up the rock-strewn road to the ranch house, the horse swung into a full gallop, and the sudden jolt bounced the lid off the Whitman's box. Clara let out a shriek as half the chocolates flew into the dust.

****

With a sheepish grin, Clara presented the half empty box of candy to her onetime friend. "Looks like you ate most of them," Geneva said. Clara explained what had happened, and Albert backed her up. Geneva managed a tepid thank you, and then inspected the various shapes and sizes of chocolate. She picked a square one and bit into it. "Nugget." She wrinkled her nose. "Not my favorite," but she finished the nougat-filled chocolate anyway on her way to the kitchen.

After supper, Albert worked on his ledgers. Clara cleared the table without being asked, and she was heating water on the stove when Geneva walked into the kitchen. "Albert told me you promised to help, and I'm glad to see you are doing it. I have a baby to care for. I can't cook and clean and do everything else by myself."

Clara poured hot water into a large pot and began washing the silverware. Geneva picked up a tea towel, but before drying a single fork, she said, "You will be interested to know your would-be suitor Curtis disappeared the day after you left." It was a tidbit of information she'd been dying to share with the ex-friend standing next to her.

Curtis hadn't been a spec of dust in Clara's dreams of returning to Colorado, and when his name didn't produce a reaction, Geneva added more dirt. "Albert said it was for the best. He found out Curtis was a half-breed. Part Choctaw. Did you know that?" A thin smile curled the corners of her lips.

Clara shook her head. "He told me he was Black Dutch."

"Seems that's what Indians, well…part Indians, anyway, or ones that aren't real dark, call themselves these days."

"Where is Aunt Lou? How long has she been gone?" Clara asked.

Geneva gave a little snort and put down her towel. Opening the cupboard where she'd stored the remaining Whitman chocolates, she popped one in her mouth. "Sometime after Curtis left, Lou married a cowhand who only worked here about a month. At least this one was closer to her in age." She gave Clara a chocolate-toothed smile. "They moved to Custer County. I guess her husband decided it was safer to buck logs than buck broncs. I doubt there's much money in it, though."

To Clara, Aunt Lou's marriage was both good news and bad. Good, because her aunt needed to settle down and start a family. Bad, because it meant her riding partner was gone.

"Did you know Alma had two unsuccessful pregnancies?" Geneva picked up her towel.

Clara nodded. "Aunt Mid told me."

"She didn't give birth to them like I did my first baby boy. It's harder…much harder to lose a child once you hold him in your arms."

"I knew about that, too, Geneva. I was truly sorry

to hear it."

Lost in thought, Geneva dried a cup, then a saucer. She put them in the cupboard, drew a deep breath, and continued. "Alma finally carried a child to term...a daughter. She named her Violet. Isn't that simply the sweetest name? Albert and I chose the name Christopher for our son because it is much in fashion these days. I can't wait to have a little girl, though. When I do, I will call her Rose."

Talk of having more babies when her pa would be fathering them put an end to Clara's interest in local news. "I need to go to bed now," she said when the last pan was dried and put away. "It was a long train ride on a hard seat. It was hot and dusty, and the train lurched back and forth to such a degree I had trouble keeping my balance when Pa and I walked to the dining car."

Chapter Ten

Before breakfast the next morning, Clara dashed to the horse barn. She felt a surge of elation with her first sniff of barn smells, a thrill that disappeared when all of the stalls were empty. Albert's foreman, the man who taught her how to ride, was the only cowboy in sight, and he was getting ready to leave.

Vincent reached under his chestnut mare, found the cinch, and threaded it through the rings. Noticing the girl's downcast expression, he stopped readying his horse. "You lookin' to go for a ride?" he asked on his way over to her.

Clara nodded, taking some comfort in the fact he remembered her.

"We're a bit horse shy this month. I'm headin' to the other side of the valley to buy some. I'll look for a mount for you."

"Where's that bay I used to ride?"

Vincent stroked his light brown moustache. "You mean Hero? He got into somethin' this spring and died of the heaves."

Clara pictured the reddish-brown horse she'd ridden for close to a year. "Not my good boy Hero!" She started to cry.

Vincent had never seen the girl cry, not even after she'd been thrown from a horse. Having little experience with women, he had no clue what to do with one that was crying, and to make matters worse, this one was the boss's daughter. He figured he was at least ten years older than she was—too close in age to have fatherly feelings for her. Since his own father never showed him or his brothers any affection, he had little to draw from, anyway.

For a man skilled with a lariat, his hands suddenly felt useless. He let them dangle at his sides for a moment, and then shoved them into his trouser pockets. When Clara stopped crying, he pulled off his bandana and handed it to her, a dirty rag that left dark smudges on her eyes and cheeks. He took a quick look around the barn. Seeing nothing faintly resembling a clean handkerchief, he ran up to the ranch house, pulled a tea towel off the clothesline, ran back and gave it to Clara. She buried her face in the snowy towel, breathing in the familiar scent of Watson's soap.

"I thought of somethin' on my way back," Vincent said. "Your pa's got a packhorse I bet you could ride. Lou used to ride 'er once in a while."

"So the horse is used to someone riding sidesaddle?"

"Yep."

Vincent delayed his horse-buying trip long enough to run the suggestion by his boss. Clara tagged along, ready to argue her cause. Albert agreed to give up his packhorse as long as Vincent found a suitable replacement. He also gave his daughter permission to ride alone with the understanding she stay within a five-mile radius of the ranch house.

That evening, Clara was back in her sidesaddle on a strawberry roan named Bridget. Pointing the horse west she rode toward the distant San Juan Mountains, threading through the rabbit brush, greasewood, and sagebrush that peppered the land as far as the eye could see. When she'd gone less than five miles, she reined in the horse. Bridget shook her head to clear her muzzle, and then stood perfectly still while Clara watched a soft pink Alpine glow brighten the San Juan's snow-covered peaks. In the hush of twilight, the only sounds were cattle bawling in the distance and the hiss of windblown sand scurrying through the underbrush. Breathing deep the faint scent of sage, Clara felt a thrill rise all the way to her hairline.

****

She would have more such evenings, but only on long summer nights when all of her chores were done. Within days of returning to the ranch, she was doing laundry again as well as whatever tasks Geneva could slough off on her. It was hard to be cordial to a former friend who'd begun taking her role as stepmother so seriously. Clara finished her work quickly, and her only reward was an hour or so of solace to saddle up Bridget and ride across the hills and dunes of the San Luis Valley at a faster pace than might be expected for a packhorse and a girl riding sidesaddle.

One evening Vincent asked Clara if she would like some company, and before long he was riding with her whenever his duties allowed. Every time he approached the house with Bridget in tow, Geneva found some reason she needed help that very minute.

Clara envied Geneva for many reasons, currently her role as mistress of the house. Back when the two of them were single, it was for her boldness around men; the way she always forgot to whisper when the two of them were in the hayloft. The cowboys would hear her and coax them down. How easily Geneva chatted with the men and made them laugh! Clara assumed marriage would temper her, hobble her lip some, change her hairstyle, loosen her corset; however, she continued to wear bodice-hugging styles and did nothing to tame her frizzy hair. She also continued to flirt with Albert's men when he wasn't around.

Clara was about to go riding with Vincent after a particularly arduous day when Geneva came up with yet another chore for her to do. "I am not your slave," Clara said, clenching her fists. "I am trying to be agreeable, but if you keep troubling me, I will tell Pa I have seen you sashaying around his men." She pointed at Vincent. "Including that one."

Geneva blinked with surprise. She mumbled something under her breath that included the word damn, and avoided Vincent after that, speaking to him only when ranch business made it necessary.

Chapter Eleven

Vincent and Clara took advantage of the long summer days, riding sometimes until the sun disappeared behind the San Juan Mountains. Returning after dark they would slow their horses to a walk while they engaged in brief conversation. Clara had to pry Vincent's stories out of him, but he told her more about himself than he told his men—that his father had been a section hand on the Chicago, Rock Island and Pacific Railroad; that he'd left home at thirteen and never gone back; that he'd been punching cows for ten years.

"I kept my nose clean and worked myself up from ranch hand to foreman." He smiled shyly. "I have your pa to thank for that."

When it was her turn to share, Clara described the idyllic childhood she experienced before her mother died, her close relationship with Nettie, the parks and playgrounds in Philadelphia, and the blissful summer she spent on the Jersey shore. After a few weeks of stories told on moonlit rides, their need for a safe haven drew them closer together, she to get away from Geneva, and he to end ten years of bunking with men who reeked of sweat and animal gore.

On a crisp Sunday morning in the September of Clara's sixteenth year, she and Vincent decided to give their horses a rest and fish for trout on La Jara Creek. Clara made a picnic lunch of beef sandwiches on skillet bread, pickles, and a dozen oatmeal cookies. Vincent rigged two fishing poles, and then he and Clara strolled along the creek until they spied a grassy spot near a thicket of aspen trees. Sunshine reflected off the aspens' white bark as they spread their blanket on the grass.

They fished for less than an hour in the fluttering shade of the trees before they put down their poles to eat lunch. Vincent ate every crumb of his sandwich and four cookies. Clara finished her lunch, picked up her pole, and cast her line into the water again, even though the fish hadn't been biting. The warmth of the sun coupled with the murmur of slow-moving water made her sleepy, so she drew in her line and rested her head on Vincent's shoulder. She could feel the hardness of his lean, yet muscular arm. She'd never sat this close to him before, not even the few times they'd been seated next to one another at Sunday supper. They did, however, more or less hug every time he helped her dismount, both knowing full well she could do so on her own.

In the warmth of the noonday sun with this girl he knew better than just about anybody leaning against him, Vincent felt as if something was sucking out his innards. He glanced down at her, and seeing her eyes were closed he lingered, watching the shadows of the leaves flicker across her suntanned face. It was a nice face, more athletic than pretty, with a strong chin and eyes the color of sage, eyes that always seemed to be deep in thought when they were open. Unlike other women he'd known, and there hadn't been many, she was physically strong, not a cry baby; not afraid to get her shoes muddy. At that moment he wanted to loosen her braids and kiss her on the mouth. Smoothing his moustache, he took a deep breath and said, "What would you say to you 'n me gettin' married?"

Clara's eyes opened wide. She sat bolt upright, hoping Vincent didn't think she was immodest for leaning against him. Was he serious, or just checking to see if she was awake? His head was turned away from her. Perhaps he was looking at the water, or his fishing pole, maybe nothing at all. She couldn't read his intent without seeing his face, so she got up and moved between him and the creek. The process of getting up, rearranging her skirt and petticoats, and sitting back down, gave her a few seconds to think about what he said; clear her mind; catch her breath. He wouldn't look at her, so she put a finger to the side of his chin and gently moved it in her direction. She saw no smirk on his lips and nothing but tenderness in his bright blue eyes.

She considered Vincent a good friend—kind, quiet, sincere—definitely her pa's best cowboy, but did she love him? He didn't give her the same tingle of warmth she'd felt around other young men—some classmates, some she met at the Jersey shore, even Curtis.

On the other hand, if she and Vincent were to marry, Geneva would turn inside out with jealousy. A relaxed smile spread across Clara's face as her quiet deliberation segued from Geneva to Christopher. Clara made every effort to avoid her stepmother, but she was genuine in her affection for her half-brother. She loved his clean baby smell after giving him a bath, and the only joy she got from washing clothes was pinning his frocks and didies on the clothesline and watching them flutter in the breeze like small white birds.

She looked into Vincent's eyes. "When?" she asked, without blinking. Her gentle reply was nearly carried downstream by the babbling creek.

Vincent laid his pole on the grass, and with one calloused mitt he grasped her by the wrist. "Are you sayin' yes?"

Clara nodded. She felt redness boiling up her face, yet her eyes never wavered from his.

"We should do it right away," he said, matching the intensity of her stare, "before Albert gets back from Omaha. He's not keen on his cowboys bein' married." Vincent's slow, husky manner of speaking caused a blip in Clara's heartbeat.

"You are his favorite, Vincent. Pa won't mind, especially if you are married to me." The sweet smell of wet leaves filled the air as she got to her feet. Vincent joined her at the water's edge, pausing before he curved an arm around her waist. For several minutes, they stood side-by-side, gazing at the little scallops made by ripples breaking against rocks.

"Where will we live?" Clara asked, her Pennsylvania Dutch practicality trumping the rose-tinted Colorado moment.

"I've been thinkin' the old homesteader's cabin," Vincent said. "You know it?"

Clara was indeed familiar with the abandoned log cabin a mile and a half down the road from her pa's house. Spider webs draped every corner, and the place was thick with dust and rodent droppings. She and Geneva used to peek inside its broken window when they walked that far. Sometimes they made up stories about the person or persons who'd lived there. Below the cabin's broken window was a table made of four stout limbs nailed to a slab of wood and three mismatched chairs. The girls imagined a gang of thieves counting their takings around the table. There was one bed made from the same combination of limbs and boards as the table. It didn't look wide enough for two people, making the girls wonder if the homesteader became lonely and returned home.

Clara and Vincent shared their ideas as to how the cabin could work for them. There was a wood stove. Before winter set in they would have to chop a lot of wood. Vincent said he could replace the broken window and do something to keep the wind from whistling through the chinks between the logs. The cabin had a dirt floor. With rugs hard to find and terribly expensive, they would have to make do with cowhides.

"After we are married," Clara said, "we can bring my bed and straw mattress from home; cut up the homesteader's bed and use it for firewood."

****

At the close of what had been a remarkable afternoon, the newly betrothed couple returned to the ranch house. Geneva was in the kitchen preparing supper when Clara delivered the news. Her eyebrows shot up, then scrunched in a frown. Lips pinched, she stared into the depths of the soup bubbling on the stove and gave it a powerful stir.

"Do you know if there is a church in Conejos?" Clara asked. "If not, we can ask the Justice of the Peace to perform the ceremony."

"When will that be?" Geneva asked, without turning her head.

Clara was smiling so hard her cheeks ached. "Day

after tomorrow."

Geneva stopped stirring and set down her spoon. "Before Albert comes home?" She turned to Clara, eyes narrowed. "I wouldn't want to be in your shoes if you don't wait for him." She opened the oven door and bent down to check on her cornbread. When she stood up, her scowl was gone.

"Do you have a witness?" Her mouth twitched as if trying to smile.

Clara and Vincent both shook their heads.

"You have to have a witness." Geneva's half smile grew full. "I can do that for you."

****

Two days later, the small wedding party left for Conejos in Albert's spring wagon. Vincent and Clara sat up front, Vincent handling the reins. Geneva sat behind them with baby Christopher in a bushel basket on the seat beside her. Three years had passed since the same wagon made another, much longer wedding trip. Geneva sat in the front seat that time, wondering for days what Clara's reaction would be when she found out she'd married her pa. During the half-day trip to Conejos, her thoughts were again on her ex-friend, this time on the explosion that was sure to roar through the San Luis Valley when Albert learned what his daughter had done.

Part II

Hot Irons, Cold Nights

Chapter Twelve

Albert hung his best hat, the short-brimmed Stetson he saved for business trips, on the hall tree near the front door. Back from Omaha with a top-dollar beef contract in his pocket, he was halfway across the great room's plank floor when Geneva told him Clara had gotten married. He dropped his grip. After a stunned silence he said, "How dare she!" His tone was cold as clay. Spewing a liberal portion of tarnation, he stormed outside, lit a cigar, and began pacing the long front porch, muttering threats and puffing like a locomotive. Geneva was right on his heels, savoring the steam.

"Stop following me," he said, his face red with rage. "Go down to that shack and tell that daughter of mine to get herself up here this minute! If Vincent is there, collect him, as well. I will mind the baby while you are gone."

Geneva grabbed a handful of skirt and petticoat in each hand and marched down to where Clara and Vincent had been living for less than a week. She nearly fell in her haste, her mind focused on the fear of God she hoped to see on her ex-friend's face when she smacked her with every threat and curse Albert uttered. Clara was outside chopping firewood when she arrived, and without pausing to catch her breath Geneva launched into a rant that lasted several minutes. Shaking her frizzy blonde curls, flailing her arms, and cursing like a cowhand, she unleashed Albert's reaction to the surprise marriage. "And he wants to see you right away," she added after she ran out of insults and cuss words.

Clara's dark brown braids were wound into the respectable coronet of a married woman. She set the axe she'd been using across a wedge of wood and started for the cabin. "Tell him I will be there shortly."

"He said immediately!"

Clara turned and gave Geneva a penetrating look. "I said I will be there shortly." She yanked open the cabin door and walked inside. She took off her soiled clothes and changed into the red plaid shirtwaist her father had given her when she turned sixteen. While buttoning the front, she sorted through the histrionics in the performance she'd just witnessed. She knew marrying Vincent would make her pa angry. She'd spent the last few days preparing for his rage; however by the time she saddled Bridget, she was certain Geneva had embellished his words with a few smoking oaths of her own. "Let her swear all she wants," Clara muttered, climbing onto the side-saddle. "I am the one who ended up with Vincent."

Albert was waiting for her on the front porch. Gracefully, she dismounted and tied Bridget to the rail. Head held high, she walked up the porch steps, and rather than cowering there, she went to her pa and stood a few feet in front of him.

He pulled a cigar out of his vest pocket for the second time that day. Using a pearl-handled pocketknife, he cut the tip off one end before lighting it with a paraffin match. He puffed on the cigar until he was sure it was lit, and then pointed it at Clara. "This is madness!" His forehead was a raft of wrinkles. "I thought you had more sense. You are too young to get married, with or without my permission, and why in the name of heaven did you pick an unschooled cowboy?"

Clara looked at his face, not down at his boots. She knew he would bring up her age, but what did he have against cowboys when he depended on them for a living? She folded her arms across her chest. "Geneva was exactly my age when the two of you made that trip to Santa Fe." She took a deep breath. "And Vincent may be a cowboy, but he isn't my cousin."

Albert's face reddened. His black eyebrows nearly merged into one as he gave Clara a scorching look of appraisal, puffing on his cigar until a cloud of smoke cloaked her shoulders. He wanted to spank her with his carpet slipper. He'd done that two or three times when she misbehaved as a child. To him she was still a child, but a spanking was out of the question.

"I never should have let you come back here."

Clara lowered her eyes. Hands at her sides, she stood her ground. Albert glowered at her with a watchful, guarded expression as if the heat of his gaze could force an apology out of her, perhaps even a change of heart. He waited longer than he wanted to, and heard neither. "Go then," he said at last. "Go to your blessed cowboy, and your pig-headed insolence be damned."

Relieved she'd made it through the confrontation without crying, yet knowing there would be more to come, Clara hurried down the porch steps, mounted Bridget, and left.

****

Albert was at odds when it came to dealing with

Vincent. He had great respect for his foreman, needed him for an upcoming drive to Kansas, yet he was furious with the man for having the gall to marry his daughter, and behind his back, no less. Vincent had apologized to him the minute they crossed paths. Albert countered with a piercing look and a good tongue-lashing. After that he spoke to his foreman only when giving him orders.

Vincent accepted the silent treatment as mild compared to what he probably deserved. He was rounding up cattle most of the time, anyway, and after a week of sleeping on a straw mattress next to a warm female body, there was no way he was going back to the bunkhouse.

Albert, curious to see how Vincent and his daughter were living, made a surprise visit to the old homesteader's cabin. As he strode the length and breadth of what he regarded as a pimple of land on his thirty thousand acres, he tried to find something to criticize. Instead he saw a new sheet of glass in the shack's lone window and fresh daubing between the logs. The door no longer sagged on its hinges, and there was a new corral between the shack and the wreck of a barn that would have to see their horses through the winter. Even so, when Clara offered him a cup of coffee, nothing but his shadow crossed the threshold.

"Since you already hauled your bedroom furniture down here," he said after a cursory look inside the one-room shack, "you can keep it. The furniture may give you some comfort; however I am confident you will not last a year in this place."

He started toward his buckskin stallion. Halfway there, he turned around for another look and saw Clara standing in the doorway in her dirty apron. "It appears you want to be on your own, Daughter. With Vincent gone for weeks at a time you will most assuredly be on your own. And mark my words, if you don't like living like a pauper, don't expect to move back with me and Geneva."

A knot formed in Clara's stomach. Her pa had always been firm with her, but never unkind. For a fleeting moment, she imagined herself dressed in rags, and then quickly recovered, vowing she would move to another town, another state, before she would live in the same house with Geneva again.

Albert mounted his long-limbed horse with the ease of a younger man, and in the ten minutes it took him to ride from the homesteader's cabin to his spacious log house, his attitude softened at the image of Clara in her dirty apron, trying to make a home out of a tumbledown shack. If she'd married according to plan, he would have given her an elaborate church wedding, preferably in downtown Philadelphia. The wedding would have been preceded by an engagement party, and other social events organized by his friends and business acquaintances. Thinking he should do at least something for her, he decided to bring his family together for a supper that would serve as a wedding salute as well as a sendoff for the trip to Dodge. It wouldn't be a grand affair; however eight adults sharing food and drink amounted to a party in the remote stretches of the San Luis Valley.

Geneva was sitting in the great room embroidering a tea towel when Albert walked in and told her to begin making preparations for a family supper. "Do not call it a wedding party," he cautioned, "although that is part of my intent."

Geneva gaped at him. She had expected her husband's wrath to last considerably longer than a week. "WE didn't have a party," she said.

Albert hardened his jaw. "You are partly to blame for what happened, Geneva. Instead of going to Conejos with those two, you should have argued against their marriage, a marriage you must have known I wouldn't approve." He picked up the book next to his chair and sat down. "I leave for Kansas in less than a week. Don't tarry with the arrangements."

Tears sprang to Geneva's eyes as she dissolved into the sofa.

Chapter Thirteen

Clara spit on the base of her iron to check the temperature. It had to be hot enough to remove wrinkles, yet not so hot it would scorch the only dress shirt Vincent owned. Satisfied with the sizzle, she spread a thin coat of beeswax on the iron's base to keep it from sticking. A second iron heated on top of the wood stove, ready to trade places when the first one cooled.

Tuesday, not Saturday, was typically the day she ironed, but she wanted her husband of two weeks to make a good impression. Vincent would be the only person at the supper table who wasn't from the east coast, and the only one who hadn't gone to school past third grade. Now that he was her husband, and not just someone who worked for Albert, the family would look at him differently. None of his own folks would be there, since they couldn't afford to travel from Ohio to southern Colorado.

Clara's ironing board was a wide, flannel-covered plank balanced on the backs of two chairs. After ironing Vincent's shirt, the sixteen-year-old began pressing her dress, the jade-colored one that made her hazel eyes look more green than gray. The high-necked dress had bothersome ruffles around the bodice and sleeves that made it difficult to iron, but she'd sprinkled the dress with water the night before to keep it damp and easier to press.

Her first Tuesday as head of her own household, she'd ironed two of her husband's cotton work shirts. She did the same for his neckerchief which she had a hard time getting him to part with long enough to wash, let alone iron.

"You didn't have to do that," Vincent said when she handed him the clean pressed rag. He smoothed his light brown moustache. "The fellas I know give their bandanas a slosh in the creek once in a while, and that's all the cleanin' they get."

"I have smelled some of those cowhands. No doubt they are the same men who wear their union suits for a year before washing them." She gave Vincent a loving smile. "You are Pa's cow boss, dear husband. You should look the part."

"Nobody says nay to me. The new fella…the one goes by Reb? He even calls me guv'nor."

"Reb? Did he fight for the South?"

Vincent shook his head. "Wasn't even born then. Comes from Tennessee. Guess he's proud of it."

While Clara ironed her frock, supper guests arrived in twos and threes at her pa's house. It had been four years since Albert Wesley Wallin moved his daughters into that house; and since that time several marriages had taken place, babies born, new households established, and a prosperous cattle business built.

It was pleasantly cool as Clara and Vincent rode their horses up the rutted trail to the ranch house. In front of them, a line of clouds flirted with the tips of the Sangre de Cristo Mountains while the sun warmed their shoulders from behind. Clara had no regrets that September afternoon for the social niceties she might have left in Philadelphia when she traded genteel city life for the wilds of Colorado. She was excited to see her aunts. Lou would be there with her cowboy-turned-lumberjack husband from Custer County, and Alma and Morris from their ranch nine miles away. She figured her pa was still in a black mood, and that put a damper on her cheerfulness. She was also concerned about Vincent's comportment. His tendency to hold back around strangers hid his lack of education. Coming from working class stock, he'd learned what manners he had by watching his superiors remove their hats in the presence of women or rise from their chairs when ladies were being seated at the table. He didn't have a dress coat to wear to supper, though, and she knew that bothered him.

Clara hadn't seen her pa since his surprise visit to the cabin, and after she and Vincent joined the party, she was relieved to see him, surrounded by his sisters and cousin, enjoying himself. He had plenty of people besides her to converse with and a cleaned up son-in-law who walked in the door shiny as a cowboy celebrating the end of a cattle drive.

Geneva's supper consisted of roast beef, boiled cabbage, and buttered carrots. Vincent and Clara were seated next to each other at the long plank table, Vincent, stiff as a stalk of celery. Clara watched him hold his fork in an awkward grip as he steered each bite into his mouth with great concentration. He didn't drop a single slice of carrot during what he later described as "the longest meal of my life."

Dessert was a two-egg cake—one layer, a little brown around the edges, sprinkled with loaf sugar. Clara's aunts presented her with wedding gifts drawn from the trunks they brought with them from Philadelphia—an emerald green silk shawl from Lou, and a set of embroidered sheets from Alma. Vincent studied the rosebud-embroidered sheets for some time before touching them with his rough fingers. He imagined lying on the silky sheets when he was buck naked, and the thought was almost as sensual as the intimacy he and Clara had been sharing between ordinary sheets. Clara was as delighted with the gift as he was, and when their eyes met, her face reflected the same glow of pleasure she saw in him.

Geneva picked up one of the pillowslips and inspected the quality of the embroidery. She laid the pillowslip down and caressed the pink rosebuds and dainty green leaves on the matching sheet. Turning to Clara with a haughty grin, she said, "In my candy opinion, sheets like these don't belong in a shack with a dirt floor."

Clara's toes curled in her shoes. "But we haven't slept a single night on that floor." She reached for Vincent's hand. "Have we, dear husband?"

Vincent blushed from his hairline to the collar of his freshly ironed shirt. Out of a corner of her eye Clara saw Geneva's lips disappear into a thin line.

Chapter Fourteen

The newlyweds slept on their beautiful new sheets for two nights before it was time for Vincent to leave for Dodge. During the two and a half weeks they'd been married, they chopped enough wood to last until he returned. Vincent filled the rain barrel with water from nearby La Jara Creek and made a nest in the half-ruined barn for two setting hens he begged off the camp cook. A good part of his monthly pay had gone into the sacks of staple goods hanging from the cabin's rafters. There would be a few eggs to supplement the provisions, but without a cow or goat, no milk.

The morning he was to leave, he and Clara stood inside the cabin saying their goodbyes. "As long as I'm doin' what I'm doin'," Vincent said, his blue eyes beholding eyes the color of sage, "I'll be gone a lot. There's no drives in winter, though, so when I get back I'll be home most of the time." He stuffed a handful of biscuits into one of his saddlebags. "Home…never thought I'd be sayin' that word again."

A smile moved from Clara's eyes to her lips. "Stay safe, Dearest, and don't spend a single minute worrying about me." She hoped she sounded more confident than she felt, considering the stories she'd heard, and the images of strangers, Utes, bears, or wild fire those stories brought to mind.

Vincent gave his young wife a parting kiss, and

then mounted his horse. Before he and his mare reached the road, he looked back to see Clara was still standing on the front stoop, waving goodbye.

****

Geneva handed Christopher to his father.

"What a big boy he is getting to be!" Albert lifted the infant high over his head, bringing giggles of delight. Having lost three sons from his first marriage two to diphtheria, and a fourth son from his second marriage, Albert doted on this one.

"You need to know Christopher's whereabouts at all times," he told Geneva. "Do not get lost in your fancy work and lose track of him." He placed the child in her waiting arms. "What plans have you and Clara made to look after one another? If you were not so God-awful afraid of horses you could bundle up Christopher once in a while and ride down to the homesteader's shack and see how she is doing. Clara is a capable girl, maddeningly independent, but she has never lived alone."

Geneva shrugged. "It's not that far. I'll walk down there, or she can ride up here."

"While the weather holds, you had best be doing the walking. Our son could benefit from the fresh air. You, as well."

Geneva gave Albert a careless nod. She presented a cheek to him when he opened the door to leave, and the minute she heard the clunk of his boots on the front steps she smiled. *No man to cook for now, or clean for. No dirty trousers to wash. More time to do what I like to do. Maybe I'll knit something for myself or the baby.*

****

It was unusually warm for the first of October, and

after Vincent and his horse were out of sight, Clara walked inside the cabin and closed the door. She washed and dried the breakfast dishes and put them away. That took less than fifteen minutes. Then she sat at the teetery table for a while before going outside to check for eggs.

Twenty-five yards or so from the cabin sat an old barn with over half of its siding missing. As Vincent once said of the dilapidated structure, "A feller could throw a cat through one of those walls and never touch a hair." Fortunately, enough of the barn's roof remained to shelter their horses and the chickens if it rained or snowed.

Clara checked the hens' nests and put the one brown egg she found in her apron pocket. Returning to the cabin, she placed the egg in a small bowl, saving it for her next breakfast. Then she turned her attention to whatever needed to be done in a log box small enough to fit inside her Aunt Mid's drawing room. Philadelphia houses like Mildred's stately home were cleaned once a week, however, those houses had foundations and wood floors, plastered ceilings, and paneled walls that kept the outside where it belonged. Abandoned for over a decade, the log cabin Clara and Vincent were living in had been wall-to-wall spider webs and rodent droppings before she went after them with her broom. Even so, she saw daily signs the previous tenants were still around.

One benefit of living in a fifteen by fifteen-foot space was the minimal time required to clean it. Finished with the sweeping and dusting, Clara got to work cleaning the beeswax off her irons. While preparing for Vincent's departure, she hadn't had time to give them a thorough scrubbing. She sat at the table, and using a large square of sandpaper, spent the next hour scrubbing off the stubborn, baked-on wax.

She kept the irons in one of the two dressers she'd taken from her bedroom along with her bed. The six-foot chest of drawers also stored a washbasin, cooking implements, whatever food goods weren't hanging from the ceiling, and a few mismatched dishes. A second bureau held their clothing and underpinnings.

She put the irons away and then sat in Vincent's chair, the one nearest the window, where she could look out and see the violet-hued mountains in the distance, or much closer, the wagon tracks etched in grass that led to her pa's house. She wondered briefly what Geneva was doing a mile and a half up that road.

Chapter Fifteen

The brutal winter of 1886-87 nearly wiped out the cattle business in the Montana and Dakota Territories. Situated farther south and nestled between two mountain ranges, Albert's cows had escaped the worst of the cold and snow. He lost around fifty head to starvation, and though this was a setback, it was a loss that barely merited a string of cuss words compared to ranchers whose entire herds froze to death.

Albert was grazing over three thousand head of valuable beef cattle that spring. He made one drive to Kansas in July of '87, and with markets in the East paying a premium for beef, he decided to make a second drive in October. Accompanying him were Vincent, a dozen cowhands, a Mexican cook, horse wrangler, and fifteen hundred head of cattle. If the weather held, and he and his men drove the herd an average of twelve miles a day, he figured they'd reach Dodge in a little over a month. Minus cattle on the return trip, they should be watering their horses in La Jara Creek by Thanksgiving.

While preparing for Vincent's trip, Clara asked to go with him. "I could help with the cooking."

Vincent leveled his bright blue eyes at her. "You dunno what it's like out there. Up at daybreak…starin' at the butts of cows from sunup to sundown…so much dust yer eyes are on fire…two meals a day…maybe some jerky and a swig of water in between. Then it's a cold sleep on a hard piece of ground."

It was the most words Clara had heard him string together and enough to change her mind, especially when he said, "And there's no privies out there, not a one."

****

The morning Albert and his men left for Kansas, the leaves of the cottonwood trees were shimmering like gold dollars. They drove the herd eastward across Trinchera Creek, then southeast on a route determined by grass and water, dipping into the New Mexico Territory when conditions there were more suitable for cattle. The low water levels in the rivers and creeks made them easier to cross than in July, however, some of the creeks had dried up completely, creating a different challenge.

Heading east also meant moving out of an intermountain valley into endless miles of flat prairie with dreary stretches of emptiness in every direction. Prairie grasses tall enough in summer to tickle a cow's belly were somber remnants of themselves in October. Dry as week-old biscuits, the thin brown grass still made good fodder.

All day the men rode, the next day and the next, ten to fifteen miles a day, depending on terrain. Vincent was often dog-tired after restless nights trying to sleep on cold ground, so tired he napped in the saddle, letting whatever horse he was riding plod along with the herd. The cattle were trail-broke by the time they reached the prairie, and the cows parted without spooking when his horse passed through the lumbering mass.

Vincent had a casual way with cows and horses

that set him apart from other men. Since leaving home at thirteen, he'd spent more time with animals than people. He had no idea how many drives he'd made and how many cows he'd punched during those ten years of never-ending dusty days and frigid nights. He was riding drag this time, bringing up the rear and choking on dust thick enough to chew. He would spit and spit and still feel grit on his teeth when he tapped them together. Often the air was so dark with dust it resembled the trail hand's lament, "If I could slice it, I could pass it off as toast."

Punching cows was all Vincent knew. Before his fulltime job with Albert, he signed up for cattle drives, dreading the tedium, yet needing the work. He was married now. Numbed by the heaving sea of rust-brown cowhide plodding in front of him, his mind often drifted from the herd he was supposed to be protecting to the fancy sheets and warm body he left behind. He wondered if thoughts like this were why Albert didn't hire married men.

The Indian summer sun parched his skin, and heat rose in quivering waves ahead. Dust boiled around the cattle. Most of the route was mind-numbingly level, and the static presence of the distant mountains made him and the men feel as if they hadn't made a lick of progress no matter how many miles they covered.

One day they passed by a towering outcropping that looked as if it had been blown there during some violent eruption. A gigantic rock in the middle of a prairie reminded Vincent that he, too, was in the wrong place this trip, and after six oppressive days, puzzling over why the top hand was riding at the back of the herd, he got up the nerve to ask about it.

Albert leveled a penetrating look at his foreman. "Now that you are married to my daughter, I cannot appear to be favoring you over the rest of my men."

Vincent nodded, believing the real reason he was riding drag was *because* he'd married the boss's daughter. He gave Albert a mock salute, and then rode back to the rear where he swallowed his speculation along with another yard of dust.

Reb Carlton, a Tennessee farm boy with a rash of pimples under a beginner's beard, was also riding drag. "We could use a mite a rain, Guv'nor," he said one afternoon when he and Vincent crossed paths. "I could drink a quart a water without comin' up fer air."

Two weeks into the drive, Reb came upon eight maverick steers in a willow grove. With some prodding on his part, the mavericks blended right in with Albert's herd. Reb kept an eye on the eight steers, and when he and the rest of the men stopped for the night, he showed off his find.

"Most likely scattered durin' a stampede," Vincent said. "Looks like they ran off a few pounds. Either that or they was puny to start with." He blew his nose into the tail of his bandana. Albert took a look at the underweight additions. "Steak is steak," he chuckled. "They will still bring in a few dollars."

A harsh wind lashed Vincent's face when he crawled into his bedroll that night and laid his head on the cold leather saddle he used for a pillow. His toes felt froze in his boots. He folded his lanky frame into the fetal position, imagining himself curled around Clara or bellied up to any bar in Dodge with a swig of whiskey warming his gullet.

Chapter Sixteen

Clara saddled Bridget for a ride. The morning was clear and bright, the temperature, agreeably crisp, and her horse full of energy. Returning two hours later, she removed Bridget's saddle and let her sprawl in the grass and pine needles, legs up, to scrub the sweat and dirt off her back. Then she led Bridget to the barn where she checked her hooves for rocks and gave the horse a good brushing before putting her back in the corral.

Figuring it was about noon, she smeared bacon grease on a couple of leftover biscuits and made that her midday meal. The pot of beans simmering on the stove would be supper. Nibbling on the biscuits and finishing the morning coffee, she read both sides of a page of the *Alamosa Journal* that had been wrapped around a slab of bacon. The news was three months old, but it occupied a few minutes of her time.

A large ad for Royal baking powder made her wish she had any brand of the ingredient. Baking powder made fluffier biscuits than the soda and vinegar she'd been using since moving out of her pa's house. Next to the Royal ad was an article describing Queen Victoria's golden jubilee. Clara read the article twice and then set the page aside, folded her arms on the table, and rested her head.

****

Christopher was crawling and curious as a ferret.

Geneva built a pen for him out of Albert's books—some of them leather-bound first editions—and a complete set of encyclopedias he'd purchased from a Colorado drummer. She stacked the walls of the pen high enough to keep Christopher contained while she engaged in her favorite pastime.

She rarely finished a needlework project, preferring to move from knitting, to crocheting, to tatting, always saving something to look forward to the next day. Without Albert to cook for, she didn't have to set the table. Instead she ate her meals in the kitchen, sometimes next to the stove. She cooked whatever was easiest, mostly scrambled eggs or cornmeal mush.

She was accustomed to Albert being gone, but she always kept an ear out for trouble. Before every drive and every trip he made to Chicago, Kansas City, or St. Louis, he lectured her on the potential for danger—bears, wolves, Indians, cattle rustlers or men who were down on their luck. While he was gone, her hearing grew more acute, to the point of making her jittery as the days dragged on.

At night, with Christopher asleep in his crib, she did needlework by lamplight. The curtains were closed and the great room quiet except for a crackling fire and the ticking of a grandfather clock. Two weeks after Albert left for Dodge, a large, half-burned log fell off the grate and thumped against the wall of the firebox. Startled by the thud, and failing to recognize its source, she scrutinized her surroundings, paying special attention to windows and doorways. Seeing nothing unusual, she purled half a row, and then stood up, knitting in hand, and tiptoed to the front door. She pressed an ear against the cold planks, listening for strange noises. She heard only the hoot of an owl, but she triple-checked the latch before going to bed and spent the rest of the night with her eyes open.

Chapter Seventeen

While Vincent was climbing into his bedroll for the twentieth time since leaving La Jara, Clara stood in front of the cabin watching the sun's disappearing act, always entertaining, never the same. A cold front had chased away the Indian summer. She'd put on long stockings that morning and dressed for chillier weather in a corduroy skirt, heavy sweater, and peplum jacket. She wrapped a wool shawl around her shoulders and watched an array of clouds slowly turn from apricot to peach as the sun's parting blush warmed the horizon. She could have viewed the nightly performance through the cabin's window, but the only glass Vincent had been able to find to repair it with was wavy. Outside, however, the view was perfect, and she could breathe the fresh scent of pine rather than the smoke-tinged air that persisted inside.

It would be dark soon. Clouds that had been brilliant went from glorious to gray in a matter of minutes. The wind picked up, fanning her face. A cone blew off a lodgepole pine and ricocheted from limb to limb before landing with a soft thud on a bed of needles. Tightening her shawl, she stood a moment longer, listening to the hiss of frost-killed grass rustling in the wind.

The sun's descent marked the end of another drawn-out day. With no one to talk to, she dedicated herself to repetitious tasks, doing them more meticulously than necessary. Tending to Bridget's needs, feeding the chickens, sweeping, cooking, hauling water, and filling the woodbin next to the stove still didn't fill every waking hour. She had most of the afternoon to write in her diary. Schooled in the virtues of patience and tolerance, she wrote sparingly, avoiding the temptation to complain. When afternoons dragged on, she might spend an hour looking for blackberries even though they were past their prime, or watch ground squirrels gather seeds and then protect them from other ground squirrels. She reread the grease-stained page from the *Alamosa Journal* until she could almost recite it. The slab of bacon the page had been wrapped around was gone, leaving nothing but jerky or salt pork to flavor beans and soup.

She groomed Bridget nearly every day while her sidesaddle languished on a peg in the cabin. The first week or so Vincent had been gone, Clara spent her idle hours riding the same grassy dunes the two of them raced across before they were married. Now, the entire San Luis Valley, with its drifting sun devils and cruelly indifferent sky, seemed desolate. Most of the cattle were gone. The vegetation had turned brown, and the white-cheeked sand hill cranes she and Bridget used to scare up had flown to Texas for the winter.

Clara shook off the bits of bark dust clinging to the hem of her corduroy skirt and went back inside the cabin. She lit the coal oil lantern on the table and watched its reflection appear in the curtainless window. A moth hurled itself against the lantern glass, bumping it several times before disappearing into the brown shadows. With no sofa to sit on and no space for one anyway, Clara spent many hours at that table. Besides eating her meals on it, she washed dishes there, rolled out biscuit dough, bathed herself, brushed her teeth, cleaned her irons, ground coffee beans, and occasionally wrote in her diary. Sometimes she sat at the table for an hour or more at a time, staring out the window, studying the clouds for signs of winter and wondering whether her pa and Vincent had crossed into Kansas.

The lamp wick sputtered. Clara got up to stir the fire and add enough wood to last through the night. She slid the door latch into place and leaned a loaded shotgun against the doorframe, preparing to sleep away part of a day too long to endure. She blew out the lamp, changed into her nightdress, and unlaced her shoes. Still wearing her long stockings, she climbed under the pile of quilts and blankets on her bed.

She lay there for several minutes, listening to the agonized wail of coyotes. They sounded close. She tucked the bedding under her chin and waited for sleep. Instead, the howling kept her awake, as did the intermittent drips of a passing rain shower rolling off the roof into the rain barrel. Stiff with cold, she reached for Vincent's pillow. She buried her face in the goose down and let go the tears she'd been holding back .

"Oh, Pa," she cried, "I am dreadfully sorry I disappointed you."

Chapter Eighteen

The day after it rained, Geneva opened the front door and peered through the milky morning fog, hoping to see the silhouette of an approaching horse and rider. It might be Clara, driven out of her shack by the cold, or it might be a messenger delivering the telegram her husband promised he would send when he got to Dodge. Not only would a telegram bring news of a safe arrival, it would be delivered by a male considerably older than her infant son, someone with whom she could exchange a few words.

"Surely the messenger will stay long enough for a cup of coffee, maybe even a meal," she whispered to Christopher, squirming in her arms. Braced on her hip, the baby kicked off one of his booties.

Geneva gave a final glance down the empty road, and then picked up the tiny sock and closed the door. Son in arms, she stood in front of the fireplace, soaking up warmth. The fireplace was a masterpiece of rock work that included a built-in alcove for wood storage. The alcove meant fewer trips to the woodpile, but she hated dealing with the ashes. She would leave them until they completely buried the grate, and no matter how slowly she scooped the residue into a bucket, or how carefully she carried the bucket outside, the ashes always floated about like goose feathers.

Whenever she did housework of any kind,

Geneva's thoughts turned to Clara who probably had to work all day to keep that shack she was living in clean. She wondered how her ex-friend was getting along without Vincent, and figured she missed him something fierce.

****

Clara's only contact with anything warm-blooded was her daily interaction with Bridget and the chickens. Checking for eggs every morning she found only one, and always under the same hen. "If you don't start producing soon," she warned the slacker, "I will have you for supper." It was a threat that fell on deaf ears.

On her thirty-third day of solitude, Clara wrote in her diary: *I vowed I would not complain while Vincent was gone, however my will is waning. Thus far I am triumphing over the loneliness and cold. Bridget and the chickens provide me with a bit of companionship. The rest of my days are as brown and boring as the eggs I gather.*

Several times a day, the sixteen-year-old donned her wool cape and walked to the road. She looked left—in the direction Vincent would be coming—and then right, where the wagon tracks continued for just over a mile before climbing the hill to her pa's house. Every day she thought about riding up there. She could say she'd come to check on Christopher, ask if she could be of help, ask to borrow something. As long as she was there, she might exchange pleasantries with Geneva. Any conversation was better than none, and there was a good chance Geneva knew of their husbands' whereabouts.

Every day she decided against making the trip.

As the cold deepened and laundry froze on the

clothesline, Clara ironed her rosebud-embroidered sheets, spreading them across her mattress and pressing one section at a time. The weekly chore made her feel closer to Vincent and warm enough at times that drops of perspiration coated her upper lip. With the smell of hot cotton rising to her nose, she envisioned Geneva ironing in her warm kitchen.

The cabin's tiny wood stove had to be fed incessantly, yet Clara still had to wear a wool sweater and jacket to keep warm. Ice had formed inside the windowpane. One night, when two pair of wool stockings weren't enough to keep her feet warm, Clara got out of bed, heated an iron, wrapped it in rags, and placed it under the blankets near her feet. She slept better that night than she had in over a week.

The next morning, she was shocked to discover the iron had burned through the rags and scorched the bottom sheet. Staring at a dark brown spot the size of a frying pan, she leaned against the edge of the mattress, wavering between shrieking and sobbing.

That afternoon she wrote about the misfortune in her diary. *Day 45—The bitter cold has taken a cruel toll. Yesterday I discovered my precious chickens had frozen to death. Last night I ruined one of my wedding sheets by using an iron as a bed warmer. What if the mattress had caught fire? If I had burned to death, no one would have known about it until Vincent returned. What if Geneva fell ill and there was no one to take care of my little brother? I must go see her. No one is perfect, leastwise myself.*

****

A skiff of snow glistened on the fence posts the morning Clara rode up to the ranch house. Her hooded wool cape was no match for the cold breath of winter, and the sun's rays, bouncing off the snow made her eyes water. Shading her eyes with the flat of her hand, she rode toward the curl of smoke ahead, shivering with anticipation at the thought of a blazing fire.

She approached timidly, with a tightness in her chest she blamed on the cold air. She tied Bridget to the hitching post, and then rapped on the front door. No answer. She knocked again, louder this time, and within seconds the door latch clicked. The door opened just enough for Clara to see one blue eye peeking through the crack. The eye opened wide and the door wider.

"I almost forgot what you looked like," Geneva gushed, embracing pink-cheeked Clara the way she used to when they visited one another. "You're cold. Would you like a cup of tea?"

Clara raised her brows. "Tea sounds good for a change. I would have brought you something I baked, but I have no eggs. My chickens froze the other night."

"Don't be a ninny. I'm sorry about your chickens. Would you like a few eggs to take back with you? I would have come to your place if Christopher weren't so heavy. Yesterday I slipped and fell." Geneva lifted her forearm and pulled back the sleeve of her dress to reveal a bruise two inches across. "What if I'd broken my arm? Nobody would have been here to take me to the doctor."

The two women walked into the kitchen. "I finally got word from Albert. He and Vincent are supposed to be here in a day or two—hungry and dirty, no doubt. I've been worried about you, Clara, truly I have. Can you stay for a while? I'm dying for someone to talk to, and I've got so much to say."

A faint smile crossed Clara's lips as she removed her cape and gloves and draped them over the back of a chair. "And I am dying to hear it…but first let me tell you what happened to one of my beautiful embroidered sheets."

Chapter Nineteen

A month into the drive, Vincent found himself in familiar territory. He and the men had spent the better part of their twenty-eighth day driving the herd along a rock-strewn trail with the Arkansas River to the north and the Cimarron River to the south. Dodge City was a day ahead; none too soon for a man who could smell his own stink.

They set up camp for their last night, and then Albert and his crew squatted around a greasewood fire, warming their hands and feet and drinking coffee. Alcohol of any kind was forbidden, so the men would have to wait until the herd was sold to drown their boredom. Those who smoked had used up their tobacco by this time. Albert still had a few cigars, but he didn't want to smoke in front of his men.

Exuberance around the campfire was high as the Rockies. Even the flat-out loners joined in the banter, envisioning, as did every man there, money in his pockets and an end to the monotony. Tomorrow night every one of them would be shorn, shaved, showered, and three sheets to the wind. Dodge held enough booze and women to last until dawn as well as a chance to add to their pay if they got lucky at cards.

Vincent finished his coffee, flicked the dregs into the dirt, and stashed the cup in his pack. He mounted a fresh horse and coordinated with the other nighthawk assigned to the last night of sentry duty. Both men wore shirts buttoned up to their necks and sheepskin jackets. For extra warmth, Vincent tied a bandana over his ears before donning his gray planter's hat.

The two men headed for opposite sides of the herd. A biting wind tugged at the scrawny grass while Vincent and the other sentry guided their horses around the cattle in a slow, clockwise circuit. The cattle were bedded down for the night, some cows barely stirring, some edgy. One of the skinny steers Reb found stood up briefly, then plopped down with a thud. Once in a while a cow looking for a more comfortable spot muscled between cows already down, causing groans of annoyance. Humming or whistling a tune helped calm a restless herd. Some cowboys took to singing, but Vincent thought that was a cockamamie idea.

****

"I lost count a how many shots he had," Reb told Albert. "It was part my fault. I jes' wanted to be able to say I got drunk at the Long Branch."

Albert's face was a sour knot. "You take one arm, and I will take the other." He glared at Vincent, slumped in a ladder back chair with his legs splayed and his wide-brimmed planter's hat covering his crotch. "What was he drinking?"

"White mule." Reb gave his boss a lopsided grin. "Tasted like sin." He grabbed one of Vincent's arms and helped him to his feet.

Albert draped Vincent's other arm over his shoulder and hefted half of the dead weight. "I expect my men to celebrate at the end of a drive, but this one does too much of it. He should sleep it off by morning. If not, tomorrow will be the longest, most miserable day he ever spent in the saddle."

Albert and Reb escorted Vincent down the trampled dirt road that ran through Dodge. Along the way they passed saloons less notorious than the Long Branch, each one spilling laughter and tinny piano tunes into the cold night air. They walked Vincent by several storefronts, including the red glass door of the Red Light Bordello, and then dumped him onto a cot in a twelve-man tent on the outskirts of town. Reb removed Vincent's boots and threw a dirty quilt over him before claiming a nearby cot for himself. Albert retraced his steps and spent the night in a small yet comfortable room in the Dodge House Hotel.

Chapter Twenty

Clara's afternoon in front of a roaring fire warmed her to the core. She left before nightfall, buoyed by the fact Vincent might be home as early as the next day. That night and the two that followed, she delayed going to bed where sleep consumed some of the wait. Instead, she wrapped up in a blanket and sat in a chair next to the window, gazing at moonlight pale and luminous as the meringue on a custard pie.

On day three of her vigil, she was sitting there watching it snow when a series of hoots, thinned by wind and distance, caught her attention. The hoots were followed by the unmistakable sound of her name, then Bridget's welcoming whinny and a hearty, "Hello, the house!"

Clara's heart grew large as the valley when she opened the door and her arms to the bedraggled cowboy with a dusting of snow on his hat and ice crystals hanging from his droopy moustache. His sheepskin jacket was soaked, as were the ends of his light brown hair. He smelled of sweat and campfire smoke, but she hugged him harder and longer than she'd held him before, and didn't flinch when he buried his frosty face in her neck. The front of her shirtwaist was almost as wet as he was after they parted.

He handed her his hat, and she peered into bright blue eyes locked on hers. She thrilled to the chime of his spurs as he walked over to the stove, took off his gloves, and laid them on the hot iron cooktop. It had been forty-eight days since he left for Dodge on a yellow-leafed morning in October.

"I am ever so glad to see you," Clara cooed, embracing him from behind. "I can't wait to hear of your adventures—on the trail as well as in Dodge…mostly in Dodge. You must tell me everything about that place. Was there music? A stage show? Did you have wonderful meals? What were the ladies wearing?" Vincent gave a few "yep" and "nope" replies, nodding occasionally while he rubbed his hands in the heat rising from the stove. The ice on his moustache melted, and he flicked the drips onto the stove where they vanished in sputters.

The cabin's close quarters offered no privacy, and since it was not yet dark, Vincent asked Clara to turn her back while he changed clothes. He hung his wet, dirty garments on the iron bedposts and returned to her in clean, dry long johns.

"Would you like to wash yourself?" Clara asked. "The water in the kettle is hot. I can't go outside the way I did when the weather was nice, but I will busy myself at the table until you finish."

She handed Vincent a washbasin, rag, and bar of soap. He poured hot water in the basin and dipped the rag in it. Other than the snow pelting his face that morning, it was the first water to touch his skin since Dodge. He rubbed the lavender-scented soap on the rag and washed himself with it. The soap smelled like Clara. The coarseness of the rag was reminiscent of his mother's rough hands, bathing him as a child.

Clara waited until she heard him buttoning up his

trousers before she turned around to watch with loving eyes as he lathered his face, shaved around his moustache, and then trimmed it with scissors. Clean again and dressed in warm clothes, Vincent went outside to take care of his horse while Clara baked a skillet of cornbread. It would go well with the split pea soup she made that morning.

Their first supper together in over a month and a half was relatively quiet. They grinned at one another from time to time, but kept their innermost thoughts to themselves. "I will leave the supper dishes until morning," Clara told Vincent after they finished eating.

She felt enticingly vulnerable and immodest as she blew out the lantern, shed her corset and shoes, and slipped into her nightdress. Before Vincent left for Dodge, the marriage bed had been awkward for them. Clara had barely been hugged and kissed before she got married, and Vincent's only experience was with soiled doves who pretty much told him what to do. Those lessons didn't last long, and he was usually too drunk to remember the finer points when he woke the next morning. Shedding the loneliness that had been her constant companion, Clara was an enthusiastic partner when she pulled her freshly shaved cowboy into her arms. Vincent was almost giddy to be lying on a mattress again, and so moved by this new kind of affection he came close to crying. They made love twice, and in a mutual need for warmth and intimacy, spooned together until dawn.

The next morning they shared experiences from the forty-eight days they were apart. Clara did most of the talking. "Is that all you remember?" she asked after Vincent summarized two days in Dodge in about a minute and a half.

"Well, Dodge ain't as busy these days."

Clara had heard Dodge City described as a cross between Sodom and Gomorrah and a Wild West Show. It had to be more interesting than La Jara, a place that couldn't even be called a town. A two-hour ride from the cabin, La Jara was nothing more than an old boxcar being used as a train depot and a tiny general store.

Clara had been alone in the cabin for weeks. With Vincent home, she had to adjust to sharing it again. The two of them usually sat at the table or warmed themselves by the stove. If they both happened to be out of their chairs at the same time, they developed a peculiar sort of dance as they moved about the limited space: three steps forward, duck to avoid the sacks of flour, sugar, and cornmeal hanging from the rafters, keep right to avoid a collision, and give your partner a whirl if you meet in the middle. It was always a slow dance, never a jig, and the dance sometimes ended with a kiss.

To give his bride a small taste of Dodge and shorten a few afternoons, Vincent showed her how to play poker. With the first hand he dealt Clara gave names to the face cards: Queen Victoria, King George, and Prince Albert.

"Why'd you name the jack after your pa?" Vincent asked.

"I didn't. I named the jack after a different Albert." Clara left the table and returned with the page from the *Alamosa Journal* she practically knew by heart. She read aloud from the article on Queen Victoria's Golden Jubilee. "Her beloved Prince Albert predeceased the celebration." She raised her eyes, and seeing an inscrutable expression on Vincent's face, she added, "Albert was Queen Victoria's husband. She called him Prince for some reason. I am of a mind the jack is similar to a prince where royalty is concerned."

"Who's King George?"

"It says right here that King George of Greece was one of the attendees."

Vincent pulled the page in front of him. "I can read." He read the entire article, using his finger as a pointer under each line. Then he moved the paper aside and dealt two hands of cards.

With nothing in their pockets except dreams of the future, they used dried beans for their wagers. Clara mastered the game quickly, winning beans about as often as she lost them. She soon grew tired of moving small piles of beans back and forth across the table, and the day Vincent won with a full house higher than hers, she gave the poker stakes a rinse and cooked them for supper.

Chapter Twenty-One

As the days stacked up, Clara and Vincent looked forward to feeding the horses, using the privy, or bringing in wood—any opportunity for diversion. The second week in December they got a break when Albert rode down to the cabin and invited them to a belated Thanksgiving supper, more a summons than an invitation.

"Of course we will come," Clara said. "Please tell Geneva I will bring dessert. I haven't eggs or I would bake a cake. I have the ingredients for a pie, though."

"Bake two," Albert said. "Reb Carlton will be there along with the four other hands on my winter payroll."

The post-Thanksgiving supper consisted of roast Canada goose with cornmeal stuffing, buttered squash, and canned corn. After everyone had eaten their fill, Clara and Geneva cleared the long plank table and replaced the dirty dishes with dessert plates and clean forks. It was the first time the two women had seen each other since Clara's impromptu visit.

"I hope you like apple," Clara said to no one in particular as she set her pies in the middle of the table. Reb clapped his hands together like a gleeful child. The other cowhands ogled the pies as if their portion might send them to Glory Land.

"Apple is my favorite," said Albert.

"Dried," Clara added. "I'm a tad shy of fresh."

Geneva ate half of her slice, and then pushed her plate away. "We still have a few apples in our cellar. They were a bit shriveled last time I checked, but maybe you could bake us another pie…this time with fresh apples." She smiled haughtily. "In my candy opinion, fresh tastes better than dried. How many do you need?"

"Half a dozen will do," Clara said stiffly.

Not a crumb of the two pies was left when the ranch hands returned to the bunkhouse and the women washed dishes. Albert poured two glasses of brandy and lit his customary evening cigar. Vincent declined his boss's offer of a cigar, but accepted the brandy. The two men talked briefly about the hay supply and protecting cattle from wolves over the winter. Finished with cow talk, Albert asked the women to come back. Clara was drying her hands on a towel when he handed her a large box. "Something I picked up in Dodge."

"You shouldn't have brought me anything, Pa." Clara took the lid off the box and pulled out a stylish bonnet. Not partial to hats of any kind, she didn't mind the one in her hands. It was made of straw and didn't have the silk pleats and imitation flowers that gussied up other bonnets.

Geneva rolled her eyes. "Albert brought me a present, as well." She lifted the front of her skirt to display the lace ruffles on the bottom of a black petticoat that didn't come close to covering her ankles. Vincent steered his eyes elsewhere.

"Telling would have been sufficient," Albert growled. Frowning, he turned to his son-in-law. "What did you bring my daughter?"

Vincent turned up empty palms. "I

didn't…I…uh…" Clara's cheeks reddened. "Vincent is new at being married, Pa. I'm sure he will do better next time."

Shamefaced, Vincent nodded, clenching and unclenching his hands while he watched Clara place the bonnet over her dark brown hair. "You look pretty as a pi'ture," he said, in a stab at making amends. Clara gave him a reassuring smile.

She removed the bonnet, and then she and Geneva returned to the kitchen. The two young women were in the middle of a polite conversation when Geneva said, "In my candy opinion, you look like a ninny in that bonnet."

"What?" Clara plunged a pot into the soapy water. Shocked by the unprovoked remark, she shot Geneva a vengeful look. "Better a ninny in a bonnet than a jezebel in a petticoat," she sputtered. The two women glared at one another until Clara picked up the pot and began scrubbing it. "Will you ever learn the correct expression is can·*did* opinion, not can·*dy* opinion? Only a ninny says 'in my can·*dy* opinion.'"

"So what!" Geneva snorted. "I may not have graduated from tenth grade, but I'm not living in a shack." A tense silence prevailed while the women finished the pots and pans. With the exception of their afternoon of tea and talk, it had been months since either one had been in the presence of another woman. The whole time their husbands were gone they had longed for conversation, especially conversation with a woman, yet they were back to using silence as a weapon.

When the dishes were done and it was time to leave, they exchanged cool goodbyes on the front porch. Geneva didn't mention the apples she offered earlier, and Clara didn't ask for them.

Chapter Twenty-Two

The cold weather continued, and Clara found herself envying her husband's responsibilities. Seven mornings a week Vincent escaped the cabin's smoky interior to hitch a team of horses to a flatbed wagon, load it with hay, and drive it to wherever Albert's cows were huddling. He used a pitchfork to toss the feed to the cows, and then returned to the hay barn for another load. He and his men hauled hay all day. Between trips, they pulled cattle and horses out of mud holes, broke through ice on slow-moving streams to water the cows, waded through wet or frozen brush to set fence posts right, all the while avoiding ground hog holes, boulders, or other hazards. When hungry wolves ventured onto the property, the men formed hunting parties to track and shoot them. At the end of days so cold Vincent had to breathe through a wool scarf tied over his mouth and nose, his pant legs would be frozen stiff, and his rigid leather boots a struggle to remove.

Regardless of how wet or cold Vincent was when he walked through the cabin door, Clara figured dealing with the elements was better than a log wall prison. On the other hand, she appreciated the time to herself—more space to do her work and especially the privacy to bathe. She wrote in her diary every day, usually mundane lists of the tasks she accomplished. Sometimes she confided more revealing observations.

-Vincent is no slacker; however gentility does not come naturally to him. He can be a gentleman when it serves his purpose, but he is awkward in its execution.

-The manner in which he uses his fork like a shovel is a rasping annoyance to me.

-I am weary of always being the one charged with minding the stove.

She never let on how she felt, never complained about the cramped living conditions, the boredom of her routine, or a stove too small to beat back the cold. She and Vincent spoke mostly about food, cows, the maintenance and comfort of their horses, daily chores, and occasionally a bit of news Vincent picked up when he worked with Albert or one of the hands.

Climbing into bed at the end of the day, they made love if Vincent wasn't bone tired. They curled together for warmth, and then Vincent fell asleep. Clara lay awake, listening for intruders or horses in distress. She ignored the familiar sounds of wind rattling the stovepipe and small animals scurrying across the roof.

The fire went out one night, and the couple awoke to a dusting of frost on the tops of their blankets, deposited there by the frozen concentration of their breath. Clara got out of bed and dressed in the semi-darkness. Her fingers were numb as she threw a handful of wood shavings into the stove and lit them with a wooden match.

"What day would this be?" she asked Vincent when he joined her.

"Sunday."

"What *date*, rather." She was squatting in front of the stove with her everyday dress, petticoat, and apron fanned around her on the hard dirt floor.

"I dunno." Vincent stood behind her, rubbing his hands together as if willing the kindling to ignite.

Clara pictured the fireplace in her pa's house and the afternoon she'd spent sipping tea in front of a fire crackling with gusto. "How long until Christmas?"

"A week...maybe less. According to your pa, yesterday was the first day of winter."

Clara sat back on her heels, arms sagging at her sides as she stared into the sputtering fire. "At least the days are shorter."

Part III

Make Do and Mend

Chapter Twenty-Three

Vincent gave Clara a calendar for Christmas, all twelve months printed on a single page bordered in bluebirds and apple blossoms. It was the only bit of color decorating the cabin walls. Every morning Clara took a moment to gaze at the birds and blossoms before marking a large black X over the previous day, a ritual she continued until the sun, the best of all mood enhancers, warmed the cabin again.

By mid-March, calving season was well underway, a bustle of birthings that put Vincent, Reb, and the rest of the cowhands on high alert for wolves. Carnivores were always a threat to cattle, but in the spring, when there were newborn calves around, wolves turned into frenzied stalkers, sneaking through underbrush or darting from boulder to boulder like a pack of ghouls. When they happened upon a cow in the throes of labor, they would attack from the rear, eating the cow and her unborn calf alive. Thanks to the vigilance and marksmanship of Albert's men, the gruesome assault didn't happen often.

Vincent skinned the wolves he felled. He cured the pelts in the barn, and as soon as he could get away for a day, he planned to take them to Conejos, collect a bounty for the ears, and sell the hides.

"Never thought I'd be a wolver," he said to Clara after skinning his fifth wolf.

"You are not one of those men. Those scoundrels would simply take the ears and avoid the ugly job of skinning." She gave her husband a playful nudge. "You do smell like one, though."

Except for skinning wolves, Clara had been working right alongside her husband, rounding up calves and helping brand them. Whenever they came upon a maverick calf, Vincent roped it, and she, wearing a pair of his old leather gloves, hung onto the rope while he built a small fire. Starting with the kindling he carried in his saddlebag, he touched a match to the chips, blowing on them until they erupted in a crackling salute to ten years of branding calves in the open range. Using whatever combustibles he could find, he soon had a fire hot enough to heat a branding iron. Clara was impressed; although she questioned why his skill at coaxing fires didn't transfer to their stove.

She held her breath every time Vincent applied the hot iron to the right hip of the calf. Both the calf and cow would be bawling, and sometimes the mama cow muscled in close, bumping her or Vincent with its shoulder or nose. Nauseated by the stench of burning hide, Clara was thankful her pa's ++ brand was small. The minute Vincent pulled the iron away she released the rope and let the calf run back to its mother. The mama cow stood still as a post—just her cow eyes blinking and her tail flicking as the calf glued itself to her side.

She and Vincent branded close to a hundred calves that spring. The rest of Albert's crew, also working in pairs, branded four hundred more. Twice Vincent showed Clara how to help a cow get through a difficult birth. He also taught her the life-saving trick of tickling the nose of a newborn calf with a weed or blade of grass to get it to take its first breath. Sometimes the effort to save one of the little animals was for naught. "Calves do stupid things," Vincent told her, "like getting stuck in mud holes, falling off cliffs, sniffing at rattlesnakes."

At the end of their last day searching for calves, Vincent and Clara loosened their reins for a leisurely return to the cabin. They rode side by side, letting their horses pick the best route through the greasewood and rabbit brush. Patches of new grass grew between the hardy shrubs, along with purple scurf pea and other wild flowers. Clara decided it was a good time to tell her husband what she'd been keeping from him. He would have made her stay home if he'd known. She hadn't even been totally open with her diary when she wrote: *Spring is here at last! Calves are suckling and squirrels are nurturing their young in underground burrows. The music of the birds has returned to the valley, and this year I am in harmony with their song.*

"We are going to have a baby," she told him when they were halfway home. "If my calculations are correct, it will be born in December."

Vincent blushed from his neckerchief to his ears. After a long string of seconds, he said, "I s'pose that's to be expected." Their horses plodded through a hundred more yards of underbrush. "I s'pose we'll be needin' some baby things. Maybe your pa'll give me a raise." He glanced at Clara, and then looked away.

"We still have your wolf money, Dearest. I was hoping we could combine that with Pa's Christmas money and buy us a sewing machine."

Vincent chewed on what he knew was a plan rather than a suggestion. Some decent duds and a bottle of Red Eye were more what he had in mind.

"It will pay for itself over time," Clara added.

They rode another half mile in silence until Vincent said, "Can you sew trousers on one of those contraptions?"

Clara nodded. "I believe so…after I learn how to use it. Punching cows is hard on your clothes, Vincent. Every week I have to mend something of yours, and not just stockings."

"Well, I'll be needin' somethin' soon, or I'll be wearin' my union suit to Easter dinner." He flashed a grin at Clara and laughed.

Clara laughed, too, at the thought of him, or even a man with more bravado, sitting at the table in a red flannel union suit.

The closest thing to Sunday clothes that Vincent owned was a burgundy silk vest he'd won in a poker game in Abilene. After the game was over, he was about to leave the saloon wearing the classy vest when the previous owner tried to rip it off his back. Four buttons popped off in the ensuing struggle, and Vincent didn't notice they were missing until the next time he wanted to wear it.

The poker game had taken place several years before he married Clara, and she, who knew the vest's history, didn't think her husband had worn it since. She was certain the vest would still fit him, so she took it out of the trunk under their bed. If she could mend it, Vincent would have something stylish to wear when they went to Albert and Geneva's house for Easter supper. Geneva was also with child, ready to give birth within days.

Opening her sewing basket, Clara rummaged through its contents and found hooks and eyes, a wooden darning egg, a pin cushion bristling with needles, four colors of heavy cotton thread, a skein of black wool yarn, a paper of straight pins, two sizes of scissors, and a thimble, but no buttons. While looking for Vincent's vest, she had run across the wool gabardine traveling suit she wore when she and her pa took the train from Philadelphia to La Jara. She thought the embossed brass buttons on the suit's jacket would look good on Vincent's vest. It probably wouldn't fit her, anyway, now that she was pregnant.

She carried her sewing basket over to the table and lit the coal lamp. The buttons on her jacket were slightly smaller than those on Vincent's vest, but she figured they would work if she shortened each buttonhole with a couple of stitches. The brass buttons winked in the glow of lamplight as she cut them off the jacket spread across her knees. She recalled the day Aunt Mid gave her the suit as a tenth grade graduation present. Barely sixteen, hair still in braids, how grown up she'd felt when she put it on and looked in the mirror! She made a silent promise to replace the buttons when she could afford them, or if she ever had occasion to wear the suit again. The lantern flickered, then dimmed.

Chapter Twenty-Four

With a doctor from Alamosa at Geneva's bedside, she delivered a healthy baby girl five days before Easter. She was too weak to prepare the Easter meal, and though Clara wasn't feeling well either, she agreed to cook it. There would be nine people, including her and Vincent, sitting around the table that Sunday: her pa, her half-brother Christopher, Aunt Alma and Uncle Morris, and their children, Violet and Todd. Albert and Morris would be wearing dress coats and Vincent his burgundy vest.

Clara's Aunt Lou would be there, too, and alone. In February, Lou's husband of less than two years was killed when a log slipped its chain and rolled over him. Alma, knowing that meant Lou had no way to support herself, had asked her sister to move in with her and Morris. "You can help with the children," she wrote when she extended the invitation. "The arrangement will benefit both of us." Thinking Lou might never become a mother, Clara decided not to mention her own good news.

Albert selected the largest ham in his smokehouse for Easter dinner. Lou baked bread and hot cross buns, and his sister Alma brought home-canned pickles, applesauce, and peas. Clara baked the ham and made gravy for the mashed potatoes. After she took the ham out of the oven, she baked a cinnamon cake for dessert.

Lou helped Clara in the kitchen. "Without Geneva," she whispered to her niece when they were alone, "it's almost as if you and I are back cooking for Albert before he married her."

Clara smiled and nodded. "I have to bake everything in a Dutch oven. Cooking barely qualifies as work with a real oven."

The meal was perfect, and after everyone had eaten their fill, Albert carried his little daughter into the great room to show her off. It was the first time he'd held Rose in his arms, and she, unfamiliar with his smell and the firm hold he had on her, began to cry. Clara took the baby from him and held her close, swaying gently until the crying stopped. Studying her half-sister's pink face, she wished she knew if the baby in her womb was a boy or a girl.

Clara carried Rose to the master bedroom where Geneva rested under a coverlet with her head propped against a bolster of pillows. "How are you feeling?" Clara asked, partly out of polite concern, partly because she might learn something about giving birth. She placed Rose in Geneva's arms and then stood by the side of the bed.

Geneva gazed at the baby's round face. "Isn't she pretty?"

"Oh yes, dreadfully so. Did giving birth to a girl feel different?"

Geneva rolled her eyes. "This may be baby number three, but it doesn't seem to get any easier. I'm still in pain." She slipped her cream-colored nightdress off one shoulder so Rose could nurse. "Will you be a dear and get me some more cake? Nursing gives me an appetite."

A quarter of the cake was left. Clara cut a piece of

it, and when Albert saw her walking toward his bedroom with the plate, he said, "Make short the woman talk, Daughter. I am about to announce something that will be of interest to you."

Clara set the plate on Geneva's nightstand and hurried back to the great room. Alma and Morris were seated on one of the leather sofas, Vincent on the other. Alma and Morris were whispering to one another when Clara sat on the sofa next to her husband. Albert cleared his throat, and they stopped.

"I have decided to pursue a promising business opportunity," Albert began. "In January, I purchased several parcels of suitable grazing land along the San Miguel River. As soon as our new calves are strong enough to travel, I plan to move my entire herd up there. The grass is better, and when the cattle are ready for market I can ship them from Montrose. The parcels of land I bought are not contiguous, which means half of the cattle will be settled near Naturita and the other half at Wright's Mesa."

Vincent nodded. He didn't know how far Naturita and Wright's Mesa were from Montrose, but he was sure they were a heck of a lot closer than Kansas.

"I already told Morris and Vincent about this," Albert continued. "Morris has decided to remain on his ranch. I like the fact he will be close enough to check on the consortium that has leased my land. Vincent will be in charge of moving the herd to the new locations."

Clara smiled at her husband. How gentlemanly he looked in his collared shirt and silk vest. "I haven't heard of Naturita and Wright's Mesa, Pa. Do many people live there? What kind of houses do they have?"

Albert pulled a cigar out of his breast pocket and lit

it. "Housing is limited. We will have to wait until next year to build." He pointed his cigar at Clara. "I guarantee whatever we find will be better than that shack you are living in."

Clara's smile disappeared. She moved closer to Vincent and threaded her arm through his.

****

Back when Albert's first wife died and he decided to leave Philadelphia, it was Colorado's trees that had interested him: Douglas fir, blue spruce, white, ponderosa, and lodge pole pine—hardy varieties that flourished at high altitudes. People were moving to the western states in droves, and with that in mind he planned to buy as much forested land as he could afford. Then he would build a mill that would convert his timber into the shingles, siding, joists, and flooring needed to house the settlers.

During his first visit to Denver, he met one of the owners of the Conejos Cattle Company, and soon after learning how much money he could make in the cattle business, he was in a dusty train car on the Santa Fe line bound for La Jara. Five years later, this man who could trace his roots to the original Penn colony, a college polo player who hobnobbed with Philadelphia society, had become one of the largest property owners in Colorado.

Chapter Twenty-Five

By the end of July, the calves born that spring were mature enough to be moved. Getting them and the rest of Albert's herd to the grass growing along the San Miguel River meant driving two thousand head of cattle north and west, through wooded ravines and sloping meadows, granite-walled canyons and land crisscrossed by deer runs. Vincent laid out a plan that would follow the northern portion of the Rio Grande for the first few days. When the terrain became too steep, he and the rest of Albert's men would have to carve an undetermined path through high country to their final destination. After the cattle were settled and lodging secured, they would send for the women and children.

Albert and his men left La Jara on August first. Cloud shadows drifted across the San Luis Valley. A light wind stirred up dust devils and shuffled the leaves of the cottonwood trees like playing cards. Vincent's grin was hidden behind his bandana when he and his favorite mare plunged into the chaos of the bawling cows. His new responsibilities would entail the same kind of work he'd done for the last ten years, but driving cattle to the railhead in Montrose would allow him to sleep with his wife in days rather than spending months with a gaggle of cowboys around a campfire.

The exodus of men and beasts kicked up a huge dust cloud. Gradually the herd moved out of the intermountain valley into a cleavage of canyons, and Vincent lowered his bandana to take in the view. Moving cattle was always a dusty proposition, but to him, this part of Colorado was comfortable as an old boot compared to the never-ending stretches of parched land he'd ridden across in Texas, Kansas, and parts of Montana Territory.

Game was plentiful. Two weeks into the drive the cook shot a deer that fed the crew for three days. The cook's good aim also added sage grouse and cottontail rabbits to the usual menu of beans, salt pork, biscuits, and gravy.

Reb took another bite of a venison steak that nearly filled the tin plate balanced on his knees. "Right good grub this time."

Vincent nodded. He sat next to Reb with his own plate of food and took off his hat, exposing a high, white forehead and sweat-matted hair. Digging into his supper, he said, "A feller might stick with punchin' cows 'til he was forty if every drive was like this one."

Later that evening, when it was time for some shuteye, Reb left the circle of men around the campfire and walked a few yards to a secluded spot where he'd stashed his saddle. Vincent, relieving himself in the bushes nearby, saw his best young cowboy pull a bottle of whisky out of his saddlebag and take a swig. "Hey!" he hollered.

Reb stashed the bottle and carried his saddle toward the campfire where some men lingered over coffee while others unfurled their bedrolls.

"Stay right there," Vincent ordered, buttoning his trousers. He walked to where Reb stood with his saddle.

"I'm fixin' to lay my head on this," the young man

explained. His back was to the campfire, making it difficult to read his face, but the slump of his broad shoulders confirmed Vincent's suspicions.

"You know the rules."

"It's a far piece to the next waterin' hole, Guv'nor."

"Uh-huh." Vincent unbuckled the flap on Reb's saddlebag and confiscated the bottle. "I'm takin' this for safe-keepin'. I won't tell Albert this time, but this better be the last."

The next afternoon, Albert and his men swung the herd away from the stream they'd been following into a long, tree-lined meadow. The grassy flatland gave the cattle a chance to rest a spell and fill their bellies after miles of slim pickings. Standing in his stirrups, Albert eyed the conifers bordering the meadow and stretching into the distance until they were the size of toothpicks. "You ride ahead," he told Vincent. "See if you can locate some daylight in those trees. A forest like that is worse than a labyrinth when it comes to moving cattle."

Vincent followed the tree line for several miles. Finding no corridor, he entered the depths of the green-black forest to see how far back it went. The pinto he'd saddled that morning was quick on her feet as she maneuvered through timbered undergrowth and densely packed trees that shut out the sun. The bright green lichen clinging to the trees' bark made them easy to spot, yet he was repeatedly smacked in the face by low-hanging branches.

Coming onto dark, he discovered a dry riverbed. He urged the pinto up the bed for half a mile to check its width, the horse's hooves kicking up sparks as it trotted across the rocks. Although a riverbed wasn't the broad expanse of land he'd hoped for, he decided it was wide enough to accommodate Albert's plodding migration.

Too late to circle back, Vincent unsaddled his horse and unfurled the pile of grubby quilts he slept in when he was on the trail. His eyes wandered down to the permanent curl at one end of his bedroll. Staring at the curl as if he'd never seen it before, he wondered if this drive would end up being his last. He was still tossing that idea around in his head when he lifted Reb's bottle to his lips.

Chapter Twenty-Six

Albert's herd was knee-deep in grass on both sides of the San Miguel River by mid-September. Once the cattle were settled, he sent a wire to his wife, instructing her and Clara to take the train as far as Montrose, then go by stagecoach to Placerville where he'd meet them with the buckboard.

NO ROADS HERE his telegram stated, *ONLY TRAILS*.

The two young women waited for the train inside the dingy boxcar that served as La Jara's depot. They sat on the station's lone bench, Geneva with Rose in her arms, Clara seated next to her with sixteen-month-old Christopher climbing on and off her lap. Resolved to the consequences of an uncertain future, the women kept their worries to themselves during the hour they waited for a train that was never on time. When they did say something to one another, it was usually about moving details.

"What will you miss most until our possessions arrive?" Clara asked.

Geneva replied without hesitation, "My knee tub. I had to leave it behind. Albert said it was too heavy to move, even by ox cart." She smiled down at baby Rose. "And the baby's crib. That will come later. What about you?"

"My horse. Definitely Bridget. They needed her for

the drive, which meant she had to go back to being a packhorse. Vincent said she was none too happy about it, either."

"That's horse-feathers." Geneva chuckled, glancing at Clara for an acknowledgement of her cleverness. "Worrying about a horse is horse-feathers."

"I heard you the first time. I will also miss my sewing machine until it arrives with our furniture. Vincent was such a dear to buy it for me. I've already used it to sew a baby blanket for your first grandchild."

"Will that train never arrive?" Geneva grumbled.

A few minutes later Clara said, "How do you picture the town of Naturita?"

"I don't expect it will be large or I would have heard of it before." Geneva glanced at the ceiling of the boxcar masquerading as a waiting room. "Nothing could be smaller than La Jara. I can't believe this train stop even has a name."

"Naturita is such a pretty name," Clara said. "I imagine it has frame houses, at least a few of them, with picket fences and shade trees in the yards."

"That would be a welcome change," Geneva said as a shrill whistle signaled the approach of their train.

It was partly cloudy when the women and children, the only passengers getting on in La Jara, boarded the train. They had no way of knowing that farther up the Santa Fe line, a massive thunderstorm was pounding the countryside from Telluride to eastern Utah and as far north as the Colorado River. Strong winds were uprooting trees. Lightning strikes ripped across the sky, and much of the area would have been blackened by fire if not for the buckets of water the storm produced.

About halfway to Montrose, rain splashed the

windows of the train car Clara and Geneva were sitting in, but by the time they arrived, the storm had passed. Walking through puddles of water on the streets and sidewalks of Montrose, they soaked their shoes and the bottoms of their skirts during the short walk to their hotel.

The next morning, they boarded a stagecoach bound for Placerville on roads so muddy, that after traveling about twenty-five miles to the south, the driver left his passengers in Dallas, telling them they would have to find some other way to their destinations. Eight men, including a judge, were waiting in Dallas for a ride to Telluride where court was being held. Having no stagecoach transportation, the men did some lawyerly arm-twisting and convinced a teamster with a lumber wagon to take all of them, including the women and children, to Placerville.

Three miles outside of Dallas, the wooden wheels of the lumber wagon became so clogged with mud that the driver told the fashionably attired lawyers and businessmen they would have to get out and walk. "The women and children can stay on board," he said. And on mostly canyon roads, with the men plodding through ankle-deep muck, the entourage finally arrived in Placerville at two o'clock in the morning. The people working at the stage stop next to Leopard Creek had a trout dinner waiting for them, and they fed a muddy, annoyed group of men hungry enough to eat a shark.

Albert had left word at the Placerville stage stop that plans had changed. Since the trails were too muddy to travel by wagon, Geneva and Clara were to buy a couple of horses and ride to a log bridge that spanned the San Miguel River. He would meet them there on his own horse and accompany them the rest of the way to Naturita.

"I will stay here until spring if I have to, but I will not sit upon a horse," Geneva declared, her chin trembling with exasperation. "Has Albert no concern for Christopher? Or baby Rose? Or me, for heaven's sake?"

Five months into her pregnancy, Clara wasn't sure she should be riding a horse, either, especially an unfamiliar horse. She read her pa's telegram again, and decided eight miles on horseback was probably doable. After they met at the bridge, Geneva could ride with him. "Horses are our only option, Geneva. You have endured childbirth three times. Riding a horse is not half as remarkable."

Geneva pulled a self-monogrammed handkerchief out of her pocket. Leaning against the side of the bed she would be sharing that night with Clara, she dabbed at her tears. Still sniffling, she did a quick survey of their dimly lit hotel room with its double bed, spindle back chair next to the window, and six-drawer oak dresser. There were no pictures on the walls, and no mirror. With a dramatic sigh she took the afghan draped across the back of the chair and used it to make a bed for Rose in one of the dresser drawers. Christopher would have to sleep between her and Clara.

Clara spent a restless night on the crowded, lumpy mattress. Rising at dawn, she dressed quietly in the clothes she wore the day before, and then tiptoed through a maze of puddles to the livery stable. What she learned when she got there was as gloomy as the misty morning.

"Sidesaddles?" The liveryman let out a wheezy

chuckle. "Not in these parts, Missy. Got regular ones though. None of 'em new. But I ain't stabled a horse in over a month. Got a couple a mules. Fellow sold me a couple a mules yesterday."

"Mules might be even better." Clara had heard Vincent say mules were more patient than horses. Patience was the key here, for both herself and the mule when it came to dealing with Geneva. Clara paid the liveryman for the matched pair of brown-black mules, both animals at least fifteen hands high and more heavily built than most horses. The mules appeared to be healthy enough, although, judging by their teeth, past their prime.

"You will be pleased to know we will not be riding horses today," Clara told Geneva when she returned to the hotel.

Geneva's eyebrows arched. "Then by what means will we travel?"

"Mule," Clara said gaily, trying to sound positive. "On a roomy saddle that will make you feel safe…I mean comfortable."

"Have you gone batty?" Geneva's eyes flashed with fury. "A mule is a cousin of a horse. Stupider than a horse. They're nasty and smelly! Mean, too, I've heard."

"First of all, mules aren't mean if you treat them right. The liveryman said the ones I, that is we, bought are good-natured and obedient—perfect for someone like you who has never ridden before."

"You did this on purpose."

Geneva's arms were crossed under her bosom. Clara grabbed her by the arms and shook her. "There are no horses for sale here, do you understand? And nobody willing to risk a team and a wagon in the mud. I was lucky to find mules."

Geneva pushed Clara away. She picked up her baby daughter and held her to her chest. "My poor children."

"If you swaddle Rose, you won't have to fuss with blankets. Hold her the way you are now. I will sit Christopher in front of me. I believe he'll find riding on the back of a mule to be quite a lark." Clara took Christopher by the hand and began walking toward the door. Pouting, Geneva lagged behind during the two-block walk to the livery stable.

She let out a shriek when the liveryman helped her onto one of the mules, again when the mule took its first step, and its second, and every time the animal so much as snuffed its nose or cocked its ears. Clara choked back the urge to laugh. "We have but eight miles to go," she assured the ashen-faced woman sitting straight as a broomstick, "and I will be right beside you the entire way."

The liveryman said the trail to the San Miguel River was well-marked and well-traveled, and it was. Clara kept the mules at a pace suitable for pulling a plow. Geneva, barely breathing during the half-day trip, did everything Clara told her to do.

They heard the river before they saw it. Upon reaching its banks, they realized there was no way to get across. The recent deluge had swelled the river to flood stage, and sweeping through the gorge like a startled snake, the force of the water had washed away all but the pilings of the log bridge.

Albert had already crossed to their side. From a hundred yards upstream he saw his family and galloped his stallion in their direction. Geneva broke into tears at the sight of him.

Christopher held out his arms. "Papa!"

"Mules?" Albert smiled at Clara as he transferred Christopher from her saddle to his. "Brilliant!"

"It was a stroke of luck, Pa," Clara shouted over the roar of the water. "There were no horses to be had in Placerville." She grinned. "No sidesaddles, either."

Still wet from his crossing, Albert reached across the space between his horse and Geneva's mule to squeeze his wife's hand. "I am proud of you. I was not sure how you would react to my instructions."

"She despised the ride, Pa, but minded my advice."

"May I get down, now?" Geneva relaxed her grip on Rose.

"If you wish," Albert replied, "however you will have to get back on that mule to ford the stream."

Geneva scowled at the swirling brown water. "The stream! I don't see a stream. I see a raging river."

"I will ride across with you," Albert said, "you and the baby. My horse will do as I command and swim to the other side on his own. I trust Clara's ability to handle a mule. Christopher will cross with her."

Although Geneva's thigh muscles ached as if she'd just given birth, she decided to stay where she was. Albert dismounted and climbed behind her, curling his left arm around her and Rose while holding the mule's reins in his right hand. He took off his hat, whacked his stallion on the rump with it, and ordered him to swim across the river.

The adults, as well as the mules, watched the superb horse clamber across the rocks at river's edge before plunging into the water. Fighting the downstream pull of the current, the horse began a slow advance toward the opposite bank. When it got close, it lunged for solid ground, shedding water as it crashed through the bushes lining the riverbank.

"This is too dangerous!" Geneva cried when Albert led their mule into the muddy water. He ignored her. Clucking encouragement to the mule, he held his wife and baby tightly as the water rushed against the animal's knees, then its chest. He felt the mule tense while it negotiated the slippery rocks on the river bottom, and then shift to muscle power when its four legs began to pump.

Geneva was wet to her armpits. Shocked by the temperature of the water, she screeched, "Please...please...please" and shifted Rose higher on her shoulder. She kept her eyes closed until they left the water and the mule scrambled up the bank to dry ground.

Clara waited, scrutinizing her pa's every move. Only after she saw him and Geneva downstream, waving assurance from the opposite bank, did she press her heels into the mule's ribs, urging it toward the water. The mule wanted nothing to do with the circus it had been watching and planted its feet. She cooed to it, dug her knees into the mule's ribs, kicked it, spanked it with the reins, but no amount of prodding would convince the animal to budge.

Albert monitored her struggle for a couple of minutes, and then he got back on the first mule and led it upriver, stopping directly across from Clara. The second mule saw its partner on the other side, and inched into the swirling flow. Clara shivered; cold water rising from her shoes to her knees to above her waist. Christopher, who'd been surprisingly well behaved up to that point, screamed when water too cold to be a bath soaked him from neck to toes. Clara tried to calm him, but shrieking and kicking, the toddler wriggled out of his half-sister's grasp. She lunged to her right to grab him. She caught his shirt, but lost her balance and slipped off the mule's back.

She tightened her hold on Christopher with one hand and reached for the mule's saddle with the other. Her heart lurched. Instead of leather, she felt the animal's smooth, muscular rump. Terrified, and unable to see through the muddy water, she groped for the mule again and caught its tail. She raised her head for a gulp of air. Realizing she was the vital link in this chain of warm-blooded creatures swirling down the San Miguel River, she hung onto the mule's tail with one hand and concentrated on keeping Christopher's head above water with the other.

The roar of the river drowned out Geneva's screams, and Clara, with her face under water most of the time, couldn't see her father running along the bank, shouting encouragement. He finally jumped into the river, struggling against the current and no match for the thrashing mule.

During three minutes that seemed like an eternity, Clara held on to both child and tail until the mule's feet touched bottom again. She slogged through the waist-deep water with Christopher in her arms, her sopping dress and an equally drenched and bawling child weighing her down. Geneva, soaked as well, was at the water's edge holding a squalling Rose.

"Why did you drop him!" Geneva traded children with Clara, and covered Christopher's face with kisses before walking off with him.

"Thank God you made it," Albert bellowed. Clara was dazed and dripping wet, hugging Rose to her breast in an effort to warm them both. "I cannot thank you enough," he added while climbing up the riverbank. "After the loss of my first son with Geneva, to say nothing of your little brothers, I do believe it would have killed me if Christopher drowned."

Geneva took Christopher on a short walk, and when they returned, everyone shared the quart of canned peaches and half-dozen apples Albert had in his saddlebag. Finished eating, Geneva approached Clara who was wringing water out of her skirt. "Albert told me I should tell you I'm grateful." She had to shout in order to make herself heard.

Clara looked down at the ground and waited. A hornet buzzed around an apple core. The first hornet was joined by another before Geneva uttered a barely audible "thank you" and hurried back to Albert.

Wet and exhausted, the small caravan prepared to leave. Albert helped Geneva onto the mule she'd been riding and handed Rose up to her. With Christopher sitting in front of him, he approached Clara, sitting atop the mule that dragged her across the river. His hazel eyes held a spark of mirth. In a voice loud enough to be heard over the rushing water, he said, "Only God knows for sure, Daughter; however I do believe persistence had a hand in what happened here today. For once your stubborn nature was an asset."

Chapter Twenty-Seven

Clara and her family rode into Naturita around nightfall, and her hopes for a bona fide town faded with the dying light. It took her mule, its partner, and a buckskin stallion no time at all to carry their human cargo past the three unpainted structures bordering the trail. The only two-story building they passed had SALOON painted on a crude sign over the door. The door was open, and a light burned inside. Riding farther, the small procession came upon a one-room log house similar to the one Clara had just left.

"A local rancher built that," Albert explained. "He intended it to be a schoolhouse, but could only afford to pay a teacher for a few months. I'm told it has been empty for some time."

Clara rested a hand on her swelling abdomen. Although it was almost dark outside, she'd seen enough to realize there were no picket fences in Naturita, and, as she learned later, no doctor, dentist, undertaker, lawyer, or lawman.

She and Geneva rode into the main cow camp behind Albert, who'd wisely stopped in Naturita to buy a lantern. Vincent was waiting there for her. After he helped her down, and the two of them shared a modest embrace, he took care of her mule, and then joined her and the others gathered in Albert's house. Clara was shocked at the house her father had purchased. Twenty feet in length, it was a one-room building separated into living and eating quarters by blankets hung from the rafters. Geneva conducted a quick inspection of the crude space that was to be her new home, and ignoring Albert's repeated assurances of "This is only temporary," she took to bed fifteen minutes after they arrived.

Housing of any kind in that area was scarce. Albert had chosen the oddly shaped place for his headquarters because it came with a bunkhouse and large corral. There wasn't a cook shack, though. With winter approaching, he couldn't expect his cowboys to stick around for trail food, and as soon as the herd was in place, he'd begun sharing the cooking and eating half of the house with his men.

Vincent had rented a two-room house with no outbuildings ten miles away. It being too late to travel there, he and Clara spent the night on the floor under a pile of coats with a bearskin rug for a mattress. Encircled by her husband's arms for the first time in six weeks, Clara forgot her disappointment in the town of Naturita. They spooned together for warmth, but with others sleeping nearby they couldn't share the welcome home lovemaking they'd enjoyed when Vincent came back from Kansas.

The next morning, Albert told Vincent he was keeping Bridget. "You can borrow my buckboard for the trip to your place. With a child on the way, Clara should not have ridden a mule as far as she did, but there was no other option. You should be thinking about a wagon of your own." Vincent nodded absently. To him, a wagon meant falling deeper into the well of domesticity. So did having a child.

He and Clara ate a hearty breakfast of bacon and tortillas, and then he bundled her into Albert's buckboard and set out for the house he'd found. The sun was up, yet the crisp fall air was heavy with frost.

Less than a hundred yards into the ten-mile trip, Clara pointed south. "What mountains are those?"

"The San Juans."

"Still? All the way up here?"

"Yep, same ones. This place is crawlin' with mountains. Those over there"—he pointed west—"they call the Un·cum·pog·ray Plateau." He turned to Clara sitting next to him and grinned. "Hell of a thing to spell."

The temperature remained cool for most of the trip, although by mid-morning, Clara had to weave her fingers into a sunshade and rest them on her brow to prevent the dazzling sun from ruining her view of the horizon. Riding farther, she noted the land didn't stretch as far as her father's spread in the San Luis Valley. Instead, there were sizeable parcels of grassland surrounded by rim rock mesas, deep canyons, and lesser peaks. Marveling at the much higher peaks looming in the distance, Clara was surprised when Vincent told her Naturita was slightly lower in elevation than La Jara.

He pointed to a steep rise on their right. "People 'round here call these high places hills, or bluffs." He steered the horse around a spot in the trail too rocky for a wagon. "In Ohio we would've called 'em mountains."

It was the native grasses growing between these high places and the proximity of land to water that gave rise to Naturita, a cow town so small it wasn't even a stage stop. Free range was the rule in that part of Colorado, and almost everyone living in the surrounding area raised cattle or the hay to feed them. Without fences hemming them in, the cows roamed up to the grassy foothills during spring and summer, drifting to lower elevations in the winter to feed on hay. When it came time for local ranchers to sell their "beef on the hoof," they drove their herds to the railheads in Placerville or Montrose.

The house Vincent rented was 80 miles from Montrose and halfway between Naturita and Wright's Mesa. The only people living close enough to call neighbors were the seven members of the Stuart family. Originally from England, Mr. and Mrs. Stuart had two sons in their twenties and three girls in their teens.

The girls—Jane, Phoebe, and Bethany—had fallen all over one another when Vincent knocked on their door asking for directions to the house he was hoping to rent. Their smiles faded when they learned the good-looking man on their porch was married, but they were pleased to hear another woman would be living close enough they could call on her.

Vincent decided to introduce Clara to the Stuarts that day before they got to their house, and when the sisters met the cowboy's wife, they were shocked by how brown she was. Thirteen-year-old Bethany, youngest of the three, asked their new neighbor, "Are you of native origin, Mrs. Reese?"

Clara blushed a shade darker. "I never wear a bonnet. The sun turns my face brown every summer. I will be white again come spring." Bethany's question brought to mind the time Clara's Sunday school teacher had mocked her for wanting to be a black-haired angel. She figured her teacher would have been horrified if a brown-faced, brown-haired girl had asked to be an angel.

****

Not yet showing she was pregnant, Clara waited until the girls invited her to tea to tell them she was expecting. They insisted she stay with them during her confinement, and three and a half months later, under a sky heavy with snow clouds, Phoebe, Jane, and Bethany, their flawless complexions pink with anticipation, took turns mopping sweat and holding Clara's white-knuckled fists while she delivered her first child.

Mrs. Stuart washed and swaddled the infant and placed him in Clara's arms. Phoebe, the middle sister, asked the new mother what she was going to name her boy. Clara had been thinking about this for some time. "Albert would be appropriate," she replied, studying the baby's face, "if the name suits Vincent."

Vincent was twelve miles upriver when his wife gave birth. He stopped by the Stuart's house the next afternoon, and Mrs. Stuart shooed her daughters out of the room to give him and Clara a few minutes of privacy. "I'd like us to name him Charles," Vincent said, looking down at his son. "After my older brother. I was thirteen last time I saw 'im." He smiled awkwardly. "Should of gone home at least once, I s'pose."

Clara studied her son's pale hair and bottomless blue eyes. Charles was a good name, she granted. Strong; even royal at times. She forced a smile. "That sounds like a proper thing to do, Dearest."

Four days after giving birth, Clara and baby Charles left the comfortable Stuart house where, including her confinement, she'd spent close to two weeks. Vincent picked up his family in the buckboard he bought from Albert, and drove them to the small house he and Clara had been living in since September. Situated in a saddle of land between two buttes, the two-room house was surrounded by boulder-strewn hills timbered with conifer and deciduous trees. Beyond the hills loomed the San Juan Mountains, closer than they'd been in La Jara, and more imposing.

Clara was pleased with her house. Larger by half than the cabin she and Vincent had lived in, and built of boards rather than logs, it had a plank floor, small front porch, and a well. There was space in the main room for the secondhand table and chairs Vincent bought in Wright's Mesa plus a wildwood rocking chair the previous occupants had left behind. To her mind, two rooms were definitely a step up, even after she discovered the house had bedbugs.

Reb and another cowhand braved the snow to have a look at the "Guvnor's baby." Reb brought along a bottle of whisky to celebrate the new arrival. "I 'preciate the one you give me," he said to Vincent as the bottle passed from man to man, "in place of the one you took." He wiped his mouth with the back of his sleeve.

Vincent glanced at Clara. "Not in front of the wife," he said under his breath.

Clara furrowed her brow. "I try not to listen to masculine conversations," she mumbled, and then she carried her son into the other room. The combination bedroom and nursery contained the iron bedstead, mattress, and bureaus she and Vincent had been using at the cabin, and a hammock for Charley. "I prefer a hammock, anyway," Clara said after using it a few days. "It rocks like a cradle and keeps Little Precious away from the bugs."

Feeling poorly for some time after Charley was born, Clara was too weak to fight the bedbugs that seemed to be in every nook and cranny. Phoebe came by frequently to check on her. Clara had heard that burning coal oil killed them, so Phoebe burned a pot of it the whole time she was there. The minute she reached her own house, she shed her clothes, inspecting the pockets and seams of every garment.

Vincent did his best to get rid of the pests when he was home, but no amount of squashing reduced their numbers, and by the time Clara regained her strength, the bedbugs had become a full-scale infestation. She and Vincent burned coal oil twenty-four hours a day, and after Clara noticed the bugs liked to climb, she began wiping the bed rails, furniture legs, and base of her sewing machine with the pungent oil. When that didn't work, she filled four empty tomato cans with it and set the iron feet of her bedstead inside the cans. She was always on the lookout for bugs, and though she'd been told coal oil was a deterrent, the bloodsucking horde seemed to thrive on it.

They fought the vermin for six months before she and Vincent gave up and moved into the next best available house in the area, a one-room mud brick hut similar in size to the one they abandoned. Clara fell silent when she saw the dirt floor. "What will we do when Little Precious starts to crawl?"

Vincent shook his head, glancing in her direction without really looking at her.

The adobe house did have a well with a pump for drawing water, and it had two small windows that had been made out of a larger one. Clara was mulling over how she might deal with a baby and a dirt floor when she noticed the thick layer of dust on the sills, rafters, and ridges of mortar between the bricks. Every surface of the Franklin stove was coated with dust or grease or some combination of the two.

She set about giving the place a deep cleaning and discovered a bull snake curled in one of the corners. She screamed, more surprised than frightened, and whacked the snake with her broom. The snake, both frightened and surprised, slithered outside through a hole in the wall.

That evening she told Vincent about the encounter. "Better a snake for a house guest than bedbugs," she said, and they shared a much-needed laugh. The next day Vincent filled the hole with rocks.

Clara kept little Charley in an empty soap crate while she did her daily chores, dragging him and the box across the dirt floor as she moved about. Without enough space inside the box to crawl, Charley used the sides of the crate to pull himself up and went straight to walking.

Chapter Twenty-Eight

Albert salvaged Geneva's good graces by showing her the five acres close to Naturita where he planned to build them a two-story, ten-room house. There was little privacy in the "long house," as Geneva referred to where they were living, and over the winter she decided she might as well help the camp cook who was a constant presence. The following summer, Geneva and the cook fed upward of twenty men at a time, even more during hay harvest.

Vincent ate most of his mid-day meals at the long house, and one pleasant summer Sunday he suggested to Clara they have supper there. On their way home that evening, Clara turned to him and said, "Had I not seen it with my own eyes, I never would have believed Geneva could put supper on the table for that many people without raising a fuss."

Vincent nodded. "Her cookin's better, too."

While Geneva was improving her culinary skills, and, as Clara confided in Phoebe, "flaunting her curves" around the men who ate in the long house, Albert gathered a wagonload of odd cuts of leftover lumber, and he and Vincent laid a wood floor in the adobe house. Vincent could barely find the time to work on it. Since moving to Naturita he'd been working twelve to fourteen hours a day, keeping an eye on cattle strung along both sides of the river for miles. The long workdays gave Clara a lot of alone time. After her work was done, she often hitched a horse to the buckboard, sat Charley next to her, and drove to the Stuart's. Their Victorian style ranch house, with its sweeping front porch and spacious interior, was a perfect place to trade gossip, recipes, and home remedies. For entertainment, the women organized picnics or potlucks that included everyone in the Stuart family as well as a handful of Albert's men. Vincent, too, when he could get away. One of the Stuart family's favorite games was charades, and if Vincent and Reb drank enough liquid courage to take center stage, Phoebe and Clara laughed so hard the sofa shook.

Albert and Geneva were always invited to these gatherings, though they rarely came. Geneva came once without him. The afternoon she showed up, she was driving a two-wheeled cart pulled by one of the Placerville mules. The mule, accustomed to hauling much heavier loads, was kicking up its heels, and even before Geneva was halfway up the road to the Stuart's house, Clara heard her shouting at the animal to slow down.

Clara and Phoebe hurried outside. "What a surprise," Clara said, amused and amazed to see Geneva bring the mule to a halt. "When did you stop being afraid of horses?"

Geneva loosened the reins and gave her ex-friend a sharp look. "A mule is not a horse. You told me so yourself. This one saved my life, which is why I trust him." She straightened the small hat perched on her head. "I call him Jack. I thought he knew his name until this morning."

She handed the reins to Clara, and with Rose in her

arms, stepped down from the cart. Christopher jumped off the other side, ran around to where his mother was standing, and hid his face in her skirt, taking an occasional peek at Phoebe and Clara. As usual, Geneva's hair stuck out around her head like a fuzzy blonde halo. The sight of it made Clara wonder, as she often did, why her father, a man who was strict about everything else, allowed his wife to appear in public looking like a hussy.

"Did Pa show you how to hitch up this mule?"

"Albert's been gone for a week…Chicago this time." Geneva smiled coyly. "Vincent showed me how. I adore my beautiful new house, but now I can leave when I want to."

Chapter Twenty-Nine

While the trails were still navigable for a mule pulling a cart, Geneva went somewhere nearly every day, but not five miles to the adobe house. It was a six-mile trip for Phoebe, who rode a horse to see Clara once a week as long as the weather held. On her first visit, she'd openly admired Clara's shiny black sewing machine, one of the newer models that could be operated by a foot treadle as well as a hand-cranked wheel.

"Mum had to leave her Singer in Manchester when we moved here," Phoebe said. "Ours was not as fancy as yours."

"I didn't ask for fancy. This one happened to be the only sewing machine in Alamosa when Vincent bought it. He sold his wolf hides to pay for it." Clara thought back to the winter she and Vincent lived in the homesteader's cabin. "That was only a year and a half ago, Phoebe. It seems longer."

Clara had been using her Singer to mend clothes and little else. Before Vincent bought it for her, she dedicated part of every Wednesday to mending by hand—darning holes in stockings, sewing on buttons, repairing rips, or mending seams. Fabric was hard to come by, but with Charley growing out of his frocks and another child on the way, it was time to make the Singer start paying for itself.

"Have you ever made curtains?" she asked Phoebe during one of her friend's visits. Clara showed her the scorched bed sheet she'd been thinking about converting into curtains. Laundered many times, the embroidered rosebud trim was still pink. Phoebe held the sheet up to one of the windows. "This should do," she said. "Even after you cut out the burnt spot, there should be enough for both windows."

Together they measured, cut, sewed, and hemmed, four rectangular panels. Phoebe suggested they convert the rosebud trim into tiebacks, and within a few hours, curtains framed the two small windows of the adobe house.

"My mother never sewed," Clara said. Eyes glistening, she stood in front of one of the windows, gazing at the pine-studded mountains in the distance. "I wish I could show these to her. I think she would be proud of me."

Flushed with success, Clara decided to tackle something more ambitious, and with Phoebe's help setting the sleeves, she made Vincent a jacket out of a gray wool blanket. Vincent wore the jacket constantly, even on fall days warm enough for shirtsleeves. He wore it to a Christmas party at the Stuart's, and when the parlor grew warm with merriment, he took the jacket off and hung it over the back of a chair. Clara didn't think it belonged there. She picked the jacket up, and noticing it felt heavier than it should, she checked the pockets. There was a metal flask in one of them. She didn't have to open it to know what it contained.

Peeking left and right to see if anyone was watching, she carried the jacket out to the screened porch and draped it over the wraps and jackets hanging on a coat rack. "Oh, Vincent," she sighed, as she buried her face in the jacket's gray wool sleeves.

Part IV

To Market, To Market

Chapter Thirty

Clara's perception of love came from books she'd read, some from her father's collection while she still lived at home, others in the school library where her Aunt Mid couldn't see what she was reading. As a girl she was especially fond of Jane Austin, and after racing through every one of Austin's books, she wondered why her aunt wouldn't let her and Lily read novels.

Thirteen years old when she got her first look at Vincent, and sixteen when she married him, her soft-spoken cowboy held a mystique not unlike that of Mr. Darcy in *Pride and Prejudice* or Willoughby in *Sense and Sensibility.* He was easily their equal in looks. He embodied the same quiet detachment, and what he lacked in money and manners was offset by his competence with horses and cattle. He didn't give her the heart-flutters heroines in her favorite books experienced, but she was firmly committed to the man she married and the vows she'd made.

In thinly settled parts of the West, men and women didn't waste time thinking about why love happened or whether it would last. They were lucky to find it. Phoebe and Reb met at a picnic, and after a year of stolen glances at social gatherings, the shaggy-haired boy from Tennessee asked the girl from England to be his wife.

Phoebe said, "Yes," and right away Reb taught her

how to say, "gettin' hitched." He laughed every time she said it with her British accent.

Before Phoebe made public her engagement, she'd spent many afternoons with Clara, helping her with her sewing projects or borrowing the Singer to work on hers. In the quiet of the adobe house, they talked for hours without Phoebe ever mentioning her growing fondness for Reb. Clara knew something was going on, though, by the eye-catching garments her friend sewed and how she always seemed to finish them before some get-together Reb was sure to attend.

Reb was far more open with his thoughts than Vincent, who never said much about anything, let alone something personal. "I'm feelin' a heap a friendliness for that girl," he told Vincent after being around Phoebe a few times. His ears reddened when he described her "apple dumplin' shape…hair the color a dark honey…her funny way a talkin'. Dontcha get a kick outta hearin' them people talk?"

Vincent gave him a wry smile. "Strikes me, you've got a funny way of talkin', too."

Mrs. Stuart had a trunkful of fabric and patterns, some of which Phoebe shared with Clara. Clara wanted to surprise her friend with a wedding gift she made by herself, and since the provisions store in Naturita sold only denim and canvas, she asked Vincent if he'd take her to Wright's Mesa.

"Should you be goin' anywhere?" he asked. "You bein'…you know…in the family way again?"

Clara cupped her hands over her abdomen. "I will be fine. I trust your ability to negotiate a trail."

Vincent got Albert's permission to leave work for a day. Clara made sandwiches, and they left at dawn for

Wright's Mesa, a town some of the locals were calling Norwood. Five hours later, Vincent brought the buckboard to a squeaking halt in front of the town's general store, one of several businesses strung along an ordinary street named Grand Avenue.

Vincent helped his wife and son down from the wagon. "I've got one more stop. I'll be back by the time you finish shoppin'."

Clara took Charley by the hand and walked to the back of the store where the piece goods and sewing paraphernalia were shelved: rolls of fabric and spools of thread in an array of colors, a small assortment of ornamental tapes and trims, and a basket of porcelain, bone, and brass buttons. She checked the price on a roll of rose silk taffeta. Silk would have made a lovely blouse for her friend if it hadn't been so costly. Instead she settled for off-white cotton batiste, almost as soft as silk.

Walking around the store with the roll of batiste in her arms, she eyed many of the items on display. She avoided temptation and only bought the fabric and a small bag of penny candy for Charley.

The buckboard wasn't in front of the store when Clara and Charley walked out. They stood on the boardwalk watching other wagons and horses pass, but no Vincent. After twenty minutes of inactivity, Charley started to whine. Clara took him back inside the store and did more shopping. She bought the silk taffeta, several yards of wool, calico, and linen, buttons to replace those she cut off her suit for Vincent's vest, raisins, baking chocolate, vanilla beans, and a square of oilcloth for her table. This time when she and Charley left the store, Vincent was waiting for them.

He watched in disbelief while Clara and the store's owner loaded package after package into the back of the wagon. "Did she leave anythin'?" Vincent asked in a weak attempt at hiding his displeasure.

"Your wife has excellent taste," the man replied, measuring his words as carefully as he'd measured the fabric he sold her.

Clara lifted Charley into the wagon. She raised the hem of her skirt, and with a hand from the merchant, climbed up to the seat. Charley, sitting next to his father, provided a small barrier between her and Vincent. Mouth set in annoyance, she reached across her son and handed her husband what remained of the twenty dollars he'd given her.

Vincent counted the money twice. "That's all that's left?"

Clara didn't answer, nor did she look at him.

"You spent thirteen dollars?" he said, louder this time.

Clara kept her eyes on the horses. "How much did *you* spend, and what have you got to show for it? The wagon bed was still empty when I placed my parcels there."

Vincent mumbled something unintelligible and snapped the reins. The buckboard jerked forward nearly launching its passengers onto the horses' backs. Charley's eyes were round as baseballs when Clara moved him back onto the seat. She put an arm around him, and leaning against her, he slept most of the way home, a good excuse for why the long ride back to the adobe house was decidedly quiet.

Chapter Thirty-One

On a day in May imitating one in July, Clara circled the Stuart's back yard. "What a glorious day for a wedding!" she said to Bethany, who was walking alongside her and Charley. Sunlight bounced off the white-capped peaks surrounding the high desert oasis of orchard, garden, and fresh-mown lawn. The apple trees were in bloom, filling the air with their delightful scent, and a slight breeze had the feathery seeds of the cottonwood trees dancing about like fairies. "No chapel could match this splendor."

The Stuart's back yard was on a grassy slope separating their house from the orchard. At the top of the slope was an arbor covered with pine boughs that Phoebe's brothers had built for the occasion. After the guests assembled, the bride and groom stood beneath the arbor to exchange their vows, Phoebe wearing the rose silk blouse Clara had made for her, and Reb, with his hair slicked down and freshly shaved, in a crisp white shirt and black string tie.

The brief ceremony was performed by a retired navy captain, a friend of Mr. Stuart's. When Reb kissed his bride, a hoot erupted from the cowhands. A party followed, with enough food to feed a cavalry detachment: beef ribs, roast pheasant, vegetables from the Stuart's garden, apple and mint jelly for the buttered rolls, a variety of canned pickles, English toffee, and marble cake served with clotted cream. The Stuart men opened a barrel of homemade hard cider for those with a taste for it, and the party that began in sunshine ended under a sky thick with stars.

Vincent wore his burgundy vest that day and Clara, seven months pregnant, wore a loose-fitting dress she made out of the linen she bought in Wright's Mesa. Nearly everyone in a twenty-mile radius had been invited, Albert and Geneva, too, although Albert spent most of the afternoon trying to convince Mr. Stuart to part with his two thousand acres. While Albert bargained, Geneva, wearing a dress the color of peacock feathers, flitted from guest to guest like a blue butterfly. Vincent and Phoebe's brothers manned the cider barrel, and Clara helped Mrs. Stuart with the food.

After most of the plates were empty and the bride and groom had opened their gifts, the air cooled. Clara covered her shoulders with the emerald green shawl her Aunt Lou had given her when she and Vincent got married, and remembering that happy day, she went looking for her husband. She found him on the east side of the house. Geneva was with him, she leaning into him, he leaning against the house, she with her hand on his arm and whispering in his ear. She moved her hand farther up his sleeve, and he laughed in a sloppy sort of way at what she said.

Clara gawked at the two of them, her heartbeat quickening at the sight of her one-time friend's betrayal. She must have made a sound that alerted them to her presence, because Vincent tilted his head in her direction, and Geneva whooshed off in a rustle of blue taffeta.

Clara took a moment to compose herself before

marching over to her besotted husband. "Stand up straight." She grabbed him by the arm and led him to a chair in the nearly empty back yard. "Sit here." She sat him down on the wooden seat. "Stay away from Geneva. And stay away from the cider. Please don't embarrass me further."

Head down, shoulders slumped, hands dangling between his knees, Vincent stared at the grass.

Finished with her husband, Clara went after Geneva. She began inside the house, wading through a handful of guests standing in the kitchen. Her father and Mr. Stuart were there, conversing with the navy captain who'd performed the ceremony. Others were enjoying a second piece of cake. There was no one in the sitting room. She opened the front door and saw Geneva in a high-back wicker chair facing away from her. She wouldn't have seen her if not for a flare of blue taffeta peeking around the chair's legs.

Clara tiptoed over and stood in front of her. "Why did you leave in such a hurry? Could it be because I caught you batting your eyelashes at my husband?" Hands on hips, cheeks flushed, Clara was barely able to say anything at all.

Geneva, with her wild mane of hair and eyes full of surprise looked like a caged bobcat. She crossed her arms under her substantial bosom. "Don't be a ninny. I already have the best man in the state."

Clara shot her a withering glance. "If that is right, why were you flirting with mine?"

"I wasn't flirting."

"Yes you were. You were flirting like a sage grouse with its breasts exposed and tail feathers fanned in the air."

Color rose from Geneva's low-cut neckline to her eyebrows. She stood up and started toward the front door, but Clara got there first and blocked her path.

"How dare you say such a thing," Geneva spouted. "Albert thinks you can do no wrong, but you have a vulgar mouth."

Clara moved her face close enough to Geneva they were almost nose to nose. "What were you doing then? I want an answer. I deserve an answer."

Geneva pulled her head back as far as it would go. "Ask your precious husband. He'll tell you all I was doing was asking why he won't talk to me anymore. Ever since I moved out of the long house he avoids me like poison."

"Because that's what you are!" Clara adjusted the shawl that had slipped off one of her shoulders. "Hopefully he knows he should stay away from poison."

"He must have forgotten it this afternoon."

"He wasn't himself."

"He was soaked. Piss-eyed. Boiled as an owl."

Clara gawked in astonishment. "And you call *me* vulgar?"

Unspoken words hung between them like barbs on a wire until Clara said she needed to check on Vincent. She gave Geneva one last smoldering look and then hustled down the porch steps. Geneva waited a moment, before slipping into the house with a satisfied grin on her face.

Vincent had fallen asleep in the chair by the time Clara returned. She helped him into the buckboard, rounded up Charley, said her goodbyes, and drove her family home. She waited until the next morning to find out if Vincent's story matched Geneva's.

He shrugged. "She was doin' all the talkin'." He dipped a bite of biscuit into his egg yolk. "I might of drunk too much cider yesterday, but that was my only sin."

Clara took a breath as big as her expanding abdomen would allow. "Your participation in anything more than conversation with that woman has become a matter of concern to me."

Vincent's fork was suddenly still. "Do you think I'm a pinhead? She's married to my boss!" He took another bite. "Your pa, for Chrissake!"

"Please don't swear, Dearest. I want to believe you." She patted the back of his hand. "I *do* believe you, but in the future you must remember to display propriety when we are around others."

Chapter Thirty-Two

Two months after Reb and Phoebe's wedding, Clara received a letter from her Aunt Mid stating she and Lily were coming to Colorado. She felt a surge of happiness when she read the first few lines and then, considering the layout of the adobe house, realized she didn't know where she'd put them. Reading further, she relaxed when her aunt wrote they would be staying with Albert and Geneva.

Clara drove the buckboard to Naturita to discuss plans for the visit. She waited until she was sure her pa would be there. She hadn't seen Geneva since their set-to at Phoebe's wedding. Geneva made tea for the three of them, and then sat grim-faced while Albert did most of the talking. Clara, after securing the information she'd come for—what day her aunt and sister were to arrive and who would pick them up at the train station—drank one cup of tea and left.

"Finally we will have guests in our spare bedrooms," Albert said when Clara made ready to leave.

Geneva improvised a smile. "I couldn't bear for Lily to stay anywhere but here." She linked arms with Clara, walking with her to the buckboard while Albert toddled behind them with Charley.

"How much longer?" Geneva asked, glancing at the bulge separating the pleats in Clara's skirt.

"About a month." Clara removed her arm from Geneva's attempt to appear friendly.

"I hope you have a girl so she and Rose can play together. Will they be half-sisters? Cousins? Distant cousins? How could they be distant if they play with each other? Oh, who cares."

"If it's a girl, she will be your first granddaughter," Clara said, and the smile disappeared from Geneva's face.

Albert gave Clara a gentle boost into the wagon, and during the five-mile ride to the adobe house, she pondered, as she'd often done, what it meant to have a girl. She wasn't sure it was wise to bring a girl into this untamed world full of hard work and rumpled men. She remembered how she used to follow her family's Negro servant around, pestering her with questions while she did her chores. Nettie never sighed, never complained, at least not openly. Clara figured Nettie had it easy compared to how hard she worked every day. Eager to see her sister and aunt, Clara was equally excited to have them meet Charley, a good-humored youngster who dragged the rag chicken she'd sewn for him wherever he went, a child who tossed pebbles at nothing in particular and giggled over the same. She hadn't cut her boy's wavy brown hair since he was born and still referred to him as "Little Precious" when he did something that warmed her heart.

"Don't molly-coddle him," Vincent would say when he saw her brushing Charley's hair. "If he looks like a girl wearin' britches he'll be everybody's goat."

"He's not quite two, Vincent. If our second baby is a girl, you can cut his hair."

****

A flurry of hugging took place in front of Albert and Geneva's house when Clara saw her aunt and sister for the first time in three years. Mildred hadn't changed a bit, but Lily had grown into a well-mannered young woman of fourteen going on fifteen whose blonde hair had turned light brown. "Give us a day to rest, and Lily and I will be out to see you," Mildred said, insisting on a visit to the adobe house instead of asking her obviously pregnant niece to make another trip to Naturita.

Feeling obese and exhausted, Clara cleaned her house until it sparkled. Then she baked a batch of molasses cookies. She dreaded the look on her aunt's face when she got her first glimpse of the cramped, one-room house she and her family inhabited. Having no cupboards or closets to store things in, nearly everything she and Vincent owned—clothes, hats, towels, tools, bags of food, dried meats, cooking implements—hung from rafters or pegs on the walls. Clara had to lead her guests around a trunk, sewing machine, rocker, two bureaus, and a stove to get to the table. Mildred and Lily had to tame their skirts in order to keep from knocking something over. Clara had given up wearing petticoats for the same reason.

She poured her aunt a cup of coffee and offered the same to Lily. Shocked into silence by the size and appearance of her sister's house, Lily asked instead for a glass of water. Sitting straight as the slats in her chair back, Mildred complimented Clara on her cookies. Otherwise the conversation that had flowed freely during supper at Albert and Geneva's house was noticeably restrained. Lily said almost nothing.

Mildred nodded at the two bureaus separating

living quarters from sleeping quarters. "I hear it is more common to use a blanket or quilt."

"Did Geneva tell you that? The first house she and Pa lived in when they moved here was divided in that manner."

"No. I read about it in a newspaper article about westering."

Clara forced a smile. "At least this house has a well…and a pump. That is not always the case out here." Privately she wondered what her aunt's reaction would have been to the cabin she and Vincent lived in before moving to Naturita.

"I'm glad you have a rocking chair," Lily said. "I expect you will need one when you have your baby."

Clara served her aunt and sister a midday meal of chicken soup, biscuits, and more cookies. While they ate, Mildred suggested she spend her confinement at Albert and Geneva's. Clara said she would think about it. Smiling and waving goodbye, promising to see them before they left, she had no intention of spending one minute longer than necessary in Geneva's house. It had taken sixteen hours for Charley to be born; thus she waited until she felt the first contraction before she packed a bag for her and Charley, hitched a horse to the buckboard, and drove to the midwife's house.

Mrs. Hamlin, the only midwife in the area, lived three and a half miles from Albert and Geneva. Clara had made prior arrangements to use her services when the time came. She stopped twice on the way to Mrs. Hamlin's, clenching the reins and gritting her teeth until the pain subsided. When she neared Albert and Geneva's house, she realized birth was imminent; that she could go no further. Lily and Mildred helped her inside while Geneva drove the buckboard to collect Mrs. Hamlin.

Mildred sent one of Albert's men to look for Vincent. Wishing like the devil he hadn't been found, he sat on one of the sofas in the first-floor parlor, sucking in his breath every time one of his wife's anguished wails pierced the air. In between contractions, Clara's eyes were fixed on her nemesis, the only woman in the room besides Mrs. Hamlin who'd experienced childbirth. Geneva—cool, unsmiling, and barking orders as she rustled in and out of the guest room—offered no words of consolation. Clara bemoaned the fact she wasn't in Mrs. Hamlin's house; not in this one, where she felt like an interloper.

Geneva sounded genuinely pleased when she announced, "You have a sweet little daughter, Clara." Downstairs, Vincent breathed easier when he saw Lily running toward him, giddy with excitement. "It's a girl," she said. "Would you like to see her?"

Bareheaded, Vincent walked into the sweaty, musty-smelling bedroom full of females. The women cleared a space for him, and no one spoke when he tiptoed over and kissed his wife on the cheek. His eyes fell on the wrinkled baby, slimy as a newborn calf, lying facedown on her chest. He put a hand out as if to turn her over and confirm her sex. Then he shoved his hands in his pants pockets. "I guess it's a girl," he stammered. Clara nodded, smiling.

He stood a minute more and then started to leave. When Clara asked where he was going he said, "To get Charley a haircut."

Mildred turned from the window where she'd been watching a furry little animal scurry up the side of a tall pine. Looking down at her niece, she said, "Thursday's child has far to go. Do you remember the rhyme? You were born on a Thursday, too, Clara, and look how far you have gone." She paused. "I suppose that was not the intent of the verse, however."

Clara shook her head. "No, Aunt Mid, 'Far to go' is perfect for a girl living far away from just about everything."

****

Every Thursday, Nettie and the other cooks and housekeepers in Philadelphia spent the day shopping, beginning at the grocer's, then going to the butcher shop, the lamp oil dispensary, sometimes stopping at a tobacconist, hardware, or dry goods shop, or a florist if guests were expected. For Clara, going to market was a once-a-month experience, requiring half a day each way by horse and wagon. If she found what she needed when she got there, she bought it by the ten-pound sack or barrel.

Nature provided what couldn't be purchased, changing what was on the supper table every season. In spring the newly sprouted pigweed was a good substitute for the spinach being served in Philadelphia, and Clara used the tender leaves and white roots of dandelions for salads. Fishing was especially good that time of year, for trout that had spent the winter under ice.

When grass was growing knee-deep to a steer, it was prime time for gardening. The Stuart family had a large garden and fruit orchard. With seeds and starts from them, Clara planted a garden of her own. The summer after Emily was born, she grew her first sugar peas.

"There's nothing quite like the pop of fresh peas in ones mouth," Phoebe said when Clara handed her a sample. "Or strawberries. My mouth waters at the thought."

Besides planting a garden every spring, Phoebe's family raised chickens and dairy cows, made delicious toffee, and traded what they had for what they didn't. In autumn, the trees in their orchard were heavy with fruit. Albert shared the beef he butchered with his men, and Vincent traded some of it to the Stuarts for apples. Clara sauced them and made pies. Occasionally she made a fresh apple pie for her pa and Geneva.

Winter was the one season Mother Nature's cupboard was bare, when everyone had to cinch in their belts a notch and live off what they caught, canned, brined, or dried. The snow kept people inside, and with time on her hands, Clara decided to make her own soap out of mutton tallow, lye, and dried lavender. The result, she was proud to say was, "A pure white soap that smells sweet and doesn't take the skin off your hands."

Chapter Thirty-Three

Albert had discovered the real gold in Colorado was land, and after building his house in Naturita, he scoured the state for good deals, buying up farms and ranches from people willing to sell. As his landholdings grew to monumental proportions, he relied more and more on Vincent to handle his cattle business. Clara felt like a "California widow," a label she'd heard people use to describe women whose husbands had gone west with a promise to send for them later. With Vincent working in distant parts of the county much of the time, her sister back in Philadelphia, and Phoebe and Reb living on the other side of the river, her only company was her children.

Lily hadn't wanted to leave. "When I finish school, I am coming back here to live," she said, choking back tears. "I have missed you, Clara, ever so much. I will miss Charley and baby Emily, too, and every one of Pa's cows and horses."

Mildred's age-lined face had taken on a stern expression. "Wait a few years, Child, before you decide something that important."

Clara kissed her sister on the cheek. "Living here isn't easy. Do you know what it means to make a silk purse out of a sow's ear? Well, I have to do something like that every day." She put an arm around Lily's shoulders and walked her toward the wagon that would be taking her and their aunt to the train station. In the short time they had alone she whispered, "Do what's in your heart, Lily. I have no desire to go back to Philadelphia."

There were days, however, when Clara wished she had someone like Nettie to help her. A baby, toddler, and household to run filled nearly every minute of her day. She didn't ride for pleasure anymore. Now, when she needed to go someplace she drove the buckboard. Vincent was also working sunup to sundown. Cattle drives in Montrose County were shorter, but keeping track of thousands of cows grazing both sides of the San Miguel River meant twelve to fourteen-hour days, seven days a week. He was sick of walking around in trousers stiff with cattle juices and boots reeking of cow manure. He'd had enough of stampedes, dust storms, blizzards, cattle with the scours, lost calves, cattle rustlers, floods, and droughts. Now, with Albert busy elsewhere, he also had to deal with no 'count, flannel-mouthed cattle buyers.

****

It was a snowy day in December, two months after Emily was born that Vincent had the brush with death that led him to call it quits. Over the years, he'd been thrown from a horse countless times, trampled twice, and almost drowned once when his horse rolled on top of him while fording a river. He didn't dwell on those experiences, and he wasn't thinking about much of anything that day as his chestnut mare plodded up a steep slope.

Packed snow and ice covered the narrow trail separating straight up from straight down. Looking up he saw slanting sheets of white. Looking down he could barely make out the worm of a river a mile below. With a start he realized his horse was precipitously close to the edge of the trail, and it took a vicious jerk on the mare's reins to keep man and beast from plunging to their deaths. The mare staggered, then regained her footing. Vincent felt the sting of fear in his armpits as he turned the horse around.

"No more," he said to Clara after telling her what happened. He was warming himself at the Franklin stove. "I'm thinkin' 'bout raisin' hogs."

Clara stood next to him, heating up his supper. The expression on his face said he was serious. Before they were married he'd shared stories about his childhood—the little scratch of dirt he grew up on—how his mother raised hogs and his father took whatever jobs a one-legged veteran could find—how his mother made enough money raising hogs to pay the bills while his father lashed out at politicians, pastors, and children that didn't mind.

News to her that cold December night was how much her husband hated the job he'd been doing as long as she'd known him. How could he quit? What kind of life would they have? Her heart began beating so hard she could hear it in her ears. "Have some supper," she said with quiet insistence. "Everything seems worse when you're tired and hungry."

Vincent pulled out a chair and sat in his usual spot at the table. Clara ladled beef and cabbage soup into a bowl and set it in front of him. Before he had a chance to look at her face, she hurried off, busying herself with tasks she'd left until the children were asleep. She avoided his eyes when he handed her his empty bowl and spoon. Her back was turned as she washed them in a pan of water.

"How will we manage?" she asked, scrubbing the bowl longer than necessary to clean it. "What will Pa do without you?"

"I'm gonna ask him to go in with me."

Clara lifted her hands out of the lukewarm water. "Why would he do that, Vincent? Why would he want to raise hogs when he can raise cattle?"

"He can do both. A lot of his land is jus' sittin' empty. I think he'll go for the idea."

Hearing her father might be involved in the new venture lessened Clara's concern, and after drying Vincent's bowl and spoon, she walked over to the table and kissed the top of his head.

****

It took Vincent three weeks to screw up enough courage to talk to his boss about raising hogs. He and Albert had been going over the books, and with profits mounting and snow piling up outside, he decided it was a good time to make his case.

Albert wanted nothing to do with the idea until Vincent said, "Last I checked, hogs were selling for a bit over five dollars apiece."

Albert raised his brows. "They can be raised on less land than cattle?"

Vincent leaned across the desk. "Far less. I'll need some help, though, if you decide to do this."

"What do you mean?"

"Not help with the hogs...help with the herd." Vincent pointed at the open ledger. "I can't do both."

Albert took a moment to reflect on everything Vincent had told him. The prospect of raising hogs wasn't particularly attractive, but utilizing unproductive land made a lot of sense, land he reasoned would appreciate over time. Why not make money on it in the meantime? He picked up a pen and did some quick calculations.

"Nate Sorenson has proven himself time and again. I could put him in charge of the north side of the river." The skin tightened around his eyes as he turned them on Vincent. "When we, that is, you start raising hogs, which you say takes minimal effort, I will still need you on the south side."

Albert's compromise wasn't what Vincent had hoped for, but it was a start; an opportunity to do something different, maybe change his life for good. After snow began melting in the spring, he found ways to squeeze time out of his workdays to build hog pens and plant sugar beets. Finished with those projects, he bought four dozen feeder hogs, then fed and watered them while still managing to look after half of Albert's herd.

The hog pens were far enough away from the adobe house that Clara didn't have to deal with the smell, and as long as her husband spent more time with cattle than hogs, she could still think of herself as the wife of a cowboy.

Geneva saw it differently. At every opportunity, especially in front of the Stuarts, she referred to Clara as "the hog farmer's wife."

In September of 1892, Vincent sold his first lot of hogs, netting three dollars a head. With dollar signs dancing in front of their eyes, he and Albert made plans to expand the operation. Instead, they found themselves in the middle of a nation-wide economic collapse that began the following February when the Philadelphia &

Reading Railroad went bankrupt. Other railroads fell like dominoes. So did a series of banks. The price of silver plummeted, and by July, a side of pork was selling for three cents a pound, butchered and dressed. The price of beef dropped intolerably low, and Albert had to sell his entire herd, even the heifers.

He sold the last thousand head in October to a buyer who'd been downright miserly with his greenbacks. Albert didn't turn around for one last look at his heifers, bawling in the holding pens next to the Montrose train depot. "This is not my Waterloo," he said to Vincent, walking alongside him. "Geneva and I can live on what I collect from my leases. When the price of beef gets back to where it should be, I will rebuild my herd."

As they approached their horses, Albert pulled an envelope out of his pocket and thrust it into his son-in-law's gloved hand. "You are the last man left, Vincent, and the best of the lot. I kept you on as long as I could. This envelope contains a bank draft for two month's wages. I trust you will find suitable employment before it has been spent. Fortunately, my daughter seems to know how to stretch a dollar."

Vincent had seen this coming. Nevertheless, it was hard to digest the full impact of being fired for the first time in his life. He stood next to his horse, staring at, but not opening, the envelope in his hand. When Albert's stony face told him there was nothing more to be said, he mounted his chestnut mare, touched the brim of his hat in a respectful salute, and rode off.

****

A cattle drive to Montrose usually took about a week; therefore Clara didn't worry about Vincent until he was four days overdue. She dreaded having to ask her pa and Geneva if they knew where he was, but on the fifth day she put her children in the buckboard and drove to Naturita. Geneva, wearing a fashionable ankle-length dress and shiny new boots, answered the rap of the brass doorknocker. Clara glanced down at her own, toe-skimming skirt, its hem brown around the bottom, and realized she'd been in such a hurry she hadn't removed her apron. If that wasn't bad enough, the apron was stained.

With Emily in her arms and Charley at her feet, she asked Geneva if she'd seen Vincent. Geneva gave her a piercing look. "Did you think he was here? I haven't seen him in weeks." She moved aside when Charley pushed past her skirt to look for Christopher. "Albert is in La Jara, so I doubt he's seen him, either."

"Vincent should have been home days ago."

Geneva motioned Clara inside, ushering her into a sun-drenched parlor. "You must not know," she mumbled.

"Know what?" Clara took off her apron. "If you know something, Geneva, tell me. I'm in no shape to be toyed with right now." She sat down on the velvet-covered sofa and plunked three-year-old Emily next to her. "Act like a lady," she whispered sternly.

Geneva sat on the other side of Emily. Leaning over to face her step-granddaughter, she said, "Rose is taking a nap, Sweetie, or the two of you could play."

"For the love of God, Geneva, talk to me!" There were sparks in Clara's eyes.

"I already told you, I don't know where he is." Geneva rested an arm on the back of the sofa and looked out the tall, multi-paned window behind it, fixing her gaze on two birds, their claws outstretched, wings flapping, squabbling over something. "It's a doggy-dog world, you know. Albert told me so. He says hard times are coming. For us all. I don't think it's fair, though that I have to be the one to tell you..." she inhaled deeply, "...that he had to fire Vincent."

The color drained out of Clara's face. "No! He couldn't have!"

"I don't think he wanted to," Geneva added, her tone softened.

Clara covered her mouth with her hands and slumped against the cushioned arm of the sofa, her heart pounding in her chest. Panicky questions flew through her brain—what was Vincent's reaction? Where was he? Was he all right? Did this mean they were ruined? She'd always thought of her father's house as a refuge, even with Geneva around. Now, sitting in his high-ceiling parlor with its Turkish carpet, damask chairs, pillowed sofa, and hand-painted lamps, she felt like a stranger. "May I have a glass of water?" she asked, her mouth suddenly dry.

About the same time Geneva left to get some water, Charley and Christopher ran into the room. Clara reached in her skirt pocket for a stick of peppermint. She watched her hand shake as she broke the candy into thirds and gave a piece to each child. The boys bounded off with their shares while Emily sucked and drooled on hers.

When Geneva returned with the water, Clara drank all but the last few swallows, which she gave to Emily. Hunched over the empty glass in her hand, she hesitated before saying, "I am expecting again."

Geneva blinked with surprise. "Oh my." She sat

down on one of the damask-covered chairs. "Oh my," she said again. "You don't sound very happy about that."

"I told Vincent about it a week ago. I was pleased then."

A few seconds of awkward silence passed before Geneva said, "Have you asked about him in town?" She tilted her head. "He nurses the bottle a bit too much. I think you know that. Maybe you should try the saloon."

Perched on the edge of the sofa, Clara lowered her eyes. "I have never set foot in a saloon. I certainly would not subject my precious children to one of them."

In a sudden burst of charity Geneva said, "If you go, I'll go with you. I can stay in the wagon with our children while you're inside."

Clara sat still as a stone for the few minutes it took Geneva to round up Christopher, Rose, and Charley. She barely remembered climbing into the wagon and driving it a short distance to the handful of buildings that made up Naturita. Reaching the saloon with Geneva on the seat beside her and the children in back, and seeing no one else around, she hitched the horse to the rail out front and ducked inside.

Squinting as she entered the dimly lit saloon, she recognized two men sitting at one of the tables as having worked for Vincent. They were gawking at her as if she had two heads. With a quick look around, Clara took in the raw interior of the room, its walls gray as an old barn and almost as rough. Other than the chairs at three small tables, the only other seating was a bench resting against the back wall.

Clara walked up to the bar. The heavyset bartender

on the other side of it wore a bib apron over his shirt. "Lookin' for somebody, Ma'am?" The man had a full beard, rust in color, and his voice conveyed strong Irish roots. He leaned across the bar to hear her better.

"Have you seen Vincent Reese lately?" she asked.

"Day b'fore yesterday," he said. "Didn't say much, mind you, 'til he had a couple o' belts." The bartender picked up a glass and cleaned it with a rag. "Tol' me 'bout losin' 'is job." He raised his eyes. "Pray to heaven you knew that, Dearie."

Clara nodded gravely.

"Said he had a couple o' kids and another one comin'." He glanced at Clara's middle. "Said he had a uncle in Durango might help him. Ever been there? Helluva town, that one." He put down the glass he was polishing. "It took some gumption to come in here, Ma'am, but don't you be goin' to Durango by yerself."

Chapter Thirty-Four

Before Vincent got married, all he needed was a horse, a saddle and a bedroll. If he didn't like his boss or the men he was riding with, he could roll up his bedroll and leave. Now he had a wife and two children, soon to be three, no job and no prospects for one until the price of beef went back up. Most ranchers didn't hire married men, certainly not those with families. None of that mattered anyway, because the thought of herding cows again was more than he could bear.

Vincent had been in Durango twice to buy horses, and while there, he'd stopped in to see his Uncle Jacob, one of his father's brothers. Both times his uncle, a bald man with tremendous shoulders, offered him a job in his paint and paper hanging business. "Spent eight years in Chicago learning the trade," he told his nephew. "Six in Denver, and the last ten right here. This town's growin' faster'n buckwheat, Boy. After I teach you the ropes, we could be partners. Then when I git ready to retire, you can buy the business from me."

The third time Vincent rode into Durango, he wasn't greeted by the prosperous sounds he'd heard on his first two trips: the chorus of hammers striking nails, men shouting at each other, the clattering of wagons jostling for position on crowded streets. Disheartened at the decline in activity, he wasn't totally surprised when his uncle greeted him with less enthusiasm.

Jacob's wife Grace rustled up some supper and afterward, as the two men sat on the front porch, his uncle said, "The cattle business ain't the only thing hurtin', Boy. My business is takin' a lickin', too."

Both men slept in ragged bouts that night—one over his predicament, the other over how he could help him with it. Just before sunrise, Jake, as Jacob preferred to be called, came up with a plan. He discussed it with Grace before presenting his thoughts to Vincent.

"Me and Grace don't have any kids," he said, "but I can still imagine bein' in your shoes. "I'll hire you. I can't pay you nothin', but you can live with me and Grace until business picks up. I know it will. It always does. It has to."

Vincent answered with a grin, and that morning, while Jake showed him some of the work he'd done around Durango, the possibility of shorter hours, much of it indoors, sounded mighty good to the former cowboy, especially the part about owning a business. While Vincent stood admiring a hallway his uncle had papered in the Strater Hotel, Jake said, "We might be able to build a small house for you and your family in a year or so."

"I'll work like a mule," Vincent said, as he was about to leave. "I'm gonna write my pa. Tell him what you're doin' for me." He forced a smile. "How long since you seen him?"

Jake hung his head. "Thirty years at least." He raised his eyes. "You?"

"Twenty. Maybe more." Vincent ran his hand through his light brown hair before putting on his hat. "Don't know why I said I'd write him. Wouldn't know where to send a letter if I did."

****

Vincent was wandering in and out of the adobe house when Clara returned from the saloon. During the bumpy, five-mile ride back, she mulled over what to say when she saw him, *if* she saw him again, this hardworking cowboy who'd lost his job and then shared his troubles with a barkeep instead of coming to her.

She kept her arms crossed when Vincent hugged her, and didn't uncross them the entire time he told her about his trip to Durango. Relieved he hadn't gone on a binge, she wanted to be happy for him, especially for his good fortune at finding another job; however the changes he described were frightening.

He searched her face and eyes, hoping to see pride. He would have settled for acceptance.

"We will make it work," she said, more to herself than to him.

She spent the next three days packing for the move. She wanted to say goodbye to Phoebe and Reb before they left. Vincent didn't want to go. He'd had to lay off all of his men, some who'd ridden with him for years, and he'd been avoiding Reb ever since. Clara said she was going see them with or without him, and Vincent relented.

Phoebe and Reb had been living on the opposite side of the San Miguel River since they got married. The river was low and running slow when Vincent drove the buckboard across. Willow bushes lined the riverbank, their leaves burnished by the onset of fall. The brown and yellow leaves swirled around the wagon, clinging to the wheels and the legs of the horses.

The Reese family arrived at Reb and Phoebe's

small frame house a little before noon. Reb stood in the doorway. Missing was his usual lopsided grin as he studied the face of the man he used to call Gov'nor.

"Don't think of me as your enemy," Vincent said. "I got the ax, too."

Reb shaded his eyes with the flat of his hand. "Z'at so." He waited a second or two before motioning the visitors to come inside.

Phoebe threw together a simple meal. "Sorry I haven't milk for the children," she said. Sitting around the table after a meal of crumpets with jam and crisp fried side pork, Reb poured tobacco onto a cigarette paper and rolled a smoke. He offered his tobacco pouch to Vincent who shook his head.

"I been thinkin' 'bout joinin' the army," Reb drawled, leaning back in his chair.

"You sure about that?" Vincent said. "A recruit don't even make a handyman's wage."

Reb shrugged. "Maybe so, but if I stick with it long enough I could get to be an officer. That's where the real money is." He winked at Phoebe. "My bride's powerful keen on bein' an officer's wife."

Phoebe returned an adoring smile. "You're crackers, Reb. Do you know that?"

Reb grinned like a burro eating cactus.

The women washed and dried the dishes, and then took their chairs outside where they could watch Charley and Emily.

"How will you manage if Reb joins the army?" Clara asked. "Will you stay here?" She glanced at Phoebe's abdomen. "And what about the baby on the way?"

Phoebe smiled shyly. "My sister Jane is gettin'

hitched. Mum and Dad will have masses of room after Jane leaves…room for Reb, too, when he gets leave."

They talked for over an hour, about what had been going on in their lives and what the recent changes might bring. Clara told Phoebe about her trip to the saloon, confiding in her how quarrelsome Vincent got (she stopped short of calling him belligerent) when he drank too much.

"Reb doesn't get angry," Phoebe said, "he just acts silly…talks gibberish. I ignore him."

Too soon it was time to say goodbye. Clara and Phoebe embraced, promising to write. Their husbands shook hands and bragged about what they would be doing the next time they met—Vincent owning his own business and Reb wearing a captain's bars.

On their way home, Clara told Vincent there was one more trip she had to make before leaving Naturita. The following morning, when he flatly refused to go with her, she left him with Charley and Emily and drove the buckboard to Naturita. It was the second time that week Clara had been in her pa's house, and this time Geneva ushered her in without a word of welcome.

She perked up after hearing Clara and Vincent were moving over a hundred miles away. Albert didn't express an opinion. He didn't even acknowledge the fact his son-in-law had found another job, a minor miracle considering the state of the economy. All he wanted to talk about was how bankers were ruining the country.

Clara spent an awkward hour there, and when Geneva offered more tea, she excused herself, saying she had much left to do in preparation for the move. With tears brimming in her eyes on the way back to the adobe house, she slackened the reins. Thankfully the horse knew its way home.

Chapter Thirty-Five

Moving to Durango meant living in southwestern Colorado again, although not as far south as La Jara. Durango was a real town, one that owed its rapid growth to gold and silver rather than cattle. According to Vincent's uncle, "People came lookin' for gold like ants on honey. Even came from other countries. There's still some gold and silver 'round here and lots of coal. The coal means jobs in the smelter…jobs on the railroad."

Not counting fly-by-night prospectors, drummers, and Utes, there were approximately 2500 people living in Durango when the Reese family arrived. Jake and his wife Grace lived in a two-bedroom house near similar homes, an island of civility in a sea of tents and miners' shacks.

Grace was a solemn-faced woman with droopy eyes and a wattle under her chin. She put Clara, Vincent, and the Singer in the second bedroom and laid one of the straw mattresses they brought with them in a corner of the living room for the children.

Clara felt nauseous most of the time; something she hadn't experienced during her first two pregnancies. She sometimes slept another hour or two after five a.m. when Vincent left for work. Then she dragged herself out of bed to make breakfast for Charley and Emily. If she hadn't had to cook for the children and keep them out of Grace's silver hair, she might have stayed in bed until noon. Grace offered to make breakfast and let her sleep longer, but Clara didn't want to be even more of a burden to this woman whose household had been turned upside down.

Most afternoons Clara gave Grace a breathing spell by walking into town with the children. Not long after settling in to her new routine, she wrote a letter to Aunt Mid, describing what she saw every day. *Durango is a fascinating mess. Hastily erected shacks sit next to buildings meant to last, and the boardwalks connecting them are crudely built hiding places for snakes. Every street is a quagmire churned by horse hooves and wagon wheels. I have to hold onto my children's hands every time we cross Main Avenue or risk being run over by a careless horseman.*

I am impressed with one building in particular, a red brick hotel, the Strater, named after the man who built it. It is the grandest building I have seen since leaving Philadelphia. It does look out of place, though. Perhaps the rest of the town will catch up with it someday. Vincent has done some work there. He tells me the hotel has a three-story privy!

The town was blessed with many shops; however most of the merchandise was too expensive. To make do, Clara sewed mittens out of the good parts of worn-out overalls, lining them with flannel for extra warmth. Aunt Mid's Christmas presents helped: dresses for her and Emily, a crisp new shirt for Vincent, and knickers or a jacket for Charley. Clara used the twenty dollars she got from her pa every Christmas to buy shoes from a mail order house in Pueblo. Even after adding a few cents for shipping, their prices were much lower than those in Durango.

She tried to make herself invisible in a house that wasn't her own. Grace didn't seem to want her help with anything other than menial tasks. Stiff with righteousness, the woman hurried through her household chores every morning to free herself for an afternoon of reading. She was willing to share anything she'd already read, and Clara accepted her offer when the children were napping or at play. Grace's reading material was mostly dime novels—short, melancholy stories often set in old castles. Filled with heartache, the stories did little to brighten Clara's mood.

****

Six months after moving in with Grace and Jake, Clara gave birth to another boy. Grace had no clue what to do when someone went into labor, but she did know where there was a doctor. Having a doctor in attendance had a calming effect on Clara, and she delivered her third child in less time and with less pain than the first two. Grace stood a few feet away from the bed, watching in fascinated horror. Clara saw the sickly expression on her face and wondered if the doctor would have to attend to another patient before he left the house.

Grace quickly recovered. She washed the six-pound boy and wrapped him in a towel. When she handed the baby back to his mother, Clara told her she was thinking about naming him Albert. "My pa's name is Albert, strictly Albert, never Al or anything else he doesn't immediately set straight." Gazing at the tiny bundle in her arms, Clara found it difficult to imagine him big enough to merit her pa's name.

Job by job, Jake's painting business rallied as the

economy limped toward recovery. Much of the work that came his way was for new stores springing up as well as repeat business at the Strater Hotel. It took Clara a while to get used to seeing her husband in canvas coveralls and a painter's cap instead of denim trousers and a gray, wide-brimmed planter's hat. "It's easier to clean paint off skin than hair," Jake told his new apprentice, and Vincent shaved off his handlebar moustache.

Clara and Vincent shared many a laugh during his first few months as a painter. There were missteps on ladders, spilled paint, paint in his eyebrows, and funniest of all his misadventures, the wrestling matches he had with wallpaper.

Her husband's skills improved, and little by little Jake bought materials to build a cottage on a half-acre of land within walking distance to town. Whenever he and his nephew had a day off, they worked on it, and a year and a half after moving to Durango, Clara had the charming little house she'd been hoping for ever since she got married. Built of lumber rather than logs, the four-room cottage had clapboard siding, a cellar, front porch, and in the back yard, fresh water pumped into a cistern by a windmill.

"I'll make you a deal," Jake told Vincent after the house was finished. "When you buy the business the house'll be yours. It'll be right there in the contract."

"Much obliged, Uncle Jake." Vincent shook his uncle's hand with enthusiasm. After he and his family moved into their brand new home, he added to Clara's happiness by putting a picket fence around the front yard. Although painting a picket fence was not his favorite job, he painted it, too. A year later, he and his uncle built a small barn in back for their horses and the cow they bought to provide milk for the children.

****

The next four years passed as quickly as the sun sets when you take the time to watch it slide below the horizon. Grace smiled more often, especially when Clara's children were around, and she read less after Clara taught her how to use the Singer. Vincent painted six barns during those four years, ten shops, twelve houses, and seventeen rooms in the Strater Hotel, where he also mastered the art of hanging wallpaper.

He and Jake had spent ten hours scraping and painting a high-pitched storefront one day when he said to his uncle, "Don't you ever get tired of the mess?"

"Turpentine gets rid of most everthin'," Jake answered, "'cept maybe the paint under your fingernails." He inspected his nails one hand at a time, and then gave Vincent a long, hard look. "I don't cotton to bellyachin', Son. You're lucky to be workin'."

Vincent shook his head in protest. "Didn't mean nothin' by it. Forget I ever said it."

Clara planted a hearty vegetable garden in back of the house. It was the summer before Charley's second year in school, and to fill up his days, he spent many an hour dragging a bucket a third his size around the garden, watering the vegetables. Emily wanted to do everything her big brother did, and being too small to carry a bucket, she carried the ladle.

Bert—as little Albert came to be called—was more fragile than his siblings, colicky, and quick to catch cold. He'd taken longer to walk than Charley or Emily, and being slight of build, he preferred playing inside to more robust activities.

Bert was sixteen months old and taking his first steps when Clara delivered another son, a husky boy she and Vincent named Seth. Seth walked at ten months. Soon he was chasing after his siblings, and like Charley and Bert did when they were his age, riding around the house on Vincent's shoulders or sitting next to him when the family went somewhere in the buckboard.

In another letter to her Aunt Mid, Clara wrote: *I am beyond content with my dear little house and burgeoning garden. A late frost put a stutter in my strawberry crop, but my beefsteak tomatoes were perfect this year, redder than I have ever been able to grow them in Colorado. Now that I have a cellar, I am canning some of what I grow. Unfortunately, the first batch of peas I canned blew up and made a mess of my new cellar.*

Vincent is gaining skill as a painter, an occupation that keeps him closer to home than when he worked for Pa. He is a strict, yet loving father to our children. They are the true riches in this town.

Chapter Thirty-Six

Clara walked to the post office once a week to pick up mail and post letters of her own. Lily and Mildred, and Phoebe for a while, were loyal correspondents. In Phoebe's last letter she'd said she was expecting another baby, and when Clara didn't hear from her, she assumed her friend was too busy to write now that she had two children to chase.

Albert wrote occasionally, Geneva once, after her daughter Lilian was born. In a Christmas card dated December 1896, Clara learned her father and his family had moved again.

Although the economy has improved, I decided to get out of the cattle business and go into banking. Banking is an excellent fit with real estate. I had considerable funds on deposit at the First National Bank in Montrose, and when the bank asked me to be on their board of directors, I accepted. I leased my holdings in Naturita and built a fine Victorian home on South Fifth Street in Montrose.

He failed to mention his wife had given birth to a third daughter. Clara learned that in a letter from Lily, along with the baby's name—Sabrina. Through a series of letters from Lily and Mildred, Clara had kept track of her sister's comings and goings during two years of Normal School, a year teaching third grade, and in greater detail, her betrothal and marriage to Henry

Newcomb, a man she met through her friend, Bella. In one of Lily's letters she wrote she and her husband were moving to Montrose. In it she included an article clipped from the *Philadelphia Inquirer* dated June 15, 1897.

The marriage of Miss Lily Anne Wallin to Henry James Newcomb of Cape May, New Jersey took place yesterday at St. Stephens Episcopal Church. The Right Rev. Benjamin Hayes officiated.

The bride is the daughter of Albert Wesley Wallin, formerly of Philadelphia, currently residing in Montrose, Colorado. She was attended by Miss Bella Busconi. Edward S. Bragg acted as best man. Following the ceremony, relatives and intimate friends feted the couple at a champagne breakfast.

After a honeymoon trip to New York City, the couple will make their home in Montrose, Colorado where Mr. Newcomb, an accountant, has accepted a position at the First National Bank.

****

In November of that year, all four of Clara's children came down with bad colds. Charley caught it first from one of his schoolmates. He gave it to Bert, then to Seth, who had just turned two. Emily was the last one sickened by the debilitating virus that affected the lungs. The doctor who delivered Bert and Seth told Clara to rub turpentine mixed with hog fat on her children's chests. She applied the pitchy-smelling mixture day and night, but it did nothing to relieve their endless coughing. She tied moist rags around their throats, and when they lost their appetites, fed them milk sweetened with sugar and a few drops of whisky.

After a week of coughing until they were too weak

to stand, Charley and Emily recovered enough to go back to school. Seth and Bert got worse, so weak they slept all but a few minutes a day. Their little bodies on fire, they complained of being cold. Vincent went for the doctor again, and this time the diagnosis was pneumonia.

Clara's vigil intensified. She moved the boys' bed next to the kitchen stove for their warmth and her nearness. Grace came to the house every day, helping Clara in small ways; sometimes simply by sitting with her. Late one night, as Clara's eyes grew heavy and the squeaks and clanks of the windmill weren't enough to keep her awake, she put a pot of coffee on the stove. Seth smelled it cooking and whimpered, "Mama, you got cossee? Me want some."

She mixed a little coffee with milk and sugar and fed it to him with a teaspoon. He took three swallows and brought it up again. "Please, God," she murmured, "help my baby get through this."

Going to church hadn't been part of Clara's life in Colorado. She sent Charley and Emily to Sunday school now that they lived in a community with a church, but she hadn't gotten back into the habit herself. She prayed silently for all of her children, even when they were healthy, fervently now for Seth and Bert. Sometimes she prayed her husband would end his bottle habit; though she sensed it was wrong to take up God's time with something like that.

Energized some by the coffee, she sat at the kitchen table; and in the dim light of the oil lamp, dipped a pen into her ink well and wrote to Lily. She twice used the word terrified, then scratched it out and replaced it with fearful, even though terrified was how she felt. Ending the letter, she wrote: *Do you believe God answers the prayers of people who do not go to church? I often wonder if He thinks me unworthy. I still pray sometimes; I feel better when I do. I am praying with every ounce of strength I possess that God is listening to me tonight.*

****

Seth died before Clara could mail the letter. After she prepared her son's body for burial and handed him over to Vincent, she burned the letter in the stove.

Bert, always more delicate than his siblings, remained close to death. Clara stayed with him while the rest of the family gathered around a small grave in the back yard. There was an inch of snow on the ground and a sky threatening more. The three adults and two children were bundled in hats and jackets; and for extra warmth, Grace brought along a blanket she wrapped around Charley and Emily. Grace read a passage from the Bible and Jake gave a short prayer. Afterward, Vincent mounted his horse and took off without a word to his uncle who'd helped him dig Seth's grave in the frozen ground, nor to Clara who had committed herself to Bert's bedside.

Vincent rode south. Before leaving town, he stopped at the Strater Hotel's Diamond Belle Saloon for two bottles of frontier whisky, and Fulton's Market for a pound of dried beef. He had his sheepskin jacket, bedroll, and whisky for warmth as he and the roan gelding that had replaced his chestnut mare took off for anyplace that wasn't Durango.

Jake tried to find him, scouring the saloons for days to no avail. Clara hovered over Bert, sometimes resting her head on his chest, wetting it with her tears.

She couldn't sleep. She spent her nights on an emotional seesaw, blaspheming God one minute, begging him for Bert's life the next, cursing Vincent, then praying for his return. Two agonizingly long days went by before she allowed Grace to take Charley and Emily home with her. A day later she asked for them back. Bert was recovering, and having all three children around kept her hands busy and her emotions in check.

Vincent returned the night of the fifth day. Clara rushed to the door when she heard his boots on the front porch. She pulled back the bolt, and in the light of a lantern, she saw a husband who could have passed for one of the bedraggled drifters who hung around Durango, men she walked to the other side of the street to avoid. She felt numb rather than guilty at not being happy to see him, and didn't even ask where he'd been when he walked past her. Instead, she bolted the door and went to bed, folding worry into disappointment and disappointment into heartache, stacking her emotions like sheets and towels and storing them inside.

****

Somehow Vincent managed to go to work the next morning—six a.m., as usual, at Jake's. "I got nothin' for you," Jake said, the minute he heard the squeaky-hinged door to his toolshed open. The painting business was always sluggish in winter, and feeling poorly that morning, Vincent was relieved to hear there wasn't a job on the docket. He watched Jake pull two cans of paint off a shelf and set them in his utility wagon.

"Not today, not any day from now on," Jake said with a slow shake of his head.

It took a few seconds for Jake's words to register, but Vincent sucked in his breath when they did.

"Why?" The question gummed in his throat, so he asked it again. "Why, Uncle Jake? Can't a fellow have some time to hisself when his kid dies?"

Jake fixed his gaze on a dried splotch of paint near his boot. "Sorry, Vince, but I'm firm on this."

"I thought we had a deal!" Vincent motioned toward the cans of paint, ladders, and sawhorses stored in Jake's shed. "I like this kind of work, and I work hard at it."

Jake raised his eyes. "You started out that way. The way you been showin' up for work lately is takin' a bite outta my business. That five-day vacation was the last straw."

"Some vacation." A sudden gust of wind blew a skiff of snow through the half-open shed door. Vincent trudged over to the door and closed it. "What about my family?"

"What about 'em? You didn't seem to miss 'em near on a week. Where was you, anyways?"

"Not far. South a-here. Some settlers let me stay in their barn when it started to snow."

"For five days?" Jake loaded a ladder into his wagon next to the paint cans.

"Three. Took a day each way to get there." Vincent spread his hands in despair. "What about the house you and me built?"

Squaring his broad shoulders, Jake met Vincent's stare. "I haven't decided what to do about that. Grace likes your kids a lot." Recognizing a trace of his brother's face in his nephew's anguished expression, he came close to relenting, but after a long minute he said, "Git along with you, now. I got work to do."

Vincent spent the rest of the day in the Diamond

Belle Saloon. Two days later, he was back to punching cows for one of the long-time ranchers who ran cattle north of Durango in the Animas River Valley. Within a month of being back in the saddle, he was looking for work again when he fell asleep in his saddle, and half the cows he was supposed to be watching strayed onto another rancher's property.

The noose of responsibility around Vincent's neck grew tighter with every passing year, the birth of each child, every failed endeavor. He reckoned the whole world was against him—Albert, who had enough money to keep him on the payroll; the banks, for ruining his hog business; barbed wire, for ending the open range; God, for taking his youngest child; Uncle Jake, for his lack of sympathy; Clara, for thinking she was too good for him. She'd never said it, never complained, but the notion had burned in him since the day they married.

The weather didn't help. He had a little money saved, but day after cold gray day with nothing to do except watch his savings dwindle, added to his mounting frustration. So did his wife who was taking in ironing and sewing to help with the bills. Damn her for acting cheerful all the time.

Awake one morning before her husband, Clara raised herself on one elbow to look at him. He was growing back the sad moustache he'd shaved off when he became a painter. With or without facial hair, the lines etched on his thirty-three-year-old face hadn't spoiled the looks of this man she and Geneva used to vote Albert's handsomest cowboy. Reflecting on her marriage to him, Clara thought it was too bad Geneva was afraid of horses, or she might have been the one who caught his eye.

Clara rose every day before dawn, let down her dark brown hair and brushed it a hundred times before gathering it into a bun at the nape of her neck. The work she'd taken on was her refuge. Some days she was ironing by three a.m. Fueled with strong coffee, she sewed from nine until noon, and then spent the rest of the day doing her own mending, cleaning, and cooking.

In April, she and Vincent got a bit of good news when Jake told them a building contractor in Gunnison was advertising for a painter. Vincent left the following morning with his uncle's letter of recommendation. A week later he was working again, but until he was sure it was a job with a future, he decided to wait before moving his family.

Jake let Clara and the children stay in the house she dearly loved as long as she paid him a little something for rent from what she earned sewing and ironing. Accustomed to binding her wounds, real or imaginary, she bandaged a smile on her face every day as she set to work mending a stranger's clothes or ironing tablecloths for the Strater Hotel.

Vincent learned that Gunnison, like Durango, was another town built around the lure of silver. When the vein ran out, the coalfields north of town and the railroad hauling it to the east kept the town's economy humming. After living there for two months, Vincent decided the contractor could provide him with steady work, and he sent for his wife and family.

Numb with disappointment, Clara packed the buckboard. All she could take with her were their mattresses and bedding, some kitchen supplies, her trunk, the rocking chair, and three boxes stuffed with clothes. She had to sell the iron bedstead and cherry wood bureaus that had been hers since she was a girl, as well as most everything else she and her husband had accumulated during their five years in Durango.

She asked Grace to store the Singer. "I hope you will make good use of it until I can find a way to get it to Gunnison." She made one last walk through the cottage she loved, and then climbed into the buckboard. The first day on the road, the children took turns sitting up front with her. By the second day the boys had found places to hide amongst the items stacked in back. They remained there most of the trip while Emily sat next to her mother, chattering like a squirrel. Clara was thankful her children were well behaved, because she was in no mood for sniveling.

Part V

New Brooms Sweep Clean

Chapter Thirty-Seven

Clara spent eight days on a rocky trail, driving a wagon piled high with belongings and towing a cow. All she wanted was to relax when she got to the house in Gunnison. Vincent came outside when he heard the wagon pull up. He and Clara shared a brief embrace, and then he took care of the horses and cow while she and the children went inside.

The first thing catching her eye was the gaps between the planks in the floor. "I can see the ground through them," she said when Vincent returned. "A rat...even a skunk could crawl through one of those openings."

"I'm plannin' to cover the floor with canvas...next payday," he said. He picked up Bert and offered his free hand to Emily. She took it with a timid smile.

Clara's eyes raked the room's rough-hewn walls and rusty potbelly stove. "We'll need more than a canvas floor to keep us warm when winter sets in."

Outwardly composed, Vincent's face flushed with indignation. "We'll be in another house by then."

Slightly larger than the adobe house and half-eaten by the elements, the place was badly in need of repair. It had been built out of cottonwood instead of something more stable, and over time, the boards and beams had warped and sprung loose from their nails. Vincent repaired or replaced the worst of the twisted boards before his family arrived. He also painted the house inside and out, with results that were far from spectacular.

He used one of the quilts Clara brought from Durango to divide the one-room shelter into sleeping areas. He and Clara slept on one mattress, and their three children shared the other head to toe: Charley and Bert at one end, Emily between them on the other.

Convinced the house was barely suitable for a squatter, Clara lacked the enthusiasm to make it feel like a home. She cleaned when necessary, but spent more time than she should have, sitting on the porch, listening to the rustle of aspen leaves and the soft nickering of the horses. If she was inside, and not engaged in some task when her husband returned at the end of the day, she busied herself with make-work so her eyes would be elsewhere when he stumbled across the threshold.

A churn of emotions tugged at her when she observed him, the strongest being a desire to distance herself from this man who was neglecting his duties as a husband and father. Lying beside him at night, she didn't cling to him anymore. She pulled her foot away if it happened to touch his and spent the rest of the night, arms at her sides. Half asleep, she would hear a wind-chilling wail and wonder if it came from an animal or from her. She usually got an hour or two of sleep just before dawn, and the first thing entering her mind when her feet touched the floor was the tedious day ahead.

****

It was July, the busiest month of the year for a painter, when Vincent rolled into work with a hangover and found himself unemployed again. Avoiding the sun that made a painter's day a good day, he spent that afternoon in the shade of a pine tree half a mile from his house with his horse, the lunch his wife had made him, and a bottle.

Charley and Bert were sitting on the front steps when he staggered home, his roan gelding trailing behind, dragging the reins. The boys scooted apart to clear a path for him. The door was open. Inside, Clara watched him walk up the six steps, familiar with the way he feigned sobriety at the end of the day. He stopped just inside the door. Still wearing his paint-spattered work clothes, he stood, arms hanging from his shoulders like sausages. His downcast eyes told her what had happened.

"What's a man to do?" he muttered. Several tense seconds passed without her saying something reassuring the way she usually did.

"Do about what?" Clara asked in the clipped manner of a schoolmarm probing for the correct answer. "Say it or you will never come to terms with it."

Vincent gave her a dismissive wave. "Say what? What the hell you talkin' about?"

Clara glanced at her boys sitting on the stoop, Bert with his back turned, Charley sitting sideways, hugging his knees and peering inside. Emily had just set four plates on the table. She stopped what she was doing and gaped at her father with wise, seven-year-old eyes.

Clara shot her husband a don't-curse-in-front-of-the-children look.

"Go outside," she said to Emily. "Pick some of those daisies growing along the road. Put them in water and set them on the table." Emily's clear blue eyes darted from one parent to the other. "Shut the door please on your way out."

Clara set down her mixing bowl and walked over to where her husband was doing his best to appear sober. "I can't change you, Vincent," she said, coolly. "Only you can do that. Do you care only for yourself?"

Vincent spread his feet to get a better balance. He took off his painter's cap and shoved it into the bib of his coveralls. "I shoulda let you stay in Durango."

Clara's eyes sharpened. "Of course. Without me and the children around you could do as you please. I must be a fool for following you to this shack."

He raised a hand as if to strike her. "Don't call it a shack!" He'd never hit her before, although there were times Clara worried he might. He'd also become less patient with the children, spanking them over trivial wrongdoings, and harder than he had in the past.

She walked over to the apple crate nailed to the wall where she kept her dishes. "Whither thou goest," she mumbled. She reached into the cupboard for another plate. "Ludicrous."

Vincent took a few careful steps across the canvas-covered floor to the table set for four and plopped into a chair. "Why do you always...talk...talk so... Dammit, Clara, why can't you use reg'lar language?"

Clara plunked the plate down in front of him and returned to the stove. Vincent rested an elbow on either side of the plate and held his head between his hands. "We never shoulda left Naturita."

"What would you have done there? Pa moved away the year after we did." Clara tested the griddle with a drop of water. The sizzle told her it was hot enough to fry the corn cakes they were having for supper. "Do you blame my father for our troubles?"

"Maybe." Vincent massaged his aching temples with the butts of his palms. "Your pa has plenty a money. He left us to the wolves. Can't you see that?" He raised his head. "Course you can't. Bet you blame Geneva, though."

Clara bristled as she ladled a few lopsided circles of batter onto the griddle. "You should be thankful such a man was your boss. Pa kept you on the payroll for years in spite of your bottle habit. He did so because you were his best cowboy…his most dedicated cowboy." She shook her spatula at Vincent. "Where's that dedication now?"

Checking for bubbles in her corn cakes, she waited for him to say something, although she didn't expect it. She flipped the cakes over and looked at him again. He hadn't budged an inch.

She took a deep breath. Closing her eyes she contemplated what lay ahead, and envisioned herself following her husband from job to job, worried all the time—about money, a place to live, school for the children, hoping the meanness she'd seen in him wouldn't get worse.

"Make yourself useful," she said, loudly enough to bring him out of his trance. "Go tell the children to wash their hands for supper."

Chapter Thirty-Eight

It was sweltering on the second floor of the First National Bank, even with the windows open, and the boardroom was abuzz with flies from its teak-paneled walls to its lofty ceiling. The flies went for Albert's face as soon as he walked into the room. He used the mail in his hands to shoo them away.

He hung his knee-length frock coat on the clothes tree, loosened his tie and collar, and took a seat at his desk to read the day's mail. Technically, the desk wasn't his. He shared it, along with the room he sat in, with five other men on the board who met there once a month. He was the only one who used the space as a personal office.

He had all of his mail sent to the bank, away from the prying eyes of his wife and the careless acts of rambunctious children. In the light of a green-globed lamp, he separated the mail into two piles: business and personal. In the business pile he placed what appeared to be a bank draft and several fat packets containing real estate paperwork. One envelope, delivered by courier, held an invitation to a benefit for the recently organized Montrose fire department. Since it was addressed to him and nobody else on the bank's board, he decided it should go in his personal pile.

He recognized the familiar slant of the handwriting on one of the envelopes. It was postmarked Aug. 8,

1898 Gunnison, Colorado. He opened that one before attending to his business correspondence. Inside he found a half-page letter from Clara.

Dearest Pa,

I am sorry to begin this letter by burdening you with bad news; however Vincent and I have agreed to live apart. As soon as I can arrange for transportation, the children and I will be moving to Montrose. Lily and Henry have invited us to stay with them until we find suitable lodging.

I look forward to seeing you again. Do you realize it has been six years? Charley and Emily have grown since you last saw them, and you will finally get to meet the grandson I named after you.

> *With love and respect,*
> *Your daughter, Clara*

****

Lily and Clara stood in front of the Wonder Mercantile, the largest store in Montrose, observing the stylish clothes on the mannequin in the window. Earlier that morning, they'd enrolled Charley and Emily in school, and after leaving Bert and Lily's infant son with a trusted neighbor, they had an hour to kill before meeting their father for lunch.

The pulsing huff of a steam engine signaled the departure of the morning train. Delivery wagons clanked and rumbled down wide dirt streets, kicking up dust and horse droppings as the sisters strolled along wooden sidewalks, their footsteps adding to the thuds and thumps of other boots and shoes.

"You seem so calm," Lily said, "even cheerful. Given your situation, aren't you the least bit nervous?"

"I suppose I should be terrified, but right now I feel

like soaring…as if you and I are girls again, walking home from school. Other times, especially when sleep won't come, my thoughts are far from cheerful." She put an arm around her sister's waist. "Thank you for showing me around Montrose, Lily. I needed something like this."

It was coming on fall, shawl weather, yet comfortable. Noticing how the townsfolk were dressed, Clara realized how significantly fashion had changed while she was living in cattle country and mining towns. Every woman was wearing a hat of some kind. She felt like a peasant next to Lily who wore a classic boater and short lace gloves. The only gloves in Clara's trunk were wool mittens, and the one hat she owned, a hood really, was made of rabbit fur.

She studied the cut of the skirt on the mannequin in the window. Like other skirts and dresses she'd seen that morning, it was slimmer in the hips than her handmade clothing. Her corset no longer fit, and without one of those, the wasp waist on the store's mannequin would be impossible.

"My greatest worry is how I am going to support myself and the children." Clara turned from the window to look into her sister's eyes. "I am certain of this much, Lily. I will scrub floors on my hands and knees if it lets me control my own life."

Lily's eyes widened. "Aunt Mid would take you in."

"Probably…temporarily. Then what would I do— become a maid? Disgrace our family? I would rather scrub floors in Colorado where everyone seems to work hard."

"Pa would never allow that."

"He might. He might consider it a fit punishment for a daughter who married without his blessing." She paused, remembering how angry he'd been when he found out she'd married Vincent. "And for marrying badly, as he likely says."

"You are too hard on yourself, Clara. I think Pa liked Vincent. When he told me about your separation, he said Vincent was like a dog that comes when you whistle."

Clara felt her stomach contract. "I find that insulting. I'm sure Vincent would too."

Lily turned pink from her neck to her smartly coiffed light brown hair.

Clara reached for the store's door handle. "Let's go inside. I have to save what little money I have, but I can look. Today I want to surround myself with pretty things."

Wandering about the crowded interior of the Wonder Mercantile, Clara spied a counter full of hats. She picked up a large felt hat with a fake pheasant mounted on top and showed it to Lily. "Would you wear this?"

Lily hid a giggle behind her fingertips. She chose one with a mauve silk ribbon covering the entire crown. "Try this on," she said. Clara held the hat at arms length before settling it over the knot of dark brown hair at the nape of her neck. "It frames your face beautifully."

Clara inspected her reflection in a hand-held looking glass, tilting her head this way and that, smiling vaguely at her reflection. Then she removed the hat and smoothed her hair. "I was not being entirely candid with you, Lily, when I said I felt like a schoolgirl again. Inside I am quaking at the thought of seeing Pa, and him seeing me in these bedraggled clothes." She put the hat back on for another look. "I suppose Geneva is the picture of fashion."

"No doubt that's how she sees herself. In my opinion, she has terrible taste." The question Lily had wanted to ask ever since Clara arrived suddenly sprang from her lips. "Do you think you and Vincent will get back together some day?"

Clara removed the hat with its pinkish purple crown and shook her head with resolve. "He has changed, Lily. These last two years he made life miserable for me and the children in ways I am too ashamed to disclose."

Lily grabbed Clara by the shoulders. "Dear, dear sister. You will always have a place in my heart…and in my home."

Deep in thought, Clara returned the beribboned hat to its stand. She and Lily left the store, and back on the sidewalk, she said, "Vincent was steady as a post when I married him. He worked twelve or fourteen hours a day for weeks before demon rum took over. Demon whisky, that is. Pa put up with it. Jake, too, because he was such a good worker most of the time. Then Seth died, and Vincent seemed to surrender his soul."

Lily and Clara locked arms and continued their walk, stopping to read a poster on the Buddecke and Diehl Opera House and poke around in several more shops. At length, Clara said, "Vincent sold the buckboard to pay for our train tickets. I thanked him for that."

Their next stop was the First National Bank, an impressive brick building with a three-story tower on one corner. "It looks like a castle," Clara said. It was cool inside the dimly lit bank, and the air held the lingering smell of cigar smoke. Clara felt a flutter in her stomach when she gazed at the slate floor, teak walls, and stunning walnut furniture. It was the first time she'd been inside such a prosperous bank.

Before going up to their father's office, she and Lily stopped to say hello to Henry who was standing behind the fence-like grate of a teller's cage. Tellering was his morning job. After lunch, he moved to an office on the second floor and worked on the bank's ledgers. His reddish-blond beard was neatly trimmed, and wearing a navy blue suit and matching waistcoat, he gave the impression of a man who could be trusted with other people's money.

"Albert asked me to catch you before you went upstairs," Henry said. "An opportunity came up, and he had to leave." His wide mouth spread in a customer service grin. "He asked me to invite you—the whole family, actually—to dinner instead. Tonight. At his house."

"Geneva will be furious," Clara whispered to Lily.

Lily shook her head. "She has a cook now and a live-in maid. The maid does all her cleaning and watches the children if she needs to go somewhere."

Clara's smile dissolved in a flash.

"She likes to do her own shopping, though. It gives her an excuse to dress up and parade around town."

Henry placed a pale finger over his lips. "Someone might be listening," he mouthed, nodding toward the next teller window. Lily and Clara exchanged awkward grins, and for the first time since arriving in Montrose, Clara had second thoughts about leaving Gunnison.

Chapter Thirty-Nine

Albert peeked through the oval glass window in his front door. "Pa!" Clara cried. She looked at Lily. "He's got whiskers!" She felt whole again just being in her father's presence. Tears clouded her vision when he bent down and gathered her children into one big hug. She'd scrubbed them pink and dressed them in their best clothes.

"God almighty!" he bellowed, smiling in approval at Charley, Emily, and Bert.

His eyes hardened when he turned them on her. Holding her by the elbows, he gave her a stiffer welcome than he'd given his grandchildren. "God almighty," he repeated, quietly this time. He directed a grimace at what she was wearing. Clara pulled Emily in front of herself in a futile attempt to hide the cut of her dress and the cheapness of its fabric. It was the nicest dress she owned, but she'd seen enough fashion that day to know she probably looked like the scrubwoman she was destined to become.

"You might have at least borrowed a dress from Lily." He took a moment to check for other signs of deterioration. "Nevertheless, it warms my heart to know you and the children are safe."

There was a glint of silver in Albert's mutton chop sideburns, moustache, and goatee, yet the hair on top of his head was still black. Clara supposed a bit of silver was to be expected on a man past fifty.

"Don't run off after supper," he said to Clara. "I have a proposition to discuss with you." He gave her a serious look, before turning his attention to Bert, hoisting his namesake in the air. "Well, young fellow, you are not as husky as your brother." He put Bert down and led him and Charley toward the sitting room. Walking past the broad central staircase he yelled, "Geneva! Our family is here!"

Clara told Emily to go with her brothers while she and Lily waited for Geneva at the foot of the stairs. In less than a minute, Geneva descended wearing a rose and cream dress with a small train in back and a hat teeming with multi-colored feathers. Her blonde, fiddle fern hair was twisted into a roll at the back of her head, and she had a fringe of curly bangs on her forehead. Clara drew in a breath. She glanced at Lily, hoping for a clue as to whether their stepmother's attire was appropriate for a family gathering. Lily's lips were twitching.

Suppressing a smile that would surely be too big, Clara extended her hands to Geneva. Geneva's hands were soft as silk. Clara was relieved when their polite reunion ended, and she could slide her rough, dry hands into her pockets.

Lily broke the silence. "We must convince Clara to buy the hat she tried on today, Geneva. That new color, the one they call mauve, is perfect for someone with her dark coloring."

Geneva gave Clara's dress the same look of disdain Albert had given it. "That would be a waste of money," she said, and for the second time that day, Clara wished she were back in Gunnison.

The maid rang the bell for supper. With her face still burning, Clara gathered her children together and waited with everyone else for the host and hostess to enter the dining room. Albert saw what his wife was wearing, and stopped her before she walked through the arched doorway. "Take off that war bonnet," he ordered, and Clara had to bite back another smile.

Centered in Albert and Geneva's spacious dining room was a rectangular mahogany table surrounded by twelve matching chairs. The family had grown to thirteen. The thirteenth member was Lily's infant son perched in an oak high chair near his mother. Christopher and Charley, eleven and almost ten, sat next to one another, whispering and occasionally trading jabs, friends again after Albert noticed them sizing each other up before supper and made them shake hands. Emily and Rose took to one another right away; whereas Bert and Lilian, the two four-year-olds who'd never met, wanted nothing to do with each other. Albert's youngest child, Sabrina, almost three, sat atop a cushion in the chair next to Geneva.

The main course was lamb, served with mint jelly, roasted potatoes, and creamed spinach. Charley gave his mother a pained look after his first bite of lamb. Emily saw the expression on her brother's face and opted for the potato. Clara cut Bert's meat for him, and then gave each of her children a look that said, *Eat everything on your plate, even if you don't like it.*

Between bites of the meal, Albert and Henry discussed the recent war with Spain. Henry wanted to talk about the skirmishes, whereas Albert focused on signs the economy was improving now that the war was over. "Lots on Main Street that sold for hundreds of dollars before the war have recently sold for thousands." He flaunted a superior grin. "Some of the property was mine."

Henry shared what he'd read in the *Saturday Evening Post* about Teddy Roosevelt's march up San Juan Hill. His face beamed, and his reddish-blond beard bobbed with enthusiasm as he recited some of the details. "I'd have given my right arm to be there," he said, his chest puffed out as if he had.

"Do you even know how to shoot?" Albert asked.

Henry's pale complexion turned pink. "I went pheasant hunting once." Speaking in short bursts, he described the bird hunting trip in detail, sometimes raising his arms as if sighting a shotgun and punctuating his story with an occasional "boom!" Albert grunted an acknowledgement, and then switched the conversation back to the economy.

The women and children ate in silence, with the exception of Rose who kept asking if she and Emily could be excused. Geneva ignored her. The maid served angel food cake for dessert, and then the children ran off to play.

Clara picked up a few plates and started for the kitchen. "The maid will take care of that," Albert said with a frown. "Try not to let your actions trumpet your circumstances. Come. Follow me. I have something to talk to you about."

Feeling fragile as a snowflake, she followed him to the small library next to the sitting room. He pointed to the overstuffed chair she should sit in, and then took the one facing her. She rested her hands in her lap and sat perfectly still while he made a production out of lighting his cigar. Feeling like a worthless piece of real estate, she lifted her face for an expected tongue-lashing worse than the one he'd given her eleven years ago.

"I only plan to mention this once." He locked eyes with her. "This is what happens when you think you know more than I do. You would not be in the predicament you are in today if you had stayed in Philadelphia and married someone from there…like Lily did."

Clara nodded, certain in her own mind she would never be happy with a namby-pamby like Henry.

"I have given some consideration to your plight, Daughter. You cannot stay with Lily indefinitely. I am not implying that you would, however, four extra mouths to feed is too many. Since three are my grandchildren, I believe I have the right to intervene."

Clara raised her hand. "Pa, I would like to say something. I may not have gone to Normal School like Lily did, but I am capable of making money. In Durango, when painting jobs were scarce, I took in ironing and sewing. Unfortunately I had to leave my sewing machine with Vincent's aunt. I kept my irons, though, and I can cook and clean. When I enrolled Charley and Emily in school this morning, I noticed the school was looking to hire a janitor. I could iron during the day and clean the school at night."

"Hush up, Clara. Hear me out." Albert set his cigar in a marble ashtray and got up from his chair to close the library door. On his way back he stood in front of his daughter, forcing her to look up at him. "A woman in Ophir Loop needs someone to lease her hotel. It's a small one. A hotel would provide you with housing as well as a means of employment." He lifted an eyebrow.

"It requires much work—long days, and every day." He waited for her to say something before returning to his chair.

A reflective look washed over Clara's face. Cleaning hotel rooms was already something she'd thought about. Hard work didn't scare her, and she was willing to do almost anything. She remembered visiting Mrs. Hamlin, the midwife who delivered Emily. Mrs. Hamlin had taken in boarders after her husband died in order to keep her house. Hotel guests were the same as boarders except for how long they stayed.

"Where is Ophir Loop?"

"South of here," Albert said, "half a day by train. Two trains a day go as far as Ophir. Then you have to take the stage or get someone to drive you to Ophir Loop. More people live in Ophir. Silverton is the closest town of any consequence."

"You've been there?"

"Yes. To check on some property that was for sale." He puffed on his cigar. "I stayed at the hotel—it's the only one in Ophir Loop—a time or two. I found it suitable lodging."

Geneva opened the library door a crack and stuck her head inside. "Lily and Henry would like to go home." She fixed her eyes on Clara.

Albert frowned. "Tell them we're almost finished." When his wife didn't leave right away, he raised his voice. "Close the door, Geneva! Clara will be along shortly."

Geneva's blonde head disappeared, and the door slammed. Still frowning over the interruption, Albert said, "You need to think about my hotel proposal."

"I have. A hotel is a splendid idea, Pa. I would like

to see it with my own eyes, though, and if Lily will watch the children, I'll go there straight away."

Chapter Forty

Off the train in Ophir, Clara hired a big-bellied fellow with a horse and wagon to drive her to Ophir Loop. It was either that or wait four hours for the next stage. The wagon was a ragged buckboard with peeling paint and grimy yellow wheels. There was nowhere to sit except next to the driver on a hard seat in the open air.

"It seems cold for September," she said as they started out.

The driver turned to her with a grin. His broad smile revealed gaps that once held teeth. "There's two seasons 'round here, Ma'am, winter and gettin' ready for winter. Even in August the temper'ture hardly gits 'bove sev'nty."

She asked the man to show her some of Ophir before they left town, and he drove by a dry goods shop, a mercantile, a dance hall, and two hotels, one of them advertising hot meat pies. Another sign, this one on the livery stable next to one of the hotels, read: "Horse Shoes While You Wait." On the way out of town they passed a church and a schoolhouse, both clapboard buildings painted white.

Few such signs of civilization existed along the three-mile stretch between Ophir and Ophir Loop, a road that switched from rocks to ruts and back again, from hard pulls to steep descents, never dropping below nine thousand feet. Unaccustomed to the altitude, Clara became conscious of every breath she took. She sat with her hands in her lap while the wagoner talked nonstop about record snows, mining companies, his horses, or the people he knew. She nodded occasionally, focusing her attention on the colossal mass of peaks rising from the canyon floor. Everywhere she'd lived in Colorado there were mountains, some closer than others. Now, if everything went according to plan, she would be living *in* them, maybe *on* them. By the time she reached Ophir Loop she was sure of one thing—if the altitude didn't take a person's breath away, the grand sweep of those mountains would.

Her mountain high vanished when the wagoner drove through the huddle of huts in the shadow of a railroad trestle called the Ophir Loop. Every building was a shoddy combination of logs and wood. Many were empty. Clara thought it a stretch to call the place a community. Village maybe? Settlement?

As they approached what the wagoner said was the train depot, a sickly-looking yellow dog ran out of the building growling and baring its teeth. "Git!" the driver yelled as he steered his horses off one muddy path onto another.

Clara turned around to see if the dog was following. "Why doesn't the train I took to Ophir come here?" she asked.

"That depot ain't for passengers," the wagoner replied. "Trains stoppin' here are only haulin' ore to the smelters." Continuing down the trail, they passed a general store with "MINING SUPPLIES" painted on its front window. According to the driver, it was also the post office. Most of the buildings in Ophir Loop were within walking distance of a stream he referred to as Howard Fork. "Runs into the San Miguel River south a here," he told her.

The trail ended at the hotel Clara had come to see. It was at the top of a rise. The driver brought his horses to a stop in the wide turnaround fronting the hotel. "It was built when this place was in its glory days." He flashed another toothy grin.

Clara took his words as a sign of pride. After he left, she stood for a moment, inspecting the hotel's exterior for symptoms of neglect. The clapboard siding was in good shape. There was a false gable over the entrance and dormer windows on the second floor, none broken. Overall, it was larger than she pictured when her father referred to it as a small hotel.

The sign next to the front door read, "Good Beds, $1.00 a Night." Clara shivered inside her cloak as she walked across a short stretch of ground and up eight steps to a covered porch that ran the entire length of the two-story building. When she pushed open the door, her eyes fell on an enormous mahogany desk that took up half the space in the entry. She swiped a finger across the desk's surface to check for dust, and then rang the bell to announce her arrival.

"It came all the way from Chicago," someone said. Clara drew back her hand, turning to see an attractive, auburn-haired woman, elegantly coiffed, walking toward her. The woman was wearing a full-length bib apron over a lace blouse and long brown skirt.

"It was meant for a brothel." The woman's eyes crinkled with mirth as she told the rest of the desk's story. "The mayor's wife made him close the brothel before this gargantuan thing even got here. The madame moved her business to Silverton, and sold me this fine piece of furniture for a fraction of its value."

The hotel owner took Clara's hand and shook it the way men customarily greeted one another. "I am Amanda Pierce. I assume you are Albert's daughter." The woman's fashionable attire and high cheekbones were an older version of the shop mannequins in downtown Montrose.

"Yes. I was Clara Wallin before I married. I am Clara Reese now." Her voice wavered when she spoke her married name. "I have come here to look at your hotel before I sign the lease."

"Rightly so. I would be suspicious of anyone who didn't." Amanda picked up a ring of keys, motioning for Clara to follow. "After I show you around, you may wander about as long as you please. Albert has stayed here on occasion. I believe he found my hotel to his liking."

She showed Clara seven of the eight guest rooms on the second floor, skipping the one with its occupant sleeping inside. Then she took her downstairs and showed her the last two guest rooms, office, parlor, dining room, and kitchen.

A tall, angular woman stood in front of the kitchen range, stirring something that smelled strongly of garlic. The woman wore a long white apron identical to Amanda's and a scowl that seemed etched in her wrinkles. Amanda gave Clara a minute to look around the kitchen before leading her into the adjacent dining room.

"I didn't interrupt my cook to introduce you," she said privately. "Hannah is haughty, even to me. I put up with her because good cooks are hard to find. Many people stop by asking for work—more men than women. They say they can cook, but few know how to cook for a large group."

While listening to what Amanda was saying, Clara casually inspected the dining room's shiny tabletops and spotless floor. She and the owner were standing next to a sideboard that held towering rows of serving vessels, and when Amanda wasn't looking, Clara used her dust-checking finger again. Same as with the reception desk, the finger came back clean.

Chapter Forty-One

A week after her exploratory visit, Clara and her children were comfortably residing in the hotel. Amanda agreed to stay on for a few days to familiarize her lessee with what it took to manage the place. She lived in one of the downstairs guest rooms. She put Clara and her family in the one next to the parlor. After Amanda left, the boys were to move into her room, and Clara and Emily would stay where they were.

Clara's first morning on the job, she left her sleeping children at five a.m. and discovered she was late for work when she walked into the kitchen and saw Hannah's bony fingers kneading dough and Amanda taking a pan of biscuits out of the oven. Appearing fresh as a biscuit herself, Amanda smiled and poured her new manager a cup of coffee.

Clara had barely raised the cup to her mouth when an Asian boy burst through the back door. He stopped mid-stride to stare at the stranger in the kitchen.

"This is Mrs. Reese," Amanda said. "She will be your boss after I leave."

The boy lowered his impeccably barbered head in a slight bow. "Haro, Missus."

Amanda rested a hand on the young man's shoulder. "Yoshiro comes from Japan. He is a very capable worker." The boy nodded, inspecting his new boss with quick, dark glances.

"Hello, Yoshiro," Clara said, unsure whether she should bow.

"You may go now," Amanda said to the boy. Yoshiro grabbed a biscuit, daubed some jam on it, and ate it on the run.

The women carried their breakfast into the dining room and sat at one of the tables. Before taking her first bite of oatmeal, Amanda told Clara in confidence, "Yoshiro is my best employee. Although he's only fifteen, I would replace Hannah before I'd replaced him. He clears tables, washes dishes, takes care of the animals." She pointed at the pepper-box in the middle of their table. "He fills these, fills mustard pots, gathers eggs, mops floors. You may not have noticed, but the hills around here have been totally cleared of trees. Every two weeks or so Yoshiro has to drive the service wagon farther up the slopes for firewood."

"I can see why you value him. Does he speak English?"

"He knows a few words; otherwise I use hand signals and sweets." Tiny wrinkles formed under Amanda's eyes when she smiled. "I pay him for the work he does, of course, but sometimes I think it's the sugar that keeps him here."

While the women talked over coffee, the miners and other workers staying at the hotel left for the day. Each man carried a tin filled with the lunch Clara had helped pack that morning: two sandwiches, two hard-boiled eggs, a dill pickle, and a square of jelly cake.

"Breakfast and supper are included in the rent," Amanda explained while she and Clara made the sandwiches. "I charge an extra twenty cents a day for a midday meal."

One man entered the dining room several minutes after the others left. He wore a decent-looking jacket rather than overalls, and his neatly trimmed salt-and-pepper beard marked him as older than the other tenants. He ate his breakfast quickly, and then carried his tableware into the kitchen with a polite nod for the two women as he passed their table.

Amanda waited until she heard the squeak of boards in the stairwell. "That was Mr. Beale. He's lived here for as long as I can remember. He works nights, stays in his room all day, reads a lot. You'll hardly know he's here."

The women finished their breakfast, and then Clara met the last employee of the hotel, Sophie, a girl from Sweden who was almost as broad as she was tall. "She hired on as a laundress," Amanda said after Sophie left to do chores. "She also cleans rooms and helps Hannah. In a hotel this size, everyone has to pitch in wherever work needs to be done."

She led Clara to the far end of the narrow kitchen and opened the back door. "You need to know what goes on outside as well as inside. "I own all of the land from here to the creek." She swept her arm across a barn, two privies, what appeared to be a chicken coop, and beyond. "It's more than enough land for the animals it takes to run a hotel.

They walked down a short path separating the barn from a corral full of horses. "Some of these horses belong to the guests," Amanda said, "some to the hotel."

The barn had a good roof and a slightly weathered coat of paint. Amanda removed the bar across the barn's double doors, and when they opened, sunshine poured over a wagon parked inside. "This is what Yoshiro uses to haul wood. It can be fitted with runners and converted to a sleigh when there's snow on the ground."

Clara took some pleasure in the familiar smell of hay and cow manure, and inside the shadowy interior she and Amanda walked through a storage area to a room with several empty stalls. "This is where Yoshiro does the milking," she said. "The chickens are in a separate building on the other side of that door. He feeds them and makes sure they have water."

Impressed with what she'd seen so far, Clara was dismayed to find the hotel had no well. The nearest creek was up a slight hill about a city block away. In exchange for hauling water, Amanda had been giving meals to a middle-aged Italian fellow. Several times a day he'd fill two five-gallon oilcans with creek water and carry them back to the hotel. The man trudged back and forth to the creek so many times on washday he sometimes fell asleep at the supper table.

****

By the time Clara finished the bulk of her training, she thought she knew the help better than she did the owner. Amanda had been generous with her instructions, less forthcoming with details of her personal life other than saying she was widowed with a married daughter. Curious how this lovely, hard-working woman ended up in Ophir Loop, Clara asked her where she planned to go next.

"I'm moving to Montrose," she said. "I bought a building there near the center of town. I'm going to turn it into a women's shop."

"If you don't mind my asking, did your husband

217

will this hotel to you?"

Amanda arched her brows. "This hotel has always been in my name. Harold built it for me. He was mining silver by the bucket back then and needed a way to keep me occupied." She smiled wistfully. "And happy."

Chapter Forty-Two

Amanda left on an afternoon of howling snow. Travelers caught in the blizzard filled the hotel for a week, and in an effort to accommodate more guests, Clara decided to turn the small downstairs office into a sleeping room. First she moved the desk and chair in with her and Emily. Then she scrounged furniture for her new source of revenue by taking one of the bureaus out of her room, and a piece here and there from some of the rooms upstairs. Nothing she took would be missed, and none of it was from her permanent boarders' rooms.

Five men lived in the hotel full-time: the night watchman, two men working their own silver claim, an assayer, and a clerk for the Rio Grande Southern Railroad. Full-time boarders paid by the month. Guests who rented by the night were usually people passing through, or officials with the railroad, or mining bigwigs. Occasionally one of the men living in the miners' dorm at the base of Yellow Mountain spent a dollar for a soft mattress and another for a decent meal. These men showed up with everything they owned crammed into a duffel bag. They paid in advance, as did all guests, regardless of the elegance of their luggage.

Supper by supper, Clara got to know her boarders by observing their habits and catching bits of conversation. Bespectacled Mr. Cogswell, who spent his days dispatching rail cars, devoured his food in a frenzy, wiping his mouth with a napkin and asking for dessert before the other tenants and guests were halfway through supper. After two or three nights of this, Clara said next to his ear, "You might as well slow down, Mr. Cogswell. If you want dessert, you'll have to wait until we set it out for everyone."

The miners were a dissimilar pair. Mr. Kearney, slight of build and clean-shaven, always wore a four-button waistcoat and tailored trousers when he came down to supper. Mr. White was a towering man with a bushy red beard. His uniform was a flannel shirt and suspenders. The two men usually arrived late, and being the only permanent residents to work up a sweat every day, ate twice as much food as the others.

Clara had learned a little about her boarders when Amanda went over the hotel books with her before she left. She kept a separate ledger for the boarders with a column assigned to each room. Checking the column totals, Clara realized only Mr. Wickham, the assayer, was behind in his rent.

"He pays something every month," Amanda told her, "more than enough to cover his food; however the sum of his arrears is nearly two hundred dollars." She showed Clara her tally sheet. "I know he has the money. Maybe you will be more successful at collecting it than I."

Clara gained more insight into her tenants' lives when she and Sophie cleaned their rooms. Mr. Kearney's room was always orderly, whereas Mr. White left his clothes wherever they fell. Mr. Cogswell's room was neat bordering on Spartan. He even made his bed every day, flawlessly as a maid. Mr.

Wickham's room was always messy. He picked up his clothes once in a while to have them laundered, even though the hotel provided laundry service. One day Clara stopped him as he headed out the door with his clothes stuffed in a pillowcase.

"We can wash those clothes for you, Mr. Wickham," she said with a friendly smile. "For a small fee, say five cents per shirt."

"Too much," he grunted. "The Chinaman charges a nickel a bundle."

The night watchman's room was tidy, although crowded with personal possessions, including a stack of dime novels on a corner table—more booklets than books—and a bookcase full of bound volumes. Clara found the stale smell of the books enticing. Whenever Sophie wasn't around, she thumbed through a few pages, wishing she had time to read. Since Mr. Beale slept during the day, his room was the last one they cleaned. He was always up and dressed, with a special welcome when they knocked on his door. The one he greeted them with most often was, "Hello, Ladies, I've been waiting for you all my life." Clara laughed the first time he said it. After that, she just smiled.

She and Sophie cleaned the tenants' rooms every Friday. It was difficult to do a thorough job during the coldest months. Sophie still did laundry every Monday, and then on Friday she and Clara dusted furniture, swept floors, emptied ashes, polished lamp globes, and filled lamps and lanterns with coal oil. Yoshiro mopped the floors downstairs with vinegar and water, and by suppertime on Friday, the hotel smelled faintly like a pickle jar.

To demonstrate she wasn't above doing dirty work,

Clara helped Sophie clean the two privies. This entailed sweeping them out, scrubbing around the two holes in each latrine, and replenishing the paper supply with whatever they could find: catalogs, nickel weeklies, calendars, almanacs, newspapers, even dog-eared dime novels. Finished up top, Clara tossed a cupful of lye powder down the holes.

"Smell better now, Missus," Sophie would say, even when it didn't.

During Clara's first weeks of cleaning privies, sweeping floors, and climbing stairs, she frequently interrupted her work to catch her breath. The thin air made it difficult to concentrate, and if she walked too fast, her heart pounded. At 9,000 feet, she also had to make adjustments in the kitchen. At that altitude, water boiled at 190 degrees; thus it took longer to cook almost everything. Her first attempts at simple things like boiling an egg or making mayonnaise had been frustrating. Clara raised her hands in exasperation after every failure, while Hannah cackled in amusement. Clara laughed, too, ending what had been a failure to communicate with the older woman. Hannah sometimes griped about it, but she showed Clara how to adjust cooking times and temperatures, or add ingredients to certain recipes. We will never be friends, Clara decided, but at least we will be able to share the same kitchen.

Chapter Forty-Three

Snow fell off and on for weeks. As the snow piled higher, the list of names on the hotel register also grew, most of them miners who couldn't work their claims when their fortunes were under ice and snow. Even with the extra space of the renovated office, there weren't enough rooms for the influx. Some men had to double up. Although they shared both room and bed, Clara charged each man a dollar per night for the room, a dollar apiece for the food, and nobody argued.

Men accustomed to sleeping in the miner's dorm or under the stars, were a rough bunch. Clara continued Amanda's policy of no drinking or gambling on the premises. The men grumbled about having to walk a mile to get a drink, yet when the snow got too deep, they managed to shovel a path to the saloon.

There was no such thing as snow days for children living in the mountains. There was no school at all from October to May. As a way to occupy her children's time during those months, Clara assigned them chores. Emily took some of the load off Yoshiro by clearing tables and helping him wash dishes. Charley kept the wood boxes full and showed guests to their rooms, sometimes carrying part of their luggage.

Without a bare patch of ground for a game of marbles, Charley made himself a sled out of a wooden crate. When it was too stormy for sledding, he constructed forts out of the firewood stored in the woodshed. Emily played with rag dolls her mother made before she gave up the Singer. Sometimes she held tea parties for her dolls, using a miniature tea set Amanda gave her. Made of hand-painted porcelain and trimmed in gold, the set included four cups and saucers, a teapot, creamer, sugar bowl, and tray.

"This set is exquisite," Clara said the day Amanda offered it to Emily. "Shouldn't your daughter have it?"

Amanda shook her head. "She outgrew it long ago, and her boys won't use it."

Clara's youngest boy Bert had few toys, and still being too small to do chores, he followed his mother around the hotel while she did hers. Often that meant the kitchen, where Hannah usually gave him a snack.

"He looks like a waif," she'd say. "This'll put some meat on his bones."

Bert's favorite way to occupy his time was to feed the stray cats hanging around the back door yowling for scraps. Sometimes he shared one of the snacks Hannah had given him. He made a pet of one of the females. She became tame enough that he could drape her around his neck like a wool muffler. His pet became pregnant, and Sophie told him, "Soon many cats."

Unlike her children, Clara had no time for play. She shouldered the work without complaint, but wished her new life included some adult conversation. She spoke to overnight guests at the time they registered; seldom was the guest a woman. Otherwise she got few words out of the help or the permanent boarders. Mr. Wickham did his best to dodge her. The miners, Mr. Kearney and Mr. White, avoided everyone, waiting until there was an empty table before sitting down to supper. Occasionally Mr. Cogswell complimented the food; otherwise he dipped his chin and gave her a polite "Ma'am" whenever their paths crossed.

Mr. Beale, who worked nights, was an exception. Since he ate his meals at odd hours, he was often the only person in the dining room when Clara entered. Thinking he must have the loneliest job in the world, she interrupted her work to chat with him. His eyes crinkled with pleasure the first time they talked. His robust tone of voice didn't match the lines on his face, and Clara found herself looking forward to the twenty-minute conversation breaks.

At the end of days that began and ended in the dark, her back ached, her head ached, and her hands felt like lobster claws. In bed at night, she listened to Emily's soft breathing and wished it was someone snoring, someone she could wrap her arms around and cling to until morning. She tried not to stare at the occasional couple staying at the hotel, at the tenderness displayed when the husband removed his wife's wrap or escorted her to the supper table.

Since leaving Gunnison, she'd received three short letters from Vincent, one while she was staying with her sister in Montrose. She answered the first letter after she moved into the hotel. In it she wrote about her employment and where she and the children were living. Vincent's second letter, addressed to "The Hotel in Ophir Loop," arrived in mid-November. In it he said he was working as a mule-skinner for the Tomboy Mine in Telluride, a town closer to Ophir Loop than Gunnison.

A third letter arrived a scant two weeks after the second. *Telluride is a lot like Durango*, he wrote. *You*

would like it here. So would the kids. We could rent a
little farm. I could buy you a horse.

Clara didn't answer it; nor had she answered his
second letter.

When chopping onions for meatloaf, she let the
tears run down her cheeks. She ached with longing, but
didn't know why. Was it the good times she read
between the lines in Vincent's letters—riding their
horses through moonlit sage, playing charades with
Phoebe and Reb, the cottage he built for her in
Durango? Maybe it wasn't about him at all. Maybe she
longed for the week she spent with Lily and Henry in
Montrose. She was regretting leaving that town with its
good schools and newspaper, its variety of shops, and
the Buddecke and Diehl Opera House she hadn't had a
chance to enjoy. If she lived in Montrose, she could see
her father once in a while. Maybe if he saw her more
often, he'd forgive her for marrying Vincent. For a
fraction of a second, she wondered if it was the
afternoon chats with Mr. Beal she missed. She'd put an
end to them when his adoring smile began making her
cheeks heat up.

****

Toward the middle of December, her nostalgia
took a more positive turn. Preparing for Christmas, she
draped pine boughs in the entry and over the dining
room windows. The aroma of gingerbread and other
delicious smells floated through the hotel, as she and
Hannah filled the cellar with baked goods. There was a
box of ornaments in the cellar, and imagining a
Christmas tree in a corner of the dining room, Clara
asked Yoshiro to hitch up the sleigh and bring back a
small conifer.

Yoshiro had learned about Christmas trees the previous December when Amanda helped him find a tree of the proper size and shape. True to the tradition, he returned with a six-foot spruce. Mr. Beale was eating supper when the young man dragged the tree into the dining room. He left the table, offering to help, and built a simple wood stand for the tree. He made sure the tree was standing straight, and then went back to his table and finished his meal.

Sophie, her moon face beaming, walked into the dining room carrying the Christmas ornaments. She set the box on the floor. Mr. Beale pulled out his pocket watch and checked the time. "May I hang some of those ornaments?" he asked.

"No know," Sophie said with a puzzled look.

Mr. Beal was unsure whether Sophie hadn't understood him, or just didn't know if she should give him permission. He decided to ask Clara. She was in the kitchen on a stool, peeling potatoes. She put down her knife and looked up when he entered.

"I'd be pleased to help decorate the tree, Mrs. Reese. I don't have to leave for half an hour." His dark brown eyes, droopy at the corners, sparkled with energy.

Clara felt her face redden. Not only had she been nosing around this man's reading material when she cleaned his room, he'd been sneaking into her dreams of late, dreams she pooh-poohed as some strange manifestation of altitude sickness.

"That would be kind of you, Mr. Beale."

She went back to peeling the potato in her hands.

"Will you tell them I am allowed?"

Clara put down the potato and wiped her hands on

a towel. With Yoshiro and Sophie watching, she took one of the ornaments out of the box and handed it to the night watchman, nodding and smiling while he hung it on a branch.

Yoshiro smiled broadly. Pointing toward the ceiling, he said, "Up now, Missus," and he hurried outside to shovel snow off the roof. With quiet resolve, Sophie squatted next to the box of ornaments and picked out the prettiest ones before Mr. Beale could get his hands on them.

Chapter Forty-Four

Clara used words, gestures, and facial expressions to communicate with Sophie, Yoshiro, and the Italian man who hauled water in exchange for food. Another method she used was to give Sophie the label off an empty can or bottle before sending her to the cellar to bring back one just like it. This saved time and avoided tears of frustration from a heavy girl challenged by steep steps.

One gray day in February, Sophie returned from the cellar empty-handed. "No loud, Missus." She handed Clara a grease-stained label. "Sophie looks long time."

"Lard, Sophie, not loud." Clara tugged at her earlobe the way she used to when playing charades. "Lard sounds like hard."

Sophie nodded. She mumbled the word correctly, and then repeated it as she left the kitchen.

When Clara was sure the girl was gone, she lit a lantern and went down to the cellar to double-check. Lard was as vital an ingredient as flour, so she was dismayed to find out the girl was correct. She started back up the steps, and saw Sophie peering down at her from the doorway, hands braced on hefty hips.

"No *lard*, Missus," she said when Clara reached the top. Her triumphant smile made Clara laugh, even though running out of lard meant a trip to the nearest town in the middle of winter.

Luckily, there had been a break in the weather. Clara asked Yoshiro to ready the sleigh for a trip to Ophir town where she could buy lard and a few other items. Wearing her rabbit fur hood, wool gloves, two sweaters, a wool cape, and a pair of men's long johns under her skirt and petticoat, Clara climbed into the sleigh. Yoshiro was bundled up, too. His lively Asian eyes were all that could be seen between his sheepskin cap and a wool scarf wrapped around the bottom half of his face.

They left Ophir Loop when the sun was at the apex of its arc. Flanked by mountains of great height, most of the flat was in shadows. Within a couple of hours, the wedge of light brightening its center would crawl up the eastern slopes and disappear.

Freed from the hotel's stale interior, Clara took great gulps of air so pure she could see thirty miles or more of the stack of mountains surrounding the grubby settlement of Ophir Loop. The sunlight, bright snow, clean air, and respite from work cleared her mind, and during the three-mile trip to Ophir, snuggled under a fur lap robe, she took stock of her new life, bypassing its shortfalls and focusing on her achievements.

Clara had Yoshiro make several stops during the hour they were in Ophir, the last one being an attorney's office. They left town at dusk. By the time the lights of the hotel were in view, the arc of sky between the mountains was blue-black and maddened with stars. With the creeks and the Fork clogged with ice, the only sounds threading the night air were the tinkle of sleigh bells and the swish of runners on frozen snow.

Yoshiro helped Clara carry her purchases into the hotel. Then he took care of the sleigh and horses. Clara shed her outer layers of clothing and stored the supplies. Sipping on a cup of coffee, she sat at one of the tables in the dining room and wrote a letter to Vincent. She'd received his letters months before, and it took her almost that long to come up with the right words in the one she wrote to him. She didn't want to anger him, but she had to let him know she was serious—that their marriage was over—that if he wanted to see his children he'd have to come to Ophir Loop. In a week or two she would write him another letter, this time informing him of the papers she planned to sign the next time she was in Ophir town.

Chapter Forty-Five

The plip, plip, plip of melting icicles signaled the beginning of what amounted to spring in Ophir Loop. A misty rain, hard to distinguish from low clouds, hovered over the gorge once or twice a week. Snow was still being measured in feet above the timberline, but bursts of wild green dusted the slopes. The creeks gurgled again, and the pussy willows growing along their banks were silver with catkins.

Inside the hotel, months of exposure to wood heat and coal oil lamps had left a greasy film on everything. Windows were thrown open, and rugs and coverlets taken outside for a good beating. Curtains were washed, floors scrubbed, quilts boiled and stretched across tree stumps to dry. Every pillow and mattress was emptied, the ticking bleached, boiled, dried, and filled with clean hay or sheep shearing. The cans, cartons, baskets, and barrels that filled the cellar were shifted from one corner to another while the shelves were wiped down with vinegar water. Then the same containers were replenished and reorganized.

All of this extra work made Yoshiro and Sophie a bit cranky, and one morning while Clara was in the cellar preparing a shopping list, she heard them arguing upstairs. Her helpers rarely talked to one another unless something came up that affected their work. Suddenly they stopped talking, and she heard Sophie clomping down the steps to the cellar. Breathing hard, the girl rushed over to her. "Jap boy no good, Missus. Want squeezing Sophie." Her farm-girl cheeks were rosy with agitation.

Yoshiro was right on her heels, shaking his head, his small eyes round with concern. "Sophie no know beans, Missus! No want squeezing Sophie. Want squeezing machine!"

Clara looked from one to the other. "What's going on here?" she asked.

Yoshiro launched a skillful pantomime, explaining he didn't want to squeeze his co-worker; he wanted a scrub bucket with an attached wringer for the mop. Noting the serious look on the boy's face, Clara came close to laughing.

"Squeeze *mop*," she said to Sophie, smiling broadly as she mimicked wringing out a mop by hand.

Sophie frowned at Clara, then at her would-be assailant before clomping back up the steps to the kitchen. Yoshiro waited until he saw her shoes disappear from view before he followed. Clara wrote 'mop bucket' on her shopping list.

****

With considerable cleaning to do, and only a few good-weather months to do it, Clara welcomed the beginning of school. Not only did school keep her children occupied, it meant another steady boarder, the schoolmarm, from April to September.

Olive Nelson was a first-year teacher from Nebraska, horse-faced and loud. She taught all eight grades in one square room where her students sat on benches. Three of the room's interior walls were whitewashed. The one facing the benches was painted

233

black. Since paper was hard to come by, students brought writing slates to class and delivered their homework assignments orally.

At five years of age, Bert was the youngest student in the school. Clara thought about him while she cleaned the sideboard at the far end of the dining room. How small he was for his age! She hoped the bigger boys weren't bullying him. A spasm of grief gripped her at the memory of Seth chasing after his siblings. He would be three and a half if he'd lived. He was still the real baby of the family.

One by one, Clara emptied and cleaned the shelves of the sideboard. To take her mind off a mindless task, she dwelled on more thoughts of her children. All three of them were well-behaved and healthy. Even Bert. Charley was the levelheaded one. She worried about him, though. His eyes lacked the innocence of other children his age. Emily, her shining light, was helping with simple cooking chores. She would be nine in a month. Clara was twelve when she learned how to cook. Her aunts, Alma and Lou, taught her back when they all lived together in the ranch house near La Jara.

That was before Geneva moved in. Clara stilled her rag. She allowed herself a moment to imagine what it would be like to have a maid and a cook, and then got down on her knees to clean one of the sideboard's lower shelves.

She felt a tug on her apron ties. "How was school, little man?" She turned around, expecting to see Bert's impish face. Instead it was Mr. Beale sporting the boyish grin.

"Why would you do such a thing, Mr. Beale?" She got up from her knees and retied her apron. "Can't you see I'm in the middle of something?"

"I couldn't resist. Rarely are you so preoccupied you don't hear someone approaching."

"Is it time for your supper already?"

"No, I will be eating with the rest of the guests tonight." He sat on one of the dining chairs.

"What time are you expected at the mine?"

"I traded with Lars tonight. We've traded before when one of us needed to do something during the other man's shift. Usually it's Lars. This time it's me."

"Does that mean you have to work twenty-four hours straight?"

He nodded, his smile revealing clean, slightly crowded teeth. "I was wondering"—he cracked his knuckles—"the stage is running again, and there's a dance tonight in Ophir town. You've been working so hard I thought you might like to go."

Clara gave a start of surprise. She had to clamp her lips together to keep from smiling. In case a smile broke free, she turned back to the sideboard and wiped down a shelf she'd already wiped.

"No? Nothing to say?"

"I am married, Mr. Beale." She swished her rag in the pan of water. "You know so."

"I'm asking if I can escort you to a dance, Mrs. Reese." He leaned forward in his chair. "Not be your beau."

The assertive way he spoke made the hair on Clara's arms prickle. She hadn't been out of the hotel except for the times she and Yoshiro went for supplies, and the only social invitation she'd received in nearly a year was to a potluck she declined because she didn't want to go alone. Mr. Beale's offer brought back

235

memories of the dances she attended while staying with her Aunt Mid. "Hops" they'd called them. She always had a good time at those dances, despite her aunt's constant presence.

"I haven't danced in a long time." Clara turned to face him. "I do enjoy dancing, but I shouldn't leave the children."

Mr. Beale laughed softly. Every time he laughed, the curve of his cheeks nearly rose to his eyes. "Ask Miss Nelson to watch them. Tell her to give them more schoolwork if they misbehave."

****

Later that evening, Mr. Beale was chuckling again, nervously this time, when he and Clara walked into one of the dance halls in Ophir. Sporting a striped waistcoat and dark wool trousers, he was dressed like the rest of the men. Clara, wearing the ruffled white blouse and slim skirt Lily had insisted on buying for her in Montrose, outshone the women.

Mr. Beale was not quite as tall as Vincent, although he walked tall. When the music started he held Clara close, guiding her through the waltz, the schottische, and other dances, round and square. She followed his lead, laughing out loud when she missed a step, her cheeks aglow as she and her partner bounced and swayed to the lively tunes of a fiddler.

When the fiddler went home, and the dance floor emptied, they squeezed into the last stagecoach to Ophir Loop with three other passengers. Sitting in the dark next to her dance partner, closely enough their thighs touched, Clara glanced at him from time to time. His profile was defined by the moonlight streaming through the window on his side of the coach, but she couldn't see the expression on his face. She imagined him putting his arms around her when they were somewhere other than a dance hall or crowded coach, and she didn't think she would push him away.

Part VI

Live, Love, Bake

Chapter Forty-Six

With the aroma of baking bread filling every corner of the hotel, Clara celebrated her first year as manager in the kitchen. It was a cool September afternoon, but the sunshine spilling through the windows, combined with the heat from the oven, made the kitchen almost unbearable. Using the hem of her apron, she blotted perspiration from her upper lip. Then she folded a pat of dough in half, kneaded it with the heels of her hands, and folded it again, a process she repeated until the dough reached the texture of an earlobe. Pushing and punching, dusting the dough with flour, she had her mind set on fixing her hair and changing into a clean apron before Mr. Beale came down to supper.

Across from her, Hannah was working on another pat of dough when the bell in the entry rang. "Someone's out front," the cook said when Clara didn't stop to answer it.

"I heard it." She gave the dough a final punch. "Will you please finish this for me?"

Clara rinsed her hands, and then hurried to the entry hall where she nearly crumpled in astonishment. "Geneva! I had no idea you were coming!" Delighted to see a familiar face, even that one, she reached for her former friend, stopping short of embracing her. "Where's Pa?"

She whisked open the front door, expecting to see her father bringing in their luggage. Instead there was only the gap-toothed wagoner turning his wagon around. He waved up at her and grinned. She waved back with less enthusiasm.

"Didn't Pa come with you?"

"No. He stayed in Montrose." Geneva's lips were puckered as if she'd just bit into a lemon. "With the children. At least that's where he said he'd be." Scowling, she removed her gloves with a flourish.

"Is he well? Please tell me he's all right."

"Your old pa is fit as a fiddle." Geneva slapped her gloves against the palm of her hand.

"Why did you come here then? Surely it wasn't to see me."

"Why shouldn't I come here? My money's as good as anyone else's." She ran a hand across the polished surface of the reception desk, slowly, pensively. Then she turned to Clara with her arms extended and tears in her eyes. Warily, Clara embraced her. Geneva clung as if holding onto a lifeline.

"You're frightening me," Clara said after a minute passed.

"Frightening you?" Geneva gave her ex-friend a little shove. "You still think something's wrong with *him*, don't you? You're frightened for *him*. Why can't you imagine *I* might be the one who's hurting?" She folded her arms across her chest. "Just because you have that man on a pedestal, doesn't mean I have to. You're not going to like what I'm about to tell you, but I'm going to tell you anyway. Your dear pa is seeing another woman."

Clara's hand flew to her heart. "Surely you are

mistaken!"

"I saw it with my own eyes. That man is a scalawag, and I'm going to prove it!"

"Shhh! Lower your voice." Clara glanced into the nearly empty dining room. "I assume you are planning to stay here. I'll ask my Japanese boy to carry your bag upstairs. After you're settled, we need to continue this conversation in private."

"I have only this satchel." Geneva pointed to the mohair carpetbag near her feet. "I can carry it myself. I've been carrying it all day."

Clara showed her to the room with the nicest bedding and curtains. "The pitcher has water in it." She pointed to the washstand with its pitcher, basin, and soap dish. "After you freshen up, come down to the parlor. I'll make us a pot of tea."

Heart hammering in her chest, Clara went down to the kitchen where the teakettle always simmered on the stove. Hannah was in the middle of a second batch of dough, kneading in a steady rhythm, mouth tight, eyes on the task. Clara gathered up the makings for tea and set them on a tray, certain the cook had overheard everything Geneva said.

The parlor was usually empty that time of the day until the boarders got off work. Clara carried the tray into the small cozy room, and set it on a stand between two overstuffed chairs. Still in a daze, she sank into one of the chairs, agonizing over Geneva's accusation. *Pa is too honest for such a thing*, she told herself, *too responsible, too old. Now that he's not dealing with cattle most of the time, Geneva probably expects him to dote on her*. Clara poured herself a cup of tea. *Why did she come here? What does she expect me to do?*

Geneva didn't dawdle. Sitting on the parlor's upholstered sofa, she watched Clara pour another cup of tea. "Is there no one in Montrose you can confide in?" Clara asked.

Geneva rolled her eyes. "I didn't come here for advice. I'm here because this is where it all started."

"What do you mean?"

"Albert met that woman in this hotel. For all I know he bedded her here."

Clara gasped. "Must you speak so brazenly? Have you forgotten I am his daughter?"

"I'm sure he was seduced," Geneva said without blinking an eye, "and since you know her—I'm talking about that pompous woman who owns this hotel—I came here for some answers."

Stunned, Clara took a moment to process the accusation. Amanda had talked about opening a shop in Montrose, and she certainly was attractive enough to catch Pa's eye, any man's eye.

The sound of someone knocking interrupted her thoughts. "Today must be my lucky day," Mr. Beale said, standing in the doorway. "Two lovelies having tea."

Ever since Mr. Beale and Clara had gone dancing, they'd met in the parlor for twenty minutes or so every afternoon before he ate supper. They used their given names (Mr. Beale's was Jonas) while they were alone, but agreed not to use them around others. They talked about many things during those hurried half-hours, but his favorite topic was whatever he happened to be reading. He spoke with such enthusiasm that every story, even those in dime novels, sounded as if they'd been written by a noted author.

Clara smiled at him. "Is it that time already?" Smoothing the front of her apron, she stood up to make formal introductions, trying not to clatter her cup and saucer when she set them on the tray. "Will you keep Mrs. Wallin company, Mr. Beale, while I get your supper ready?"

Geneva's eyes moved back and forth between the man and Clara, her lips tightening into a thin line. Jonas's early supper was an excuse for Clara to get away, time to ponder Geneva's outrageous claim. She gave her stepmother a cautionary look before leaving for the kitchen. "We will finish our conversation later, Mrs. Wallin."

In the warmth of the kitchen, Clara opened cans and sliced bread for poached tomatoes. Mulling over Geneva's accusation, she searched her memory for anything her father said about Amanda. The night he suggested renting the hotel, he hadn't even given the owner's name, and he was all business when he drew up the rental agreement. Amanda hadn't talked about him, either, other than mentioning he'd been a guest.

Clara knew her father well: the pride he took in his appearance, his horsemanship, his need to be building something—a house, a cattle empire, a fortune. She'd spent one week with Amanda and found her to be smart, considerate, and far too elegant to engage in something sordid.

Geneva was another story. If anyone were going to be unfaithful, it would be her. Thinking back on how blatantly she flirted with cowboys, especially Vincent, Clara wouldn't have been surprised if her former friend was flirting with Jonas that very minute. She hadn't foreseen them ever meeting one another. Did he think she was pretty? Clara set the pot of bread and tomatoes on the stove. *Is that woman going to be a thorn in my side for the rest of my life?*

Chapter Forty-Seven

Since the parlor was filled with guests after supper, Clara suggested she and Geneva go upstairs to her room where they could talk in private. Papered in brown and beige roses, the room was sparsely furnished. An armoire sat against one wall, and next to it a washstand, both pieces made of oak. The simple bedstead was wrought iron, painted white. An oil lamp, the only light in the room, sat on a round, cloth-covered table in front of the window. The table had one chair.

Clara lit the lamp and closed the curtains. As a soft glow brightened the room, she pulled the spindle-back chair next to the bed, where Geneva sat with her white ankle boots dangling over the edge.

"He was always at the bank," she began. "I used to wonder why. Now I know. I was about to open the door to his office when I saw them through the letters painted on the glass. Amanda was sitting next to him, not on the other side of the desk where she should've been. They must meet there all the time."

"It's a bank, Geneva. They were probably discussing business."

"What kind of business? Monkey business?"

A ripple of irritation crossed Clara's face. "She owns property in Ophir and Telluride, and a shop in Montrose. She managed this hotel for years. Made money at it, too. Did you meet her?"

"I didn't go in."

Clara shook her head.

"Well, what would you have done? I was humiliated."

"I would have asked for an introduction. She is perhaps the most interesting woman I've ever met."

Geneva pursed her lips. "All I know is Albert stayed in this hotel while she was here, and more times than he needed to. If you won't help me, Clara, I'll find somebody who will."

****

Making good on her threat, Geneva spent the next two days asking every boarder and employee at the hotel to tell her about Albert's stays—how long, which room, who he talked to, who he ate with, and what their previous landlady was doing while he was there. She had trouble communicating with Yoshiro and Sophie, however, she thought she'd discovered the mother lode in Hannah when she found out Amanda spent a lot of time in the kitchen. Instead, the cook's two or three-word answers riled Geneva to the point her questions escalated into spiteful demands. After that, Hannah wouldn't give her a crumb.

Undaunted, Geneva moved her interrogation from the kitchen to other parts of the hotel. She spent less than a minute with Miss Nelson, who hadn't boarded there long. Mr. Beale didn't recognize Albert from the picture Geneva showed him, and neither did the two miners.

"I remember him," Mr. Wickham said after glancing at the picture. "Snooty gent. I saw him and Amanda talking in the parlor one night. It was late. I was on my way to bed."

"Oh!" Geneva grabbed his shirtsleeve. "What were they talking about?"

Mr. Wickham pulled his arm away. "I don't know. I didn't even wish them goodnight." He cleared his throat and backed away. "I have to leave now."

Geneva followed him as far as the stairwell. "Surely you remember more than that, Mr. Wickham."

"I have to go to work now, Ma'am." The assayer hurried up the creaky stairs for his jacket. Geneva followed, hounding him with questions, shouting at him through the closed door of his room. She kept after him until he left the hotel and was out of earshot. That evening she waited for him to return, but Mr. Wickham, being practiced in the art of avoidance, disappeared for a few days.

Mr. Cogswell recalled sitting across from Albert at supper. "Twice, I believe. We talked mostly about the railroad I work for—whether it was a good investment—that sort of thing." He studied the face of the woman who'd been scouring the hotel like a detective. "It appears you're trying to dig up some dirt about our former landlady. If you are, you're looking under the wrong rug, Mrs. Wallin."

At breakfast the next morning, Clara found Geneva sitting alone at one of the dining room tables. She had her chin on her chest, and in front of her, a plate of half-eaten johnnycakes. Clara carried a cup of coffee and plate of scrambled eggs to the table and sat across from her.

"I've decided to go home," Geneva declared before Clara took her first bite of food. "I've wasted the last two days talking to nincompoops."

"You need to cheer up, Geneva." Clara put down

her fork. "From what I can tell, you haven't found a single thing to support your fears."

"Fears? I'm not afraid. I'm angry."

"You're ripping yourself to shreds over nothing."

Hearing a loud bang in the kitchen, Clara jumped out of her chair to investigate. "It was just Hannah setting a heavy pot on the stove," she explained when she sat back down.

Geneva shook her head in disgust. "A vile woman. I don't know why you put up with her."

Yoshiro entered the dining room with a bag of salt and a funnel and began filling the saltshaker on a nearby table. "Not now, Yoshiro." Clara shook her head and motioned for him to leave. The boy nodded several times, and then headed for the kitchen. "Thank you," Clara said, loudly enough he was sure to hear. "One thing I am confident of," she said, returning to her conversation with Geneva, "is that my father keeps his promises. Remember the vows he made when he married you?"

Geneva pushed away her half-eaten plate of johnnycakes. She narrowed her eyes. "Well, you must have forgotten yours. Maybe it's a family trait. Poor Vincent, living all by himself. Maybe I'll write to him."

Clara dug into her scrambled eggs. "I am too busy to sit here and quarrel with you, Geneva. I have a hotel to run. I'll ask Yoshiro to drive you to the train station. I would ask you to give my love to Pa when you see him, but I know you won't."

Chapter Forty-Eight

Albert hustled down Second Street with a tweak to the brim of his bowler hat for every person he passed—some who revered him, others who feared him. He worked the sidewalk like a politician, stopping here and there to shake hands and exchange superficial greetings. It was a sunny day, perfect for socializing, but he didn't want to get bogged down in small talk.

He was on his way to the shop with Millinery & Ladies Furnishings painted on the front window. He pictured the shop's owner as he'd last seen her, wearing a high-necked blouse, fitted above the waist and tucked into a slim skirt—a stylish combination that accented an hourglass figure. She wore her auburn hair piled in a soft bouffant, with a runaway strand or two trailing her cheeks.

He took a deep breath as he entered. A cluster of tiny bells mounted on the door announced his arrival, and within seconds Amanda walked toward him, weaving through the displays of merchandise with the poise of a queen. Her face registered surprise. Her grip was soft and warm when she shook his hand.

"Hello, Albert. Always a pleasure."

"The pleasure is mine." He removed his hat. "How is the ladies' business today?"

"Rather quiet. Are you to be my first customer?" Her smile was welcoming yet professional. "I received some lovely blouses this morning. I was unpacking the carton when I heard you come in."

A quick look around gave Albert more than he cared to see of feathers, flowers, and lacy unmentionables arranged on tables or hanging on racks. "I thought we might go out for something to eat," he said casually. "No doubt you would appreciate a break from all of this."

Amanda's brows shot up. "I can't leave the shop unattended. Not only am I the only one here, I would be more comfortable discussing business at the bank. Why aren't you having lunch with your wife?" Before he could answer, she said, "We are not in Telluride anymore, Albert, or Ophir town. People would talk, even though there is nothing to talk about."

After a small pause, Albert said, "My wife is in Ophir Loop…at your hotel…visiting my daughter. Does that surprise you? It certainly surprised me." He flashed back on the night Geneva told him she was going there; how fiercely they'd argued about it; what a shrew she had become of late.

"I would like to talk to her when she gets back"—Amanda moved a step closer—"find out how the hotel is doing, how Clara is doing. Could we have lunch when she returns?" She arched her brows. "The three of us?"

Albert hesitated. "Let me think on that." He put his hat back on and started for the door. Before opening it, he turned to her. "Would you like me to bring you something to eat?"

Amanda shook her head. "That is thoughtful of you, Albert, however, everything I need is right here."

Dining alone at a café near the bank, Albert

reminisced about the two years he'd known Amanda;
how he'd invented reasons to spend time in San Miguel
County where he was far enough removed from
Montrose he could be seen with her in public. He
remembered how heads turned when she entered a
room, and what a thrill it was to be the man at her side.
He'd felt that way about Geneva after marrying her. He
liked to watch his cowboys squirm while they
pretended not to be ogling his wife's breasts and wild
blonde hair. Now that he was a man of money and
property, a woman like her seemed frivolous, even with
her hair tamed in a roll on the back of her head.

Ever since his first conversation with Amanda, a
lengthy one lasting well into the night, he'd wanted to
know what it felt like to bed a woman so nearly his
equal. It was a fantasy that bedeviled him for months
until finally, after no indication of interest on her part,
he soothed his torment by telling himself a man his age
was better off having an affair of the mind. Besides,
none of the women he'd known during his fifty-three
years had matched his fantasies.

Finished with his lunch, Albert took his time
walking to the bank and up the two flights of stairs to
his office. While going through his mail, his thoughts
strayed to the afternoons and evenings he'd spent with
Amanda, and the longer he thought about her, the more
convinced he was that her business savvy was what
interested him most—an instinct for buying and selling
that was almost as flawless as her face. He stopped
short of gilding the lily, however, when over a glass of
sherry that evening he wondered if he would have that
same level of respect if she were a man.

Chapter Forty Nine

Geneva had blown through the hotel like a dust devil, stirring up residents and making Hannah mad enough to quit the following week. The announcement took Clara by surprise. Although Hannah had snubbed Geneva after their heated argument, she hadn't indicated anything was wrong until the day she resigned. The reason she gave was that she was moving to Norwood to live with her son and daughter-in-law. Hannah was in her sixties, and moving in with her son made sense, however, Clara questioned the timing of her decision.

She presented the testy but reliable woman with a new apron and a smiling fair-thee-well before her cook walked out the back door for the last time. After the door closed, Clara sank to her knees, eyes brimming with tears as she scanned the room that was soon to be her prison. She knew the kitchen well: skillets, pots, and cooking implements hung from an overhead beam that ran down the center. On the wall near the back entrance was a stone fireplace where she and Hannah did some of the cooking over hot coals. To the right, against the wall separating the kitchen from the dining room, sat the double deck wood-burning stove. Larger than most, it had a restaurant-sized oven below the cooktop as well as two warming ovens mounted above, one on either side of the stovepipe.

To the left, a row of windows cast light on a three-foot-long cutting board. Crosshatched with knife marks, the board sat on a counter running the length of the window wall. Under the counter, a curtain hid the slop bucket, washbasins, cleaning supplies, and miscellaneous culinary staples stored in bins and crocks.

"How will I ever manage all of this?" she said as if Hannah were there to tell her.

It was coming onto noon. She stood up, dried her eyes, and weighed options for lunch. She always kept canned oysters on hand, and there was plenty of milk and butter in the cellar, so she decided to make oyster soup. That, along with yesterday's whole wheat bread and leftover spice cake would have to do. Before moving into the hotel, Clara usually baked batter breads for her family. If she had yeast, she saved it for the kneaded bread she made Saturday for Sunday supper. Now, especially without Hannah, she would be baking some kind of bread every day—biscuits for breakfast, bread for sandwiches, rolls for supper, and cakes, cookies, and pies for dessert.

She poured half a gallon of milk in a pot and set it on the stove. She stared into the whiteness, waiting for the milk to heat while mulling over the two and a half days that had turned her world upside down. Stirring continuously to make sure the milk didn't burn, she remembered Geneva, newly married and trying to bake biscuits in a Dutch oven, muttering, cursing at times, when the clumps of dough came out burned on the bottom and raw in the middle. She and Aunt Lou had laughed about it.

Clara experienced failures of her own while

learning to bake at a high altitude: dough that wouldn't rise, yeast that died, bread with so many holes in it there wasn't any place to spread the butter. Her stepmother's cooking gradually improved while their relationship did not. Perhaps she should have been more tolerant of Geneva back then, but at the moment, furious over losing Hannah and dreading what that meant, Clara never wanted to see her former friend again.

She added oysters to the milk and simmered them a short time before ladling the soup into bowls. Her guests ate the soup, bread, and cake with gusto. After lunch, Sophie and Yoshiro washed the dishes. When they finished, Clara explained how their work would be divided with Hannah gone. Since she would be cooking night and day, they would have to do all of the cleaning. She told them her children would be doing more, too. She gave Charley the job of mucking stalls, and put Bert in charge of feeding the chickens and gathering eggs. Emily had been doing a little cooking. Now she would have to do more.

To compensate Sophie and Yoshiro for the extra hours they would be putting in, Clara gave them small raises. When she realized their raises totaled less than she'd been paying Hannah, she stopped fuming about Geneva and focused instead on the money she was saving.

****

Clara fell behind on some of her other responsibilities such as getting after Mr. Wickham to pay his rent. Every month, she told him when rent was due and how much he owed. After that she lost track of him. Occasionally, a chance sighting would catch him dawdling somewhere, smoking a cigarette as far down as his fingers would allow.

"Yessum," he'd say when she reminded him. Then he would give her half a dozen promises made through a thin display of tobacco-stained teeth. She was certain the assayer would never pay up.

One cold night in November, he entered the dining room, giddy with rum. It took him a minute to get his bearings before he stumbled up to the sideboard and filled his plate. Eyeballing the crowded room, he saw an empty chair at the miners' table. "Make way for a cappytalist, boys!" he sputtered as he plopped onto the chair next to Mr. Kearney.

Conversation in the dining room stopped. Not a fork moved as all eyes rolled toward the sloppy drunk sitting at the miners' table. "Pure sulphuret of silver!" Mr. Wickham bellowed, slurring his esses. "Bet you gents throw them rocks cloggin' your rocker away." He let out a boozy guffaw and jabbed an elbow into Mr. Kearney's side.

Mr. Kearney jabbed him back. "Hobble your lip, little feller, or you could get yerself killed." The miners exchanged glances, and then Mr. White leaned across the table with a pretentious smile for the cappytalist. "You can tell us, though. We got our *own* claim." He examined Mr. Wickham as if seeing him for the first time. "This just happen today? Who hired you? Where'd he find it?"

Suddenly less boisterous, Mr. Wickham brooded over his plate. When Mr. Kearney asked him what pure sulphuret of silver looked like, he said, "Like ordinary rocks. Kinda blue…kinda black."

Barely speaking above a whisper, the miners

grilled Mr. Wickham for several minutes without the assayer disclosing who brought the ore for testing or where it had been discovered. When his eyes glazed over, Mr. Kearney bumped him with his shoulder, and instead of waking up, Mr. Wickham slumped face forward onto the table, vomiting as he fell.

Both miners leaped out of their chairs. Several people sitting nearby did the same. "Damn fool!" Mr. White sputtered. "Shouldn't drink if he can't hold it."

Mr. Kearney glowered at the scrawny man passed out on the table. "He's such a skinflint. Hard to believe he spent enough money to get drunk."

"I'm thinkin' it was the hooch talkin'," said Mr. White. "Little man talkin' big. Maybe he'll drown in his own juice."

Hearing the commotion, Clara left the kitchen, turning on her heel as soon as she saw what had happened. In seconds, she was back with a mop. She cleaned up the vomit, and then returned with a pan of water and a rag. She washed Mr. Wickham's face, helped him to his room, and dumped him across his bed, making sure to lock his door when she left.

The assayer didn't go to his office the next day; nor did he come downstairs for meals. Sober and somewhat contrite when Clara checked on him a day later, he told her the story he was dying to tell someone; how he'd thought the rocks were worthless at first and gone weak in the knees when he saw the test results. "Before I gave the fellow the results, I told him I'd buy half his claim. We shook on it, and half a day later he led me to an entire hill of the precious ore." He gave Clara a wolfish grin. "I may not be rich right this minute, but I will be."

Clara folded her arms across her chest. "If you have the money to buy valuable land, then you must have enough to pay what you owe in rent. How soon can I expect you to settle your account?"

Mr. Wickham's grin disappeared. Clara worried he would, too, until he walked into the kitchen the next day and handed her a certificate for one hundred shares of Silver Bell mining stock. "I've been buying these for years." He eyeballed the certificate one last time before signing it over to her. "This should take care of what I owe and then some."

Clara had to bite her lip to keep from smiling. "Where will you be living?" she asked, thinking she might have to hound him for what he owed if the stock turned out to be worthless.

"A long way away from here," he said with the wariness of a rich man living in mining territory. In less than an hour he packed up his belongings and left.

That afternoon, Clara lit a lamp in the parlor and showed the stock certificate to Jonas. "Is it real?" She held the certificate up to the light.

Jonas read the signatures at the bottom. "I'm not an expert, but it looks real to me."

"Do you know where I can sell it?"

"Why would you want to sell it? It'll be worth more if you hang onto it."

Clara shook her head. "Half of this belongs to Amanda. After I pay her what she's owed, I'll save the balance."

"You might think about using some of it to hire a new cook."

"You don't like my cooking?" She gave Jonas a playful smile.

He smiled back, loving her with his eyes. "You're a splendid cook, Clara, but you're at it constantly."

Clara's eyes wandered to the parlor window and the grayness hovering outside. "We'll be snowed in again soon. I don't want to hire somebody who just wants a job that's warm."

"You're making excuses."

"I can handle the work, Jonas." She put on her business face. "More importantly, I am the one in charge here."

Jonas studied the determined set of Clara's mouth and the way she sat on the edge of her chair, shoulders squared, ready to argue with him if necessary. How he loved this woman, especially when she asserted herself. Did he dare ask her to marry him? If he didn't marry her, he'd have to move. Lately he'd been having trouble sleeping during the day, knowing she was on the floor below, slaving in the kitchen.

"If we were married, I could be of some help to you."

Clara's heart gave a jerk. Although Jonas was smiling, she could tell he was serious. She tried to remain serious, too, but her face betrayed her by turning red. "My divorce isn't final for months." She put her hands on her cheeks to cool them.

Just then Emily walked into the parlor. "Your rolls are done, Mother, and I need to use the oven."

Clara gave her daughter a blissful smile. "Be a dear and take them out for me. Mr. Beale and I are discussing something important."

Emily heaved a sigh and hurried off. As soon as she was out of earshot, Jonas said, "We could get married in New Mexico Territory. Marriage and divorce laws are more lenient there."

"Oh, Jonas!" Clara was pink-faced and beaming. A titter in her stomach bubbled into laughter. "My pa did the same thing when he married Geneva."

Jonas knelt down on one knee. This made Clara laugh even harder. "Stop!" she said between giggles, "you're being outlandish!" He brought Clara's hand to his lips and kissed it, and when he looked up at her, he saw a glow in her eyes that said yes.

Chapter Fifty

Right away Jonas urged Clara to make plans. She told him she needed more time. "I need to make sure the children are safe if we leave them alone. On top of that, someone has to cook while we're gone."

"Don't be too picky," Jonas said every time she mentioned the cooking. "Your boarders won't revolt over a few mediocre meals."

Clara couldn't make up her mind, and in the middle of her muddle, she mailed the Silver Bell stock certificate to Montrose, along with a letter asking her father to sell it for her. *I hope the stock has value. Whatever it turns out to be worth, please give Amanda fifty percent of the proceeds, and put my half in a savings account at your bank.*

Albert was pleased to have an excuse to see Amanda again. It had been two months since she'd turned him down for lunch. He decided to drop by her shop with her share of the money, arriving about the time she normally went home. She was gracious, as always, astonished when he handed her the money. "How did Clara manage this?"

"She made no mention of it." Albert noticed how delicately Amanda held the money, not clutching it the way a more desperate person might. She counted the bills delicately, as well. "Will you be coming to the bank to deposit this?"

Amanda shook her head. "I have another use in mind. Please thank Clara for her efforts. I intend to write and ask how she got Mr. Wickham to pay." There was a hint of frost in her voice when she added, "I have to close my shop now, Albert."

Albert fidgeted with the brim of his hat. "I trust the amount is correct?"

"Absolutely. More than I thought I would ever see." Her eyes moved from the banker's gray-tinged whiskers, to his starched collar, wool overcoat, and perfectly creased trousers before returning to his face. "I am sorry, Albert, but I must ask you to leave. I have been here all day."

"If the amount is correct, is something else wrong?"

Amanda opened her cash register and placed the money inside. "I met your wife."

For a fraction of a second Albert let down his guard. "I see," he said, envisioning what might have taken place. Not wanting to hear the details, he affected a half-hearted smile. "Well then, I am pleased I was able to surprise you with the money you were owed." He put his hat back on, nodded a formal goodbye, and left.

****

The encounter Amanda mentioned to Albert wasn't his wife's first visit to the shop. Geneva had purchased a pair of gloves there when it first opened, and would have been a regular customer if she hadn't stopped by the First National Bank a few days later and seen the shop owner and Albert sitting at his desk, he looking at her as if she were his favorite dessert.

His wife's second visit came soon after she

returned from Ophir Loop, and this time she hadn't gone there to shop. Since Amanda was with a customer, Geneva walked over to a display of purses where her eyes rested on a beaded portmanteau. She picked up the small purse and opened the clasp, visualizing her own comb and mirror in the folds of the satin lining. Then she remembered why she was there, and put the purse back down.

Every few seconds she stole a glance at the beauty who was trying to steal her husband. As soon as the customer left the shop, Geneva walked to the counter where the cash register sat. "I'm not here to buy anything," she said before Amanda even had a chance to say hello. "Do you have designs on my husband?"

Amanda knitted her perfect brows. "Who are you? And how dare you make such an accusation!"

Face pale, hands clenched at her sides, Geneva stood her ground. "I am Albert Wallin's wife. How do you feel about that?"

"Feel? I feel nothing." Amanda scrutinized her accuser. Everything about the woman, from her combative attitude to the gaudy brooch at her throat, bespoke a lack of refinement. "I've seen you someplace," she said. "I never would have guessed you to be Albert's wife. Why have you waited this long to confront me?"

Geneva lifted her chin. "I didn't know what was going on until I saw you with him…in his office."

"What were we doing…in his office?"

"You were sitting beside him on the wrong side of his desk. You should have been sitting across from him."

"We were probably going over a real estate

contract. The wording in those pages can be confusing. Albert told me his wife went to Ophir Loop a while back. Was that also after you saw me in his office?"

"Yes. I knew he'd stayed at your hotel. More than once."

"And that is the sum of your case?" Amanda regarded Geneva with cold speculation. "You've gone to a lot of trouble for nothing, Mrs. Wallin. I do not have designs, as you put it, on your husband. I don't plan to marry again, and if I were to change my mind about that, I wouldn't choose Albert."

Geneva's face went scarlet. "Why not?" she squeaked. She backed up a few steps, then a few steps more. Then she scooted for the door, jangling the bells on her way out.

The next day she wrote Clara a bread-and-butter letter, more note than letter, thanking her for her hospitality. She ended with, *I pray you will never tell your pa what you and I talked about while I was in Ophir Loop. Albert is the best man in all of Colorado.*

Chapter Fifty-One

Every night before going to bed, Clara donned a shawl and lit a lantern for a dutiful trip to the second floor of the hotel. With no wall sconces up there, the hallway was dark except for the glow of her lantern and the strips of light under the doors that snuffed out one by one as the hour grew late. There was never a light under Jonas's door. While passing his room, she wondered what he was doing at that moment and pictured him sitting on a boulder, or a log, guarding a cave-like opening blacker than night. Sometimes she imagined him in front of the same opening, flailing his arms and stamping his sturdy leather boots to get warm.

Clara had never been to a mine, let alone the Silver Bell. If she had, she would have known the mine Jonas guarded was a huge hole in the ground covered by a shaft house, not a cave. She wasn't interested in mining, nor had she been attracted to the night watchman when she began stopping by his table nearly a year ago. She just wanted to talk.

She'd begun by asking simple questions—how he liked his meal, where he was from, why he moved to Colorado, what he liked to do in his spare time. She learned he was from Missouri (Mizzura being his way of saying it), raised on a farm where he walked behind a plow and milked cows. He was seventeen when he got his first paying job as boiler stoker on a riverboat. He'd taken up carpentry during his twenties, and moved to Colorado in his early thirties, hoping to find silver.

"Did you find any?" she'd asked him.

"Didn't find a lick on my own. I was lucky, though. Got a job at the Tomboy mine. Every man I knew wanted to work there. I spent eight years in that godforsaken place, most of it in the dark—dark when I went to work, dark in the belly, dark when my shift ended. I had another stroke of luck when the night watchman job opened up at the Silver Bell."

Clara gave him a wry smile. "Working in the dark again."

"During my shift, yes." He studied her face for a hint of scorn. "I prefer the night shift, Mrs. Reese. The foreman leaves me alone, and I don't have big shots looking over my shoulder. When I work nights I get to see the sun every day."

Another time she stopped by his table, she asked, "What does a watchman watch for, Mr. Beale?"

He laughed, and the rounds of his cheeks hid the lines under his eyes. "Theft, mostly. I give every miner a once-over at the end of the shift—no smiles…no nattering…let them know I mean business. Once in a while I go through their lunch pails."

"Is theft a problem?"

"It would be, if the men thought they could get away with it. There could also be trouble from outsiders. I listen for strange noises and keep a shotgun handy."

At first Jonas thought Clara was stopping to chat with him because it was part of her job. Then she asked more personal questions—what books he'd read, his opinion of them, whether he'd ever been involved in a serious relationship—and he wasn't accustomed to that kind of attention. He started watching her more closely. She gave the impression of plainness until she smiled. When she smiled, she was quite appealing. There was sureness in the set of her shoulders when she walked into a room, and he could tell by the graceful way she moved that she came from good breeding. Her daytime uniform was an ankle-length dark skirt, simple blouse, always pale in hue, and a long white apron. He remembered seeing her in a dress once, a green one that called attention to her gray-green eyes. Regardless of what color she wore, he saw wisdom and compassion in those eyes.

To Jonas, women were sweet-smelling creatures subject to fainting spells or tears, concerned about frivolous things and fragile as porcelain dolls. His mother had been that kind of woman, obsessed with manners and other people's opinions. His father had been patient and affectionate, a man who gave his wife a wink or a pat on the bottom every time he came in from the field, his father's way, Jonas realized later, of connecting with a woman who didn't find much joy in life.

Watching those little displays of affection, Jonas grew up thinking flirting was natural. It was casual, noncommittal, and it almost always produced a smile or a giggle, and rarely, but blessedly, something more intimate. Still a bachelor at forty-five, he would have married one of those sweet-smelling creatures, fragile or otherwise, if women hadn't been scarce in every place he ended up working.

He believed Clara was everything he hoped for in a wife—nice figure, even after bearing children, excellent cook, kindhearted—to him and everyone else—and from what he'd seen over the past year, no porcelain doll weaknesses. If only she would stop dragging her feet when it came to marrying him!

His work schedule prevented him from spending much time with her, although they talked for a few minutes in the parlor every night before he ate supper, and she always wished him well before he left for work. Standing in the hotel entry, or on the porch if it wasn't snowing, they exchanged endearments, sometimes a kiss, and frequently Jonas mentioned New Mexico, teasing her about her Victorian notions of propriety.

"You had enough gumption to file for divorce. Seems to me that would be the hard part. Who's keeping track of when you filed, other than you and me? Maybe Vincent, though I rather doubt he's counting the days."

"What about the person who marries us?" Clara asked. "He will know."

"He won't care. All he wants is his fee."

"What about the witnesses?"

"Hell, Woman. They probably just want to feel like good citizens for a minute or two."

Clara walked to the other side of the mahogany reception desk and began thumbing through the guest register. "You realize if we were to marry I would have two husbands at the same time." She flipped through the pages of the register so quickly she couldn't possibly be reading them.

He stopped her by grabbing her hand. "You'll only be married on paper…and in two different states. It's not as if you'll be sleeping with both of them." He chuckled at the sight of Clara's gaping mouth. "Only me."

****

Jonas was changing into his work clothes one afternoon, hoping for another night at work with no snow, when his thoughts were interrupted by a cry of surprise. It came from the turnaround below his window. He peered outside and saw Clara standing next to a delivery wagon. A stranger wearing a gray planter's hat was climbing down from the seat.

He finished buttoning his pants and hurried downstairs. "I heard you shout." He approached Clara and the stranger. "Is everything all right?" He shaded his eyes for a better look at the man.

Clara put on a cheerful smile. "Jonas…this is Vincent. You've heard me speak of him." The two men shook hands, Vincent looking intently at Jonas, whose eyes were wide with surprise. "The shout you heard was when I found out he'd brought me my sewing machine." She pointed to a bulky item wrapped in a blanket in the bed of the wagon. "I had to leave it in Durango a while back."

"How long did it take you to get here?" she asked Vincent.

"Two and a half days." His eyes remained on the man with the salt and pepper beard.

Nobody spoke until Jonas, reading the anguish on Clara's face, asked Vincent if he needed help unloading the machine.

Vincent shook his head. "Naw, I got it handled." But he made no move to do so.

Jonas felt a prickle in his armpits. "No doubt the two of you have a lot to talk about, and I need to get some supper before I go to work." He started toward the hotel, but before he'd gone six steps, he turned around. "Will I see you tomorrow?" he asked Vincent.

Vincent looked at Clara who was looking at the ground. He shrugged.

Jonas made his way to the kitchen and helped himself to the rabbit stew simmering on the stove. He carried his bowl to his usual table and ate in stony silence. That night his twelve-hour shift felt like twenty as he walked the path he'd worn around the perimeter of the mine, checking the hands on the shaft house clock every time he passed the entrance. Numb to the cold biting his face, his mind was elsewhere. Had Clara known her husband was coming? Would she change her mind about divorcing him when they were alone? Would her heart melt when she saw him with their children? Could he, Jonas Aloysius Beale, be this close and have the only woman he ever loved snatched from his arms?

****

Back at the hotel the next morning, he cautiously opened the front door and stood in the entry for a moment before walking through the dining room to the kitchen. Cheered by the smell of frying bacon, he was relieved by the sight of his beloved tending the skillet, and nobody he recognized in the dining room.

Clara seemed unruffled and unchanged, still the woman in charge. He filled his plate with bacon and scrambled eggs and plopped two pieces of toast next to them. She poured herself a cup of coffee and followed him into the dining room.

"How did it go?" he asked the minute she sat down. The stress lines on his forehead deepened as he waited for her reply.

"As well as could be expected. He didn't ask me to reconsider. He said, 'I know you're done with me. I just want you to remember something good about me.'"

"Is he still here?"

"Yes, he's leaving as soon as he readies the wagon."

They sat in silence, Jonas eating his breakfast while Clara drank coffee.

"I have to think about lunch," she said when the silence went on too long.

Jonas reached across the table and took her hand. "How do you feel about all this?"

Clara returned his gaze. "I'm a bit sad, actually. Vincent and I were married for thirteen years. He bought that sewing machine with money he made skinning wolves. He says he's a new man, but I smelled alcohol on him as soon as he climbed down from the wagon." She gave Jonas an encouraging smile. "You needn't worry, I'm not going to run off with him." *She* was worried, though, about Vincent. He didn't look healthy. His face had a sallow cast to it, and the whites of his eyes were dull.

Chapter Fifty-Two

"How long will it take us to get there and back?" she asked Jonas a few days after Vincent's visit.

"Three days, if we hurry." His heartbeat quickened as he took her in his arms. Gazing into her eyes, he kissed the tip of her nose. "Are you sure you're ready to do this naughty thing?"

Clara blushed. "With school starting again, Miss Nelson is here to watch the children. I've been asking around, and I found a former chuck wagon cook in Ophir to cover for me." She raised her brows. "Can you be gone from work for three days?"

"If I can't, I'll quit." He lifted her up and twirled her around. "Thank God you've come to your senses!"

Jonas had worked with his boss for years, both with him and for him, but he'd have to find someone to work his shift before he dare ask for time off. He asked Lars, since they'd traded shifts in the past, and though Lars couldn't do it, one of his cousins could. Jonas got a commitment for three days off without pay, and then he and Clara finalized plans.

The temporary cook was at the hotel before breakfast the morning they were to leave for the New Mexico Territory. "I never did nothin' like this," the man said when Clara walked him through the dining room to the kitchen. "Remember...I told you I can't cook the fancy stuff." His unreadable eyes moved from the fireplace to the stove to the counter along the window wall. He unhooked a frying pan from the beam above the stove, turning it over to inspect the bottom. "Where's the fixin's?" he asked.

Clara showed him the staples she kept under the counter, and set out what he needed for biscuits. Then she led him downstairs for a quick look at the pantry, including the bread and cookies she'd baked, more than enough to last the three days he'd be there.

She scrutinized the man while he stirred together a batch of biscuits, thinking, *if he changes his mind, I'll strangle him*. She sighed with relief when his biscuits turned out fluffy and brown. He was whistling and frying sausage when Emily walked into the kitchen.

"This is good coffee," he said, lifting his cup.

"My daughter Emily can show you how to make it. You will find her quite helpful."

Two days before she and Jonas were to leave, Clara had told her children she and Mr. Beale were getting married, and they'd accepted the news with less resistance than she expected. Their primary concern was sleeping arrangements.

"Does this mean I have to share a room with Charley and Bert?" Emily asked.

Charley frowned. "I'm twelve, Mother. Do I have to have her in my room? Bert doesn't want to share, either...do you, Bert."

Bert, six, gave his brother a whole-hearted grin and nod. "Will we have to mind Mr. Beale, Mama?"

"You have to mind him like you would any adult. You don't know him as well as I do, but you will find him to be kind."

To avoid ruffling feathers, Clara put Emily in the

room that had been the office. When it was time to leave, she hugged her children goodbye. Still doubting the hotel could run without her, she put on her wool cape, picked up her satchel, and joined Jonas on the front porch. Although it was May, and most of the snow had melted, it was still cold.

A light mist speckled their faces during the ride to Ophir town where they were to take the train to Durango, stay overnight, and cover the final forty miles to New Mexico Territory the next day by whatever means they could find. It was raining when they boarded the train. Raindrops the size of lemon drops hammered the roof over their heads while they took their seats.

"I will probably fret the whole time we're gone," Clara said, five minutes into the trip.

Jonas squeezed her arm. "Don't ruin our time together with worry." The rumbling wheels and pounding rain nearly drowned out his words. He reached into his jacket pocket and brought out a piece of paper folded in thirds. "This is where we'll be staying." He unfolded an advertisement for the Strater Hotel and laid it across Clara's lap.

"The Strater Hotel? What a wonderful surprise!" She picked up the flyer for a closer look, remembering how impressed she was the first time she saw the hotel. "I used to wonder what it would be like to stay in such a place every time I walked into town." Clara smiled blissfully, and the smile stayed on her face for such a long time, Jonas credited her with chasing the rain away when the sun broke through the clouds halfway to Durango.

He carried their small bags from the train station to

the hotel. "You're spoiling me," Clara whispered the instant she and her husband-to-be set foot in the grand lobby of the Strater Hotel. Jonas left for a moment to sign the register, and Clara made a slow circle around the high-ceilinged room, taking in every detail from the gas lamp chandeliers to the hand-loomed carpet.

"It's like a palace," she said to Jonas when he returned.

Savoring his small victory, he grinned so hard his whiskered cheeks nearly covered his eyes. "A fitting place for my queen." He passed his arm through hers, guiding her up to the third floor where they lingered in front of Clara's room. They held hands for a moment, engaging in sweet talk rather than sharing a kiss in such a public place.

"This is the last night you will be sleeping anywhere but next to me." Jonas unlocked her door and handed her the key.

What he said and how he said it sent a shiver through Clara's core. "I know that," she whispered, "and I will fully embrace the company." Standing in the doorway, they hugged one another, gazing into each other's eyes until a rustle of skirts, coupled with fragments of conversation drifting down the hall, caused them to part. A man and woman passed by, and then Jonas gave Clara a peck on the cheek. "This will have to do until tomorrow, sweet lady." He winked at her before walking down the hall to his room.

Clara had a hard time sleeping that night on a strange mattress in a strange room. Listening to the street sounds echoing from below, she looked up at the ceiling, wondering if Vincent had painted it. Perhaps he'd papered the walls...or the hallway outside the door. She debated calling on his Uncle Jacob and Aunt Grace. They still kept in touch, but if she called on them, she'd have to explain why she was in Durango. There wasn't time for a visit, anyway. She and Jonas had to keep moving.

As soon as it was light enough to see the ruts in the road the next morning, they rented a double buggy and two horses for the trip across the border. Jonas was handsomely garbed in a navy blue suit with a blue and gray striped waistcoat, and Clara wore a close-fitting beige linen dress she'd sewn for the occasion. The soon-to-be-married couple welcomed the sunshine warming their hands and faces as they drove south.

A wake of dust boiled behind their buggy as they sped to Aztec, the closest town in the New Mexico Territory that had a Justice of the Peace. The air grew warmer with every mile they traveled. Jonas took off his jacket an hour after they left Durango. He stopped at a stage station halfway to Aztec. There, he changed teams and removed his vest. Clara had to suffer the whole trip in her corset.

Arriving in the clump of ramshackle buildings known as Aztec, Jonas helped Clara down from the buggy. She brushed off the powdery layer of dust that had accumulated on her dress during the morning's race to get there. "Which of these buildings do you suppose is the courthouse?" she asked Jonas. "None of them look impressive."

"No signs on any of them, either," he added.

A scruffy man holding a shotgun appeared in the doorway of one of the houses. "Whadda you want?"

Jonas didn't move a muscle. "We're looking for the Justice of the Peace," he said, trying to sound friendly. "We're here to get married." The man lowered his shotgun. Pointing to a trail running north, he said, "Follow that road a mile or so. That's where his farm is."

Jonas and Clara got back into the buggy, losing precious time as they drove into the countryside. After two wrong stops, they found the right farm. The man who was to marry them had to change out of his coveralls, and then they followed him to a rundown building he said was the courthouse. Two people who worked there signed the certificate of marriage as witnesses to the brief ceremony.

There was only one public place to eat in the dusty little community; thus Jonas and Clara's wedding supper consisted of bacon, prunes, and boiled potatoes. They ate in less time than it had taken the Justice of the Peace to marry them, and when finished, they hustled back to Durango, arriving at the Strater Hotel after dark.

Clara hugged Jonas's arm on the way to the room he'd slept in the night before. Jonas lit the lamp, while his wife ducked behind a folding screen to change into her nightdress. The thought of finally sharing a bed with her was blissfully painful, yet he had to wait a few minutes longer for her to undress.

A few feet away, Clara heard the jingle of coins as Jonas slid out of his trousers. Then she heard the clunk of his leather belt hitting the hardwood floor, followed by the squeak of the bed springs. She unlaced her corset and changed into a lightweight muslin gown. In her haste to undress, she forgot to loosen her hair. She slipped from behind the screen, pulled back the bed covers, and climbed in next to Jonas. He shook his head as if scolding a child, pulled her closer, and removed the hairpins.

His heart lurched at the sight of her hair falling in dark brown waves around her shoulders. He pulled her toward him, exploring her uncorseted body through the gauzy fabric of her gown. She pressed her face into his neck and breathed maleness tinged with sweat. She raised her head to meet his gaze, and he kissed her, lightly at first, then with growing intensity. She lifted the front of her gown and quickly discovered that the man who'd been courting her for over a year was as passionate under the covers as he was about the books he read.

Chapter Fifty-Three

Few lamps still burned in the hotel when the newlyweds returned to Ophir Loop. Jonas fell asleep the minute his head touched the pillow. Clara lay awake, worrying about occupancy. She felt it was extravagant to have family in three rooms on the first floor, especially since the room Jonas previously occupied was empty. She slept better after she rented the upstairs room to a Pinkerton man who'd been hired to keep an eye on the miners' union.

Sharing a room created problems Jonas and Clara hadn't anticipated; space, for one. Jonas's books and other personal items combined with Clara's trunk and sewing machine left barely enough space to move. Working opposite halves of the day disrupted their sleep to such an extent that Jonas switched shifts, spending his days underground again rather than nights up top, and wielding a pick and shovel instead of a shotgun.

****

While rooms were being shuffled at the hotel and the newlyweds were settling into a new routine, changes were also taking place in Montrose. In July, Clara received a letter from her father in which he appeared to take the news of her second marriage better than he had the first. *Even though I have not met the man*, Albert wrote, *the fact you have a partner again means a better chance at success in life for my grandchildren.* Then he continued with news of his own. *Montrose seems dead to me now after visiting California. The glorious climate out there is luring people to Los Angeles County in droves. I regret not saying goodbye to you or meeting your new husband, however, I am eager to leave this town. Geneva has already packed her trunk.*

I will lease my house in Montrose. I never sell. Property always appreciates in the long run. I should do quite well in California's real estate market.

I have rented a suitable house in Pasadena, near where I plan to build. My new house will have indoor plumbing. The water closet is already on its way from England.

He wrote again in December, his Christmas card displaying a watercolor painting of a palm tree. That February, he sent Clara and her family a crate of oranges. Clara hadn't eaten an orange since she left Philadelphia, and her children had never seen one. Bert picked up one of the oranges and sniffed it, grimacing when he bit into the rind. He handed the piece of fruit back to his mother.

"You have to peel it," Clara told him. "It's not like an apple or pear." She peeled the orange, and gave each child a section. All three faces lit up when they tasted the juicy pulp, and after a nod of approval from their mother, three hands reached into the crate for an orange of their own. Clara ate the one she'd peeled. Closing her eyes, she savored the fruit's tart sweetness, pleased to have something fresh and natural to share with the baby in her womb. She remembered how her mother used to put little treats in her Sunday shoes—candy, nuts, and sometimes an orange. What a wonderful childhood she'd had compared to her own children growing up in a hotel in Ophir Loop.

Clara gave each of her employees an orange, another one to Yoshiro on his sixteenth birthday. Yoshiro shared his birthday orange with his parents, hoping to soften them up when he told them he was getting a job in one of the mines, with or without their blessing. The young man's voice cracked with emotion when he broke the news to Clara. "I quit today, Missus," he said as darkness fell on his last day at the hotel. Yoshiro lowered his closely barbered head and politely waited for her response.

Clara was too shocked to say anything. Then she praised him to the stars and offered him a bigger raise. He shook his head, still avoiding her eyes. She offered him one day off a week. Yoshiro looked up briefly, then down at the floor again. "Mine makes more money."

Trembling at the thought of losing her most valuable employee, Clara thought she might faint. Exhausted, pregnant, feeling emotionally betrayed, she somehow managed to hold back the groan in her throat. She knew she couldn't match what the mines offered, and she'd lived in Ophir Loop long enough to know that other than claim-jumping or similar forms of robbery, options for making a decent living there were almost nonexistent. To her, Yoshiro was still a boy, only three years older than Charley. It was hard to imagine him working in the diggings, hundreds of feet underground, dirty and drained at the end of his shift. Like his father. Like Jonas.

Silently resolved, Yoshiro stood firm. Clara paid him what he was owed, and then with a pinched smile, handed him a fresh-baked cinnamon roll when he walked out the back door, hoping he'd think kindly of her and his old job and come back after a week or two of backbreaking labor.

For five days, Jonas watched his wife stubbornly do everything she normally did and Yoshiro's work as well. On day six, after working his shift, he ushered her out to the front porch, opened the front of his parka, and pulled her next to him, wrapping her in his jacket. Holding her close, he volunteered to leave his job at the mine and take over for Yoshiro.

"I can't work as fast as that boy did, but I can look for wood, chop it, haul it, build fires, shovel snow. I can go to Ophir for supplies. I grew up around cows and horses. I can take care of the livestock and everything else that needs to be done outside." His smile glowed white in his dirty face. "And, I can do a few other things—like fix those creaky boards in the stairwell and build you some decent kitchen cupboards."

His enthusiasm spilled from his mouth in tiny puffs of frost. While he waited for Clara to say something, a cloud drifted across the sliver of moon overhead, its shadow darkening the snow-muffled expanse encircling the hotel.

"Yoshiro made far less than your wages," Clara said, mildly amused.

"Wages you aren't paying him anymore, and if we can't get by on what the hotel brings in, I will dip into my savings." Jonas inspected his wife's upturned face. "Twelve hours a day shoveling ore is killing me, Clara, and I'm growing deaf from the pounding of the stamps."

Clara nodded, her face pensive as she tried to

imagine her husband doing Yoshiro's chores. "What about scrubbing pans and helping Sophie with the laundry?" She tilted her head back to see if he could tell she was teasing.

Jonas cleared his throat. "I wouldn't be comfortable doing that. Not if I'm honest about it, but I don't mind mopping floors."

The smile Clara had been holding back spread across her face. "I think we can make this work." She gave Jonas a reassuring squeeze before leaving the warmth of his parka to return to the kitchen.

Even with Jonas doing almost everything Yoshiro used to do, as well as the food shopping, Clara didn't have a minute to relax. There hadn't been an empty room in the hotel since October when the temperature went from cold to frigid and prospectors left their claims in droves, looking for a warm place to sleep and food that didn't freeze on their forks. Word of Clara's cooking had gotten around, and she started keeping the dining room open until nine p.m. Often, she took the last loaves of bread out of the oven near midnight, and then dragged herself out of bed at five a.m. to boil water for coffee and start breakfast.

"You're being reckless," Jonas complained. "Working this hard can't be good for our baby." He rested his hand on the swelling under her nightdress. "I'm telling you right now…if you don't hire another cook, I'm gonna find one for you."

Clara pushed his hand away. "You wouldn't know what to look for."

"People don't expect big city cooking in a place like Ophir Loop. You're spoiling these men, Clara. Me, too." He patted his rounded stomach, a midsection that used to be flat as a young man's. "I know you're tired of hearing me say this, but why not hire that chuck wagon cook? We got no complaints about his cooking when we came back."

"No praises either." Clara rolled onto her side and faced the wall. "I would have to teach him everything I know. That would be more tiring than doing it myself."

"You're making excuses again. I swear you are the stubbornest woman I've ever known."

She toyed with what he said. "I suppose I am a bit possessive when it comes to my cooking, but look at all the money it's bringing in."

"Is it worth the risk of losing our baby?"

****

The next morning, Clara told Jonas to go ahead and hire the chuck wagon cook, and without giving his wife a minute to change her mind, he drove the sleigh to Ophir town. Arriving around noon, he asked at six different shops before he found anyone who knew the man, learning to his profound disappointment that the chuck wagon cook no longer lived there.

He begged Clara to keep searching, and over the next few weeks she interviewed several applicants, all men claiming to have cooked for large groups of people, one even saying he'd been a chef in a hotel restaurant. Remembering what Amanda had told her about job seekers saying they could cook, Clara took a good hard look and rejected every one of them.

"You're being stubborn again," Jonas said.

"I'm not being stubborn. I'm being prudent. Not one of those men had a decent recipe for pie dough."

Clara baked some version of pie every day. Chicken potpie made better use of the meat on a chicken than frying or roasting, and occasionally she wrapped leftover stew or mashed potatoes in crescents of dough, fried them in hot lard, and served them for lunch. She made dessert pies every other day. She preferred fresh fruit pies, but since apples and cherries didn't grow at that altitude, her guests had to settle for raisin, dried apple, vinegar, chocolate, butterscotch, or custard.

Her own recipe (2 c. flour, 3/4 c. lard, a salt spoon of salt, 6 tbsp. of cold water) produced tender, flaky crust at any altitude. After listening to a slew of recipes that sounded more like biscuit dough, she finally hired Thelma O'Connell, a miner's wife with four children. Mrs. O'Connell had been cooking three meals a day for a family of five, and her pie crust recipe was almost identical to Clara's.

"I know how hard it is to work at two jobs," Clara told Thelma after hiring her. "What would you say to taking home what you cook as part of your pay? That way you won't have to cook for your family when you get off work."

Thelma showed a lot of gum when she smiled. "That sounds like a fine arrangement," she said. "Very fitting, Mrs. Beale, very fitting."

Chapter Fifty-Four

The twentieth century was not much more than a babe itself when Clara gave birth to her fifth child. There wasn't a doctor within twenty miles of Ophir Loop, but she knew a nurse in Ophir town, a woman she'd become acquainted with when Charley, Emily, and Bert had measles and whooping cough. In August, sensing her time was near, Clara asked Jonas to drive her to Ophir, hoping the nurse would deliver her baby. Not only did the woman say yes, she opened her home to Clara, cared for her during a difficult delivery, and kept her and the baby for another week.

Jonas named the baby Pearl. The day he brought Clara and their daughter back to the hotel and Sophie tucked them into the clean bed she'd readied for them, his eyes misted over at the sight of his wife and child, Clara in a lace-trimmed nightdress with Pearl nestled in the crook of her arm. He leaned across the bed and kissed his wife on the forehead. He stood up, and took a moment to collect himself, captivated by the child he thought he'd never have. He'd grown fond of Clara's other children, too, and felt a pang of sympathy for their real father.

"What did Vincent do when he saw his kids?" he asked. "He hadn't seen them for…how long was it?"

"Not quite a year," Clara said. "The night Vincent arrived, I told the children to gather in the parlor…that I had a surprise for them. They didn't say much when they saw who was there. Vincent gave them each a hug, and handed Charley a bag of candy. He told him to share it with Emily and Bert, and that brought some smiles."

"Do they ever talk about him? Say they miss him?"

"Not often. He was quite strict. Used a switch if they misbehaved, and not always a small one."

Jonas gazed at Pearl's tiny face. "I can't imagine this little angel ever doing anything bad enough to be punished." After a silence, he added, "Of course I wouldn't lay a hand on any child."

Clara stayed in bed for three more days. With Thelma O'Connell covering for her in the kitchen, she had time to write letters informing everyone in her family of Pearl's birth. Aunt Mid and Lily wrote back right away. Her pa's letter came two months later, one sentence devoted to his newest grandchild, and a page and a half to rapturous descriptions of California and the house he was building.

A second letter from California arrived on the heels of the first, this one from Geneva. Clara read it quickly, hearing the written words as if her former friend was speaking them.

Dearest Clara,

We are finally settled in our new house. How I wish you could see it! It has sixteen rooms. Albert had the workmen tear down two cottages to make space for it. One of our neighbors is the mayor.

Our house is one of the only homes in Pasadena with piped water. Summoning water from a faucet is such a lark. I titter every time I turn the handle and water pours out.

She went on to describe the indoor privy down to the last tile, and signed the letter *Affectionately yours.*

"Dearest Clara? Affectionately yours?" Had Geneva been spending too much time in the California sun? Then Clara read again the part about summoning water, and decided that sounded more like the self-absorbed woman she knew. So did the woman's cunning postscript: *Thank you for keeping your promise, Clara. Albert seems as happy here as I am. I would die if he knew I once doubted him.*

Geneva sent a letter to Clara once a year at Christmas, and Clara did the same. Geneva wrote about the people she'd met and trips she'd taken to San Diego and San Francisco; about beaches, cafes, museums, fountains, and a vast ocean warm enough to swim in. Clara's letters focused on the splendor of the mountains and the pleasures, rather than the hardships, of living in a world where water was always cold and getting it involved a great deal more effort than turning a handle.

"I'm writing to Geneva," she said to Jonas late one night. They were sitting across from one another at the small table in their room. They shared the same lamplight, he reading a book while she wrote. "Can you help me think of something to say?"

Jonas laid his book face down on the table and set his magnifying glass next to it. "What have you written thus far?"

"Most of it's about you." She smiled coyly. "Do you want me to read what I wrote?"

He gave a hoarse chuckle. "Only the good parts."

She covered her mouth to hide her smile. "I won't read all of it." She paused to look over what she'd written. "It's all good. Here's a sample." She held the letter to the lamp. "Besides my children, Jonas is my greatest joy. I am blessed to have him in my life." She stopped reading to catch his reaction.

A loving expression warmed Jonas's face as he reached across the table for her hand.

"I know what you're thinking," she said. "Why doesn't she say that to me when I tell her I love her?"

Jonas tilted his head. "Not exactly what I was thinking, but close."

Clara smiled down at her letter. "I do love you, Jonas, but it's easier for me to write it than say it."

Jonas let go of her hand. "It's easier for both of us to say something romantic when we're not working our fingers to the bone."

****

Running a hotel was a full-time job for both of them, especially in the winter. When the creeks were locked tight, and the children were ice skating on Howard Fork, every room in the hotel was full. When the surrounding streams churned with whitewater, the hotel had fewer overnight guests—more time to relax, pack a picnic lunch, explore on horseback, or go dancing in Ophir town.

The hotel's full-time residents also came and went as the seasons changed. "I swear," Clara grumbled the summer Pearl turned two, "if the names in my ledger keep changing so frequently, I'm going to stop referring to our boarders as permanent."

In the wake of Mr. Wickham's departure, Mr. White and Mr. Kearney cashed in their silver and went home to their wives and families. "At least that's where they said they were going," Clara told Jonas after they left. "I hope they didn't go looking for Mr. Wickham."

Mr. Cogswell left a year later, and in a hurry, after he was robbed at gunpoint while sitting at his desk in the freight depot. His eyes were round as his spectacles when he explained what happened and said goodbye.

Miner after miner rented the rooms these men vacated. Sometimes a low-ranking government official or a railroad work crew stayed for a few weeks, followed by more miners. Miss Nelson's room went from teacher to teacher, none of the young women staying more than two summers at the Ophir Loop School.

Clara had to deal with employee turnover, too. Sophie remained at the hotel until Pearl was three. Then she married a man who worked at the Silver Bell, and exchanged cleaning a hotel for cleaning one of the shacks that made up most of Ophir Loop. Sophie's departure led to a succession of maids and laundresses: Lulu, Mattie, Frieda, Henrietta, and a girl who called herself Blue. Dependable as the creeks rising in June, Thelma stayed on.

Help wasn't easy to find, and as Clara's children grew older, they found themselves cleaning rooms or hanging laundry in between hires. They also contributed to the "board" half of the hotel's room and board. Emily picked wild raspberries growing in sunny parts of the valley every summer. At first she made jam out of them. By the time she was twelve, she was baking raspberry pies.

"Who made this delicious pie?" guests often asked, and Emily, blossoming into womanhood, wasn't shy about stopping whatever she was doing in the kitchen to walk into the dining room and accept the praise.

Jonas took the boys fishing, and taught them how

to use a shotgun. Soon there was trout on the menu in summer and roast goose in the fall. Meat was hard to come by in Ophir Loop, yet tenants and guests expected some form of it every night for supper. To save money, Clara bought beef hearts and tongues from a local farmer and corned them in brine. In about ten days, when the meat was good and spicy, she simmered it for hours, adding potatoes and cabbage for a one-dish meal.

Even the youngest member of the family knew how important it was to make sure the guests had plenty to eat. Pearl was only two and a half when she saw an older gentleman walk into the dining room after breakfast was over. Her mother and Thelma were in the kitchen, chatting over their work. The little brown-eyed girl could tell the women didn't know the man was there, so she got something out of one of the bins under the kitchen counter and took it to him.

"I think someone's in the dining room," Thelma said, hearing conversation on the other side of the wall.

Clara sighed. "I thought we'd fed everybody." Wiping her hands on a towel, she went to investigate and saw an elderly man sitting at one of the tables. He was leaning down, talking to Pearl, and in his hands was a large raw potato. It was a story told around the family table for years.

Pearl was Clara's only brown-eyed child. She'd inherited her eye color from Jonas, and when she was old enough to go outside, she wanted to do everything her father did, such as milk a cow, which she never got the hang of, and grow vegetables, which she did.

Every year, usually sometime in June when the soil thawed enough to get a spade into it, Jonas planted a sizeable garden halfway between the hotel and the creek. At the age of six, Pearl, who Clara and Jonas still called Baby, was doing most of the weeding, helping some with the watering, and picking the produce when it ripened. The growing season was too short in Ophir Loop for tomatoes, but the garden produced enough lettuce, carrots, and radishes to make a few salads. The potatoes, cabbage, turnips, beets, and onions were stored in the cellar and used for months. Clara canned peas, beets, and carrots and made sauerkraut out of some of the cabbage.

"Watch for snakes," she warned Pearl whenever her daughter went outside to work in the garden.

"You don't have to say that every time, Mama. Garter snakes aren't harmful, and Papa shoots the rattlers."

The fence Jonas built around the garden didn't protect it from snakes, however, it did keep out rabbits and skunks. Charley and Bert trapped skunks during the warmer months, not to feed the guests but to make a little money. Bert was eleven, Charley fifteen when they heard about a doctor in Ophir who paid a dollar a pint for skunk oil. To get rid of the odor, they tied the skunk's carcass to a large tree root that grew into the creek. In two days, the flow of the water washed the smell away. Then they took the carcass home, cut the thick layer of fat off the back, boiled it, and poured the rendered oil into jars.

One day they discovered a dead badger in their trap. Bert ran into the hotel, holding the animal by its tail. "Look, Mother," he said, his face glowing with excitement. "We caught a dromedary!"

Clara took the carcass from Bert, holding it at arm's length to avoid the smell of its fur. "This is a badger, not a dromedary. Where in the world did you learn the word dromedary?"

Bert shrugged. "School, I guess. I never saw a picture of one."

Clara searched through Jonas's pile of books and found a copy of *The Arabian Nights*. "You should read this. Your brother too. It doesn't have pictures, but your brain will see the dromedaries in these stories."

Bert showed the book to Charley. Then the two boys skinned the badger, and Clara cut it up for stew, adding bacon and garlic to hide the sweetness of the meat.

****

Charley spent two years trapping skunks before deciding it was time to get a real job. At seventeen he moved to Telluride where he found employment loading ore wagons for the Alta mine. It was backbreaking work, but he was making some real money, far more than he made doing odd jobs around Ophir Loop and selling skunk oil.

Chapter Fifty-Five

The summer of 1910 was warm bordering on hot in the river valleys of Colorado, scorching in the rest of the Midwest. The long stretch of warm days was better than a shot of fertilizer for the hotel's garden, enough so that by the middle of July, Pearl was picking beans every other day, and Jonas was getting ready to cut his second crop of lettuce.

A drummer selling shoes ate three helpings of green beans the night he stayed at the hotel. "Best meal I've had in weeks," he told Clara. "Might I trouble you for an early breakfast tomorrow? I'm hoping to get on the road by dawn."

Jonas rose at four a.m. the next morning to build a fire in the kitchen stove. To accommodate their guest's request, he piled on extra wood so the stove would be hot enough to fry bacon the minute the cook arrived. Then he left for the barn, figuring Thelma would be walking in the back door any minute.

He'd fed and watered the horses and was milking one of the cows when Clara awoke to the smell of smoke. She threw back her covers and dashed to the kitchen where tongues of flame were licking the wall behind the stovepipe. The teakettle atop the stove was screaming. Thelma was trying to put out the fire with the contents of the slop bucket, but each splash produced a pathetic hiss.

"What in heaven's name were you trying to cook?" Clara cried, her heart hammering in her chest.

"Nothing! The wall was already on fire when I got here!" Thelma dropped the empty slop bucket, and eyes wild, looked around the kitchen for something wet. "I was a bit late this morning." Her voice was high and hysterical. "You know I'm never late."

"Don't talk! There should be water in the horse trough. Fill the bucket with it. Hurry!"

Clara rushed to her children's rooms and flung open the doors. "Get up!" she yelled. "The kitchen's on fire! Grab something to wear. Put it on outside. I'll meet you in the turnaround!"

She hurried to her own room, shed her nightdress, and threw on a blouse and skirt, not bothering to put on a corset. Clutching the front of her skirt, she took the stairs two at a time, yelling, "Fire! Fire!" Upstairs, she beat on the doors with her fists, crying, "Wake up! The kitchen's on fire!" and she didn't stop pounding until someone in every room had opened the door.

Tearing back downstairs, she glanced into her children's rooms, and seeing they were empty, she covered her mouth and nose with her arm and dashed to the kitchen for another look at the fire.

Thelma was coming out as she was going in. "It's no use," the cook gasped, wiping her eyes. "I threw a bucket of water on the fire, but it didn't help a bit. Don't go in there. There's too much smoke." Head bent in despair, she pulled a handkerchief out of her pocket and blew her nose.

"Go out to the turnaround, then. Make sure my children are safe. I've got to get Jonas." Clara picked up the front of her skirt again and rushed out the front door, down the steps, and around the side of the hotel to the barn.

"The hotel's on fire!" she shouted.

Jonas bolted to his feet, spilling milk and knocking over his stool. "What in thunderation! What happened?"

He started for the door, but Clara grabbed him by the arm. "It's in the kitchen. Thelma couldn't put it out."

Jonas jerked his arm loose. "Let me try."

"It's too late! There's too much smoke."

"Where's Baby? Where's everybody?" His face was white as his eyeballs.

"Baby's safe. All the children are safe. I rousted the guests, but I have to go back and make sure they get out."

"How did it start?"

"I'm guessing the stovepipe got too hot."

"Oh, God!" Jonas groaned.

"Thelma was late. There wasn't enough water. Stop asking questions and save the animals. Then come help me." She turned around and ran out of the barn. " Hurry!" she cried, midway up the path.

Rounding the corner of the hotel, Clara was relieved to see Thelma and the children in the turnaround. About half of the guests were milling around not far from where they stood. She hurried inside and bumped into two men staggering down the stairs with their feather beds.

"Stop! You're clogging the stairwell!" she shouted.

One of the men peeked his head around the mattress he was carrying. "We're tryin' to help, Ma'am."

"You can help by stopping this nonsense." Clara squeezed by him on her way upstairs.

The men lugged the mattresses to a spot twenty yards or so from the hotel, and then returned to the front porch where they stood outside the door, gawking into the smoke-darkened interior.

"We should form a bucket brigade," one man said.

The other man shook his head. "Even if the creek was right next door, and it ain't, we couldn't reach the roof with it."

Holding a pillowcase over her mouth and nose, Clara appeared in the doorway. "Get out of here!" she screamed. "Why can't you follow directions?" She herded the men off the porch, and then joined Thelma and the children.

"Where's Bert?" she asked Emily.

Emily didn't hear. She was busy watching the satchels, clothes, pillows, and other items guests were throwing out the upstairs windows. A shoe landed a few feet in front of her and Pearl.

Pearl blinked up at her mother. "Our shoes are still in there, Mama. My ice skates…"

"That's not important," Clara snapped. "I asked you a question, Emily. Where's Bert?"

Emily winced as a ceramic water pitcher shattered when it hit the ground. "I don't know. He was here a minute ago."

"He said something about helping out back," Thelma said.

"I swear I will smack that young man when I see him." Clara gripped Emily by the shoulders. "You're too close to the fire. Stand over there next to those stumps. Keep an eye on Baby. I'm going to look for

Bert."

Clara was almost to the front porch steps when she heard the crunch of boots on gravel. Turning, she saw Jonas and Bert racing toward her. "I was helping free the animals," Bert said when he saw the look on his mother's face. Still small for eighteen, he smiled like a boy but his voice was that of a man. "We got 'em all out."

"The cows headed for the creek." Jonas paused to catch his breath. "The horses went to heck knows where."

"That's well and good, but we've got trouble here! The drummer's still upstairs. The couple from Iowa, too. All three are taking too long to pack up their things."

"I'll get them!" Jonas started for the porch.

"Wait!" Clara cried. "Use this!" She tossed him the pillowcase she'd been using to protect her lungs from the smoke.

Jonas was back in a flash with the holdouts, the drummer clutching a carpetbag full of shoes to his chest and the couple from Iowa loaded down with luggage. All four were coughing and gasping for air as they joined the crowd of people in front of the hotel.

Word of the fire had spread quickly. Men wearing caps or miner's helmets dropped whatever they were doing to charge up the stump-covered hill and gawk. Clara spied Yoshiro's face in the crowd. No longer a boy, his small dark eyes held the same haunted look as Jonas had when he worked in the belly of the mine.

As soon as Jonas and Bert joined Clara and the girls, Thelma went home. The family stood apart from the crowd, watching the fire race through the hotel like a train roaring across the Ophir Loop trestle. Smoke generated by the conflagration rose halfway to the clouds. Sparks landed on the outbuildings and burst into flames. One by one, the fire took the barn, the privies, the chicken coop, and the corral. It would have spread to the forest, if every tree on the hill hadn't been felled for fire wood years ago.

Emily and Pearl cried hysterically when the roof of the hotel collapsed. Clara and Jonas stood as if in a trance, their emotions fluctuating from sick-at-heart to thankful-to-be-alive as the raging fire destroyed the hotel they'd come to think of as their own.

"I shouldn't have built such a big fire this morning." Jonas shook his head. "Thelma is never late. Why this of all mornings? I feel lower than a snake's belly right now."

Clara nodded absently, too caught up in her own anguish to respond. *Must tragedy pile on tragedy?* It had been less than two weeks since she'd received a letter from Grace telling her Vincent had died. Perhaps the fire was punishment for not attending his funeral, even though the letter arrived days after he'd been buried. Her breath was coming in shallow gulps as her brain grappled with the frightening images in front of her eyes. She and Jonas had saved enough money for a down payment on the hotel. Amanda hadn't put it up for sale, but Clara was certain she would have sold it to them. Now what were they to do? And what would Amanda say when she found out her hotel had burned down?

Clara wanted to cry with her daughters, keen like a wounded animal, but Jonas was grinding his teeth, and Bert was trying to hide his tears; the whole family couldn't fall apart. Emily was wearing her new straw hat and holding nine-year-old Pearl by the hand. Clara scowled at her older daughter. "I see you saved your hat."

Emily shrank under her mother's glare. Her chin quivered again, and she let go of Pearl's hand. She found another place to stand that wasn't so close to the family.

"I'll take Pearl for a walk," said Bert.

Jonas put an arm around Clara. He raised his face to the rugged rim of mountains surrounding Ophir Loop. "You know," he said pensively, "here it is the middle of July, and we're still surrounded by snow-capped mountains. Every wrinkle on the skin of those mountains carries at least a trickle of water half the year. Those trickles join other trickles, and soon they grow into the streams that crisscross the flat. We've always got plenty of water, yet we couldn't get our hands on enough to save the hotel." Clara nodded glumly, the knot in her throat making it impossible to speak.

Mid-morning, Thelma returned to offer the family lunch and a place to stay. It would be crowded in her two-room cabin, but it was the only option. The children went home with her, leaving Clara and Jonas, standing like statues.

****

Smoke snaked out of the broken beams and debris for days. After the ashes cooled, Clara waded through the ruins, stirring them with her boots, searching for the remains of anything salvageable. The wrought-iron pots and pans made it through. The two fireplaces, now black as coal, still survived, as did the skeletal remains of the cookstove and iron bedsteads. Gone were the mahogany reception desk, the trunk where Clara kept letters and the diary she hadn't written in since Charley was born, Jonas's books, the Singer, every piece of clothing they weren't wearing, and a cellar full of foodstuffs, including six five-gallon cans of honey that cost twelve dollars apiece.

After reinventing herself in a cabin near La Jara, an adobe house in Naturita, a cottage in Durango, a shack in Gunnison, and a hotel in Ophir Loop, Clara was starting all over again.

Part VII

No Rest

Chapter Fifty-Six

Albert was in his wingback chair reading the Sunday edition of the *Pasadena Star* when three raps on the door echoed down the marble hall. He set the paper aside and picked up his rosewood cane, hoping whoever knocked wouldn't stay long. Limping slightly, he made his way from the den to the front entry. On the other side of the heavy oak door stood a ruddy-cheeked boy about ten years old.

"Telegram, Sir," said the boy, grinning from one sunburned ear to the other.

Albert reached into his pocket for a quarter. The boy thanked him, and then raced down the steps to his bicycle.

Albert ripped open the envelope. Through the lower half of his bifocals he read, *HOTEL BURNED 17 JULY. ALL WAS LOST. WE ARE SAFE WITH LILY IN MONTROSE. CLARA*

Telegram in hand, he closed the door and started down the center hall, his cane tapping a steady rhythm on the marble. The hall led to French doors opening onto a sunny courtyard where Geneva was entertaining three women from the neighborhood. Four well-coiffed heads turned in Albert's direction when he walked outside. The women interrupted their game of pinochle to watch him peck his way across the stone patio to their table. A gentle breeze stirred the leaves of the elm tree protecting them from the sun.

"I have troubling news." Albert held up the telegram.

Geneva clutched her fan of cards to her chest. "Not about the children."

Albert shook his head. "No, it has to do with Clara."

Geneva laid her cards facedown on the table. "Not something that could wait until later?"

Albert handed her the telegram. After a quick read, she looked up at him with a bewildered expression. "How will they manage? Will her husband have to go back to mining? He must be close to fifty."

Still chewing on the news, Albert didn't reply.

The other three card players sat in silence, their eyes moving from Albert to Geneva, and then back and forth around the table.

Geneva stood up. "I hope you ladies will excuse me, but I would like to continue our game another time." She gave the women her best Pasadena hostess smile, and then rang for the maid.

The center hall echoed with chatter while Geneva accompanied her guests to the front door. After they were gone, she walked into the den where her husband had returned to his chair and newspaper. She studied his profile. Still handsome at sixty-two, he was clean-shaven again, a change made when gray overtook black in his facial hair.

"I suppose this means you'll be going to Montrose," she said.

Albert took his eyes off his paper and turned them on her. "We're both going." He laid the paper in his lap and adjusted his spectacles. "We are long overdue for a trip to Montrose, anyway. After we make sure Clara and her family will be all right, we can go down to La Jara and check on Christopher…see firsthand if he's doing any better at ranching."

Geneva rolled her eyes. "You need to give the boy more time, Albert."

"Boy! Our boy is twenty-three years old." He picked up his newspaper. "I will make travel arrangements in the morning." Geneva nodded humbly and left.

Albert opened the newspaper to an advertisement for the auto he'd been thinking about buying—a 1910 Chalmers-Detroit "Forty." Soon he was absorbed in such details as seating for five to seven, 36" wheels, gas lamps, and hand-buffed leather seats, imagining himself behind the wheel of something better than the REO parked in his garage. He briefly considered buying the Chalmers and driving it to Colorado, but abandoned the idea when he remembered how bad the roads were outside of town.

At ten the next morning, he drove his REO runabout to the train station where he purchased three tickets to Denver on the Acheson, Topeka, and Santa Fe Railroad. The third ticket was for sixteen-year-old Sabrina, the only one of their children still living at home now that Rose and Lilian were married, and Christopher was in La Jara.

Before leaving the station, he sent a wire to Clara. *RECEIVED YOUR DISPATCH. ARRIVING MONTROSE BY TRAIN JULY 30.* He signed it, as he did all of his telegrams, *A. WALLIN OF PASADENA.*

The day was already heating up when he walked next door to the Hotel Green for a cool libation. Sitting

307

in the elegant bar with a highball in one hand and a cigar in the other, his attention drifted to the two times he'd stayed at the hotel in Ophir Loop and the beautiful woman who owned it. She'd been smart to buy insurance. He couldn't see her rebuilding, though, when it had taken her as long as it did to find someone to rent the place.

Then his thoughts turned to Clara. Another father might have included an encouraging word in his telegram, however, to Albert, the fire was simply the latest in a sequence of events that never would have happened if Clara had married someone with better prospects than Vincent.

Deliberating over what to do about her plight, he finished his drink and drove home. By the time he parked the REO in his garage, he had conceded she was a tough cookie, tough as every Wallin that preceded her—wild, headstrong, not afraid to take chances. *Thank God at least one of my children turned out like me.*

He asked Geneva to join him on the patio. "Let's stand over here." He shielded his eyes against the slant of the sun. Eyeing him skeptically, Geneva did as he asked.

They stood facing the garden, close enough their shoulders were touching. "What is mine is yours," Albert said. With one sweep of his hand, he took in the manicured hedges bordering the yard, the shade trees, groomed lawn, and six varieties of roses blooming in the garden. "Everything on this acre and many more in Colorado," he added. "That fire cost Clara the entire lot of her possessions. She and I have had our differences over the years, but when I see her, I intend to show some compassion. You need to do the same. I have tried to stay out of this civil war you two have been fighting these many years, however, you must be cordial to her this time."

"We've been writing to one another," Geneva said quietly, still facing the garden.

"Not often, from what I can tell. When you do, I find myself speculating as to what you write about— your fine clothes? The mayor's wife? And what does Clara write about—how many biscuits she baked?"

Geneva folded her arms in a sulk. "You think she's perfect. You've always thought she was smarter than me."

"For God's sake, Geneva, this is not a contest. You are my wife. She is my daughter."

"She's my stepdaughter."

Albert turned to her, narrowing his eyes. "Why did you feel compelled to say that? Does having a stepdaughter automatically produce an evil stepmother?" He took a good look at his wife's face, still pretty despite lines of age around her mouth and eyes. "Listen to me, Geneva, and listen well. Long before Clara was your stepdaughter she was your cousin, technically, your first cousin once removed. She is still your cousin. You, me, Clara, Lily, Christopher and the girls, *my* grandchildren, *our* grandchildren—we may not always get along, but we all share the same roots. The same sap runs through our veins. Try to remember that while we are in Montrose."

Chapter Fifty-Seven

Clara and her children hobbled into Montrose with nothing but the clothes they wore the morning of the fire, and one outfit each purchased from the paltry inventory at the Ophir Loop general store. They'd spent three nights in Thelma O'Connell's cabin. During an interminably long three days, Clara sifted through the ruins while Jonas rounded up the horses and cows. He sold the cows; kept the horses. At night the family slept, or tried to sleep, on featherbeds rescued from the hotel, squeezing into whatever space they could find on Thelma's floor. Jonas begged a ride into Ophir where he closed his account at the bank and bought a wagon to haul the mattresses and other salvaged items to Montrose. Clara and the children took the train.

Lily was waiting at the station when they arrived. "Dear, dear Sister," she murmured, enfolding Clara in a bear hug, "I haven't slept a wink since I heard what happened. Thank heaven no one was hurt." She did a cursory inspection of the bedraggled four. Except for the stylish straw hat Emily was wearing, they were variously attired in homely, ill-fitting clothes, Bert carrying a small valise.

"Where's the rest of your—" Lily's hand flew to her mouth. "Never mind. Never mind." She motioned for them to follow her. "Henry's out front waiting in the Olds."

Henry's 1908 Oldsmobile was the first motorcar Clara and her children had ridden in. They'd only seen a "horseless carriage" once about a year before the fire when a Great Smith touring car belonging to one of the guests chugged through Ophir Loop and parked in the hotel turnaround. Painted fire engine red, the seven-passenger car caused quite a stir. During the two days it sat in front of the hotel, a steady stream of Ophir Loop residents stopped by for a look.

In Henry's Olds, with the canvas top lowered and Pearl sitting in Clara's lap, the five-passenger auto held six. All four passengers sitting in the backseat braced themselves when Henry revved the engine, relaxing after nobody was ejected when the car lurched forward.

During a slow trip through town, Clara and her children found themselves surrounded by mountains again, although these ranges were distant compared to the peaks shadowing Ophir Loop. To the west they could see the Uncompaughre Plateau, bathed in mauve as the sun set behind it. To the south were the San Juans, still capped in snow. With the evening air cooling their faces and ruffling their hair, they gawked at the people and buildings they passed, Emily waving, Pearl giggling, while Clara and Bert struggled to keep their own excitement contained.

"What an amazing machine!" Clara said to Lily after Henry let his passengers off in front of their house. "Have you driven it?" Considering how much weight Lily had gained, Clara wasn't sure her sister would fit in the space between the seat and steering wheel.

Lily laughed so hard her belly shook. "Not on your life! I know the song, though." She started singing "In My Merry Oldsmobile," stopping after the second line.

"Oh, dear. I wasn't thinking. This probably isn't a time to be gay."

"No need to apologize," Clara said. "I could use a little gaiety."

She hooked an arm around her sister's shoulders as they walked up the path to the house. Henry and Lily lived two blocks from where Albert and his family had lived while he served on the board of the Montrose First National Bank. Henry still worked there, having advanced from teller to branch manager. His salary afforded a two-story frame house with four bedrooms and a detached garage. The house was blessed with electric lights, but like most buildings in Montrose, it didn't have an indoor privy. There was a well on the property, though, and by using the red-handled pump mounted next to the kitchen sink, Lily could draw water without having to haul it in a bucket. While she and Clara were in the kitchen preparing supper, she asked about the fire.

"I am better now," Clara said, relieved to be in the presence of her sister, someone she could confide in without being censured. "I was inconsolable at first, almost as devastated as I was when Seth died. Jonas and I had been saving money, hoping to buy the hotel. I had just learned of Vincent's death. It was too much to cope with at one time." She paused for a moment, lost in thought.

"You seem to have settled down," said Lily. "I was afraid you would be a weeping mess when I met you at the train."

"After the smoke cleared, as well as my mind, Jonas and I started talking about building a hotel of our own. A modern one, with indoor privies, in a town like

Montrose where there's more business, more people to choose from when it comes to hiring cooks and chambermaids."

"Indoor privies? In a hotel? That would be something to behold." Lily handed Clara a bunch of carrots. "What did Amanda say when you told her? I haven't set foot in her shop since we got your telegram."

"She was the first person I wired. Her reply was curt. I was upset about it until I said to myself, aren't all telegrams curt?" Clara took the carrots over to the sink to rinse them.

"Then what happened?"

"A day later, I received another telegram from her. In it she said she was going up there with an insurance man to view the damage. She should be back in Montrose by now." Clara began peeling the carrots. "I'm going to go see her tomorrow."

Lily's eyes widened. "I'll say a little prayer for you."

The next morning, Lily asked Clara if she'd like to borrow something to wear when she faced Amanda for the first time since the fire. Everything in her closet was too large. Clara opted for a Merry Widow picture hat and a pair of kidskin gloves, scowling at the reflection in her sister's full-length mirror.

"I'm a fashion disaster, Lily. I dread seeing Amanda, but I owe her an explanation and an apology. I would feel more confident wearing something appropriate when I saw her. That is, when she saw me."

Clara set off for Amanda's shop wearing Lily's hat and gloves along with the mannish blouse and gathered skirt she'd purchased at the Ophir Loop store—clothes with the kind of roominess a laundress would appreciate and the owner of the most fashionable shop in Montrose would likely scorn.

Lily suggested Henry drive her into town, but Clara wanted to walk. "Maybe I'll see a house for rent along the way, someplace Jonas and I can live until our hotel is built. If we can come up with the money, that is." She smiled broadly. "Do you suppose I have enough pull at the bank to get a loan?" Lily's smile was more guarded. She'd long ago learned to be cautious when it came to banking matters.

****

The way I'm dressed, the neighbors will think I'm a gypsy, Clara thought as she walked along the unpaved road, ogling the flowers she passed. Almost every house had some combination of black-eyed Susans, lavender, hollyhocks, day-lilies, roses, or peonies in their yards along with a shade tree or two.

At the corner of First Street and Townsend Avenue, Clara heard the faint sound of a piano being played in the Buddecke and Diehl Opera House. She interrupted her walk to listen to it, and stood there long enough to hear "Let Me Call You Sweetheart" and "Down by the Old Mill Stream." Then she continued on her way, her spirits buoyed by sunshine, flowers, and a couple of songs she'd never heard before. "No more dilly-dallying," she told herself. "Amanda's shop is in the next block."

She entered the shop slowly, barely rustling the tinkle bells mounted on the doorframe. She was greeted by the scent of dried rose petals, but her stomach tightened into a knot when Amanda left the customer she was waiting on and rushed to the door.

"Thank you for coming," she said with a smile. "I'll finish my transaction. Then we can talk."

Clara wasn't sure what to make of Amanda's congenial reception. Breathing a little easier because of it, she strolled among the racks and tables, picking up a bit of finery here and there and putting it down without really knowing what she'd had in her hand. There was a mirror at nearly every turn, and she glanced in each one she passed, checking for gray in her own dark hair after seeing how white Amanda's was now.

The customer didn't stay long, and as soon as she left, Clara walked to Amanda and spouted the apology she'd been rehearsing in her head.

"I am the one who should be apologizing," Amanda said. "The hotel was insured. The contents were not. I feel terrible about everything you and your family must have lost. That fire may turn out to be a blessing. What would I have done if you and your husband had decided you were tired of all the work and moved? It took me a long time to find someone—you, as it turned out—who was willing to rent my hotel. I did *not* want to go back up there and run it again."

Clara unclenched her hands as a gush of relief flooded over her. She thought it best not to mention that she and Jonas had talked about buying the hotel.

"This is a meager offer," Amanda glanced at Clara's skirt and blouse, "but I would like to give you something from my shop."

"Please don't. My family and I will be fine."

"I will not be able to look you in the eye again if you leave here empty handed."

Feeling like a weed in a rose garden, Clara perused the merchandise on display. Every undergarment she touched was fancier than anything she'd ever owned. After some deliberation she decided on a cream-colored satin corset, a practical choice for a woman who'd been without a corset for a week.

"I will let you in on something." Amanda wrapped the corset in plain white paper. "I plan to use my insurance money to renovate the space next door. The extra space will allow me to sell dresses and shoes and hire a seamstress." She tied a ribbon around Clara's package. "If you don't mind my asking, what do you and Mr. Beale plan to do? Will you be staying in Montrose?"

"Yes. This is a good place for us. My sister lives here, and winters are definitely more hospitable. You will be surprised when I tell you Jonas and I are thinking about building a hotel here. We enjoyed managing your hotel, and we think Montrose could use one with electric lights and indoor plumbing."

Amanda arched her brows. "A hotel such as that would require a considerable sum of money."

A rush of color flooded Clara's cheeks. "I know. Jonas and I are good at saving, though. We should be able to mortgage what we don't already have saved. Plus my husband is handy with a hammer and saw."

Amanda placed her fingers on Clara's arm. "Do you plan to serve food in your hotel?"

"We haven't put our ideas on paper yet, but yes, we will definitely serve food."

"I am pleased to hear that. This town could use a good restaurant."

Chapter Fifty-Eight

"What was her shop like? What was she wearing?" Emily asked when her mother waltzed into Lily and Henry's tastefully appointed parlor. "Did she mention your dowdy clothes?"

The smile Clara had been wearing since leaving Amanda's shop disappeared. "Don't be rude, Daughter. Amanda wasn't, and she had every right to be." She took off Lily's picture hat, and then sat next to her on the sofa. "Jonas isn't here yet?" she whispered.

Lily shook her head. "No, but Pa and Geneva are." She tightened her lips in a look of dismay. "They're a day early. Henry went to get them. Do you feel like baking a cake? All I have for supper is ham hocks and lima beans."

Clara sniffed the air. "Mmmm…makes the whole house smell good. What kind of cake would you like?"

Emily, sitting in an overstuffed chair near the front windows, got up and rushed to her aunt and mother. "Do you have all the ingredients, Aunt Lily? Chocolate, perhaps? Allspice? I'll happily go to the store for you. The same one you took me to this morning?"

Though Emily had been in Montrose for less than twenty-four hours, she already had her eye on a fellow who worked at the largest grocery store in town. While living in Ophir Loop, she'd been engaged twice, both times to men too rough around the edges to suit her mother. Jonas hadn't liked them either, and turned both men down when they asked for her hand.

"But I'm almost twenty," Emily lamented after the second refusal.

"You're still young," Jonas told her, "and too pretty for words. The bachelors around here don't have much to choose from. *You* should be the one doing the choosing and darned picky about it."

"I have enough chocolate, Emily," Lily replied. "Thank you for suggesting it, though, Chocolate cake would be a good ending to a humble supper."

"Eggs?"

"I have eggs, as well."

Emily was about to ask her aunt if she needed anything at all when a series of loud honks caught her attention. She hurried to the front windows and pulled aside one of the curtains.

"It's Henry," Lily said from across the room.

All three women filed outside with Emily leading the way. As soon as they opened the front door, they realized it was Henry's car horn they'd heard, but Albert was the one sitting behind the wheel. Henry was in the passenger seat, Geneva and Sabrina in back, Geneva holding onto her wide-brimmed hat as if protecting it from a blustery wind. Albert was wearing a Panama hat and grinning like a prankster.

"I thought I would give our boy Henry a driving lesson," he shouted over the chug-a-chug-chug of the idling engine.

"Right," Henry sputtered, "by roaring through town as if we just robbed a bank." He jabbed a nervous finger in the direction of the garage, and with a grinding of gears, Albert drove the Olds up the gravel driveway.

Within minutes, the joy riders joined the rest of the family for a flurry of handshakes, slaps on the back, and my-how-you've-growns—each member of the family speaking louder than the next to be heard. "It's good to see you, Clara." Albert gave his eldest daughter a warm embrace. Geneva also appeared genuinely glad to see her.

Clara was on her way to the kitchen to bake the cake she'd promised Lily, when Jonas appeared out front in the wagon, and the chaos of welcomes began again. Although it was the first meeting for Jonas and Albert, Clara had been married to her second husband long enough she was past worrying whether they would get along. Even if they were to clash, she figured her pa lived in California, and if everything went as planned, she and Jonas would be in Montrose. She couldn't help watching them, though—two men with mostly silver hair, Albert, stoop-shouldered and leaning on his cane, shorter than he used to be, yet slightly taller than Jonas.

She stood across the room from them, too far away to hear what they were saying yet pleased to see they were both participating in the conversation. Her attempt at lip reading was foiled when Geneva strolled over and tapped her on the shoulder.

"May I be of help with supper?" she asked, louder than necessary. She checked to see if Albert heard what she said. Several times during their long train ride he'd reminded her she was to be kind to Clara while they were in Montrose.

"Ah! I didn't see you coming," Clara said, surprised by the interruption and doubly surprised this woman of leisure would offer to help. She studied Geneva's face for a clue of intent. "How thoughtful of you, Geneva, however, Lily and I have supper in hand. Would you like to help with the dishes?"

Geneva blinked several times. "I suppose I could do that." She glanced at Albert who was still engrossed in conversation with Jonas, now a three-way discussion that included Henry.

"I'll count on you then," Clara said. "In the meantime, I have to excuse myself. It's almost six o'clock, and I still have to bake a cake."

"You're certain I can't help?"

"I could bake a cake with my eyes closed." Clara's calm manner of speaking belied her underlying resentment for a woman who seemed to stir up trouble every time she was around.

"I brought my needlework with me," Geneva said. "I'll work on that for a while."

Lily was already in the kitchen rounding up ingredients when Clara entered. "I've gathered most of what you'll need. Will you please get the Baker's chocolate out of the pantry? It's on the top shelf."

"Is the oven hot?" Clara asked.

"Yes. I knew you'd be in a hurry."

Clara checked to make sure they were alone. "Have you spoken with Geneva? She seems to be acting oddly."

"Not to me. She raved on and on about the fancy meals they ate on the train. No mention of lima beans. Your cake had better be delicious."

"She hugged me so hard I nearly lost my balance. She kept saying, 'I'm sorry, I'm sorry.' It made me uncomfortable."

"She's probably sorry about the fire." Lily pulled a mixing bowl out of one of her cupboards. "We all say that when something bad happens. I think what we mean is, I feel bad that you feel bad. It just comes out, 'I'm sorry.'"

Clara broke two eggs into the mixing bowl and whisked them into a froth. "I don't trust her. She doesn't care what happens to me. She never has. Well, maybe she did a little...before she married Pa." Clara stirred in the rest of the ingredients, poured the batter into a rectangular pan, and set it in the oven. Lily had gone out to her garden for salad fixings, leaving Clara to mull over her suspicions while the cake baked. Remembering the last time she'd been hugged by Geneva was when she came to Ophir Loop hoping to find proof of an affair, Clara was certain she wanted something from her this time, too.

Chapter Fifty-Nine

The chocolate cake was still warm when it was time for dessert, too warm to frost. During the main course, everyone except Albert talked about the fire and its aftermath. He nodded occasionally to show he was listening, but waited until dessert to ask what he really wanted to know.

"I hear you met with your landlady today." He cut a forkful of cake. "How did she take the news?"

At her husband's mention of the shop owner, Geneva looked down at the linen napkin in her lap. Clara glanced in her direction. "Better than I thought she would. After Amanda got my telegram, she went up there to look at the damage. I thought she would be devastated, furious with me. Instead, she seemed almost relieved."

"I wondered about that," said Albert. "She had been trying to rent or sell that hotel for years. She had plenty of insurance."

"She told me she's not going to rebuild; that she's going to use the insurance money to add onto her shop." Clara's face brightened. "Lily, you will be happy to hear this. So will you, Emily. She plans to sell dresses and shoes in the new space. She's also going to hire a seamstress."

Emily set her fork down. "Oh, Mother, I do love this town."

Pearl looked up from her dessert. "My shoes burned up. May I have some new ones?"

"In due time," Clara said. "You shouldn't interrupt, Baby."

Pearl frowned. "But Emily…"

"Emily is an adult now."

Albert considered his nine-year-old granddaughter's complaint. The edges of his mouth turned up at the sight of her chocolate-rimmed pout. "I will buy you some shoes *before* Amanda's shop is finished. In fact, I would like to buy a pair for everyone who lost shoes in the fire."

Clara looked at Jonas. She could tell by the brooding expression on his face that he was as uncomfortable as she was with such a public offer. "We are not destitute, Pa," she said, gently.

"I know that." Albert blotted his mouth with a napkin. "Jonas and I talked at length before supper. I rather like the shoe idea, though, so don't argue with me."

"Your cake was delicious," Geneva said, hoping to redirect the conversation. Her remark was followed by a chorus of praise around the table.

Albert asked for more tea, and Lily went to the kitchen to get it. After pouring him a cup, she set the pot in front of him and started clearing the table. Clara picked up several plates and followed her into the kitchen. Emily did the same.

Geneva turned to Albert. "I should help them." Checking to make sure everyone at the table had heard her offer, she sat with her hands in her lap, smiling at no one in particular.

"Go then!" Albert said in a fearsome whisper. He

was about to stand and pull out her chair, when she jumped to her feet and walked to the kitchen, pausing in its arched doorway to scrutinize a room half the size of hers in Pasadena. Lily's kitchen had two freestanding cabinets on either side of a white porcelain sink supported on legs. A double-oven iron range sat a few feet from the sink. A small window was positioned over the sink, and bay windows enclosed a breakfast alcove at the opposite end of the room. Lily stood next to the sink, filling a large pot with water by repeatedly raising and lowering the handle of a pump. Geneva felt fortunate to have piped water in her own house, but held back the urge to brag about it.

Lily lugged the pot of water over to her coal-burning range, and set it atop the cooking surface with a loud clunk. "What can *I* do?" Geneva asked as Clara hurried past her with more dirty dishes.

Clara set the dishes on the sink counter. "As soon as the water is hot enough, you can wash these dishes. Emily will dry for you, won't you, Dear?" Emily was scraping table scraps into a slop bucket. "Yes, Mother," she answered without looking up. "Lord knows I've had enough practice."

Unbuttoning the cuffs of her silk blouse, Geneva walked into the kitchen like she owned it. Clara had done enough sewing to know the blouse was tailor-made. So was the tulip-shaped skirt she wore. "Can she borrow one of your aprons?" Clara asked Lily, smiling deceptively. "We wouldn't want her to spoil her pretty clothes."

Geneva rolled up her sleeves and walked to the range. She dipped a finger in the pot to check the water's temperature. "I would say something about what you're wearing, Clara, but that wouldn't be a nice thing to do to someone who'd lost everything she owned in a fire." She turned to her ex-friend, eyes narrowed. "Would it."

Clara took a quick look at the shapeless skirt and blouse she'd worn all day. Realizing she hadn't fallen apart when she'd worn the outfit into the most fashionable shop in Montrose, she squared her shoulders, picked up a bar of Ivory soap, and shoved it in Geneva's hand. "How long has it been since you had your hands in dishwater?" she asked, her voice icy. "Do you even remember how? Do you remember you're supposed to wash the utensils first?"

Geneva raised the soap to her nose and took a sniff. Then she pointed the bar at Clara. "If the proper way to wash dishes is so damn important to you, why aren't *you* doing it? Or maybe *you* should dry instead of Emily. That way you could inspect my work."

Lily glanced from one adversary to the other, opened a drawer, rifled through its contents, and pulled out an apron. "Let me help you put this on," she said, careful not to disturb Geneva's bouffant hairdo when she slipped the bib over her head. Then she fussed with the apron strings, shaping them into a pretty bow.

"For heaven's sake, Lily, she isn't going to wear that thing to church," Clara said.

Emily gave her mother a slow, appraising look. Lily patted the apron's bow, and then turned to Clara with a shushing finger over her lips.

Clara thoughtfully digested her daughter and sister's unspoken remarks. *Lily just shushed me like she would a child. Why is Emily so quiet? Do they think I'm being ornery?* Aiming a scowl at Geneva, she grabbed a tea towel. "Don't leave me the pots and pans the way you used to."

Lily motioned to Emily they should leave. After the two of them joined the rest of the family in the front parlor, Geneva checked the dishwater temperature again. Nodding in approval, she hefted the pot off the stove and carried it to the sink, put a stopper in the drain, and poured in half the water for rinsing. Then she dropped the bar of Ivory soap into the remaining hot water and swished it around until suds appeared. With a defiant smile, she picked up a handful of silverware and dumped it into the soapy water.

Sounds of laughter and muffled conversation filled the parlor, but the kitchen was silent while the silverware, then the glasses moved from the wash pot to the rinse water to the drying towel. When it was time to wash the plates, Geneva said, "Remember how we used to talk until the last dish was in the cupboard? Well, the water's getting cold and we haven't said a word."

"I have nothing to say that you didn't hear during supper." Clara put Lily's crystal water glasses on a tray and carried them to the hutch in the dining room. On her way back, she picked up a dry tea towel.

"Why are you being nasty to me?" Geneva said. "I'm trying to be nice. Albert says we should stop acting like enemies. He says you and I belong to the same tree."

Clara took a dinner plate out of the rinse water, shook off the excess, and dried it. "That doesn't sound like Pa. He's too direct to speak in metaphors."

Geneva rolled her eyes. "Must you always use words most people have never heard of?"

"Pa is never ambiguous," Clara offered.

Geneva picked up a dessert plate, plunged it into the soapy water, and gave it a furious wash.

"You needn't scrub the roses off that plate," Clara said.

Geneva flicked a sidewise glare and kept scrubbing.

"Pa usually says exactly what's on his mind. That's all I was saying."

"Then why didn't you say it that way?" Geneva rested her forearms on the edge of the dish pot. "I knew exactly what he meant. I was hoping you and I would talk about it. He thinks our family—you and me, mostly—are parts of the same tree. I think we're the roots. He said something or other about roots."

"Roots, not branches?"

"Roots! I remember now. He said we're all connected by the same roots."

"More so than most families," Clara muttered.

"What did you say?"

"I said, that certainly describes our family. Our roots are so connected they're like the snarls on an old cat."

That remark started a squabble that lasted until the water needed to be changed. Geneva dumped out the used water, refilled the wash pot, and set it back on the stove. While her back was turned, Clara picked up a few clean dessert plates and put them back in the dirty pile.

"We need to stop arguing," Geneva said while they waited for the water to heat. "I have to tell Albert we did more than just the dishes. He and I have been married for twenty-five years. So have Morris and Alma. Surely you've gotten used to it by now."

The grandfather clock in the hall began its top-of-the-hour chime. Clara waited until the sequence ended and nine bongs announced the hour. "I have grown accustomed to your marriage, but I will never be totally at peace with it."

Geneva took the reply with straight-faced politeness, nodding absentmindedly. When she didn't bite back, Clara felt emboldened. "As long as we're talking about your marriage, I've always wanted to know something—did Pa ask you, or did you ask him?"

"What?" Geneva's eyebrows rose dramatically. "Did you honestly think I could be that bold? Albert and I were getting along well during the trip to Santa Fe, so my brother suggested it to him. Morris said it would make Alma feel better about marrying *her* cousin if Albert did it, too. He reminded your pa how scarce women were. Said it would save us making another long trip."

Clara thought back to Jonas's proposal, and how thrilled, even though slightly embarrassed she'd been. Geneva's betrothal hadn't been half that romantic, not much better than being a mail order bride.

Geneva picked up one of the clean dessert plates Clara had put back in the dirty pile. "I thought I washed this." She glanced at the rest of the pile. "These look clean to me."

"Everyone certainly must have enjoyed my cake," Clara said, sounding serious, "so much so they licked their plates." Geneva studied the expression on Clara's face. Sensing mischief, she smiled, tentatively at first, before breaking into a full bubbling laugh.

Clara laughed with her. "You used to do that to me all the time."

They shared other enjoyable memories, embellishing most of them, while they finished the dishes. Geneva had just scoured the last pan when Albert appeared in the doorway, saying it was time to leave for their hotel. She rinsed the pan, and then took off her apron and unrolled the sleeves of her stylish blouse, wet despite the effort to keep them dry. With a persecuted look, she walked to her husband and showed him her shriveled fingertips.

"They will recover." He kissed her on the forehead. Then he turned to Henry standing next to him. "I want to go by my old house tomorrow before we board the train for La Jara. I still consider it one of my finest accomplishments."

"We can do that." Henry placed a hand on Albert's shoulder. "I'm driving though, right?"

Albert threw back his head and laughed. "If you insist."

The men left to get the car. Geneva gathered her needlework, put on her hat and gloves, found Sabrina, and ushered her outside. Clara followed them into the cool night air. Both women wanted to end on a good note, although neither one knew how to do it. Sabrina filled the gap with questions about the ranch in La Jara, a place she'd never seen. Geneva patiently answered her questions until Henry's Oldsmobile chugged down the driveway and stopped in front of the house. Albert helped his wife and daughter into the backseat, and before Geneva sat down, she leaned forward and said to Clara, "We should write more often." Clara nodded in agreement.

****

Later that night, in a house dark and quiet, Clara

and Jonas had their first opportunity to talk in private. Lily had given them the guest room. Jonas was lying on his side, eyes closed, with his good ear facing Clara. "Your father is a prince of a fellow," he whispered. "I've always thought of him as something of a miser."

Clara yawned. "Pa isn't a miser; he just believes every person should earn his own keep."

Jonas opened his eyes. "You think I'm talking about the shoes, don't you."

"The ones he offered to buy us? Of course."

"Well, I'm not. I haven't had a chance to tell you this, but he wants to help us buy the hotel."

Clara raised her head off the pillow. "Oh, Jonas, you didn't ask him, did you?"

Jonas heaved a sigh. "I just met the man, Clara."

"I know, I know." She lay her head back down and chewed for a moment on the fact her father had offered assistance to someone who was practically a stranger rather than discussing the arrangement with her. "What did he say?"

"He asked me a lot of questions about our finances. Said he would make up the difference between our savings and what we can borrow from the bank." Jonas reached out for her. "Woman, we are going to have the finest hotel in all of Montrose County."

"With a piano in the parlor?"

Jonas chuckled. "With a piano in the parlor."

Chapter Sixty

It took Clara and Jonas until December to secure financing for their hotel, find a suitable location, meet with an architect in Denver, and make several changes to his plans. The final design was for a hotel with fifteen guest rooms and a manager's living quarters. The manager's quarters would be on the main floor along with an office, a spacious parlor, three guest rooms, and a restaurant large enough to hold fifty diners. The other twelve guest rooms were on the second floor, six on each side of a long hall with a lavatory at each end. Both lavatories were to have a flush toilet with wall-mounted water closet, and a marble sink. The plumbing diagram called for an identical lavatory on the first floor next to the hotel's only bathtub. The claw-foot bathtub was housed in a separate room not much larger than the tub itself. For a small fee, guests could bathe there.

The final plans were spread across the kitchen table in Clara and Jonas's rented bungalow. Going over the plans with them was Barnaby Harriman, the man they'd hired to supervise construction. "Lean as a gnawed off shinbone," as Jonas described him, Barnaby had built or helped build several noteworthy structures in Montrose, including the addition to Amanda's shop. "We'll hafta wait 'til May to start on it," Barnaby said, head bent over the plans. "We could dig out the basement, but it's too cold to pour concrete. It'd be flat out ridiculous to dig a hole 'n just watch it fill up with snow."

Clara hugged herself with sweater-clad arms. "It doesn't seem fair that Amanda's addition is finished, and all we have to show for our efforts is raw land."

"You're not being realistic," Jonas said, slightly annoyed. "Amanda didn't have to get a loan—a big one, big enough to choke an elephant. Besides, all Barnaby had to do was knock down a wall, build three more, and put a roof on." He nudged the man standing next to him. "You could do a job like that with one hand tied behind your back—right, Barnaby?"

"Well, there was a bit more to it than that," Barnaby grumbled.

"Have you seen this page yet?" Clara set the drawing of a restaurant-sized kitchen in front of Barnaby. "I look forward to hearing what you think of it when I come back from the store. I'm almost out of flour again, Jonas. Can you believe how well my pies are doing?"

To bring in a little money until the hotel was finished, Clara had been baking and selling pies. She started small, relying on Lily and Henry to spread the word to their friends, but by Thanksgiving she was baking a dozen pies a day in her tiny kitchen, selling most of them to the town's largest grocery store.

Emily was lending a hand with preparation. After the pies cooled, she made deliveries in a handcart Jonas outfitted with shelves to keep the pies upright on trips down bumpy roads. Helping her mother wasn't entirely selfless on Emily's part. She had dated several young men since arriving in Montrose, but the one she was keen on worked at the store that sold the pies.

"Of all the fellows who've come courting," Jonas told her after the young man had been to the house a few times, "one stands out from the rest."

"Who might that be?" Emily asked, affecting an innocent grin.

"Edwyn. The fellow who works at Mrs. Allen's store. Does most of it, from what I can tell."

Born in Wales, raised in Montrose, Edwyn decided early on he wouldn't follow his father and his father's Welsh and Cornish friends into the mines. When he heard Mrs. Allen was opening a grocery and sundry store in the center of town, he pressured her for a job before the building was half finished.

In February, he asked for Emily's hand, and this time Jonas said yes. "We'd like to get married toward the end of May," Edwyn said, "when the snow has melted off Horsefly Mesa. That's when the wind dies down, and we can be outside again."

"Wouldn't a garden reception be simply lovely?" Emily said, feeling rather modern as she pictured herself in an outdoor wedding like the ones she'd seen pictured in the *Ladies Home Journal*.

"May is fine," Clara said. "We'll talk about the reception later." And in the middle of baking pies and finalizing details for a hotel, Clara found herself planning a wedding, one with a church, a minister, and most likely a garden reception. The only real wedding she'd attended was Phoebe and Reb's where both the ceremony and the party that followed took place in Phoebe's back yard.

Since Lily had been married in a church, Clara went to her for help, but was told Aunt Mid had done all of the planning. Clara wrote to her aunt asking for advice. The shaky handwriting in the letter Mildred sent back was difficult to read. The sarcasm, however, was clear. *How pleased I was to hear Emily is to be married. As you will recall, I was there the day she was born. I am also pleased she has decided on a traditional wedding and not followed in the footsteps of her mother and grandfather.*

I can no longer travel; thus cannot be there to advise you as to the planning and execution of a wedding. Since you lack the discipline to be properly wedded yourself, twice no less, I am sending you this highly regarded book. Hopefully it will answer all of your questions.

Along with the letter was a generous check and a copy of *Our Deportment: or the Manners, Conduct, and Dress of the Most Refined Society.* Clara read the chapter devoted to formal weddings, and then set the book aside. Even if she and Jonas could afford such a wedding, it would be a sideshow in Montrose. She did, however, encourage Emily to mail a few invitations. After receiving his, Charley, still hauling ore for the Alta mine, sent his sister ten dollars and a note that read, "Since you'll probably be getting all gussied up for your shindig, this might come in handy."

"Oh, Mother, I hope he can afford it," Emily said when she saw how much he'd sent.

"Your big brother has always had a generous spirit," Clara said. "He's making a good wage. Send him a thank you note and stop fretting."

Emily used the ten dollars to purchase a stylish travelling ensemble to wear on her honeymoon. Amanda pulled it together—brown suit with tan pinstripes, beige turban, and brown lace-up boots with a

334

French heel. Amanda's seamstress made Emily's wedding dress, an ankle-length white dimity gown with lace yoke and sleeves. Pearl watched with interest as her sister picked out the dress pattern, fabric, style of lace, white satin slippers, and veil.

"I want a wedding dress, too, Mama," Pearl said, during the final fitting.

"You will have to wait for that," Clara said, "until you get married...hopefully many years from now."

Amanda smiled graciously. "I could have my seamstress make her a dress out of the same bolt of fabric. It will be my treat."

Clara took the dress home after it was finished, and a few days later showed it to Lily. "Is Pearl going to be in the wedding party?" Lily asked, admiring the sheer white dress.

"No, I think she just wanted some of the attention she saw being lavished on Emily."

"This is probably a touchy subject," Lily said, after a respectful pause, "but what a shame Vincent isn't here to see Emily get married. If he were still alive, would you have asked him to give her away?"

Clara hung Pearl's dress in the wardrobe Jonas built over the winter, a simple oak cabinet with a hanging rod mounted above two large drawers. It was the only piece of furniture in the room other than the bed. "If Vincent was still alive," Clara said softly, "he would be too sick to get out of bed, let alone walk Emily down the aisle."

Lily placed a comforting hand on Clara's arm. "Do you feel like talking about it?"

Clara glanced at the limp curtain strung across the bedroom window. Stained along the bottom and hung from a string, it matched the cheerless character of the room. "I don't mind. It's been almost a year since he passed." She drew a deep breath and closed her eyes as if summoning the past. "I think I told you he moved to Telluride, then back to Durango after we separated. I don't know what he did to support himself unless his Uncle Jake took him back. Nevertheless, a week or so before the hotel burned down, I got a letter from Grace telling me Vincent had passed. She wrote he'd been ill for over a year with liver cancer. He spent several months in Mercy Hospital before he died."

"That makes me sad. I never met Vincent, but it's still sad."

"I know. He was a good husband before his bottle habit got the best of him. After I read Grace's letter, I walked up to the creek where Jonas wouldn't see me cry. I love Jonas with all my heart, but all I could think of after reading the letter was the early years Vincent and I spent together; having our children; how upset he was when Seth died. Remembering that terrible time in our lives made me cry even harder." Clara closed the wardrobe doors. "Vincent would have been forty-seven if he'd lived to see Emily get married."

"Pa might like to give her away," Lily suggested. Pink glowed in her chubby cheeks when she smiled.

"He has already walked two daughters down the aisle and has one to go. Besides, Geneva wrote me they're not coming. Pa sent a case of champagne, though. It came all the way from New York. No, Lily, I want Jonas to give Emily away."

****

"I think I've earned it," Jonas said when Clara asked him. "I've treated her like a daughter for ten years. Suffered through her moods. Suffered through weeks of silence after I rejected those two ruffians." Other than being fitted for a new suit, Jonas had steered clear of anything having to do with the wedding. While his wife and stepdaughter argued over trivial details, he and Barnaby were clearing trees and digging the hotel's basement. He got involved in a minor way when Pearl showed him the dress she'd be wearing to the wedding.

"Miss Amanda made it for me, Papa. It's almost as nice as Emily's." She gave him an angelic smile. "Of course it would be wrong to be *as* nice."

Moved by his ten-year-old daughter's wish to look like a bride, Jonas decided to buy her a little ring— plain, like Emily's gold band, but threadlike in thickness. She showed the ring to nearly everyone at the wedding reception.

****

Emily and Edwyn's wedding took place May 20, 1911 in St. Paul's Episcopal Church, the church Lily and Henry had been attending since moving to Montrose. It was partly cloudy that day, chilly during the reception held in Lily and Henry's yard. The shade trees back there were just beginning to green. The freshly mown lawn and scattered clumps of daffodils barely resembled the pictures Emily had seen in the *Ladies Home Journal*, but it was quite enough garden for the happy bride.

Chapter Sixty-One

During the four months following Emily's wedding, the hotel went from a hole in the ground to a two-story brick structure with a concrete basement. Main Street fairly hummed with activity as construction workers crawled all over the site, hammers hammering, boots clunking on plank walkways, men shouting to one another, as workers applied their skills to wood, brick, wire, and metal. Coveralls sagging on his scarecrow frame, Barnaby was there every day, inspecting materials, checking plans, yelling orders, and then grabbing a hammer to work alongside his men, a crew of craftsmen that included Jonas.

Jonas and Barnaby had been working together since before the rest of the crew was hired. They'd cut down most of the trees and brush on the property, leaving a stand of box elders at the back. While they excavated the basement, the trees budded. Leaves rattled in the breeze when the roof went on, and glowed in yellow splendor as the walls were being plastered. Since the middle of September, Jonas had been working on the bannisters, using a lathe to make the dowels, and an adze, gouge, and drawknife to carve the handrails.

"We made a hell of a good choice in Barnaby," Jonas said to Clara one night. He was lying in bed, propped on one elbow, watching her brush her hair. He was having trouble keeping his eyes open after another ten-hour day at the construction site.

"He *should* be good," Clara said, "considering what we're paying him." She gave her brush a rest.

"He's perceptive," Jonas continued. "Today he suggested we widen the front porch…make it go all the way to the street. That way the stage, or automobiles, can drive right up to the landing and drop passengers off."

Clara nodded casually as she let the idea bloom in her head. "Our guests should appreciate that—especially in bad weather." She began brushing her hair again. "Are you still working on the stairwell?"

Jonas groaned as he rested his head on the pillow and stretched out. "Yes, I am. Stairs are done." He closed his eyes. "I'm almost finished with the bannisters. Wait 'til you see the entry. Not 'til I'm done, though. I want you to see it in all its glory."

****

Four days later, Jonas miscalculated a swing of the adze, a tool so sharp it cut through his boot and gashed his right instep. "Damn!" he yelped, ripping off his boot to inspect the wound. "Be careful, stupid!" he scolded himself. He checked his work area for something to absorb the blood, and grabbed a discarded paint rag. He wrapped the rag around his foot, tying it tight. Then he picked up his adze and went back to work, one boot off, one boot on.

Clara was aghast when he walked into the kitchen that night with his foot bound in a bloodstained rag. She sat him down, removed the rag, and re-bandaged his wound with a clean cloth. "Shouldn't you have a doctor look at this?"

"Don't fuss," he groused, "it's just a scratch."

The foot swelled during the night, and Clara urged Jonas to stay home the next morning.

"I've only got a few pieces left to carve," he said, "and as soon as they're done, you and I are going to Denver to buy furniture." He gave her a glowing smile. "Won't that be something? And we're gonna paint that town red while we're there." He winced as Clara re-bandaged his foot and wrapped it in buckskin.

"What in hell happened?" Barnaby asked when he saw Jonas's makeshift boot.

"Adze slipped. Nicked my foot."

"Sore?"

"Hurts like the devil. Swelled big as a pumpkin last night."

"Pour some whiskey on it."

Jonas made a face. "Wife won't allow it in the house."

"Git yerself some anyways!"

Jonas finished another section of bannister, and then left the site early, stopping at Edwyn's store on his way home. Clara looked askance at the "rare old blended Irish" cure-all he had tucked under his arm when he walked into the kitchen.

"You should have bought turpentine," she said. "That got rid of the children's diphtheria when I swabbed their throats with it." She cleansed the pus from the wound and poured whiskey over it. She doused it again before he went to bed, but the next morning the swelling had climbed to his knee.

"You need to stay home until this heals," Clara said, wagging a finger in his face.

"I don't have a choice," Jonas muttered. "I can barely stand. My heart is pounding like a jackhammer.

Tell Barnaby for me. Right now I need a swig of that whiskey." Clara frowned. "For the pain, Woman!"

Clara filled a teacup with whisky and handed it to him. After he gulped it down, she put her hand on his forehead. "You're burning up. I'm going for the doctor."

She lifted her narrow skirt and ran most of the mile to the closest doctor's office. The doctor was behind a closed door when Clara dashed in, but the minute he finished with his patient, he fired up his Model T and drove her back to the bungalow.

A short man with thinning brown hair and steel-rimmed glasses, Doctor Meyer inspected Jonas's festered wound. "Why didn't you come see me with this?" He reached into his medical bag, pulled out a thermometer, and put it in Jonas's mouth. Five minutes later, the gauge read 103 degrees.

"He needs to stay off that foot," Doc Meyer said. "Clean the wound with soap and water and put some of this on it." He handed her a small bottle of carbolic acid. "The swelling should go down in a couple of days."

Jonas spent a restless night, most of it without a sheet or blanket. The next morning, his speech was garbled. He told Clara everything was blurry. She ran into town again, this time to the bank, and together she and Henry managed to get Jonas to the hospital where he lost consciousness the minute the attendants placed him on a stretcher.

The admitting doctor checked Jonas's swollen foot and took his pulse. "Is this your husband?" he asked Clara. She nodded, her face stricken. "His blood pressure is low. I probably don't have to tell you his wound is seriously infected."

Jonas was assigned to a private room. After the attendants laid him on the hospital bed, and a nurse made sure he was comfortable, Clara pulled a straight-backed chair to his bedside where she could look at him, hope rising every time his eyes fluttered open, falling when they closed.

She sat there off and on for the next four days, listening to him breathe, watching his foot turn purple, then his leg, then both legs. Every so often a nurse in a starched apron rustled in, attended to her patient and rustled out. Otherwise, a terrible silence filled the room as Jonas's breathing grew shallower.

Lily and Henry stopped by every evening, Emily, every afternoon. Doc Meyer came by twice a day to look at his patient's wound and listen to his heart. "How is he?" Clara asked, every time he came. "Not good," he answered, every time she asked. "His organs are shutting down. I would elevate his feet, but that would be too hard on his heart."

On Jonas's third day in the hospital, Doctor Meyer removed his stethoscope and glumly shook his nearly bald head. "His heartbeat is barely discernable. You need to prepare yourself for the inevitable, Mrs. Beale." Clara slumped forward and rested her forehead on the edge of the hospital bed. She didn't sit up again for a while after the doctor left.

Numbly she sat in the hard chair, time passing in teaspoons rather than the gallons of happier days. Waiting for what Dr. Meyer had called "the inevitable," her thoughts fluctuated from resignation to hope for a miracle. Frequently she took hold of Jonas's hand and brought it to her cheek, murmuring words of encouragement and blaming herself for not insisting he see a doctor.

Near nightfall of day four, the hand she brought to her cheek was cold. She held onto it for some time, and was still holding it when one of the nurses walked in and turned on a light. Gently the nurse took Jonas's hand and checked for a pulse. With a look of mute despair, she laid the lifeless hand across the patient's chest.

Clara stood up and woodenly put on her coat. She showed the nurse the vest pocket flashlight Henry had loaned her the night he and Lily found her sitting in the dark. "How do I work this thing?" she asked.

"I'll get someone to take you home," said the nurse.

"Never mind," Clara muttered. She took a last look at Jonas's too-white face, and then walked out of the hospital in a daze.

She managed to make it to Lily and Henry's house where she broke down the minute her sister answered the door. Lily cried with her, holding Clara to her breast until they both stopped crying. "I'll ask Henry to tell your foreman in the morning," Lily said when they parted. She wiped her eyes with the hem of her apron. "What should he say?"

Clara's lips twisted in anguish. "Tell Barnaby his best carpenter is dead. Tell him to send the workmen home."

Lily's mouth dropped open. "But the hotel. It's almost finished. You can't let it sit empty. You have a mortgage to pay. Pa to pay. And Pa will make you pay it."

Clara pressed her hands to the sides of her head. "I

know. I know. I'm angry. I'm spent. I don't want to deal with building a hotel…owning a hotel…cooking for a hotel. I'll tell Barnaby myself. Leave Henry be."

"Are you sure? I'm worried about you."

"Don't be."

"I'll let your children know."

"Better you than me, Lily. I don't think I could handle it. Will you please keep Pearl and Bert for another night? And tell Emily not to come over. Tell her I want to be alone."

"Henry's still at the bank. I'll call him. Ask him to drive you home."

"It's not that far. I don't want to see him, either."

Bone tired, Clara trudged through yellow leaves on her way to the sparsely furnished bungalow she'd endured for a year—a gloomy house that felt even more barren when she walked inside. She turned the switch on the light bulb hanging from the kitchen ceiling, then turned it off again. She was hungry, but nothing sounded good to her. She made her way down a short hall to the room she'd been sharing with Jonas, took off the clothes she'd worn for four days, and put on her night dress. For a minute she gazed at the pristine bed she'd made the morning Jonas went to the hospital. She pulled off the top quilt, bundled it in her arms, and walked with it to the front of the house where she collapsed on the sofa.

****

Clara slept for ten hours. After a breakfast of tea and toast, she walked to the construction site where she found Barnaby working on Jonas's bannisters. Arms crossed in front of her, she gazed upon the nearly completed entry with its evidence of Jonas's handiwork in every piece of turned wood.

Barnaby put down his tools. Realizing what must have happened, he ordered his men to stop working. "What do you want me to do, Mrs. Beale?"

The work site grew eerily quiet while the foreman and his crew waited for Clara to reply. From somewhere on the second floor came the round echo of a wayward strike on the head of a nail. Nothing from Clara.

"He did good work," Barnaby said after a minute of silence, "a bona-fide stickler."

Still no answer.

"I feel your pain, Mrs. Beale, believe me I do, but my men and I need some direction."

Clara squared her shoulders. "I'd like you to finish this hotel as soon as possible. Jonas would want that." Mouth set in grim determination, she circled the wood-paneled entry as if walking in her sleep. Several times she ran her hand along the guardrail Jonas had carved as if part of him still clung to it. Barnaby offered her a ride home, but she declined. "I want to walk. I need to walk. It gives me time to think. I have a lot to think about."

Chapter Sixty-Two

Before the hotel could begin receiving guests, it had to be furnished. Clara and Jonas had talked about a trip to Denver for that purpose. It would be a lark—a break from work, a reason for them to celebrate their accomplishment. She'd imagined browsing through shops resplendent with merchandise during the day, and then dining and dancing with Jonas in charming cafés at night.

"I don't think Jonas realized how much time it would take to find everything," she said to Lily after their first day of shopping.

"Or how many times you two would be lost. I doubt he knew Denver any better than we do. At least we know where Union Station is so we can find our way home when we're done."

Clara and Lily spent ten days shopping for restaurant supplies and kitchenware; beds, bureaus, and a bathtub. The last check Clara wrote was for a sofa and four overstuffed chairs for the parlor. "Thank goodness we didn't have to shop for a piano," she said to Lily. "The secondhand one I bought from the opera house will do just fine."

****

It took two and a half months for all of the barrels and crates of merchandise to arrive in Montrose, and after everything was unpacked and settled, the first ads for "The Only Modern Hotel in Montrose" appeared in local newspapers. The hotel opened a week before Christmas with every room occupied. Soon, advance bookings extended past Easter.

People had been clamoring for reservations while the hotel was still under construction. Indoor plumbing was a draw, as were the electric lights and coal heaters in every room. There was also a telephone in the office. Telephones, automobiles, and electricity were changing Colorado the same way they were the rest of the nation. Now, instead of miners staying in most of the rooms, there were surveyors, train crews, Mountain States Telephone & Telegraph crews, electrical engineers, and tourists.

In business again, one that was netting an excellent return, Clara walked a path cobbled with cooks, housekeepers, chambermaids, and grandchildren. Between 1912 and 1918, while America was caught up in the sinking of the Titanic, then the Lusitania, and sending troops to Europe, twenty thousand guests signed the hotel's register. Three head cooks came and went, as did a score of cook's helpers, maids, and waitresses. Clara was the only constant. Except for a day or two when her grandchildren were born, she was always at the hotel—greeting guests, collecting money, keeping the books, hiring, firing, and sometimes lending a hand in the kitchen.

Bert stayed at the hotel for two years, helping his mother. He picked up the basics of plumbing and electrical maintenance and learned to drive a motorcar. Charley learned to drive an automobile for a job he took delivering mail from Naturita to Norwood. It was in Naturita that he met and married his wife Emma, a young woman Clara described in a letter to Geneva as "stunning to look at but lacking in industry." Then she went on to report: *Charley and Emma have rented a small hotel called Naturita House. When he collects the mail in Norwood, he picks up people planning to visit Naturita and brings them back with him. Of course he recommends they stay at his hotel.*

Delivering mail, especially in winter, and managing a hotel and stage stop were too much for him to handle; therefore Bert has gone into business with him. They bought five Ford automobiles, and one of my boys—sometimes both—drive to the Norwood train station and back several times a day. That is fifty miles round-trip on terrible roads.

I rarely leave my responsibilities at the hotel, but last month Charley picked me up and drove me to Naturita for my birthday. Countless times he had to swerve to miss boulders or drive through creek water running across the road. The roads were so narrow I swear there was less than an inch between cars when we met one coming toward us. Sometimes there was not enough room for two cars to pass. When that was the case, Charley or the other driver would have to back up to a widening—not a simple maneuver if there is a drop-off on one side!

Have you driven a motorcar? I would give it a try if the roads were paved and at least five feet wider.

Clara and Geneva wrote to one another more frequently during those years, long newsy letters that were mostly about their children and grandchildren. Geneva's brood of grandchildren numbered twelve; Clara's eight—three boys for Emily and Edwyn, a boy and two girls for Charley and Emma, and one of each for Bert and Margaret. In another letter to Geneva, Clara described Margaret as "almost as handsome as Emma. Thankfully this one cooks and cleans."

You are too passionate about cooking and cleaning, Geneva wrote back.

****

While Bert and Charley were making new lives for themselves in Naturita, Pearl was helping out at the hotel as she grew from childhood to womanhood. By age twelve she attended school several hours a day and served restaurant patrons during the supper hour. When she got a little older, she liked to dish up supper for the train crews that arrived at the hotel after the restaurant was closed. One of the cook's helpers prepared the food ahead of time. Pearl served it, and then sat with the men while they ate, listening intently as they talked of work and play.

"Tell me more about the Royal Gorge," (or Black Canyon or Cerro Summit or Tennessee Pass) she might ask. "How far is the drop? Aren't you terribly frightened when you have to repair something up there? I've never been to Denver. You make it sound like an exciting place to visit."

Seldom were the men in the presence of a female, let alone a brown-eyed brunette the likes of Pearl. They relished the attention, humoring her with best guesses as to the depths of canyons or steepness of grades, and exaggerating their encounters with wild animals. Otherwise they talked of billiards, bagatelle scores, picture shows they'd seen at Denver's Princess Theater, or Sundays watching the Denver Grizzlies play baseball at Broadway Park.

When the United States entered the Great War in

1917, several train workers Pearl had gotten to know either volunteered to serve or were drafted. She wrote letters to all of them, receiving far fewer than she sent. The letters that did make it back mentioned foreign-sounding places like Cantigny and Belleau Wood, names she'd also seen in newspapers.

"They are frightfully lonely over there, Mother," Pearl said of her railroad friends, "and in far greater danger than when they worked in the canyons."

Like Pearl, most people in America knew someone who was fighting in Europe. Geneva was worried her grandson might be drafted, and in January of 1918, when the temperature hovered near the freezing mark in Montrose and oranges were ripe in Pasadena, she spoke of her concern during a trunk call she placed to Clara's office. It was a first for both of them—the first long distance phone call either had placed or received, as well as the first time they'd spoken since washing dishes together.

"I'm worried about my grandson Stanley," Geneva said a few seconds into the call. "I've heard they're going to lower the draft age. Stanley's only fourteen, but who knows how long this bloody war's going to last?"

Clara laughed. "When did you add bloody to your colorful vocabulary?"

"Be serious, Clara. I hear it all the time."

The phone line went quiet during an expensive pause. "Actually, cuss words don't sound half bad," Clara said, "when they're spoken with a British accent. Meanwhile, you needn't worry about Stanley. From what I read in the papers, the war is going better. And when it's over, neither of us will have to worry about our grandsons, because President Wilson says it's the last war we're ever going to fight."

****

From Pasadena to Montrose to Manhattan, posters urging men to join the army, navy, or air service were plastered on buildings or wrapped around utility poles. "Food Will Win the War" signs were posted in other places, urging citizens to reduce their personal consumption. Wheat was the primary concern, also meat and sugar. The hotel restaurant had been complying with meatless Tuesdays and wheatless Wednesdays, but when peach season rolled around, Clara ignored the plea to go easy on sugar and baked peach pies by the dozen.

"We aren't supposed to use this much sugar, Mother," Pearl said as she dumped a cup of sugar, half a teaspoon of cinnamon, and a quarter cup of tapioca into a bowl of slivered peaches.

Clara pulled two pies out of the oven and set them on the restaurant's spacious counter. "I'm doing my part. Look at how many peach pits I'll be donating."

Pearl glanced at the bushel-basket of pits sitting on the floor. "What do they use them for?"

Clara shrugged. "Somehow they're used in gas masks to offset that awful mustard gas the Germans are using." She blotted the perspiration from her face with a towel. "Meanwhile, I'm going to buy all the peaches I can get my hands on. My patrons have been asking for it." She handed Pearl half a peach. "Here. Eat this. Is there anything more delicious?"

****

Clara bought all of her fresh fruits and vegetables from local farmers who carted wagonloads of whatever was in season into Montrose twice a week. One fall day after peach season was over, she was nearing the street where the farmers parked their wagons. A woman was getting out of a Model T Ford. The veil on her hat partially obscured her face, but there was something familiar about her. A young man was helping the woman out of the car, and when he turned around, Clara's breath caught in her throat. He was a dead ringer for the cowboy she'd known as Reb.

She hurried across the street. "Phoebe! What are you doing here? Have you been living in Montrose and I not knowing it?"

Phoebe lifted her veil. "Clara! What a wonderful surprise!" She held out her arms, tears glistening in her eyes as the two women embraced. "I do not live here," Phoebe said, as she and Clara stepped back for a better look at one another. "My son and I are here to retrieve Reb's coffin. He—it—whatever one calls such a thing, is scheduled to arrive on the ten o'clock train." She pulled a handkerchief out of her sleeve and used it to blot her tears. "This is my son Hugh." She curled an arm around the young man standing next to her.

Hugh smiled and tipped his tweed cap. Clara smiled back, somewhat stunned as she looked into the face of Reb at about twenty years of age. The young man's cap was brown, and he was wearing a gray shirt under a black jacket. Phoebe's dress and hat were black. The Ford was black. Well, all of them were.

"Oh, Phoebe," Clara murmured, lightly touching her friend's arm. "I shouldn't have burst in on you and your son at a time like this." She hesitated, wondering what she should say next. "Vincent is gone, too—cancer. Going on ten years now. I married a second time and am widowed again."

"I know so many widows," Phoebe said. "Now I am one, too." After an awkward pause she said, "Reb made captain. He was in the sixteenth infantry…about to retire when the Army begged him to stay. The generals needed at least a few men with experience."

"Where did he fall?" Clara asked.

Phoebe shook her head. "He didn't die over there. He was wounded somewhere on the Western Front and was on his way home in a hospital ship with hundreds of other chaps when he caught the flu. He died before he reached shore."

Clara's eyes widened. "How awful! Was it the Spanish flu?"

Phoebe nodded. "The word plague is being bandied about in the pubs—bad as the Black Death, people over there are saying."

"It's here, too, you know. Montrose has imposed restrictions. Where are you living?"

"For years Reb and I moved from fort to fort. Now I am back on the family farm. You remember it, don't you?"

Clara's face brightened. "Of course I do. We had such good times in that house!"

"It's a quite nice house, actually. My brothers are somewhere in France right now, but they put a loo inside after Mum and Pops passed away."

Hugh held up his arm and pointed to his wristwatch. "We should go, Mother." Phoebe gave her son a loving look. "Hugh made it back without a scratch."

"My two boys are exempt," said Clara. "They both have families. They live in Naturita. You may have seen them and not known they were mine."

Phoebe finally broke a smile. "Please come see me next time you visit…no need to let me know ahead of time. I will drop whatever I am doing for a friend."

Chapter Sixty-Three

One week after Clara came across Phoebe and her son in downtown Montrose, the Allies broke through the last section of the Hindenburg line. November 11, 1918, newspaper headlines across the nation declared:

Armistice Signed
End of the War

Almost immediately, commerce picked up in the states. Every train, stagecoach, and automobile passing through Montrose was packed with returning soldiers, land seekers, people looking for work, and others hoping for a new beginning. These people needed places to stay, and as a result, the hotel was full every night. One guest, a woman with a reddish cast to her face, signed for a room and went straight to bed. Too sick to come down for supper, she asked for a pot of tea, and Clara took it up to her. The next morning, the woman had to be helped downstairs and lifted into the back seat of a waiting automobile.

Clara complained of feeling ill after the woman left. "I ache all over," she said to Pearl in a voice thin and raspy. "My legs are weak as a doddering old woman's." Stumbling back to bed, she slept until dark. Upon waking, she asked Pearl to put a wet cloth on her forehead. "I don't need a doctor to tell me I have a fever," she mumbled. She was asleep again when Pearl returned with the cloth. Living in a hotel for most of her seventeen years, Pearl knew what needed to be done, and she dealt with the tenants and guests for three days, stopping intermittently to refresh the wet cloth while her mother slept and slept.

"I feel much better," Clara said to her daughter after sleeping the better part of three and a half days. "I can sit up now without feeling faint." While Pearl stood by to make sure her mother was telling the truth, Clara got out of bed, and tested her legs. They didn't buckle, so she put on a fresh skirt and blouse. She took a deep breath and held it. "See, I can breathe without coughing." She slipped her feet into her shoes and bent over to lace them. Finished, she looked up at her daughter and said, "That was the nastiest cold I've ever had."

Pearl furrowed her brow. "I don't think that was a cold, Mother. I think you caught the flu from that woman we practically had to carry downstairs. Maybe you still have it. Maybe you shouldn't be up yet."

"Nonsense. I feel fine," and as soon as she finished dressing, she was back to greeting guests and planning menus.

The Montrose medical community had been seeing Clara's symptoms in others, however most patients were down more than three days, and by mid-November more than a score of deaths had been reported. Two of Clara's steady boarders took sick shortly after she did. When word of it got out, a city employee nailed a large QUARANTINED sign on the front of the hotel. Soon, the same sign hung on every hotel in Montrose. Clara tried to honor the quarantine, but when she explained to out-of-towners there were sick people in some of the rooms, they ignored her.

Some were ill themselves. Desperate for a place to sleep, they more or less forced themselves on Clara, doubling and tripling up in the rooms, sleeping on parlor furniture or the floor, and there wasn't much she could do about it.

"Why do we have to let sick people stay here?" Pearl asked after this had been going on for close to a month. "Maybe we should call the sheriff. Gunnison isn't letting anybody into town unless they agree to be quarantined for two weeks. What if somebody dies here?"

"Nobody is going to die here," Clara said without raising her voice. "After they rest for a few days, they'll be fine. I can't throw people out. Where would they go? Every hospital in the state is full, and no one is going to take them into their homes."

"This is a plague, Mother, a plague! Shops are padlocked. Theaters closed. The streets are nearly empty."

Clara smoothed Pearl's dark brown hair off her brow. "Don't be so dramatic, Baby. People don't survive a plague. The trains are still running. So is the stage."

****

As the disease spread, chatter filled the phone lines, some people claiming the disease was a secret weapon unleashed by the Germans. Children began jumping rope to a new ditty.

I had a little bird,
It's name was Enza.
I opened the window,
And in-flu-enza.

Half of the rooms in Clara's hotel held sick people,

some with the equivalent of bad colds, others nearly comatose. A newly married couple, young and healthy-looking when they signed the guest register, stayed at the hotel one night. They were on their way to Norwood where the husband planned to open a dental practice. A week later they returned to Montrose on the same train that took them to Norwood, this time in coffins.

With no help to be had, Clara moved from sick person to sick person as if walking in her sleep, sleep she needed herself. She finally managed to get a nurse to come during the day. The nurse asked for an exorbitant fee, and she paid it.

Doc Meyer stopped by once. "It starts out like regular flu," he told Clara, the concern in his eyes magnified by his steel-rimmed glasses. "Then it turns into the bloodiest pneumonia I've ever seen. It isn't always deadly, but there's no rhyme or reason as to who gets it or who survives. It's not like most diseases where the weak ones die and the strong ones live. One of my patients was a woman of eighty-something. She had it, and she's still kicking."

"I think I had it," Clara said.

"Then you drew one of the lucky numbers."

"What did you do for the elderly woman?"

"Told her to stay in bed. Gave her a little whiskey."

"Whiskey! Isn't there anything else?"

Doctor Meyer shrugged. "Eucalyptus oil helps the cough some. There's belladonna, but that can be dangerous."

"So can whisky," Clara said grimly. She paused for a moment to contemplate the doctor's advice. "I can buy eucalyptus oil. Where did you find whisky? Ever since Colorado went dry I haven't been able to get it for my restaurant."

"I had a bottle or two of my own. It's gone now."

The doctor set out for the next hotel, leaving Clara, Pearl, and the nurse to do whatever they could with limited resources. A few days before Christmas, Clara happened to be going upstairs when Pearl was coming down. Her daughter missed a step and would have fallen if Clara hadn't been there to catch her.

"I feel so queer, Mother." Pearl had one hand on her forehead, the other on the bannister. "I have a headache that won't go away. I'm having trouble remembering things." Seeing the worried look on her mother's face, Pearl quickly added, "I'm not coughing, though, so I don't think it's the flu."

Clara ordered her daughter to bed and applied the same treatment she'd been using on others: cool wet cloths on the face to reduce fever and two or three drops of eucalyptus oil in a teaspoon of sugar to ease congestion. Pearl drifted in and out of a tortured dream, struggling for breath, incoherent when she tried to speak. She'd begun coughing the minute she went to bed. Talking made it worse—a deep, wracking cough that lasted until she was too weak to draw in enough breath to cough again. Each time she woke, Clara said, "Everything is going to be fine, Baby. Go back to sleep. I slept the whole time I had it. Sleep is the key."

Sometimes Pearl woke, eyes wild, cradling her chest as she coughed long and painfully into a blood-splotched towel clutched in her hand. Exhausted by the coughing spell, she'd float off again. Clara watched her daughter's condition steadily grow worse. She put in a call to Doctor Meyer, and was shocked to learn that in caring for the sufferers, he, too, had succumbed to the disease. Another doctor said he'd come as soon as he could, but made no promise as to when. A third woefully shook his head when he heard Pearl was coughing up blood and bleeding from her ears.

Clara suffered through the next few days in sickening waves of panic. She felt as if she was watching something fragile slip through her fingers—clawing the air like a helpless fool while trying to catch it—and then watching it break on the floor. Still, she had to leave Pearl's bedside to attend to guests and other hotel business. Christmas was coming. The hotel was overflowing with guests, sick or otherwise. The cook's helper was ill, which would have been a bigger issue if people hadn't been shunning restaurants for fear the disease was being spread by restaurant workers. Clara hoped keeping busy would keep her mind off what was happening, but she moved about the halls like a ghost. Repeatedly, she left in the middle of what she was doing to check on Pearl, and when she approached her daughter's bedside for the last time and found her lifeless, she let out a wail that echoed through the hotel like the howl of a wolf in a canyon.

Chapter Sixty-Four

The undertaker's desk was covered with paperwork, and near his elbow, an ashtray overflowed with cigarette butts. Pessimism clouded his brow as he scribbled something onto a sheet of paper. He handed the form, along with a pen, to Clara, and while she read it, he reached across his desk and parted the sea of paper to clear a space for her to sign. "Too many deaths!" he muttered. "I hear Telluride and Silverton are even worse off than we are."

His long face mirrored the grim expressions on the two women sitting across from him. For weeks the undertaker and his son had been working well into the night building simple wooden coffins. Others in the profession were also working long hours, and when one of their own died after handling victims of the flu, morticians stopped embalming and used slings to lower the flu-riddled bodies into coffins.

Emily had driven her mother to the mortuary, remaining by her side while she made arrangements for Pearl's burial. Later that day she brought her wedding dress to the hotel. "This is for Pearl. I don't have a daughter to wear it someday." She laid the dress across Clara's bed.

Clara stared at the white dimity dress for a moment, her eyes filling with tears. "She wore a dress made out of this when you got married. Little did we know it would be the closest thing to a wedding dress she'd wear until she was buried in yours."

"I know," Emily said softly. "Also the closest thing to a wedding ring. Remember that little ring Jonas gave her?"

Clara nodded, tears dropping on a white blur as she leaned over to pick up the dress. "Will you help me put this on her?"

Emily held up her hands in protest. "I don't dare, Mother. Eddie and I have been careful not to expose ourselves, and thank God, thus far none of us has gotten sick." She gave her mother a hug. "You can count on us being at the funeral, though."

****

Montrose had imposed a temporary ban on public funerals. Family members of the deceased were allowed to go to the mortuary and cemetery and told to bury their dead quickly. Then they were supposed to go home and stay there. Two days after Pearl died, a horse-drawn hearse transferred her coffin to the Cedar Creek Cemetery. Clara, Lily, and Henry, wearing dark winter coats, wool hats, gloves, and scarves, followed the hearse in Henry's automobile. Also bundled in warm clothing, Edwyn, Emily, and their three young sons trailed behind in a Model T Ford.

Gray clouds hung overhead, and half an inch of snow covered the ground—clouds too high and temperature too cold for more snow. The short funeral procession met no other vehicles during the slow trip through a town showing no sign it was three days before Christmas. Faces could be seen in the windows of some of the houses they passed. When the people watching realized they'd been spotted, they quickly withdrew or pulled down their shades.

"Did you see that?" Clara whispered to Lily. "No doubt they're relieved it's not them being buried."

"Or one of their loved ones," her sister murmured.

Upon reaching the cemetery, the family got out of the cars and walked through the dusting of snow to a plot of land Clara bought after Jonas died. When she bought it, she assumed she would be the next one buried there, not one of her children. The undertaker signaled Henry to begin. Clergymen had stopped attending graveside services, so Henry said a simple prayer while Pearl's coffin was lowered into the grave next to her father's. The family stood silent for a few moments, and then trudged back across the snow-whitened lawn to their cars.

Clara invited everyone to the hotel for lunch, and when she went to order it, she was surprised to find Amanda had prepared an elegant meal for them and left it with the cook. Amanda, who had suffered with the flu for a month and survived, brought chicken sandwiches, deviled eggs, beet salad, toffee, and gingersnaps.

Henry pushed two tables together while Clara asked the waitress to serve the food, ordering coffee for the adults and hot chocolate for Emily's boys. Three men nearby lowered their voices, finished their meal quickly, and left. What little conversation took place around the two tables was hushed; most of it about the quality of the food and the woman who prepared it. Out of respect for the occasion, they didn't rush.

They were passing around a tin of cookies when Bert entered the restaurant. "Bert!" cried Clara and Emily in unison.

"It's blue-belly cold out there." Bert removed his

hat and coat and tossed them on the winter wear piled on a corner table. Peeling off his gloves, he turned to see his Montrose family sitting together, everyone, even his three small nephews, wearing dark clothing. He swallowed dryly. "What's going on?"

All eyes moved to Clara, whose lips were quivering at the sight of her younger son. She hadn't had the heart to inform him or his older brother that their sister had died. "Pearl," Clara choked. "Flu." And though she hadn't shed a tear that morning, she cried as if learning of Pearl's death for the first time.

Fighting a lump in his throat, Bert walked over to Clara and rested his hands on her shoulders. Then he asked Lily to move one chair over so he could sit between her and his mother. "I am beyond sorry," he said as he sat in the chair his aunt vacated. "I would have come yesterday if I'd known."

Clara blotted her eyes with a napkin. "I know, I know. These blasted funerals have to take place quickly." Lowering the napkin, she took a hard look at his face. "Your cheeks are rosy. I hope that's due to the weather, not a fever."

"I'm fine, Mother. Margaret's fine. So are the children, but Charley and his family are down with the flu. I've been making all of our runs to Norwood for a week." He reached for a sandwich, and then pulled back his hand. "May I have a sandwich, Mother?" Clara smiled and handed him one. He took a bite and continued talking with his mouth full. "Charley's kids took it first…then him and Emma."

Clara's face went pale. "Please tell me they're all right." She grabbed Bert's sleeve. "Please. I can't take any more bad news. How long have they had it? Is anyone coughing up blood?"

Bert's soft, empty eyes moved around the table to the rest of the family, everyone focused on what he had to say. "Frankly, Margaret and I haven't gone over there. Margaret found out they were sick from our doctor who is Charley's doctor…the whole town's doctor. Last we heard, Emma and the children were getting better, but not Charley. That's all I know. I came here because you've been around the disease for weeks. You seem to know as much about treating it as the doctors do."

"Like I did for Pearl?" Clara's lips trembled again.

Bert looked her straight in the face. "Like you helped many people, Mother." His gentle way of speaking accentuated his youthful appearance. Slightly built, with doll-like hands, he wasn't as strong as his brother who'd spent ten years loading ore and driving mule teams. But he wasn't fragile, either. "I came here to take you back with me. In your last letter you said you'd hired a manager. I'm sure he can handle things for a few days."

Clara's eyes moved across the empty tables in a restaurant that should have been bustling with diners. "I don't suppose you have any whisky at home."

Bert shook his head. "Can't get it for love or money."

Emily stood up and pushed back her chair. "May I have these for my boys?" She pointed to the remaining cookies. "We have to leave. Eddie has to go to work."

"I'm keeping the cookies this time," Clara said, "for Charley's children. Charley might like one, too."

"Of course, Mother. I should have thought of that." Emily gestured for her boys to get their coats. "I need to be more mindful of how lucky I am that my family has been spared."

"We're leaving, too." Lily scooted her chair back from the table. The puffiness around her eyes made her round face look even fuller. "Henry should have been at the bank an hour ago."

Clara hugged everyone before they left, and then hurried to her room to pull a valise from under her bed. She packed a few personal items, plus cotton towels, a bottle of eucalyptus oil, some alfalfa tea (it eased joint pain for some people), and the tin of gingersnaps. Knowing a cold ride lay ahead, she donned more warm clothing and took along a heavy wool blanket.

Chapter Sixty-Five

By crow, Naturita is about forty miles from Montrose. In 1918, it was twice that far by car or wagon due to the massive Uncompaughre Plateau separating the two communities. An old wagon road skirted the base of the plateau, and at half past one in the afternoon, under the same gray clouds that had been following Bert all day, he steered his Model T onto the frozen mud road. It hadn't snowed during his morning drive, although several inches of it covered the road at higher elevations, deeply rutted with tracks petrified into ice. By keeping the Ford's tires in the tracks, Bert managed to keep control as long as the road was relatively flat or he was driving uphill. Going downhill was another matter. At the top of every steep incline, he had to get out of the car, walk around to the back, and lower the small pinion tree he'd chained to the bumper. The tree, dragging behind through snow and ice, supplemented the brakes. At the bottom, he stopped again to reattach the tree.

By the time he and Clara reached the highest mile of elevation, it was dark. Neither said a word as the Ford crept along at five miles an hour. Bert's eyes were trained on the frozen tracks while Clara's thoughts were on Charley. She wanted to scream at Bert to hurry. She needed to see her older son with her own eyes, determine how ill he was, do whatever she could to help him, hold him in her arms, tell him she loved him. At the same time, she knew her younger son was driving as fast as he could in the dim light of headlamps on an icy road.

Knees pressed together, eyes shut tight, blanket pulled up to her nose, Clara listened to the car's pistons pound out a rhythm to the beat of her heart. She had traveled that route several times, but always in late spring or summer when sun warmed the sagebrush surrounding Montrose, and then hid behind aspens and conifers as the road around the plateau climbed higher. She tried to calm herself with memories of the drive in summer when the air smelled of pine, and the aspen leaves rattled with friendly chatter. Now, when she peeked out the window, the snow-covered ponderosas loomed overhead like tall sentinels wearing black and white uniforms, and the aspen trees were nothing but bony branches, clawing at the sky.

Suddenly, the car was gaining speed. Opening her eyes, she saw less snow, fewer trees, and a landscape of sagebrush and juniper. "How fast are we going?" she asked Bert.

"Fast as I dare," he said, his eyes on the road. "We're out of the ruts, but there's still ice in spots."

Half an hour later, the lights of the Ford shone on Naturita House, the modest hotel Charley and Emma had been managing for several years. They lived a few yards behind it. Bert stopped the car in front of their house, and left the engine running. Clara peeled off the blanket she'd been wrapped in for seven hours and walked through a skiff of snow to the front porch. Bert picked up his mother's valise and carried it to where she waited on the landing.

"I'm not going in with you," he said. The Ford's headlamps exposed his mother's puckered brow. "Don't look at me that way, Mother. I love Charley, but I have to consider my family. Please tell him I haven't fallen behind on the mail. He may be worried about that. Tell him I'll come see him when he's up and around again."

Clara patted him on the cheek. She turned and knocked on the door, and in seconds Emma opened it. The glow of the kerosene lantern in her hand heightened the dark circles under her eyes. Unsmiling, she appeared exhausted and disheartened. "I've been waiting for you. Bert got word to us he was going to Montrose to fetch you."

Emma led Clara down a short hallway. "The kids are asleep," she said quietly as they passed the bedroom her children shared. In a second bedroom a few feet away, Charley lay curled like a cutworm under a pile of covers. Emma set the lantern on a stand next to the bed. The room's one window was closed, and a coal heater was going full blast.

Clara bent over her son for a better look and saw the reddish tinge she'd come to associate with Spanish flu. "Charley-boy," she said softly. "It's your Mama."

A hint of smile appeared on Charley's lips, but he didn't raise his head or open his eyes. He mumbled something that sounded vaguely positive. "I'm going to help you get through this," Clara said, no better at sounding confident than Charley's fuzzy greeting.

She opened her valise and took out one of the towels she'd packed. "Go wet this," she told Emma. "Wring it out, and then put it on Charley's forehead. And bring me a spoon."

****

For the next two days, Clara took command of Charley and his family in a house that had piped water in the kitchen, but no indoor privy, telephone, or electricity. She cleaned up Emma's kitchen, and cooked nourishing meals for her and her three children. Charley rolled his head away whenever Clara tried to feed him anything, even a spoonful of oatmeal or one of Amanda's gingersnaps.

"You have to eat something," she whispered to him. Praying silently while scrutinizing her son's blank face, she reminded an unseen God that she had sacrificed enough.

She spent hours at Charley's bedside, smoothing his brow, fluffing his pillow, rubbing eucalyptus oil on his chest, and spooning alfalfa tea between his cracked lips. Too vividly she remembered him as a child—collecting rocks, dragging a watering can around her garden in Durango, building forts out of firewood, a toy wagon out of a match box and empty thread spools. He'd gotten a one-day job stacking bricks when he was about ten. They were living in Gunnison at the time. How proud he was to help his family, even though he'd been paid in loaves of bread.

While Clara concentrated on happier times, Charley spent his hours in a drug-like stupor—a world shrouded in fog where a pale moon, sometimes two moons, floated around his bed. He was vaguely aware of having hands and feet, but he didn't need them, couldn't feel them, attached as they were by strings like those on a marionette. Other than the caged star hissing on the table next to his bed, it was a peaceful place where whispers drifted on the breeze and a minty smell flowed from his nostrils up to his brain.

Clara stood watching him, relaxing some while he slept, cringing at the sound of his bone-deep cough when he woke struggling for air. He mumbled something that sounded like Mama. Or was it Emma? The few times Clara woke during her bout with the flu, it was her mother's thin white face she'd hoped to see. Did Charley want to look upon his own mother's face when he opened his eyes, or would he rather see Emma?

Behind Charley's fevered eyelids, a light with no connection to day or night came and went. Something told him the light was important, that he could gain back his strength and escape the creepy world his mind had invented if he could just hang onto it. Dazzling as sunlight when the light first appeared, it grew less and less intense, until two days after his mother arrived, the light went out for good.

It was near dawn when Clara, half asleep on a chair near his bed, realized Charley had stopped breathing. She shook his shoulder, hoping she was wrong, knowing she wasn't. Her throat ached with sorrow. She opened her mouth to cry, wail like she did when Pearl died, but nothing came out. Head bowed, feet cold and heavy as iron, she plodded to the kitchen where Emma was making coffee. No words were necessary when her daughter-in-law saw her face.

Still weak from the flu, Emma dropped onto a painted wood chair, moaning softly, rocking back and forth, her face twisted in anguish. "I'm six months pregnant," she sobbed. "How will I manage?"

"Hush, you'll wake the children," Clara said. Grief descended on her shoulders like a wet shawl, and her cheeks felt as if they'd been molded out of clay. She picked up Emma's coffee pot and mechanically filled two cups with steaming coffee, sweetening each with cream and sugar. She handed a cup to Emma. "Here. Drink this. You will manage; we both will." She drew in a ragged breath. "We have to." The stale assurance, all she could come up with, was the right thing to say to a widow with three, soon to be four children, but the words rang hollow, even to Clara.

Chapter Sixty-Six

It was frightening how tragedy was hurling itself into everyone's lives. Especially hard hit by the pandemic was Colorado's Western Slope where miners died in droves, their damaged lungs unable to fight the pneumonia-like disease.

Bert hired a teamster who'd worked with Charley at the Alta mine to transport his fellow worker's body to Montrose. It had snowed off and on while Clara was in Naturita, but there wasn't a cloud in the sky when Bert and his Model T fell in behind the teamster's truck. The two vehicles made it over the Uncompaughre Plateau without incident, and upon reaching Montrose, the teamster carried Charley's body into the hotel where it remained overnight in the room that had been Pearl's.

Two days later, the family, including Emma this time, made another terrible journey to the Cedar Creek Cemetery. After her second graveside service in less than two weeks, Clara returned to a hotel where half the guests were sick with the flu. Death felt like a loathsome chore she had to face every day, and with so many people tugging at her sleeve for help, including the man she was training to replace her, she was too exhausted to cry. She slogged through her days expecting nothing but tragedy, cringing when the telephone rang, praying for someone to open the door to their room if she knocked on it.

She agonized over her two remaining children, especially Bert who'd always been smaller and more fragile than Charley; however Bert didn't get sick. Neither did Emily and her family, nor Lily and hers. Clara gave her daughter-in-law Emma money to live on until her baby was born and business picked up at the Naturita House. Emma made and sold candy to bring in a few more dollars. After the first of the year, Amanda sold her shop and moved to Minneapolis. "I think the disease affected my heart," she told Clara. "I need to be closer to my daughter now."

****

As the grim hush of winter lost its grip, a few rays of hope brightened Clara's days. Denver reopened its schools in January. By the middle of March, most of the restrictions imposed by the Montrose town council had been lifted, and local papers contained fewer obituaries. Shops were open again, and people out and about, acting as if the disease had run its course.

Clara and the earnest young man she'd hired as manager during the height of the flu crisis were going over the books for March when the candlestick phone on the office desk rang two longs and a short. She took the receiver off the hook and held it to her ear. The connection was poor. She recognized her father's voice on the other end of the line, but couldn't make out what he was saying.

"I can barely hear you, Pa."

"I said, Geneva's gone!" He had to raise his voice dramatically to be heard over the static. "Don't ask me to say it again!"

Goosebumps prickled Clara's skin. She put her

hand over the phone's mouthpiece and asked her manager-in-training to come back later. Then she pulled the upright phone close to her chest, her fingers gripping its neck. "What happened?"

"She died!" Albert shouted, a message that wasn't something to shout about. "Why else would I be calling long distance? Your birthday isn't until May."

Clara nearly dropped the receiver as the bleak, wintry feeling she'd borne for months fell on her shoulders again. "Was it the flu?"

Albert cleared his throat. "I thought we had escaped it. Geneva and her lady friends went to a picture show one night, and three days later, she and the woman next door were dead."

Clara let out a cry. She put her hand over the mouth of the phone again as a profound sadness washed over her. Tears threatened, constricting her throat and stinging her eyes.

"I am moving back to Montrose," Albert bellowed. "She was the one who liked it here. I stayed longer than I wanted to for her sake."

His words brought to mind Geneva's last letter, the one she sent with her condolences after Pearl died. "Albert seems to have lost interest in this place," she'd written. "He hasn't bought or sold anything in two years. All he does is sit and read."

"I want my house back," Albert said, still hollering to be heard, "the one on Fifth Street."

Clara blotted her tears with the sleeve of her tunic. "Someone's living in it, Pa."

"I know that. Get rid of them. Who did your plumbing and electrical work when you built the hotel? I'll need to bring my house up to date."

"I'll see if Barnaby's still around." Clara paused, weighing her words. "What arrangements have you made for Geneva?" For a long moment she heard only crackle in the phone line.

"I found a sunny spot for her at the Mountain View Cemetery. She was a good wife," he said with a hitch in his voice. "She was naïve and frivolous and not very smart, but I am going to miss her."

After Clara hung up the phone, it was as if she'd sprung a leak. She went to her room and cried for half an hour over Geneva, Pearl, Charley, the young dentist and his wife, questioning why she had survived when others died. She felt fragmented, having left a little piece of herself in every place she'd lived, every family member she'd buried.

Geneva had always been the one with the charmed life. In flashes of memory, Clara saw the two of them when they were young and unmarried. How excited they'd been when their parents told them they were moving to a world of cowboys, towering mountains, and horses; how innocent their talks of life and love as they strolled along La Jara Creek. A smile fluttered on her lips when she remembered her and her friend in the horse barn, peeking over the edge of the hayloft at young men tending their horses. Geneva always sneezed or said something to let the cowboys know they were being watched. She knew they would sweet-talk the girls into climbing down the ladder.

When Clara ran out of tears, she held up her hands and spread her fingers, gazing for a moment at the wedding band Jonas had given her. She'd never taken it off. Her eyes moved from her fingers to the veins she'd recently noticed on the backs of her hands. Squeezing her hands into fists, she felt the ache of arthritis.

She stood up, took a deep breath, and thinking a cup of coffee would buoy her spirits, she walked down the hall toward the kitchen. On the wall between her room and the bustling hotel kitchen hung a large gilt-framed mirror. She usually whisked by it without a peek, but after her crying bout she thought she'd better take a look at herself. Her eyes were red-rimmed and swollen. A clump of hair had strayed from the bun at the nape of her neck. She pulled out a hairpin and anchored it back in place. At forty-something, her athletic frame didn't match the strands of gray in her dark brown hair. Looking closer, she saw more signs of time passing—cheeks that were pale, not browned by the sun, eyeglasses screening the gray-green eyes Vincent used to say were the color of sage. She shook the cobwebs out of her head and pushed open the kitchen door, poured a cup of coffee, and left without the cheerful greeting she usually had for the help.

****

It took Albert two months to shut down his life in Pasadena. During the interim, Clara found his lessees another place to rent. While searching for them, she fell in love with a house that was for sale and bought it. It was more house than she needed, yet one that would appreciate in value. The stark white, two-story colonial had three bedrooms, four fireplaces, a roomy modern kitchen, den, parlor, and a bathroom complete with a claw-foot tub like the one at the hotel. This one she wouldn't have to share.

She moved into her house shortly before Albert returned to his. From the tall, multi-paned windows in back, she could look out on a pond lined with lilac bushes and a fenced yard sprinkled with pine, ash, apple, and peach trees. The lilacs were in bloom. The fence around the back yard was made of bricks, but she'd long since changed her mind about wanting one made of white pickets. Walking across her very own shiny wood floors and peering into twelve-foot-high ceilings trimmed with shiny white moldings, she felt something akin to awe at finally having the home she'd always wanted.

****

She allowed her father a day to get settled before paying him a visit, and the first thing she did when she arrived was help him locate his glasses. She found them on a small stand in the foyer. The lenses were thick as canning jars.

"Your eyesight isn't what it used to be." She handed him the glasses.

"Neither is yours," he grumbled." He hooked the glasses over his ears. "My eyesight is fine."

Clara hadn't seen her father in nearly ten years. His hair was completely white now, and white hairs sprang from his eyebrows. It had been decades since he ranched, and almost that long since he'd ridden a horse, but he'd driven his 1917 Chevrolet touring car over eight hundred miles from Pasadena to Montrose.

"What are you doing?" he asked when Clara began rearranging some of his furniture.

"I'm making sure you won't bump into anything."

"I am steady as a rock. Leave everything where I put it."

The second time Clara visited, she brought a pie baked in her own gas oven. With knotted fingers, Albert pulled back the tea towel the pie was wrapped in and took a sniff.

"Apple?" He raised his unruly brows. Clara smiled and nodded. He gestured for her to follow him. "I have something for you too."

After a slow walk past the formal dining room, parlor, and small library, they entered a high-ceilinged, wood-paneled room containing an enormous mound of cartons, crates, and boxes. "I had the movers pack up everything Geneva owned." He pointed his cane at the pile. "I told them my daughter would know what to do with it."

Clara surveyed the mountain of goods, wilting at the thought of the staggering task ahead. A sad quietness filled the room. Without a word, she helped her father open a few boxes before he shuffled off, leaving her to sort through every item of clothing, every accessory, picture, trinket, and knickknack Geneva owned.

Oh, Geneva," Clara mumbled, sorting through one of the smaller boxes, *I don't want to see—touch—all of these reminders of you.* She felt a sudden balm of affection come over her. *I swear I can hear you laughing. You had the most infectious laugh. Must you even torment me from the grave?*

Inside the first box, Clara found embroidery hoops, knitting needles in several sizes, bags of yarn, embroidery thread, and a half-finished baby sweater with matching booties. At the bottom of the box was a sampler about the size of a tea towel. The top half of the sampler held an embroidered scene that reminded Clara of the ranch house near La Jara. The bottom half contained a verse cross-stitched in black.

Fire in the grate
Teakettle is boiling
Come before it's late
After a day of toiling

Sampler in hand, she looked for her father and found him in the library. He was sitting in a wingback chair, reading a book. "I rather like this." She held the sampler up to his face. "Do you suppose I could have it?"

Albert gazed at the sampler, laughing softly as he put down his book. "She was going to give that to you. I remember her saying it might slow you down some. She used to read me parts of your letters, expressing concern for how hard you worked. She never said so, but I believe she was somewhat jealous of your accomplishments."

"She was the talented one." Clara held up the sampler, admiring its workmanship. "I think I'll have this framed."

Albert nodded. He picked up his book and was about to sink back into his story when he realized Clara was still there. He held the book out to her as if to say, *can't you see I'm reading*?

Clara ignored him. "You know, Pa, living in this part of the country is difficult, especially for women. It's better now than it used to be, but I worked like a mule to get to where I am today. Geneva didn't have to work a tenth as hard as I did—mostly because she married you."

Silence filled the musty library, its high walls lined with books, some of them older than Albert. He closed the one in his hands, smoothing the cover with gnarled fingers. It was close to a minute before he spoke, and his eyes were fixed on the book when he did. "You have rawhide resilience, Clara. You made something out of nothing—on more than one occasion, as I recall. I helped some, but for the most part you did it yourself. You should be proud of that. Moreover, if you hadn't worked as hard as you did, you would have ended up fat like your sister Lily." He picked up his book and leafed through the pages. "I feel like something sweet. How about a piece of that apple pie?"

Clara smiled warmly. "Of course, Pa." She draped the sampler over her arm, and was about to enter the hallway when she heard him add, "and a cup of tea."

"I'll have one with you," she said, on her way to the kitchen.

A word about the author…

Ginger Dehlinger is a native Oregonian who writes about the American West—its flora and fauna as well as the people living there. She writes essays, short stories, and poetry and has published two novels.

Ginger belongs to several writing groups and enjoys hiking, reading, and travel in her spare time. She lives in Bend, Oregon, with her husband Dick and a cat named Kiki.

http://gdehlinger.blogspot.com

Thank you for purchasing
this publication of The Wild Rose Press, Inc.

If you enjoyed the story, we would appreciate your
letting others know by leaving a review.

For other wonderful stories,
please visit our on-line bookstore at
www.thewildrosepress.com.

For questions or more information
contact us at
info@thewildrosepress.com.

The Wild Rose Press, Inc.
www.thewildrosepress.com

Stay current with The Wild Rose Press, Inc.

Like us on Facebook

https://www.facebook.com/TheWildRosePress

And Follow us on Twitter
https://twitter.com/WildRosePress